WITCH FURY

"Full of action, excitement, and sexy fun . . . Another delectable tale that will keep your eyes glued to every word."
—*Bitten by Books*

"Hot romance, interesting characters, intriguing demons, and powerful emotions. I didn't want to put it down, and now that I've finished this book, I'm ready for the next!"
—*Night Owl Reviews*

WITCH HEART

"[A] fabulous tale . . . The story line is fast paced from the onset . . . Fans will enjoy the third bewitching blast."
—*Genre Go Round Reviews*

"Smart, dangerous, and sexy as hell, the witches are more than a match for the warlocks and demons who'd like nothing more than to bring hell to earth and enslave mankind. Always an exhilarating read."
—*Fresh Fiction*

"*Witch Heart* is a story that will captivate its readers. It will hook you from the first few pages and then take you on a wild ride. It is a fast-paced story but it is also a story that will make you feel emotion. Anya Bast uses words like Monet used paint. It's vibrant. It's alive. Readers will be able to see the story come to life as it just leaps out of the pages."
—*Bitten by Books*

WITCH BLOOD

"Any paranormal fan will be guaranteed a Top Pick read. Anya has provided it all in this hot new paranormal series. You get great suspense, vivid characters, and a world that just pops off the pages . . . Not to be missed."
—*Night Owl Reviews*

WITCH FIRE

MIDNIGHT
ENCHANTMENT

ANYA BAST

B

BERKLEY SENSATION, NEW YORK

THE BERKLEY PUBLISHING GROUP
Published by the Penguin Group
Penguin Group (USA) Inc.
375 Hudson Street, New York, New York 10014, USA
Penguin Group (Canada), 90 Eglinton Avenue East, Suite 700, Toronto, Ontario M4P 2Y3, Canada
(a division of Pearson Penguin Canada Inc.)
Penguin Books Ltd., 80 Strand, London WC2R 0RL, England
Penguin Group Ireland, 25 St. Stephen's Green, Dublin 2, Ireland (a division of Penguin Books Ltd.)
Penguin Group (Australia), 250 Camberwell Road, Camberwell, Victoria 3124, Australia
(a division of Pearson Australia Group Pty. Ltd.)
Penguin Books India Pvt. Ltd., 11 Community Centre, Panchsheel Park, New Delhi—110 017, India
Penguin Group (NZ), 67 Apollo Drive, Rosedale, Auckland 0632, New Zealand
(a division of Pearson New Zealand Ltd.)
Penguin Books (South Africa) (Pty.) Ltd., 24 Sturdee Avenue, Rosebank, Johannesburg 2196,
South Africa

Penguin Books Ltd., Registered Offices: 80 Strand, London WC2R 0RL, England

This is a work of fiction. Names, characters, places, and incidents either are the product of the author's imagination or are used fictitiously, and any resemblance to actual persons, living or dead, business establishments, events, or locales is entirely coincidental. The publisher does not have any control over and does not assume any responsibility for author or third-party websites or their content.

MIDNIGHT ENCHANTMENT

A Berkley Sensation Book / published by arrangement with the author

PUBLISHING HISTORY
Berkley Sensation mass-market edition / February 2012

Copyright © 2012 by Anya Bast.
Excerpt from *Embrace of the Damned* by Anya Bast copyright © 2012 by Anya Bast.
Cover art by Tony Mauro.
Cover design by Rita Frangie.
Interior text design by Kristin del Rosario.

ISBN: 978-0-425-24503-3

BERKLEY SENSATION®
Berkley Sensation Books are published by The Berkley Publishing Group,
a division of Penguin Group (USA) Inc.,
375 Hudson Street, New York, New York 10014.
BERKLEY SENSATION® is a registered trademark of Penguin Group (USA) Inc.
The "B" design is a trademark of Penguin Group (USA) Inc.

PRINTED IN THE UNITED STATES OF AMERICA

10 9 8 7 6 5 4 3 2 1

Dedicated to Jeffrey Skinner
for helping me see beauty in the way words come together

ACKNOWLEDGMENTS

As ever, thank you to Brenda Maxfield for being my sounding board and my second pair of eyes.

Thanks to Axel de Roy for creating the gorgeous interactive map of Piefferburg, which appears on my website, www.anyabast .com.

ONE

FIND her. Trap her. Compel her to reveal the location of the two stolen pieces of the *bosca fadbh* and get the fuck home. Those were his objectives.

Of course, Elizabeth Cely Saintjohn's objectives directly opposed his.

Right now he was blind, pissed off, and holding a rope embedded with cold iron. The only way this night could get worse was if she escaped him again. Niall's ear twitched and the hair on his nape rose as something scraped along the boulder to his left. He went still, his eyes searching the endless black for some sign of his quarry.

Footsteps sounded on the path behind him. He turned, cursing the lack of moonlight and Elizabeth's habit of only traveling at night. To his right, movement caught his attention and he stilled, growling in frustration. Light, ringing laughter echoed all around him. She moved fast and completely silently when she wished.

Rage clenched his gut. She was playing with him. *Again.*

"Must be nice to be able to see in the dark and move like the wind, huh?" he snarled into the empty air. Not to mention dissolve into water and move anywhere she wanted within the bounds of Piefferburg. Neat trick.

His hand tightened on the rope that was especially designed to trap a fae like her. He wore thick black leather gloves to prevent the charmed iron from touching his skin and leeching his magick away. It was meant to bind Elizabeth, an asrai, before she escaped him. It would only work if the rope touched her bare skin. Normally that would be a problem, but not with Elizabeth. Reverting to her water self and traveling through the earth left her naked every time she regained form. Unfortunately, roping this woman was harder than catching a weasel in a vat of olive oil. He'd never so much as caught a glimpse of her yet since it was always dark.

Usually, it went this way—she toyed with him for a while, making him think he might have her . . . then she escaped. It was a bizarre situation for him. *He* was usually the one doing the toying where women were concerned.

"Come on, Elizabeth. Don't play hard to get. Just give me the pieces and I'll stop hunting you."

"I kind of like it when you hunt me," came her lilting voice from somewhere farther up the path he walked. She had a sexy voice, whiskey rough and sweet.

He ground his teeth together and readied a spell in his head that would give him a little light. It wouldn't last long, so he needed to draw her closer before he released it. He was a mage, capable of versatile magick not unlike that of the Phaendir. Except his magick wasn't born of the creepy hive mind that the Phaendir used—his power was all inside him. Independent. Powerful.

And that's why he'd been sent after the asrai. He was the best qualified to capture and compel a fae like her. Best at thieving—or thieving *back*, in this case. Best at weaving illusion. Best at tracking, capture, and torture. Best for this job. Or, at least, that's what everyone at the Black Tower thought. That had been a week ago. A week filled with failure. Who knew what they thought now.

The Shadow Queen had sent him out the moment the Black Tower had learned the Summer Queen had passed off her pieces of the *bosca fadbh* to Elizabeth. The pieces were parts of a key that would unlock magick that could free the fae from

Piefferburg. He was no closer to trapping her now than he'd been on the first day.

"Why are you doing this?" he called. "Why keep your people from freedom? The Phaendir are at our gates right now. We don't have time to lose." His voice grew a degree lower and a lot more hostile. "Why work for the Summer Queen, a nice nature fae like you?"

"Who said I was nice?" The words breezed past his ear and were gone.

He lunged toward the direction of her fading voice with his rope and got nothing but air, a cool breeze, and the light floral fragrance of the soap she used. Staggering and swearing a blue streak, he barely caught himself before falling on his face. Straightening, he laughed mirthlessly. "Come on now, don't go away so fast, baby. At least give me a kiss before you fuck me."

And she was there, the warmth of her presence at his elbow, taunting him with her proximity. The brush of her silky hair against his skin. That soapy, light flowery scent of hers teasing his nose.

Ah, good. He'd been gambling her arrogance might be her end.

"Arendriac," he murmured. The charm burst from him with a little pop, lighting their immediate area with a golden glow. He reached out to pull her close in the same moment, rope in one hand ready to trap.

His fingers brushed the smooth bare skin of her waist as she backed away. For a moment she stood motionless. Her lush lips were parted, ruby red hair lofting around a pale, beautiful heart-shaped face, green eyes flecked with gold and wide with surprise.

He stared back at her, sharing an equal measure of astonishment. She was the most stunning woman he'd ever seen. He hadn't been expecting that.

Niall took a step forward, rope in hand. She dissolved as soon as he moved. A vision of beauty one moment, gone the next in a soft burst of spray. He looked down at his feet and saw the puddle of water she'd become. Then even the water disappeared, soaking into the earth, every single molecule of it, traveling through the ground to find a river, a stream, whatever flow that would take her away.

Swearing under his breath, he knelt and touched the dry soil where she'd been standing only a moment ago.

Gone yet again.

"Damn it," he cursed under his breath. The pretty lady with the pieces was out of his reach for another night. He wasn't sure which he mourned more—the loss of the pieces or the woman. The witch enticed him. She'd done that even before he'd caught a glimpse of her. Why couldn't she be some unalluring hag without the clever wit she displayed in the woods every time he chased her, without that constantly teasing scent? It was fucking distracting.

Especially since he sort of liked the woman.

Too bad he was probably going to have to kill her.

ELIZABETH regained consciousness sitting on a bed of leaves with her head bowed. Near her bare foot a beetle with bright green and gold casing edged its way through the dying foliage. She blinked, her eyes adjusting to the softly lighted area around her, and raised her head, shivering from the chill in the air.

That had been the first time she'd had a good look at her pursuer. He'd been about what she'd expected. The man was clever and had a mouth on him that never quit. Sparring with him night after night was actually sort of fun—which said a lot about the state of her personal life. Pathetic. Not that she'd ever known it to be anything different.

He was good-looking. She'd expected that based on his cocky personality. Strong of body and jaw, with tousled, thick dark hair that curled over the collar of his shirt and framed a set of expressive gray eyes and a handsome face. She'd only had the barest second to look at him, but a man like that tended to stick in your mind.

His lips were full and his cheeks sported a hint of whiskers that needed to be shaved. She wasn't sure if that look was deliberate or a result of the chase she'd been leading him on. She hoped it was the latter. Damned man needed to leave her alone.

Carefully, she pushed to her feet and stretched, enjoying the light waft of the night air around her nude body. Her clothing never dissolved with her, only her flesh, muscle, hair, and bone had the power to melt into her water self and then re-form. It was that way for every other asrai she knew, all one of them.

The other asrai lived near the ocean. The last time Elizabeth talked with her, she'd seemed distant and dreamy. Hopefully she hadn't fallen prey to a common asrai fate—losing sense-of-self to water forever. Some asrai dissolved one day and simply never re-formed, stayed water for the rest of their lives. The asrai who were all alone in the world, had no one to anchor them, had a much higher chance of it happening—or so she'd heard, anyway.

In the distance her mother's cottage glowed between the trees. The sprae congregated here, their great number driving away the black, moonless night. As she walked, Elizabeth said thank you to them, even though she doubted they understood her.

The sprae were the only reason her mother, Thea, lived. Thea was a rare and special breed of fae, a kind born only since Piefferburg had been erected. Her life force was dependent upon the sprae, the tiny sentient beings who were drawn to fae energy. The origins of the fae dependent were murky, a result of the goddess Danu's will alone.

The scent of vegetable stew hit Elizabeth's nose the moment she cleared the doorway. Her mother turned from the pot on the stove. "And where have you been this evening, my girl?" She waved a hand at clothing draped over a chair. "Go on, get dressed. I have a good stew and some even better bread." Her mother was used to her strolling around naked, since her water self was the way Elizabeth traveled so often.

Elizabeth's stomach growled at the prospect of food. She went for the pair of trousers and the man's shirt, inhaling for any remaining whiff of her father's scent, but it was long gone now.

Her mother spooned up stew into bowls and set the table. Elizabeth went to the refrigerator to get the cheese and butter for the thickly sliced bread already on the table.

"I was just out exploring," Elizabeth finally answered her mother's question.

She wasn't very good at lying and hoped her mother wouldn't press her. Her mother had ways of making people do what she wanted through the food she cooked, like tell the truth when they didn't want to tell it. It was her strongest talent. If she didn't do it with her strong intuition, she did it with her tea or baked goods.

They sat down and began to eat. Elizabeth buttered a piece of bread, keeping her eyes away from her mother's face. These days she needed to be really careful around Thea since she was keeping a secret—an enormous life-changing one.

Her mother stared at her for a long moment, then the small laugh lines around her eyes creased. "You've met a man."

The knife she held clattered to her plate and she glanced up. "What? Why would you say that?" She gave a laugh that sounded a little too tense to be genuine.

"You've got a glow about you I've never seen before, a glow of excitement. That's got to be what it is. Tell me about him!" She leaned forward, her face beaming.

Thea wanted so much for Elizabeth to drag herself away from the hermit's life that her mother was forced to lead because of her sprae dependence—the hermit's life Elizabeth had grown up leading out of necessity. Thea wanted Elizabeth to meet a man, move to the city, have children, be happy. Above all, avoid the fate of losing her sense-of-self to water.

A life in the city and a family weren't what Elizabeth wanted at all, despite the sheltered life she'd lived.

"A glow of excitement?" she echoed. Ah. Well, yes, of course. Her life had turned very exciting the moment the Summer Queen had entrusted her with two of the pieces of the *bosca fabh* and had ordered her to hide them. "I haven't met a man, Mom. At least, not in the way you're thinking."

"Oh." Her mother sighed and placed a slice of cheese on the heel of the bread. "That's too bad."

Elizabeth made a *hmmm* sound that was as noncommittal as she could make it, then swallowed a spoonful of stew. "*Mmmm*, good stew."

Her mother waggled a finger at her. "Don't change the subject on me, girl. It's time we had a talk about your future, and this is just the moment to do it."

She was familiar with this conversational opening. It had to do with the walls of Piefferburg falling and what that meant for the fae.

Elizabeth set her spoon to the side of the bowl and sighed. "Any future that doesn't include you alive in the world isn't a future I want to contemplate. Can we not talk about it tonight? Let's enjoy our food instead."

Even though she wasn't hungry anymore.

The sprae provided her mother's life force. If the walls broke, her mother would die. She'd watched her father and brother die; she wasn't going to lose her mother, too.

Her mother looked at her sadly. "It's coming, and everyone knows it. Even living way out here in the Boundary Lands I know it. What must be, will be, my girl. It will be good for you, and I'm thankful for that. The rest of it . . ." She shrugged. "I simply have to accept."

Elizabeth steadied her gaze at her mother's careworn face. The sprae dependent aged more like a human than the fae, and her mother was nearing sixty. "We'll see about that."

Thankfully her mother dropped the subject, and the two of them finished their meal making harmless small talk that had nothing to do with death or the betrayal of her people. Those were two subjects Elizabeth wanted none of right now.

After she'd helped her mother clean up, Elizabeth kissed Thea's cheek and disappeared out the door, vanishing into the woods. As she walked, she shed her clothes. Then she ran, jumped onto a log and launched herself off it, diving through the air as though into a pool. In midair she became water self, splashing into the earth.

All the tension and stress of her life vanished immediately, along with the bulk of her personality. Feeling free, she gathered herself, seeking the underground water source that flowed under her mother's property and joined it. The only time Elizabeth ever surrendered was when she transformed into water, giving up her physical self to the slow, cool slide of moisture and the path of least resistance.

She flowed through the earth, pushing through dirt and skirting rocks, her fae consciousness a bare echo at the very back of her water awareness. Finding the river that flowed near her mother's cottage, she joined it and whooshed into the current, twirling and playing, dislodging the pebbles at the bottom and somersaulting along her way—reveling in *flow*.

When she sensed she'd reached the general area of her destination, she found the now familiar underground stream and rode it as close as she could get to the clearing, then pushed to the surface. She was tired from traveling; it was hard to get through the earth and find a way to break through to the top.

Re-forming near a tree, she lifted her head and shivered. It wasn't from the cold, though it was really chilly at this time of the year—it was from her location. The place where she'd chosen to hide the pieces of the *bosca fadbh* was the same place all her nightmares had been forged.

She pushed to her feet and stepped through the underbrush, into the clearing. Every time she came here, she relived it. The flash of metal, the laughter, the bellows of pain. The blood. The bodies.

Finally, the burial.

The sounds echoed through her mind and images flashed. It didn't matter how hard she pushed them away, they always came anyway. It was not easy for her to come here, but this place served as a reminder of the reason she was betraying her people.

The Black Tower had already taken too much from her.

She needed that reminder because she was very much aware of the treachery she was committing against her people. The guilt was strong, but her fear was stronger. She couldn't lose Thea—she *wouldn't* lose her.

She walked to the base of a tall, thin birch tree, moved a rock and dug into the earth. The ground was cold, but recently turned up, so the dirt gave easily under her fingers. This was where she kept the two pieces of the *bosca fabh* hidden. Taking the pieces from their hiding place, she unwrapped the fabric that enfolded them and touched their smooth surfaces by the muted, flickering light of the sprae that had gathered around her.

They looked so unimportant, all dull gray metal and uneven edges. They looked like hunks of junk, something to be thrown away or tossed in a bin at an antique store. Instead they were imbued with powerful magick, the ancient magick of her fae ancestors. If she laid her hand on top of the pieces, she could feel it pulsing faintly. It was *possibility* just waiting to be activated.

And it was her sad job to see that it never was.

That familiar mixture of regret and relief filled her as she verified the pieces were still safe. Slowly, she refolded the fabric and replaced the objects, the voice of the Summer Queen ringing through her ears: "I know you already have one compelling reason to keep these pieces out of the Shadow Queen's hands, but you know you have another one . . . *don't you?*"

The threat had been audible. If she refused the Summer Queen, she would be killed. But it wasn't for that reason she'd agreed to hide the pieces. If it was just her life at risk, things would be different . . . easier.

The pieces hidden once more, she sat down near the base of the tree and closed her eyes, feeling with her senses for Niall Daegan Riordan Quinn's location. She'd never deliberately sought him out, but after the glimpse she'd had of him today, she wanted another. Once she had a lock on his unique presence, she dissolved, her limbs going soft and her body once again finding its water self and traveling to him.

Re-forming, she found herself at the edge of a campsite, a fire flickering merrily not far away. Standing, not making a sound, she moved from her place between two bushes and peered through the foliage at him.

She didn't worry about being caught. Niall remained sadly deluded on this point, but he would never catch her. Watching him now she decided that was somewhat of a pity. Maybe being caught by this man wasn't the worst thing that could happen to her.

He leaned up against a rock, blanket spread underneath him and the fire crackling and spitting near his booted feet. He had his eyes closed and his hands behind his head, looking restful . . . maybe just a little defeated. Her lips curled in a smile. His shirt was unbuttoned, giving her a glimpse of his muscular chest and a hint of his broad shoulders. This man was much stronger than her; no doubt about that—but she was faster and trickier.

He had dimples. She hadn't noticed that before. They gave him a mischievous look. Her gaze traced the curve of his lips, and she wondered what his hands were like, wondered what his hands on her body might feel like.

She knew she shouldn't be thinking about this man in that way. He was her enemy. He wanted the pieces she was guarding and therefore, by default, his success meant her mother's death. Still, she couldn't help fantasizing about this man. She'd been doing it from the first night he'd tracked her down and she'd heard his voice in the darkness, caught the scent of him on the wind. It was true she lived a sheltered life, but she'd met plenty of men, mostly nature fae—this man was different. This one called to her in a primal way.

This one made her wonder what it would be like to slide naked down the length of him, to feel the cup of his big hands on her body and the fit of him between her thighs. Maybe it was just because he was the one man she could never have, or maybe there was something more substantial to her attraction.

Either way, it didn't matter.

This was just fantasy. She couldn't have this man. Not even for one night.

NIALL opened his eyes, feeling the pressure of someone's presence nearby. *Elizabeth.* It had to be.

He remained still, searching the area with his senses for her exact location. Once he thought he had it—she was *right there*, between those two bushes—he sprang to his feet and lunged for her.

A woman's yelp. A flash of a long, peach-colored form. The softest brush of bare skin against his fingertips.

Then nothing.

He lay sprawled in the foliage, cursing under his breath, branches poking him in the side and leaves tickling his nose. Then he rolled onto his back. Sweet Danu, she'd been naked again. He rubbed his fingers together, recalling the lovely sensation of her skin.

He wanted more.

Two

GIDEON P. Amberdoyal, archdirector of the Phaendir, stood at the window of his office and watched the military mill in front of the Piefferburg Gates a distance down the road. To one side of the gravel lane leading to the massive gates was the Church of Labrai and its cemetery, the roosting place of all the black vultures in this region. The birds swooped in the sky, playing in the air currents, blissfully unaware of the chaos below them.

The U.S. government had sent the two hundred and ninety-fifth Heavy Brigade Combat Team of the United States National Guard along with the state and local police. Not only were they creating a net to catch stray fae—a total joke that they even could—they were preventing the Phaendir from storming the gates and committing wholesale slaughter.

They were a buffer—with guns.

What the United States thought was going to happen here was beyond him. They lacked the stomach, Gideon suspected, to go on the offensive against the fae, yet their defenses wouldn't be strong enough to contain the fae if the walls broke.

Idiots.

Something in his jaw cracked and he forced himself to unclench his teeth. It was not a pleasant sight—seeing those humans there.

He felt the presence behind him a moment before he heard a soft rustle of fabric and a knock on the doorframe.

Gideon turned to see Brother Cadwyr. He wore the traditional black cloak of a brother and even had a tonsure, worn only by the most devout. Brother Cadwyr was extremely dedicated to their cause and was currently Gideon's second-in-command. Should he disappear, Cadwyr would be left in charge. Gideon trusted him to follow the Phaendir's ultimate agenda in every way.

"Brother Gideon, everything is ready for your trip."

Gideon nodded. "Thank you."

"Good luck, my brother, and may Labrai be ever at your side."

"And at yours."

Brother Cadwyr bowed deeply at the waist and held the position for several moments, a mark of deep respect. Then he turned and left. Brother Gideon went back to gazing out the window toward the gates, trying not to think about what he was soon to do.

The wounds from his most recent flogging—a little more energetic than normal—ached sweetly with his every movement. Blood still seeped down his wrists, having soaked through the bandages he'd wrapped himself in.

The self-flagellation was more than just a prayer he made to his god, Labrai; it cleared his mind, helped him plan for the challenges that he now faced. Challenges unlike any that had faced a leader of the Phaendir before.

Clearly Labrai understood he could handle what was to come. He had chosen him to undertake these difficulties, after all. Pride swelled his chest. When this was over he would go down in history as the man who'd changed the course for Phaendir everywhere.

The time was so close.

Gideon lifted his chin a little and gazed past the magickal barrier surrounding Piefferburg that only the Phaendir and the fae could see. No inferior human eye could detect it. None of these ants scurrying around Protection City right now had any true idea of the power behind Phaendir hive magick. It was made of Phaendir faith—and *that* was unbreakable. Those walls would never fall. How could they?

The delay in storming Piefferburg chafed because he'd been dreaming of shedding fae blood for so long, but, luckily, it appeared he did have a little time to spare. Who had known that some of the fae inside Piefferburg actually wanted to stay there?

Namely, the Summer Queen.

His spies had told him that two of the three pieces of the *bosca fadbh* had gone missing. The Summer Queen had fled with them, and no one knew where she was hiding. The Seelie Court had been set adrift. The Shadow Queen sat in her Unseelie Black Tower with only two of the four ingredients for the recipe she was sure would grant her people freedom. *Useless.* All the fae were on edge, and whispers of another fae war were growing louder.

Clearly Labrai was shining down his love on the Phaendir. Gideon relaxed his shoulders a little. With such a powerful force on their side, they wouldn't be able to lose. Life would be perfect if Watt Syndrome would reignite, but not even he could hope for such splendor.

Someone knocked on his door, and Gideon turned to find Colonel McGivens of the National Guard standing in the archway. His lip curled, though he tried to keep the sneer off his face. McGivens was a burly human with a meaty build and an even meatier mind. "Can I help you?"

"Yes, you can help me," McGivens barked. "You can keep yer gawddamn brothers out from underfoot. They're getting in the way of my men while they're securing the perimeter."

Gideon gripped the back of his chair and counted to five slowly. "While your men are *securing the perimeter*, the brothers of the Order of the Phaendir are securing the magickal barrier." He paused and gritted his teeth. "You know, that thing that *keeps the fae in* Piefferburg?" He paused, tipping his head to the side and considering the colonel. "Which job do you think is more important, making sure the magick keeping the fae prisoner stays up or creating a net of flimsy humans the fae will rip through like aluminum foil should they escape?"

McGivens pointed a fat finger at him, and his flabby jowls turned red. The man never missed a meal. "I didn't come here a newborn babe, Archdirector Amberdoyal. I *know* you people can do yer mojo from a distance. There's no gawddamn reason they should be out by the wall!"

There was a reason, of course, but Gideon wasn't about to tell him what. Gideon shifted, as if unconcerned by his outburst, and adjusted his cuff links.

The general's gaze strayed to the bloody bandages around Gideon's wrists and his nose wrinkled in disgust. "We're getting ready to call in the whole division. I won't have the general annoyed by yer antics. The Phaendir are restricted, as of now, from entering a twenty-foot perimeter from the main gates and the wall. I don't gawddamn want to see any gawddamn one of ya near it from now on. Understand?" The man's limited swearing ability was rivaled only by his limited mind.

Gideon stared at him coolly.

McGivens didn't wait for an answer, probably because he knew he'd be waiting for the next century or two. Instead he whirled and strode from the room.

The colonel could get snatched by a goblin and have his spleen eaten for all Gideon cared. He needed his men close to that wall. He turned and gazed out toward the gates.

He was going to have to get close, himself. Closer than he'd ever been. He shuddered.

But he was Labrai's instrument, his hand an extension of His will. He would do what needed to be done.

NIALL stalked through the halls of the Black Tower, scowling at everyone he met and pushing past the individuals who didn't have the good sense to stay out of his way. He was here to deliver bad news to the Shadow Queen—news of his failure—and that never put him in a good mood.

A week of hunting and he'd caught nothing but a handful of moonbeams, a whiff of flowered soap, and a whisper of silken soft skin. No stolen pieces. Only defeat.

He made his way through the glossy black marble corridors of the Unseelie Court, to the ornately carved door of the

Shadow Queen's quarters. The two black-and-silver-garbed
Shadow Guard on either side of the entrance recognized him
and gave him access immediately.

He stepped into the room to find Aislinn, the queen of the
Unseelie, sitting on a chair in the middle of her large white
and rose receiving room. Those who wanted to talk to her
came here, to this intimate yet well-appointed room, which
was a far cry from the chilly, palatial throne room of the Rose
Tower, which currently sat empty.

An enormous swath of red and white velvet and silk
encompassed her slim body. Pearls draped her throat and
dripped from her ears. Her spine looked ramrod straight,
probably from the corset. Once Aislinn was dressed in her
elaborate court finery for the day, she didn't move much. Niall
knew all too well that Aislinn preferred her jeans and T-shirts
to heavy gowns and jewelry, but there were traditions the fae
never gave up. The Shadow Queen—or King, as the case may
be—dressed in elaborate finery befitting his or her station.

Caoilainn Elspeth Muirgheal, Summer Queen of the Seelie
Court, was always dressed similarly, but Caoilainn always
added a coat of frigid bitch to wear as an accessory.

Aislinn turned toward him. Her face appeared pale and dark
smudges marked the flesh under her eyes. Normally tension
never showed on Aislinn's beautiful face. Conditions right now
were just too much—they'd be too much for anyone. "Niall."
Her voice sounded edgy, yet a note of hope rang through.

He said nothing, only returned her gaze. His lack of response
and his expression were message enough—he'd failed again.
He hated stealing away that tiny seed of optimism she had.

She dropped her head and let out a slow breath, not speaking for several pregnant moments. "You know that chaos and
death are at our door."

He stepped from the foyer into the room and walked to
stand near her. "I know."

"I may soon need to unleash the goblins and the sluagh on
the Rose Tower. No fae ruler has done that since the dark days
of the Fae Wars."

The Shadow Queen couldn't release the sluagh on an asrai.
Not even an immortal army of the damned could catch Elizabeth. The Summer Queen had known that.

"I know." His gaze dropped to the faint trace of the Shadow Amulet at her collar—the mystical necklace all the Shadow rulers donned that gave them power beyond imagining. The problem was that this power was all tied to death and violence. The goblins, when used as a weapon, were horrendous. The sluagh were worse.

This was why Aislinn looked so taxed.

She'd been forced to take the Shadow Throne when her savage biological father, the former Shadow King, had attempted to kill her and raze her soul. But Aislinn wasn't really made for the brutality that came with running one of the fae courts. There were hard decisions to be made— carnage to be wrought. Rose or Black didn't matter, there was always blood on the hands of the Tuatha Dé Danann sídhe royals.

"Soon I'll have no choice but to unleash the hell of the Netherworld on the head of the Summer Queen, wherever she may be, in order to get those final pieces. This will spark a war between the Rose and Black Towers at a time when we need unity, not division. We will be a warring and divided people when Gideon Amberdoyal gets his way and splits Piefferburg like a ripe peach, probably with the help of the U.S. government. Eventually the humans will have to step in." She raised her gaze to his. "Embroiled in internal conflict, that's no way to meet our worst enemy."

"Give me a little more time."

"We were out of time the moment Charlotte brought us the final piece of the *bosca fadbh*."

"I know I can catch her."

She pressed her lips together. "She's an *asrai*, Niall. She's not getting caught unless she wants to be. You've never met anything like what she is. None of us have."

He allowed a slow smile to slip over his mouth. "Maybe, but she's never met anything like me, either. I have more magick up my sleeve, Aislinn. I'm far from defeated. I'll find a way to trap her. I swear by my life."

She smiled a little, and he felt his heart lighten. He cared about Aislinn, worried about her as his friend, not just as his queen. "I will give you a little more time, but not much more, Niall. Not much more."

* * *

GIDEON strode down the gravel pathway leading to the front gates of Piefferburg, the heels of his brown loafers making an unpleasant gritty sound with every step he took. The Labrai-damned U.S. government and their Labrai-damned soldiers were not going to stop him from destroying the fae before they could use the Book of Bindings and the *bosca fadbh* to break the walls of Piefferburg.

No one but Labrai, Himself, would stop him from achieving his goal. Not Colonel McGivens. Not the National Guard. *No one.* The fae would free themselves over his dead body.

The humans didn't know what was good for them. Insignificant, ignorant creatures with the life expectancy of a worm. They didn't want to protect themselves, fine, but they weren't going to drag him and his brothers through the muck of their compassionate stupidity either.

Waiting. Waiting. Negotiating. Diplomacy. More waiting. *Enough!*

A barely evolved monkey in a uniform stepped in front of him holding a rifle crossways over his chest. "No Phaendir allowed past this point, sir."

Gideon raised his head a degree to stare into the young human man's face. His right eye twitched. "Do you know who I am?"

"Mr. Archdirector, sir."

"Then get the fuck out of my way, soldier."

"Can't do that, sir. Got orders from Colonel McGivens that no one passes this point but authorized personnel."

Gideon took a pained breath of air and pinched the bridge of his nose between his thumb and forefinger. Sometimes he really wished he could channel the force of the Phaendir's collective magick through his body on his own. He couldn't, of course. Phaendir magick had to do with strength in numbers; it was hive magick. All he had was his brute strength.

Looking at him, one wouldn't peg him for a strong man, though, as Phaendir, he was much, much stronger than the average human male—even stronger than a soldier in the two hundred and ninety-fifth Heavy Brigade Combat Team of the United States National Guard. He was well aware of how he appeared to others—balding brown head, medium-brown eyes, average height and slight build, face that wasn't much to write home about. He'd always thought his looks were an advantage.

They made people underestimate him.

Still pinching the bridge of his nose, he punched straight out with his opposite hand, the handle of the blade he'd hidden up his sleeve firmly in his palm—tip stabbing forward, aiming for the lungs. The knife slid through the fabric of the man's uniform and slipped into flesh as sweet as a bursting berry and just as red. He might not have individual magick to wield, but he was stronger and faster than any human around.

The soldier gurgled wetly, his eyes wide with surprise. He slumped forward, against Gideon. He backed away and the human collapsed to the ground, blood trickling out of his mouth.

A soldier not far away yelled and pointed. Others spotted the fallen man, saw Gideon, and ran toward him. Gideon sprinted away from gates, around the wide, tall brick wall of Piefferburg, gunfire popping behind him.

Should he have snuck out here in the dead of night without the damn U.S. military trying to shoot holes in him? That would have been nice. It also would not have alerted the government to a very important point—he was going in and he was getting the job done. This was his message to them.

A bullet whizzed past his ear and struck the ground near his foot. Another bullet embedded itself in the wall at just the same time he found his target, a crumbling space in the barrier surrounding Piefferburg. It was well concealed by trees and had been left open over the years on purpose by the Phaendir. He and his brethren had also created a rift in the warding in this spot, allowing Phaendir to enter, but no fae to leave.

He dove into the bushes and trees concealing the spot and wiggled through the space, pushing his way through the muck, mud, scraggy trees, and bushes that grew in this part of Piefferburg. Behind him he heard the soldiers yelling, calling out to the others to see if anyone had seen where he'd gone. They would probably assume he'd entered Piefferburg; maybe they'd even find the open spot in the wall.

That was of no concern to him.

He sat for a moment, looking up at the wall from the Piefferburg side. If a fae came too close to the warding, it would repel them—violently.

Wincing, he put a hand to his side, where he'd been stabbed trying to prevent Charlotte Bennett from taking the third piece of the *bosca fadbh* not long ago. The Phaendir had used magick to speed his healing, but the wound still gave him twinges of pain when he moved wrong.

Grimacing in discomfort, mud sticking to his shoes and pant legs up to his knees, he squelched his way through to the other side of the muck until he could no longer hear the cries of the soldiers, then sat down with a thump and pulled off his shoes.

Silence. Not a bird cried. Not a leaf rustled. It was eerie. *Creepy.* Like the Boundary Lands knew he'd just entered and were watching him, weighing him, wondering what to do with him.

He looked around. Tall pine trees reached for the blue sky above his head. Small bushes of pink and lavender flowers spotted here and there, growing when they shouldn't be growing, this late in the year. The tiny sentient sprae were sparse here, twinkling here and there and giving him the willies.

All around him fae magick breathed on the back of his neck like a dragon. Goose bumps rose along his arms and legs. Nausea clogged the back of his throat.

Dear Labrai, he was in Piefferburg.

He rose, staggering backward, stockinged feet crunching painfully onto pine needles, then he bent over and lost his breakfast on the forest floor. The sound of retching filled the silent air and the scent of vomit mixed with the sweet smell of evergreen and flowers.

Remaining bent over, he rested his hands on his knees and spit a couple times to get the sour taste out of his mouth, feeling the flush of his skin give away to cold. The silence of the Boundary Lands closed around him like a fist once more. He had to get out of here.

Straightening, he shrugged his jacket off and used it to wipe his mouth, then threw it down. Picking up his shoes, he made his way through the forest, trying to forget where he was. He had a long way to go.

And someone very special to meet.

THREE

ELIZABETH knelt in her garden—one of many she tended throughout the Boundary Lands—and held her open palm over the earth, feeling the damp power of the land spiraling up into her bare skin. The water in the Boundary Lands constantly called to her other self and, sometimes, like tonight, it was hard to resist.

Moonlight glowed above her, bleaching the color from her skin. She concentrated on the back of her hand, convincing herself to stay in her physical form. She had work to do. This was one of the places where she grew fruit and vegetables for herself and others using her own particular brand of asrai magick. The food needed to be picked, planted, and distributed.

She could coax the soil to produce a wide variety of lettuces, turnips, potatoes, carrots, peas, tomatoes—even apples and peaches—out of their regular season and make them grow very fast. Centuries ago, when grocery stores hadn't existed, her brand of fae power had been highly sought after. Now she used it to feed the old and infirm residents of the Boundary Lands. This particular garden produced vegetables. She tended it every night.

Digging her fingers into the cool night-touched soil, she sought one of the potatoes under the earth, drew it out, and popped it into her basket. She had a Midas touch when it came to growing things. All she had to do was pop another sprout-ling into the ground and an additional potato would grow no matter the conditions or the time of year. Tomorrow night it would be ready to feed someone.

Just as she was replacing the seed potato, the hair at her nape rose. A presence had entered her gardening area. Her lips curled into a smile. Ah, so he'd joined her tonight after all. She'd suspected maybe he'd given in and accepted he'd never catch her. But, of course, he wouldn't give up—he couldn't. Not a man like him.

Leaving her vegetable basket on the ground, she turned on the balls of her booted feet and crept quietly into the bushes that edged her garden, listening for his tread on the forest floor. He tried so hard to be quiet, but Niall Quinn was no nature fae. He would never fail to leave some kind of passing impression to a wildling.

Peering from between the leaves, she watched him pass, charmed iron rope in his hands. So he was back to the rope trick again. She shook her head. Dealing with this man wasn't even a challenge for her. It was almost sad, really.

"Elizabeth," he called, turning around in a slow circle. "I don't want to hurt you. Just give me the pieces and I'll leave you alone. You can go back to hiding in the trees or whatever it is you do. You can keep doing that once the walls are down for that matter. What the rest of the Piefferburg fae want has nothing to do with you. You shouldn't care if the walls stand or not."

Her jaw clenched. He knew nothing about her, but she supposed that was probably a good thing. It kept her loved ones safe.

"It's pretty selfish of you, isn't it?" he called. "Keeping those pieces from your people. Who do you think you are, anyway?"

A daughter protecting her mother from premature death, but, of course, she couldn't tell him that.

He'd walked over to stand near her. If she reached out she'd be able to feel the rough texture of his jeans against her finger-tips.

"Do the right thing, Elizabeth. You're a good person. I know you must comprehend that hiding the pieces is wrong."

She eased out of the bush without a sound and crossed the path in front of him. She probably looked like a silvery shadow to Niall. He called her name and bolted after her, but she was already gone—a safe distance away from him.

"Maybe what *you're* doing is wrong. Have you ever considered that?" she called. "Have you considered what will happen to the fae if the walls break? There will be chaos and violence when we're released into a world of people who hate and fear us."

"Not all of them hate and fear us. The humans seem fascinated and confused by us, but the majority doesn't seem to hate us. As a people, they seem to regret imprisoning us, even."

He'd gotten too close. Damn, the man moved fast.

She shot away from the sound of his voice, circling back toward her garden. "Bullshit," she called over her shoulder. "Have you seen *Faemous's* coverage of the armies massing at our gates? They're all carrying weapons. Niall, maybe we're better off in here. We have our own society, our cultures are intact. We're safe here."

"We're trapped. Enslaved. And we're not safe, Elizabeth. If the Phaendir can find a way to exterminate us without pissing off the government, they will. Especially now that Gideon Amberdoyal is archdirector. Have you been that sheltered out here that you don't know this?"

His voice possessed a withering, condescending quality that made her snarl at him. "I may be a reclusive wildling, but I'm not stupid. I know the risks we face."

"Good. Then give us the pieces."

He was following the sound of her voice. She passed through her garden and out the other side. He still had no chance in hell of catching her, poor guy. "I wish I could, but I can't. You don't understand, and I wish I could make you see. If I could, you would understand that you're the selfish one, not me."

"Elizabeth—" The word cut off abruptly and his voice faded into surprise. "This is your garden? Is this why you're here so often?" He sounded like he was standing somewhere near where she'd left her basket, over by the potato patch.

She snorted. "As if I'd answer any questions about myself," she called. "How do you know where to find me every night, by the—" She turned and Niall was standing right in front of her, close enough to kiss. Her eyes widened and her lips parted. Maybe he was more formidable an opponent than she'd assumed.

He wore a cocky little smile of triumph on his handsome face. The rope he held loosely in his hands looped over her head and pulled tight around her waist and arms. "The same way I can throw my voice. Magick."

Her gaze met his and held. Her breath rushed out of her in a little surprised puff. "Tricky."

She could feel the charmed iron in the rope length vaguely sapping the strength from her body, but as long as it wasn't touching her bare skin, she was all right. Thank Danu she'd worn jeans and a heavy sweater tonight against the chill in the air.

His gaze swept down her body. "Wearing clothes for a change, I see." His full lips twisted. "Pity."

He'd probably expected her to be naked due to her mode of travel, but she'd used her ATV tonight. It was the perfect vehicle for the Boundary Lands and allowed her to stay clothed.

She was able to travel by kelpie, too. She was one of the few fae able to ride them and survive. Usually the massive black horses drowned all those who accepted their offers of a ride, but her nature was kin to theirs—of water.

She tipped her head to the side and gave him a little smile. "This won't work, you know."

He grinned, showing dimples and a devilish glint in his eyes. "Looks like it's working just fine to me."

She shook her head. "No, sorry. I'm letting you hold me right now."

His smile grew a little cockier. He raised an eyebrow. "And why would you do that?"

"You fascinate me."

"Ah. Yes, well, I fascinate many women."

"I didn't mean it that way."

His smile faded and his grip tightened on the rope. "In what way did you mean?"

Her eyes narrowed. "You really know nothing about me, do you, Niall?"

He yanked her toward him and dropped his head a degree. His mouth lingered a heartbeat away from hers, so close she could feel his breath warming her lips. "Maybe you can educate me."

She paused, enjoying the press of his body against her a little more than she should. He had a strong chest and arms, muscular and warm. For a moment she hoped he'd drop his mouth to hers and kiss her. She'd never been kissed before.

Reality jerked her back from the danger she was flirting with. She couldn't play around like this, no matter how tempting and intriguing this man was.

She smiled sweetly. "Good-bye, Niall."

"No. Eliz—"

But she was already dissolving into the world of liquid, giving herself over to the rain, the rivers, and the streams, becoming one with all the moisture in the earth . . . surrendering.

NIALL hunched over a dusty tome in one of the small, dank rooms of the Black Tower, swearing at the top of his lungs. "Asrai, asrai. Fucking asrai," he chanted, paging through the fading book. "Why is there nothing in here about the asrai?"

You really know nothing about me, do you, Niall?

That sentence still rang through his mind. No, he didn't. He was working on precious little information about her, in fact, and it drove him crazy he couldn't find more.

The door whined open, and Bella Quinn, his sister-in-law, entered with a new stack of books. "How's it going?"

He snarled inarticulately at her.

"That good, huh? Maybe I better call in some help to do research." She surveyed the piles of books he still had to go through.

"I'd rather be out hunting her than stuck in here reading." He turned a page and ran his finger down it. Yet he needed inspiration to strike—something to give him an idea of how to catch her.

She nodded. "The queen will order hundreds of people to do research if it will help you. You know she will if you ask."

Niall was aware of that, but he didn't trust anyone but himself to do this job. Call him a control freak, but he might come across a tidbit about the asrai that sparked an idea in his mind, while another would just pass over it.

He leaned back in his chair and looked up at her. She had dust caught in her dark hair. "I have a couple more tricks up my sleeve. I just want to make sure they'll fucking work this time."

"Do you know what her motivation is yet? If you can find that out, maybe you can use it against her."

He scowled. "No, and it's pissing me off. The way she talks, it's almost like she thinks the walls falling would hurt those she loves. She sounds like she might be protecting someone."

"Protecting someone from the walls falling? That doesn't make sense. No fae is safe with those walls up."

Niall considered her words for a moment before standing. "Look into it. See if there are any fae who will be directly harmed by the walls coming down. Maybe my key to cracking Elizabeth lies there. In the meantime, I've got one radical move to make. I hope it works."

"Me, too."

He surveyed the mess of books, scowling. It was anyone's guess since the damn books weren't cooperating enough to tell him what his chances were. "Go ahead and get some people to research for me. It's clear I can't do this on my own."

"I will," answered Bella, looking up from a tome. "You finally met your match, huh?"

He grunted at her. "If you find anything interesting, I'll be in the Boundary Lands. I can't tell you how fucking sick I am of trees." He moved toward the door.

"Niall?"

He turned back around.

"What's she like?"

He shrugged. "Clever. Witty. Too fucking pretty by half. I think you'd like her."

"It sounds like *you* like her."

He glowered at her. "How could I like anyone who's keeping the final two pieces of the *bosca fadbh* from us?"

NIALL slammed his map down on the hood of his SUV and surveyed it. He'd been tracking Elizabeth's moves for the last three nights. She probably knew he'd been following her, but he hadn't engaged her at all. Hadn't so much as uttered a word since the night he'd had her in his rope. Instead he'd been charting her movements. Where she spent her time and for how long.

Mostly her travels involved checking on the gardens she kept throughout the woods. She harvested the food and delivered it to homes throughout the Boundary Lands, mostly to the elderly or the bed-ridden.

How fucking sweet. And out of character for a rat bastard of a fae who would steal and keep hidden the last pieces of the *bosca fadbh*. It didn't make sense.

Nothing about this woman made sense.

Other than growing and collecting fruit and vegetables and delivering them to the needy, Elizabeth took the occasional foray to a spring or a river to bathe. He'd tried to be a gentleman and not peek. Really, he'd tried.

Mostly, he'd failed.

He was a man, after all, right? A very healthy man with certain . . . needs . . . that weren't getting met while he was out here communing with the Danu-forsaken trees every night.

Anyway, he was pretty sure she'd known he was there. She'd just been teasing him. And tease him, she had. The woman was lovely—pale skin that glowed in the moonlight, breasts that weren't huge but weren't tiny either, just big enough to cup in his hands. *Her ass.* He groaned, remembering. Perfect. Beautiful. His fingers itched to stroke it.

For the five millionth time he cursed the Summer Queen for picking a woman as gorgeous as Elizabeth Cely Saintjohn to do her dirty work.

Stabbing his finger down onto the map, he looked up into the sky. Twilight was falling fast. It was time to put the final touches on his plan. For the last three nights he'd been following Elizabeth, he'd had Aeric O'Malley and a crew of fae workers out in the woods constructing an elaborate trap.

In order to keep Elizabeth from noticing the activity, he'd cast a concealing spell over the area and had them work during the day, the time when an asrai was fast asleep.

Tonight was the night he'd catch her. He could feel it. No way could even an asrai slip *this* snare. Tonight he was going to play cowboy and herd this wild horse into a corral.

She'd be his by midnight.

This garden was the one where Elizabeth spent most of her time, so he could count on her showing up tonight. Once he did, his plan would be put into action. With the weight and resources of the entire Black Tower behind him, there was no way he wouldn't eventually prevail against one little wildling fae, no matter how tricky her methods of evasion.

In the distance he heard the engine of an ATV cut off. Soon a presence behind him made the hair on the back of his neck stand up, and the sweet scent of Elizabeth wafted on the cool evening breeze to tease his nose. She was here. Excellent.

He wished he could've kept Aeric here to help him catch her, but Niall had worried that the presence of anyone other than him would make her dissolve before he could snare her. He was her enemy, but she was growing more and more accustomed to his presence. Hell, he knew she was laughing at him and all his failed attempts to trap her.

Tonight *he* would be the one laughing.

He circled the garden and caught sight of her kneeling in the center of a pea patch, the moonlight washing out the vibrant red of her hair. There were faint gold tones in that fall of beauty; he'd noticed last time he'd seen her up close.

"Hello, Niall," she said without looking up from her plantings. "You're not fooling anyone, you know. To my ears you make about as much noise as an elephant."

"Glad to know my presence doesn't alarm you."

"*Annoy* would be a better word to use. You've been following me around relentlessly. Tracking my movements, are you? I never in all my days thought I'd have a stalker."

He lowered his voice a degree. "I never in all my days believed a fellow fae would deny her people freedom."

Her shoulders seemed to stiffen. "I guess we're both full of surprises, then, aren't we?"

"Let's stop this silly dance, Elizabeth. Just talk to me. Tell me why you're doing this."

She shook her head. "You wouldn't understand."

"Try me."

"No." She stood. Her gaze met his across the garden. "You'll never get those pieces from me while I'm alive, Niall. You seem like a nice guy even though you're Unseelie. Are you prepared to kill me to get them?"

He steadied his gaze. "I hope it doesn't come to that, but, yes. The stakes are too high. I'll kill you if I have to." He paused. "I've been thinking that's probably going to be the ending to this story."

She glanced away from him, up at the waning moon. "Too bad you don't know where they are, right? Then you could just murder me now and go get them."

He didn't blink. "Yes, a pity."

They stood staring at each other for a long moment. The element of teasing that had been present in their former encounters seemed to be gone tonight. Niall worried that he'd pushed her too far. Maybe tonight, instead of leading him on a chase to arrogantly prove she could, she'd just dissolve and be gone.

Suddenly, she dropped her basket and bolted like a jack-rabbit into the foliage.

Thank the goddess for her ego. Tonight it might mean the end for her.

He ripped through the bushes in pursuit, branches scraping at his face and pulling at his clothes. The woman was like a deer, able to leap fallen tree trunks and bushes like no one he'd ever seen. It was a damn good thing he was in shape, but even in shape it was a real chore to keep behind her. Tonight it was even more important to keep her on the run since he needed to subtly guide her to where he wanted her to go.

She veered to the left and he went wider, gently nudging her toward the right. Tonight there was no banter, no stopping to chat from a distance. Tonight he was the hunter and she was the hunted—even if she didn't truly understand that.

Little by little he herded her toward a clearing about fifty feet from her garden. His chest burned from exertion, his face felt on fire from being whacked with branches, and his clothes were torn and dirty.

Just a little more to the right and he'd have her.

ELIZABETH laughed softly as she vaulted a clump of black-berry bushes, enjoying the stretch of her muscles and the faint burn of her lungs. Niall was really serious tonight. It was a good opportunity to show him that he would never be able to catch her. Maybe she could get him to finally back off and give up. Leave her alone.

Honestly, she'd kind of miss him, though.

And, anyway, he wouldn't be the last the Black Tower sent. The Shadow Queen would never give up on retrieving the pieces. She could expect others to come after her, maybe Unseelie that weren't as pleasant as Niall Quinn.

Elizabeth fully anticipated a short life.

She dashed into the middle of a clearing. A stream ran on the other side. That was where she'd make her exit. She didn't have to dissolve directly into water, but it did seem to make the transference experience go a little smoother.

Leaping over a boulder, she almost flew into the tree line on the opposite side, the run through the woods absolutely no trouble for her at all.

And ran straight into what felt like an invisible brick wall.

FOUR

SHE impacted and bounced backward, sliding along what seemed like a smooth, hard floor. But that was impossible! Pain exploded through her, robbing her of any opportunity to examine the strangeness of what had just occurred. Instead she sucked in a pained breath, holding her stomach, and rolled to her side, trying to drag air into her lungs.

From some distant place in her stunned mind, she noticed that every noise she made sounded loud and off . . . *echoing* . . . like she was in a big metal box, not out in the woods.

Somewhere a door slammed shut. All light extinguished.

"Wha—?" She fought through her disorientation, tasting blood on her tongue from where she'd split her lip. "What's happening?"

Above her came the sound of sliding metal and a crack of moonlight. "I win," came Niall's voice. He sounded exerted and out of breath. "Your ass is mine now, Elizabeth."

"Where am I?" she managed to ask, rolling onto her hands and knees and spitting blood onto the strange, smooth floor. It *was* a big box made of metal, she noted now. Charmed iron, to be exact. Now that she'd noticed, she could feel it sapping her magick.

Oh. Sweet Lady Danu, no.

She looked around, realization slamming into her. She was in a long, wide charmed iron box camouflaged to look like forest. Even though she was fully dressed, she had no defenses against this much charmed iron.

"You're trapped." Niall sounded smug.

He must have had this built during the day, when she'd been sleeping. That whole chase, he'd just been herding her right where he'd wanted her to go.

Trapped.

Panic clawed at her throat, made a tight fist in her stomach.

She dissolved immediately, shifting to her other self, her body sliding into its watery state.

Slippery. Hard. No earth. No freedom. No surrender. Suffocating. *Dying . . .*

She re-formed, her breath coming in short, little pants. Her lungs burned, her body ached. She rolled onto her side and realized she was naked, her clothes crushed beneath her from her shift. The charmed iron touched the bare parts of her body, sapping her energy and her life force even faster and harder.

"This is going to kill me," she croaked. "Let me go."

Niall said nothing for a long moment. "Tell me where the pieces are."

"No! I can't."

The small metal door slammed shut.

She slumped to the floor and concentrated on breathing. It wouldn't take her long to die in here, with this much of her skin exposed to the iron. Her mother would grieve if she died, but at least her mother would be safe. If she died now, they'd never find the pieces. Never break the walls.

But, *oh, Lady*, she didn't want to die.

Elizabeth wasn't sure how long she laid there, her body growing weaker and weaker. Finally the sound of the larger door being opened met her ears and moonlight flooded the box.

"Stubborn woman," Niall grumbled as he knelt beside her and touched her upper arm with a gentleness that seemed odd.

He hated her, right? So why lay his hand on her arm as if he cared about her welfare? Nonetheless, he rubbed his fingers along her skin, and strange comforting warmth flooded her body.

Pushing his hand away, she reached an arm toward the opening of the box. If she was stronger, she could bolt for it. But all she could do was lie there and allow Niall to pull her hands to the small of her back and snick a pair of cuffs around her wrists.

He pulled her gently to her feet. "Walk," he commanded, pushing her toward the opening.

She stumbled out of the stifling box and drew the clean evening air into her lungs. That, combined with the absence of so much charmed iron against her skin, seemed to clear her mind. The earth taunted her under her bare feet. She wanted so much to dissolve right into it and escape, but now the charmed iron touching the bare skin at her wrists prevented that. "Bastard," she spat.

"Now, now." Niall clucked his tongue. "You had this coming."

"You made me run headlong into a wall!"

"And you got off lucky. All I see is a little boo-boo on your lower lip. Still have all your teeth, don't you? No broken nose or cheekbones? No concussion? No broken arms or legs?"

"No. I'm just bruised from head to toe!"

"Bruised is better than broken. I spelled the wall you ran into to be much softer than it would have been naturally. You didn't slam into it so much as bounced off of it. I don't have time to deal with a bunch of injuries." He flashed a cocky smile at her. "You don't have to say thank you."

"Good. I won't."

"Don't be a poor sport, now. You've been playing with me for the last two weeks. Now *you've* been played. It happens to the best of us."

Yes, but his mother's life wasn't on the line.

He led her into the clearing, where she immediately became aware of her state of dress, or lack thereof. "The least you can do is give me some clothes."

"I don't have any on me right now." He gave her a slow up-and-down. "Anyway, I think I prefer you naked."

"Of course you do, you're a pig."

He *tsk*ed at her. "You're the one who tried to dissolve into charmed iron. It's your fault you're naked, not mine. Now come on. It's getting cold out here."

He led her through the woods to his SUV. She looked longingly at her garden as they passed it, thinking about all the vegetables that would go to rot and how the people she provided them to would go hungry. She had no illusions she'd be back anytime soon to pick them.

She had no illusions she'd *ever* be back to pick them.

A heavy feeling settled into her chest. If only she'd been more cautious, less cocky. Her capture meant she would be letting people down. Not only her mother, but so many others.

He opened the passenger side and helped her get in. She was practically sitting on her bound hands. "Can you at least move my wrists to the front instead of the back?"

He chuckled. "Yeah and have you take the opportunity to escape the moment the charmed iron leaves your skin? Not even. You'll have to wait until we get where we're going for that."

"What?" she asked sweetly, "You don't trust me?"

He pulled a blanket from the backseat and covered her with it. "Trust the fae who betrayed her people? Never."

The words pricked, but she tried not to show it. She looked straight ahead as he closed the door and climbed into the driver's side. He started the vehicle and guided it down the makeshift path through the woods. She saw now that the path was much more worn than it ever had been before, showing clearly that men and vehicles had been using it regularly for some time, building her trap, no doubt. She shivered.

Why hadn't she noticed the signs before? Had Niall used some sort of magick to hide the evidence? He was a mage, after all, with powers as unique as hers. She had no idea what his abilities were.

"What are you going to do with me?" Her voice sounded emotionless, flat.

"Right now I'm going to take you to a place where you can change into some clothes, have something to eat, and get warm in front of a fire. Then you're going to tell me where the pieces are."

"And if I don't?"

His voice dropped to a softly threatening purr. "If you don't, well, then I'll make you."

"You don't seem the type to enjoy hurting women. I'm sort of disappointed to find out you are."

"I never said I enjoyed it, but there's a reason I've been sent to do this job, Elizabeth."

"What's that?"

"I'm very good at finding things and persuading people. Let's just say I always get what I want."

"Huh. Funny. So do I."

"Great, something in common. This should be fun, then, right?"

She locked her jaw and stared out the window of the SUV. He guided the vehicle onto the main road and they drove for about fifteen minutes before he pulled onto a long gravel driveway that led to a cottage. After cutting the engine, he got out, came around the other side, and helped her out.

She made her way up the path, and he opened the door for her. The inside of the cottage was comfortable, with over-stuffed furniture and rough-hewn tables and chairs. A large creek stone fireplace dominated one wall.

He led her into the living room and took an object from a small table. Holding it up, he said, "This is a charmed iron restraint." He opened it, knelt, and snapped it around her ankle. Then, touching the hinge, he murmured a series of words in Old Maejian she could barely hear, and the hinge disappeared. Now it was a flat, smooth piece of charmed iron laying flush against her skin. She had no hope of getting it off, not without Niall's magick.

He stood. "Get it?"

Numbly, she nodded.

He removed the cuffs and jerked a thumb at one of the doorways off the short hallway that led to a bathroom. "I laid clothes on the bed for you. Get dressed while I make a fire."

She moved toward the bedroom.

"Oh, and Elizabeth?" She turned to stare at him with an expressionless face. "Don't get any bright ideas about running away. You know as well as I do that charmed iron will kill you if it stays against your skin for too long."

"How could I forget?" She shuffled into the bedroom.

NIALL poked a twig into the sputtering fire, making it spit, yet not quite catch the logs. Fuck, he hated tricking her like this.

Trapping Elizabeth was like trapping some wild, free thing. He had no illusions that he'd immediately crushed her spirit—she had plenty to spare—but she did seem a little less vibrant than she had before with that charmed iron cuff around her ankle.

This would be so much easier if he didn't have a whisper of admiration for her.

He had to constantly remind himself that she was hiding the pieces, working with the Summer Queen. This woman was scum for betraying her people. He could say the words, but something stopped him from really feeling them.

And, fuck, she was gorgeous. All that alabaster skin, the fiery long red gold hair, the swell of her hips, and the curve of her ass. Her breasts . . .

Damn. There weren't even words.

He'd seen a lot of beautiful women in his life. After a while they all started to look the same to him, but Elizabeth was in a class all by herself.

After she'd shifted and ended up nude, it had been really hard for him not to look his fill. He'd managed to refrain. That would have been wrong. She was at his mercy right now, and he was enough of a gentleman not to take advantage of that.

The sound of footsteps behind him made him look over his shoulder. She'd dressed in the long, filmy white nightgown he'd given her. Eschewing the shoes he'd provided, she was still barefoot, the metal of the cuff glinting at her ankle. Her hair hung long and tangled over her shoulders. She hadn't washed away the blood where she'd split her lip, and a bruise was forming on her forehead.

She took him in, struggling with the fire, and knelt beside him, making a frustrated sound. "Don't you know how to build a fire?"

He rocked back on his heels. "Don't go camping much."

"Obviously." She rolled her eyes. In about two minutes a blaze roared in the hearth.

She stood and backed away from him, gaze holding his.

He studied her. "Why are you helping me?"

She gave him a *duh* look. "Because we'd both freeze before you could make an adequate fire on your own."

"No, I mean, why aren't you raising hell right now? Why aren't you fighting me, trying to escape, *something*."

She smiled slowly, but there was an edge to it. Her eyes glittered. "Do you think I've given up? That I've accepted my fate? Do you think I'm. . . . *resigned*?"

"I don't have the slightest clue what's going on in your head."

"You can bet your sweet little tush it isn't surrender. Not to you." Her eyes narrowed. "Don't think for a second I'm going to make this easy on you." She paused, her smile widening. "I'm going to make it impossible."

He smiled his own hard, glittering smile back at her. Yes, he would wager her will was strong, but it couldn't hold a candle to his.

Let the games begin.

ON a narrow gravel pathway that was only wide enough for one vehicle, Gideon parked the small, rusting junk heap he'd stolen back in Sioalte and vowed that next time he'd swipe something with a little more class. The door squeaked open and he slammed it shut, then made his way through the prickly bushes and overgrown hedges, into yet more of the Labrai-cursed Boundary Lands.

The air was redolent with the scent of pine and fresh flowers. A distance away, he could hear the crash of the waves on the beach. All around him birds twittered and sang, happy to be alive.

It disgusted him.

Every moment he spent in Piefferburg was another moment that the corrupt magick in this land seeped into his flesh like a cancer, fouling his very DNA. Sometime after he'd entered, a bitter grimace had settled onto his face and nothing seemed able to remove it.

It was just lucky that none but two people in the entire area of Piefferburg could recognize him. Over the years he'd been careful to keep his face off *Faemous*, the frivolous twenty-four-hour-a-day human TV coverage of the Rose Tower. The two women who had seen his face in person, Emmaline Siobhan Keara Gallagher and Charlotte Lillian Bennett, resided in the Black Tower, so he was unlikely to happen upon them. Eventually he would seek them out.

They were both on his list of people to kill.

He walked for what seemed like forty-five minutes, his mood growing blacker with every step. The weeds grew more tangled and the trees scrubbier as he made his way in. The scent of seawater teased his nose. He was growing close.

Finally the pathway opened into a clearing. Here the scrub ended and roses bloomed in profusion. Lilies and tulips competed with hyacinth, and all the trees glittered as if hung with jewels. He stopped and stared, working his tongue around the sour taste in his mouth and grimacing as if in pain. The air was malodorous with spring even though it was nearly winter.

Flashy. Beautiful. Arrogant. Over the top. Just daring the world to tell her stop.

He would expect nothing less of Caoilainn Elspeth Muirgheal. Even in hiding, she was a show-off.

Before him rose a cliff of crumbling rock. He made his way to the small opening at the bottom and stepped within. The stone of the huge, high-ceiling "room" had been polished and cleaned. The walls and floor were mostly even, but free of adornment. Fire flickered in mounted lanterns, casting long, flickering shadows over the rock walls. Two rows of the gold-and-rose-bedecked Imperial Guard stood on either side, still as statues and obviously loyal to their queen to the bitter end.

One of them moved to greet him. "Gideon Amberdoyal?" His voice echoed *doyal . . . yal . . .* The man's eyes glinted with malice, and Gideon knew an acute moment of unease as he studied the man's very pointy sheathed sword.

"I am." His voice ricocheted sharply off the walls and ceiling.

"Come with me. You're expected."

The guard walked toward a crack in the far wall and Gideon followed, their footsteps echoing. He was led down a narrow flight of stairs carved into the stone. Fire flickered over the rough stone walls from intermittent sconces, throwing shadows that crawled over the guard's back, the steps, the walls.

Somewhere nearby, below them, came a crash that seemed to make the entire stairway vibrate. "What was that?"

"Waves. We're in a cliff overhanging the ocean."

At the end of the stairway, the guard led him through a

small room, what passed for an antechamber. The wide doorway ahead of them radiated pure white light. They stepped
into a room that was much colder than the rest of the place,
and Gideon shielded his eyes, blinking.

Another wave crashed against the cliff as his sight adjusted.
The guard was gone, leaving him alone in an immense room
of polished white marble shot through with veins of rose.
Enormous pillars were scattered throughout, rising to a beau-
tiful fresco stretching the length and breadth of the ceiling.
The scene? Of course it was the crowning of Caoilainn Elspeth
Muirgheal, the Summer Queen of the Seelie Tuatha Dé Da-
nann sídhe.

She sat on a throne in the center of the immense space,
with a group of men standing at the base of the dais. Gideon
recognized the cadre of his Phaendir who had entered Piefferburg the day before he had—the ones who would be his
hive in here, allowing him to wield magick.

He also recognized the big, red-haired form of Liam Connall Deaglan Mag Aoidh, leader of the free fae, who had
entered with the Phaendir. Liam and his free fae didn't want
the walls to fall because most of them had killed fae and
would be reaped by the Wild Hunt. They'd been helping the
Phaendir thwart the efforts of the Shadow Queen and her ilk
to procure the pieces of the *bosca fadbh* but they'd failed
twice.

They'd all failed.

The first time had been in Israel, when Emmaline Gallagher had retrieved the second piece from the depths of the
ocean where it had been hidden in a charmed box. The second
time they'd failed to stop Charlotte Bennett from taking the
third piece from the base of the Stone of Destiny in Ireland.

"Well." The young, yet somehow old, voice of the Summer
Queen rang out like poisonous bells. "We meet again, Gideon.
How long has it been?"

He walked toward the group, satisfied beyond all measure
that he was tracking dirt all over her pristine white marble
floors. His clothes were dirty and ripped, his shoes ruined. He
looked like he'd crawled his way up from a grave. "Three hundred and seventy years at least."

She looked the same. Fair, young, fresh face framed with a

riot of soft blond curls. Just as the last time he'd seen her, she was swathed in head-to-toe silk and satin, gold and rose. Sapphire jewelry winked from her ears, wrists, and the slender column of her throat.

He gave her a slow, cool blink, his jaw locking. "Not long enough."

Her smile felt cold enough to frost his skin. "Indeed. It would have been better were we never to meet, would it not? Not even all those centuries ago."

"Not for the Phaendir," he ground out. He wasn't going to say thank you for helping them create Watt Syndrome all those years ago. She'd helped them for her own selfish reasons. In return they'd made a nice show of "capturing" her and "imprisoning" her in Piefferburg. "Nice place you have here." He swung an arm wide. "Very big, very . . . *polished.*"

"Did you think I never prepared for this eventuality? I had this stronghold created under strictest secrecy not long after Piefferburg was formed. Everything in this place is designed to suit my will, even the very cliffs you're standing in now. It took me centuries to erode the land to create them." She smiled. "I enjoy cliffs. They have a certain raw beauty."

Gideon grunted. He hadn't seen them, but he imagined they looked a lot like the White Cliffs of Dover. "Interesting." And yet, not. "Let's get on with business."

She waved a hand to encompass their group. "And here we are, you and I. Partners once again. We are the triad of doom, are we not? The head of the Phaendir, the leader of the betrayer free fae, and the treacherous, scheming Summer Queen?" Despite her words, there was no note of self-loathing in her voice. Instead she sounded proud, even a little amused, like this was all a game to her.

Maybe the whole Piefferburg experience had been a game to her, from Watt Syndrome to now, and she didn't want the game to end. She didn't want her little court to be distracted by the wide world, to stop worshipping her.

Liam forced his jaw to unlock long enough to answer, "United for a good cause." Bitterness and sarcasm infused his voice. He clearly wasn't happy to be here, either. After all, he and his free fae had escaped the Great Sweep only to be separated forever from their friends and family. Liam probably hated being forced to ally with the people who'd made Piefferburg possible.

Gideon understood the desire of the free fae to keep the walls standing, hate them though he did. But, one day, when he didn't need the free fae anymore, he would find a way to get rid of them.

The Summer Queen's reasons for keeping the *bosca fadbh* from the Shadow Queen were a little more elusive. They had to do with her ego, of course, the monster that had created this polished marble room on the edge of a cliff in nowhereland. Within Piefferburg she was one of the most powerful beings. Outside Piefferburg she would be lost, alone. Her Seelie Court would scatter, seduced by the gleaming, glittering modern world. Outside Piefferburg she would be nothing to no one.

To a woman like Caoilainn, that was worse than death.

Gideon would have liked to say he'd kill her, too, when this was all over—but no one could kill the Summer Queen, short of herself or . . . "The Shadow Queen hasn't sent the goblins or the sluagh for you yet?" he asked with the sweetest smile he could manage through his permanent sour grimace.

The Queen of the Unseelie had power over the goblins, able to command them as she wished. In addition, Aislinn Christiana Guinevere Finvarra was a necromancer, married to the leader of the Wild Hunt. Together they had the ability to summon the sluagh, an immortal army of unforgiven dead.

The Summer Queen might be able to fight off the goblins, but not the sluagh. Not for the long term. A protective barrier would work for a while, but eventually the flesh-eating monsters would break through.

"Pah! She's too weak. She cares too much about the rights of the goblins to order them around, and if she calls the sluagh for me she risks never locating the pieces of the *bosca fadbh*." She waved a glittering hand. "She's useless. Anyway, I have defenses against anything the Shadow Queen sends my way."

"I'm surprised one of your own guards hasn't slit your throat yet, Caoilainn." Liam's voice sounded just like how his face looked—hard, mocking. Not even his flowing Irish accent could soften it. It was a dangerous attitude to take with a woman like the Summer Queen. Yet, Gideon suspected Liam didn't care much. Either that or he was just stupid.

She swiveled her head around and stabbed him with her icy blue gaze. The air cooled to the point of giving Gideon the shivers. Her magick was related to her emotions, which meant the room in which she sat was always a few degrees colder than anywhere else. "I have surrounded myself with my most loyal. Never doubt my judgment, boy." She held up her hand and pointed to the Summer Ring, the piece of jewelry that became a part of the Seelie Royal's very body, imbuing the wearer with eternal life and power beyond imagining. "And never think anyone can harm me."

Liam spat on the floor. "I don't give a shite if you're harmed. I just want to keep the fecking walls from falling." His gaze moved through the Phaendir to Gideon's face. "Then you can all die and rot in hell."

Gideon smiled. "Well, aren't we a happy little triad of doom." As if to punctuate his sentence, a particularly huge wave crashed into the cliff, making the room shake.

"The fae whore," Gideon said, getting down to business. "Where is she?"

"The one I gave the pieces to? The asrai?" The queen waved a hand. "Running around the woods like always. The Unseelie mage, Niall Quinn, the one with the blood of the Phaendir, is chasing her, but he will never get the pieces. She's protecting her mother." Her gaze met Liam's. "Her motivation is a lot like yours. She will never reveal the location of the hidden pieces, not even under threat of death."

"How can you be so sure?"

"Long ago I looked into the soul of Emmaline Siobhan Keara Gallagher and saw that she would make the perfect assassin for the Rose Tower. For many years, she did. Don't you think I used my abilities to look into the soul of Elizabeth Cely Saintjohn to discover the strength of her will before I gave her the pieces? I'm confident in the decision I made. The pieces are safe, safer than they would be even with me."

Gideon trusted no one, not even the Seelie Queen and her powerful magick. He definitely didn't trust her judgment or opinion. He stroked his chin. "Do you know where she hid them?"

"No. Once I handed them over, she concealed them, and she won't even tell *me* where they are."

"Pity."

"Why?" She shrugged a shoulder like it was nothing. "They're safe as can be."

Gideon looked up at her with daggers in his eyes. "The only time they'll be safe is when they're in *my* hands, and in my hands they *shall* be."

"Well, I guess you should have contacted me sooner, before I was forced to hide them on my own. Now they're out of your reach."

He ignored her excuse. "Now I'm going to have to track this woman down and torture the information out of her."

Frost tipped his nose and his skin turned blue. The Phaendir near him, faces dark within their hoods, flinched. "What did I just say about doubting my judgment?" she snapped. "When I told you the woman won't give up the location of the pieces even under threat of death, I meant it."

Gideon's lips peeled back from his teeth in an attempt to smile. "My dear Summer Queen, there are things worse than death."

FIVE

ELIZABETH sat on the couch and toyed with the silver cuff around her ankle, all the while trying to kill Niall with her gaze alone.

He'd done something to the doors and windows, locked her in magickally somehow. She knew that because she'd tried to climb out the window in the bedroom. She'd been neither able to unlock it nor break the glass.

If she escaped, she still wouldn't be able to get the cuff off, of course, but she could die trying. That was better than having Niall do the deed. She had no doubt he would. For all his charm and softening of charmed iron walls, there was a ruthlessness in his eyes that warned her to stay wary.

If she was going to make a break for it, she would have to do it soon. The iron sickness was leaching away her strength little by little. A nature fae's resistance to charmed iron was lower than the other fae. Some suspected it was because the nature fae were more aligned with the elements than the rest. Soon she'd be too weak to run. She had a feeling he was waiting for that—waiting for her to weaken so he could press her for the pieces.

Poor, deluded fool.

"Where did you meet the Summer Queen when she handed over the pieces?" Niall walked over to stand near the edge of the couch, his dark eyes skating over her hungrily as they so often did.

Men were men. Place a halfway attractive woman near them and they all acted the same.

She turned her face away from him. She could tell him that much. The information meant nothing. "We met in the Boundary Lands, at a stream by New Orkney. She had two guards with her and was *not* dressed for traipsing through the underbrush. Why do you want to know?"

"She's gone into hiding." He sat down on a chair nearby.

"Well, don't look at me. I don't know where she went." She paused, looking down at her ragged fingernails. "But I'm surprised she ran, doesn't seem her style. I'm surprised she's not still sitting in the Rose Tower, thumbing her nose at everyone and proving how powerful she is."

"Caoilainn is interested in few things as much as her own neck. She knows how to survive. Most of the Seelie Tuatha Dé are upset with her for what she's done, but she's declawed them so much over the years that they can't retaliate with much more than fluffy white magick. They could grow roses at her feet, or produce a nice spring rain, maybe." He snorted. "That doesn't go for the Unseelie, who are far more unforgiving and a hundred times more powerful. Caoilainn fled to save herself from the Shadow Queen's eye. The Shadow Queen doesn't want to release the sluagh on her ass, but that doesn't mean she won't."

She raised her gaze to his. "The Summer Queen can't only fear the Shadow Queen. I know she's hard to kill, but I imagine losing her head wouldn't do her much good. I figure that will happen sometime soon. She can't take on all of Piefferburg and expect to live."

He jerked his chin at her. "And what about you? You're taking on Piefferburg, too. Do *you* expect to live?"

She snorted. "Of course not. My plan was to run for as long as possible and try my best to survive, but I always figured some Unseelie fae would eventually kill me trying to locate the pieces."

"Then why do this?"

She looked away from him, curling her bare feet under her

on the couch. Obviously, she wasn't going to answer. She changed the subject instead. "My vegetables are rotting in their plots, and the people I feed will starve."

"Guess you should have thought about that before helping the Summer Queen." When she didn't answer, he stared at her for a long moment. Finally he stood, his hands fisted at his sides. "You mystify me."

"I thought I annoyed and enraged you."

"Yeah, you do that, too. You're a woman of many talents. I'm going to get some wood."

He left the cottage door open while he was outside. Knowing she had few chances left, she sprang up and ran for it. Some invisible barrier flashed tingling pain through her and tossed her backward. She slid on the floor of the kitchen until coming to a stop near the dining room table. Pushing up on her hands, she glowered at him as he stood in the doorway with an armful of wood.

He clucked his tongue and shook his head. "You should know better, Elizabeth." He stepped over her and knelt by the cold hearth, building up a fire for the chilly evening to come.

"Are you just going to wait until I die of iron poisoning?"

He struck a match. "I hope not. I hope you'll come to your senses before then."

Disgruntled, she picked herself up off the floor and brushed herself off. "Why do you want out of Piefferburg so much? Do you really think humanity will welcome us with loving arms? Let us live where we want? Go where we want?"

He turned to her with a hard look in his eyes. "Do you really think I'll *let* them tell me any of that? I lived in the world before Piefferburg. I know what it is to go where I please and do what I want. Once I'm out of here, no one is going to dictate the terms of my life to me. In the centuries I have been locked in here, they have erected the Eiffel Tower, the Statue of Liberty. I want to see them. I want to go back to my homeland, walk on Irish soil once again, and breathe Irish air." His voice broke with emotion. "The world was meant to have fae in it, Elizabeth. It had fae in it long before the first human was a glint in some apelike creature's eye."

She grimaced at him. "I still don't understand what's so bad about life in here."

Niall said nothing. He finished building up the fire at his leisure, then stood and walked over to her, coming very close, close enough that she could feel his warm breath on her face. She fought the urge to take a step backward, hating the soft, excited curl in her belly that seemed to always be present when he came near her.

He leaned in so close he was almost kissing her. "I have no life in here." The words whispered against her lips. His eyes looked dark, haunted.

Her heart pounded out a crazy rhythm. Her body softened and her lips parted. For an awful, wonderful moment she thought his lips would touch hers. Then he was gone, across the room, and the chilly air closed around her like a lonely embrace. She hugged herself, rubbing her upper arms against the cold.

Disappointment weaved a bitter thread through her before she forced sense into her mind. Her libido needed a smackdown. This was the worst man in the world to feel attraction toward. She chalked it up to too much alone time in the woods. Stupid. Silly.

Dangerous.

She needed to watch herself. Never let her defenses falter. And tamp down this irrational reaction to him at any cost.

Drawing a deep breath, she forced her heart rate to ratchet down and walked into the living room. "You're wealthy, live in the Black Tower, have a brother here, friends. Doesn't seem so bad to me."

He looked at her. "How do you know about my brother?"

"The Quinn brothers? Everyone knows about you, even a reclusive nature fae like me has heard of you and Ronan."

The Quinn brothers were known not only because they were siblings, which were rare enough in the fae world, but because they were mages. Through some trick of fate or by deliberate motion of the goddess Danu's hand, the brothers had been born to a fae woman by a Phaendir father. That made them part-blood Phaendir and fae. It was completely unheard of. In all other known cases of Phaendir siring children with human or fae women, the offspring always turned out 100 percent Phaendir and always, *always*, male.

She took a step closer to him. "What was it like, living with them?"

"The Phaendir? We didn't live with them for very long. By the time our magick began to manifest it was clear that we were fae, not Phaendir, at our cores." His lips curled in a bitter smile. "We were called *abominations of nature* and were turned out by our father from the Phaendir enclave in Ireland."

"I'm surprised they didn't kill you."

"Looking back on it, so am I. It was the final mercy of our father, I guess."

Hugging herself against the chill in the cottage, she walked over and sat down on the edge of the couch. "So you went back to live with your mother in the fae community?"

He looked away from her. "She was dead by then, one of the very first of the fae to succumb to Watt Syndrome. No one even knew what it was back then. She just got sick and died. I don't think she would have accepted us, anyway."

"Why not?" She was so close to her mother, loved her so much and was loved in return; it was hard to imagine how any woman could reject her own child.

"She was Seelie, and the Phaendir magick in us made us Unseelie. Our magick was so versatile and could harm and kill in so many ways that we were considered to be dark fae."

She frowned and shook her head. "Your mother couldn't have been that pure and perfect. After all, she'd slept with a Phaendir."

"The story goes that our father forced her into marriage with him. They lived together long enough to sire us, just ten months apart. Then our father took us from her and forced her back to the Seelie Court. Ronan and I don't know the truth. In any case, she wasn't there for us to run to, and, even if she had been, she probably would have turned us away. Too many bad memories. She hated our father."

"Sweet Danu. You were just children. Where did you go?"

"The Shadow King had a stronghold near what is modern day Belfast. He welcomed us like long lost sons returning home."

"I'm sure he valued you for your uniqueness."

He stood and poked a stick into the fire to force a log to collapse into the flames. "Yes, and the Phaendir wanted to kill us. They castrated our father for siring us, to make sure he would never father another monster."

She grunted. "That's awful, but he did throw you to the wolves by turning you out."

"He was never a warm man, but that was an act of kindness. He gave us a chance at life. If we'd stayed, we probably would have had our throats cut in our sleep."

"Yes, the Phaendir are ever so merciful." Her voice was laden with sarcasm.

"Yes, Phaendir mercy." He looked up at her, eyes glittering and hard. "That's exactly why the fae need their freedom."

She shifted uncomfortably, looking away.

"How old are you?"

Great. Here would come some lecture about how young she was and how he had so much more life experience than she did. Sighing, she answered, "You must know I'm only in my twenties."

He walked to her and knelt beside her, taking her hands in his. "You are so young, Elizabeth. You can do anything, see anything, be anything. Do the right thing and I'll let you walk out of here. You can enjoy the rest of your life, free, and in the world. You can travel to India. You can rent an apartment in New York City, or you can fade into the rain forests of Brazil. The possibilities are limitless."

Yet all she wanted in the world was for her mother to survive. And here she was, likely to die a virgin.

Pulling her hands from his, she looked away from him, out the window.

"Don't make me do this, Elizabeth. Don't make me watch you fade away with that charmed iron on your skin."

She held his gaze steadily. "I'm not *making* you do anything you don't want to do, Niall. Stop acting like the wounded party here. I'm the one who is about to die." She cocked her head to the side. "I wonder if the Wild Hunt will come for you when I finally go?"

His jaw locked. He stood and turned away from her. "The Wild Hunt won't come for me because I'm under direct orders from the Shadow Queen to do whatever it takes to get the pieces from you." He half turned toward her. "But I'll regret it, Elizabeth. No matter how selfish a woman I think you are, I'll still regret your death. I'll regret what has to come next, too."

She sighed in exhaustion. "What comes next, Niall?"

"You know all about me, yet you don't know the nature of my magick? There's a reason I was sent to do this job." His voice held notes of tired resolution and steely resolve. "When I told you I intend to get the information out of you, I meant it. You won't let it go the easy way, so it will have to be the hard way."

He walked out of the room and left her shivering.

SIX

LIAM wandered the halls of the Black Tower, every molecule of his body on alert. There was only one person in all of Piefferburg that might recognize his face—Charlotte Bennett, the human woman who had taken the third piece of the *bosca fadbh* from the Stone of Destiny in Ireland.

He'd fought her there; the bitch had even stabbed him and left him for dead. His wound had barely healed. It hurt like hell all the time, especially when he exerted himself, but he wasn't going to let anything stop him from completing this mission.

There was no way Charlotte wouldn't recognize him if their paths crossed. That night it had been dark and everything had been chaos, but he was a distinctive man with his enormous build and his fire red hair. According to his information, Charlotte resided in the Black Tower with her new husband, Kieran Aindréas Cairbre Aimhrea. If she ran into Liam while he was poking around it could cause massive problems.

It had been hard for him to leave the Boundary Lands, where the Seelie Queen had her hideaway. Liam had been just a small boy when the Great Sweep had occurred and barely remembered what it was to be surrounded by the fae or immersed in an enchanted wood. He was a nature fae, though, and his blood remembered.

Standing in the Boundary Lands after having entered through the Phaendir's secret chink in the wall had been a heartbreakingly beautiful experience for him. He'd just stood there, arms outstretched, sprae lighting on his skin, head, back, and soaked it in. It had been like taking a warm bath after centuries of bitter cold. He'd barely even noticed the Phaendir retching in the grass all around him.

Now he came to the Black Tower, a betrayer of his own kind, yet what choice did he have? His adopted family of free fae were full of those who'd committed fae murder after the walls had gone up. If the walls came down, Aideen, his wife, along with so many others, would be swept away by the Wild Hunt faster than you could say *sluagh*. *Gone*.

So, here he was, totally alone, looking for any way he could to prevent the walls from coming down. Not only that, he was working with the fucking, conniving Summer Queen and the treacherous Phaendir. Danu, but he hated that.

The whole thing was making him cranky.

He stopped in front of the carved double doors of the Shadow Queen's receiving room. Two black-and-silver-garbed Shadow Guards stood on either side. They said nothing, didn't twitch a muscle. Liam bet if he reached for the door, they'd move all right. Instead he stood there, scowling at them both until the door finally opened.

A slim dark-haired woman stood in the entryway. He let out a slow breath of relief. It wasn't Charlotte. "Liam Connall Deaglan Mag Aoidh?"

He nodded. "I have an appointment with the queen."

"Yes." She held out a hand, which he squeezed. "My name is Bella. Come on in."

He entered the lushly decorated rose and white room. The Shadow Queen sat in the living room, with a good-looking man with long dark hair beside her. Probably the Shadow King, Gabriel Mac Braire, incubus, and Lord of the Wild Hunt. This was the bastard who'd reap his Aideen if the walls fell.

Bella led him over. "We don't get many nature fae to see the queen. If there's something specific you need during your stay, just ask for me."

"Thanks," he grunted. Their graciousness just made him feel that much guiltier. Would be easier if they were all fecking bitches and arseholes.

He walked over to stand in front of the queen. After a moment, he realized he should bow and did so. She motioned for him to sit down on a nearby sofa. He sat, examining her. The tattoo of the Shadow Amulet was faintly visible on her collarbone and neck. Swathes of silver and white fabric enfolded her slender form and a black and silver crown sat on her blond head. She was pretty and a little fragile-looking.

So this was the woman who had disposed the former Shadow King. She didn't look like much.

He remembered Aodh Críostóir Ruadhán O'Dubhuir, the former Shadow King, and his pet ogre, Barthe. He'd seemed the friendly sort, but fecking brutal as hell under his warm exterior. It was hard to believe this was his daughter.

The Shadow Queen raised her eyebrows. "Liam Mag Aoidh? You've come a long way from your home near Silver Branch. What do you require of the Shadow Court?"

He shifted on the couch and cleared his throat. He had to be careful to damp his Irish accent. Most of the inhabitants of Piefferburg had lost theirs over the years. "I think it's more a question of what the Shadow Court requires of me."

She raised a silver-blond eyebrow. "Really? How is that?"

"It's no secret that the Seelie Queen's gone rogue and run off with two pieces of the *bosca fadbh*. It's also no secret that she's passed them off to some nearly uncatchable fae to hide them for her. I can help you find that fae and get those pieces back."

Gabriel spoke up. "What skills do you possess that could help us?" The words went unspoken, but were perfectly audible to his ears—*since you're just a nature fae.*

"I have the ability to meld my consciousness with parts of the earth and locate objects." There, let them chew on that.

"That definitely is a relevant ability in this case, Liam," answered the Shadow Queen, "but Piefferburg is a pretty big area." It was. It was roughly the size of Virginia, in fact, the state just to the north of the detention area. "The woman hiding the pieces is an asrai, with the ability to become water at will and re-form anywhere within the bounds of the warding. She could have hidden the pieces absolutely anywhere in Piefferburg."

"Let me find the woman. If I can find her, maybe I can narrow down the possibilities for the location of the pieces."

"We already have a very capable man on that task."

"So send a second." He leaned forward. This was his fastest way of getting the job done. He could go out on his own to look for the woman, but the Shadow Queen had information that would make his job easier—like the location of the woman right at this moment. They were right, Piefferburg *was* a big place. He needed to convince them that he could help. "You need all the people on this that you can find."

"The one we sent is someone we trust implicitly, someone with highly specialized skills. You must understand that *trust* is very important, especially right now. The man we sent would not appreciate someone showing up who he doesn't know, no matter how helpful you could be in this situation. In fact, we're pretty sure he would act violently toward your presence."

"I can handle violent men. Send me. I want to help. I'm desperate to help. I need these walls broken." *Lie, lie, lie.*

The king and the queen shared a brief look. Then the Shadow King caught and held his gaze. "Look, Liam, thanks for offering your help. We might take it, but not quite yet. I understand you'll be staying here with us for a while?"

He gave a curt nod, his teeth grinding. This was his dismissal.

The Shadow King nodded back. "Good. Then we know where to find you in the event we need your help."

Not good enough.

FUCK. He didn't want to hurt her.

Niall entered the living room where Elizabeth was tied to a straight-backed chair and blindfolded. She'd let him do it, hadn't fought him a moment. It made guilt well up inside him hard enough to give him chest pains. He didn't want to see her suffer, this woman, yet the easiest thing would be to torture the information out of her. That's what the Shadow Queen expected of him. Torture was what he'd intended from the beginning.

He couldn't do it.

Striding past her, he went into the kitchen and leaned against the counter, bowing his head. *Damn it*. He wished the queen had sent someone else to do this job. His brother, Ronan. Anyone. Yet he suspected he knew why he'd been selected. Sure, it had to do with his special arsenal of skills, but she'd picked him for another reason, too—his compassion.

The Shadow Queen had known he would use restraint when another of the Unseelie might hurt her so badly she died before she gave up the location of the pieces. Niall was unlikely to do that.

But it was his compassion that was tying him in knots right now.

He shouldn't care about this woman. He should be willing to do whatever it took to get what he'd come for, yet one look from her big green eyes and he was toast.

That's why he'd blindfolded her.

"I can hear you, Niall." Her voice sounded steady and strong when it should have had a tremor of fear running through it. "Why don't you just come over here and do it?"

He turned and rubbed a hand over his face. "Last chance. Tell me what I need to know so I can set you free."

"Sorry. That's not going to happen."

"Screw your stubbornness, Elizabeth." His voice came out bitter and cold.

"Come give it your best shot, Niall, but you'll fail." Ah, now he could hear a note of fear in her voice. It was nice to know the woman wasn't made of stone. Maybe he would be able to reach past her defenses after all.

He pulled up a chair facing her and took her hands in his. For a moment, he studied her. Her long red hair lay tangled over her shoulders, dark against the creamy paleness of her skin, like garnets and gold woven into silk. Her full lips trembled just the slightest bit, and her hands were cold.

She was worried about what he was about to do—and she should be.

He could just make out the dusting of freckles across her nose under the blindfold. They reminded him of cinnamon.

He had an urge to count them, commit every last one to his memory.

After all, he would carry this woman with him forever after this was over. He would never forget her, would never go even a day without thinking of her.

He almost didn't do it, but couldn't stop himself in the end. It was a mistake and he knew it, but how often in his life had he knowingly made a mistake? Too often to count. So, he went ahead and made another one.

Leaning forward, he pressed his lips to hers.

She jolted with surprise in her seat, but didn't pull back.

Leisurely, he tasted her mouth, exploring those full lips by brushing his mouth over them slow and then even slower. Her fingers, twined with his, curled tighter and the softest noise escaped her throat. Her lips worked, kissing him back. Her tongue flicked out against his mouth, and a slow shiver crawled up his spine.

Dragging his hand up to the nape of her neck, he slanted his mouth across hers and parted her lips, sliding his tongue inside. His tongue tangled with hers and she made another soft noise, her tongue rubbing up against his and making his heart beat out a crazy rhythm. A warm, salty tear slid into his mouth, and for a moment he wasn't sure if it was hers or his.

Breaking the kiss, he rocked back, staring at her. Tear tracks snaked down her cheeks. His mouth was still filled with the taste of her—like wild, cold water from a stream.

"That was my first kiss." Raising her bound hands, she wiped at her cheeks with her fingers. "It was beautiful."

Surprise rocked through him. With any other woman he would take that for a lie—a desperate survivor's ploy—but he believed Elizabeth.

"Too bad it had to come from the man who is about to torture you." His voice came out leaden.

The small smile she wore faded. "Yes, that's bad luck, isn't it? Maybe a different time, a different place."

"With different stakes between us."

Fuck. Fuck, fuck, fuck!

He forced himself up and stalked to the other end of the room where he punched the wall, driving his fist through a layer of drywall. He wanted to think she was playing him.

But she wasn't.

Leaning his head against the wall and cradling his throbbing fist, he took a few deep breaths. Then he turned and walked back to her.

It was time.

ELIZABETH brushed her lips with the back of her hand and felt another teardrop land on her thigh. She wished she could be stronger than this and not cry. She wished she wasn't selfishly thinking of herself right now and the fact she was probably about to experience a lot of pain.

She wished it wasn't Niall who was about to deliver it.

Most of all, she wished she could live out the rest of her life, see her mother again, maybe even have another kiss like the one she'd just experienced. Yet she knew that was not to be her fate, not in this lifetime.

From somewhere across the room she heard a thump—like a fist hitting a wall. She jumped at the sound and the series of low curses that followed it. Clearly Niall didn't want to do this anymore than she wanted him to do it.

But she knew he would anyway.

After a few moments, Niall sat down opposite her and took her hands. This time the gentleness was gone. Now he meant business. Her body tensed as she waited for whatever torture he had in store for her. She had to endure it. She had to stay strong.

His hands gripped hers a degree harder and magick tickled her palms, skittering up her arms and through her shoulders. A small sound of fear rose in her throat and she swallowed it, her face screwing up with bitterness. Inch by inch the magick he wove around her reached deeper within, permeating every molecule of her body. It didn't hurt, not yet. Her muscles went tense, her jaw locked tight, teeth grinding, as she anticipated pain.

When was it coming? What was he going to do . . . ?

She stood in a moonlit clearing. Her blindfold had been removed. The cottage was gone. Niall was gone. She looked down at her hands. The rope that had bound them together had disappeared.

What had happened? Had she somehow dissolved even with the charmed iron on her?

No. That was impossible. Anyway, she was dressed. Looking down at herself, she saw she wore a pair of loose pants, the ones she favored, with her favorite soft navy shirt. She lifted one bare foot and saw that no cuff bound her ankle.

Above her the moon shone through a few scudding clouds. Lifting her face to it, she raised her arms, feeling the stretch of her muscles. She felt wonderful without that charmed iron touching her skin.

Stepping to the edge of the clearing, she reoriented herself. *Ah.* She was near one of her gardens! And her ATV was parked under the elm tree, just where she always left it. Hurrying over to her patch, she retrieved her basket and began to harvest ripe peas, tomatoes, and green beans. She could deliver them to Abertha, Sioned, and Donnell tonight.

As she picked, she wondered why she'd been standing in the middle of that clearing so confused. She'd come from her mother's house tonight, right? Yes, she remembered now. She'd stopped to see her mother first, after she'd woken in the late afternoon, before heading out to check her gardens, just as she did every night.

Niall . . .

The name breathed through her mind in her own voice, making her stop and raise her head. It almost sounded like a warning, but it was so far off. Who was Niall?

Frowning, she shook her head and went back to work. A pity she'd forgotten her seedlings from home. She'd have to go back for them before dawn and replant to ensure another crop tomorrow night.

When she'd finished collecting all the vegetables, she picked up her basket, intending to make her rounds, and secured it in the storage bin on the back of her ATV. Her ATV started with a roar, then settled into a kittenish purr, and she guided it down the narrow pathway that led away from the garden, headed to the next growing patch.

She spent her evening like she did any other evening, harvesting her fruits and vegetables, planting more, and delivering her food to those nature fae who needed it. Donnell was her last stop. He gave her a loaf of fresh baked bread in return for the vegetables, something she'd pass on to Marilynn, an elderly sylph who lived not far from her.

After she'd left Donnell's small cottage deep in the northern part of the Boundary Lands, she walked to her ATV, smoke curling from the chimney behind her, thinking about the pieces of the *bosca fadbh*. Cold fear crept up her spine at the thought someone would find out she was hiding them. The Shadow Queen would certainly discover her identity sooner or later, probably sooner. She'd send someone after her, maybe more than one someone.

And the Shadow Queen wouldn't send just any fae—she'd send *Unseelie*.

She felt confident in her ability to escape almost any fae, but who knew the magickal capabilities of the hunter the queen would send? It made her doubt herself. Worse, it made her doubt the hiding location of the pieces.

Maybe she should move them, just to be safe.

Deciding that was exactly the best course of action, she mounted her ATV, stuck the loaf of bread in the storage compartment, and started it up. She headed away from Donnell's, directing her path through the trees with the stars shining bright above, headed for her hiding spot in the clearing.

Yet . . . something niggled.

Somewhere in a far-off part of her mind something tickled.

Told her not to go to the clearing. Dangerous. Threatening. Someone was watching.

Waiting.

Niall . . .

She slowed the ATV to a halt and sat, engine idling, as she cradled her aching head in her hands.

Don't do it, breathed the voice in the back of her mind.

Beware, Niall . . .

Suddenly, she remembered.

Elizabeth dragged in a ragged breath, as though bursting through the surface of the ocean after diving deep. She was back in the cabin, tied to the chair, the charmed iron still banding her ankle.

She'd never been outside this building. Not once. It had all been an incredibly real illusion.

Ripping her hands from Niall's grip, she reached up and

tore the blindfold from her eyes. She stared at him, breath coming fast and labored, eyes wide, mouth open. Her mind stuttered, trying to comprehend what he'd done to her.

Niall leaned back and half closed his eyes. "Welcome to the world of magicked illusion, Elizabeth. How do you like it?"

She sputtered for a moment, unable to form a thought, let alone words. Standing, she immediately remembered the unfortunate fact that her ankles were bound. She went down hard.

Niall was there in an instant, rolling her over and asking if she was all right. He was such a considerate torturer.

"No, I'm not all right," she managed to say while he untied her hands and feet. "What the hell was that?"

He rocked back on his heels and studied her as she lay sprawled on her side. "That's just one of the many facets of my magick. I told you there was a reason they sent me and *only* me." He raised his dark brows and smiled his cocky little smile. "Impressed?"

She pushed up to a sitting position and watched him move to a nearby chair. She'd known his magick was different from any other fae's magick, but she'd never expected him to be able to take reality and just re-form it that way, like putty in his hands. He'd catapulted her into a dreamworld that was almost as real as her waking one, made her forget the last two weeks had ever even happened. He'd thrust her clear back to the beginning, right after she'd taken the pieces from the Summer Queen.

It was a complete and total mind fuck.

She'd nearly led him right to the hiding place. Which, of course, had been his plan.

She narrowed her eyes at him. "How far were you into my head? Could you read my thoughts?"

"I only wish. That would make things easier, but all I do is create the world and its parameters. I set the stage, but you fill it with information from your subconscious. Once in, I see everything you see. It's like being in a shared dream." His grin widened. "You almost led me to your hiding spot. I know you did."

She bolted to her feet, shooting him a look of daggers. "Almost. I didn't do it. I caught you."

"Your subconscious is very strong. It warned you." He leaned back against the headrest behind him, stretching like a cat. "Don't worry, eventually I'll reach even the darkest, most hidden parts of your mind. Eventually, I'll win."

He'd come really close to winning this time.

She looked down at her hands; they were shaking. Pain she could endure, but this? It was only at the very last second that sense had broken through. How could she fight against *this*?

Fisting her trembling hands at her sides, she stared down at him. "I figured out you were in my head once, and I can do it again. Don't be so sure of your success." Even now the charmed iron was making her grow weaker, but that worked in two ways. It served to make her less sure of success, but it also limited his time. She glanced down at the cuff. "I think I can hold you off long enough."

He was on her in a flash, pushing her back. She tripped over the edge of the couch and went down into the cushions. He followed her. His body was strong and warm on hers, and immediately the memory of the kiss flooded her mind.

His lips were only a breath's space from hers as he spoke. "I can make you believe anything with my magick, Elizabeth. I can create heaven or hell. I can make you imagine the worst kind of pain or give the best pleasure. I can bring your nightmares to life." He paused, his gaze fiercely focused on her eyes. "Don't make me take the dark path."

Her tongue dry and her eyes wide, she returned his gaze as coolly as she could with his huge body pinning hers. "I thought we went over this already. I'm not *making* you do anything."

He pushed up and away from her, dragging a hand through his hair as he turned from her.

She sat up. "I will resist you to my dying breath, Niall. I will force you to take every black road you don't want to travel before this is over."

Half turning toward her, he said, "Then I need to protect you from yourself . . . and from me." With that, he was striding toward the door.

It slammed behind him, leaving her alone.

SEVEN

NIALL pulled his SUV up in front of the house where Eliza beth had done her last delivery in the mind scene he'd created for her. He recognized the place from following her around. Certainly this had been the point in the scene when she'd been ready to lead him to the pieces, so maybe that meant the pieces were hidden around here somewhere.

He knew it was a long shot. She had the ability to travel anywhere she wanted within the bounds of Piefferburg with her ability. The logic that had led him here to search was pretty fucking flimsy.

But he was desperate. Every lead, no matter how thin, needed to be followed so he could avoid hurting Elizabeth.

He parked the SUV and stepped out into the early evening air. The small stone cottage up the narrow lane needed repair. Two of the shutters were gone, another was falling off, and several of the shingles on the roof were broken. Weeds choked the base of the building, vines climbing the crumbling walls.

This was one of Elizabeth's hard-luck cases. He started circling the area, checking under rocks, behind bushes, peering up into the trees. The pieces probably weren't anywhere near here, but it gave him an excuse to be away from Elizabeth for a little while—away from her beautiful, accusing eyes and the horrible temptation she presented.

He'd never thought he was the type of man to take advantage of a woman in his care. He wasn't exactly *caring* for her, of course, but she was still in his keeping, vulnerable to him. It was wrong how much he wanted her. It was wrong that he thought about her constantly, fantasized about taking her on the dining room table. It was wrong how often he had to draw back from touching her. He wanted her spread beneath him, wanted to taste her—wanted to make her come over and over.

That made him the worst kind of predatory bastard.

He stopped for a moment and breathed the cool evening air deep into his lungs over and over, the bark of the tree he leaned against rough on his palm. He needed to get this woman out of his head somehow. Maybe a trip back to the Black Tower and the welcoming arms of someone else would help, but he didn't have time for that.

"Hello, who is that? Elizabeth? Is that you?"

At the sound of the old man's voice, Niall stepped out into a shaft of silvery moonlight. "No, it's not Elizabeth, sir, but I'm a friend of hers." In the mind scene, Elizabeth had called him Donnell.

He was a Fir Darrig, one of the fae who were helpful to humans who became lost in faery. They also partied a lot and liked their whiskey. This one was ancient, probably had been ancient when Piefferburg had been created. His partying days were long over, although, by the smell of him, not his whiskey drinking days.

The old man leaned on a gnarled walking stick not far away. His eyesight probably wasn't very good, but he gave Niall a squinty head-to-toe sweep anyway. "Friend of Elizabeth's? Didn't know she had any. That girl is alone all the time. What's your name?"

"Niall." He wouldn't give his last name if he didn't have to. Once a upon a time, and even now in certain quarters, the possession of a fae's full name meant you had power over them.

"Niall, huh?" The old man rubbed his chin. "Not a nature fae."

"No, sir. I live in Piefferburg City." Clearly that was a mark against him. He hesitated, then plunged on. What did the opinion of this old man matter? He had more pressing concerns. "In the Black Tower."

The man considered him for a long moment. "Unseelie, eh? What are you doing out here snooping around my house, and where's Elizabeth?"

"I'm looking for something she lost. Two silver objects about this big." He cupped his hands together to indicate the size of the pieces. "Seen anything like that around here?"

"No. Sorry." He smacked his lips. "Any chance she'll be coming around anytime soon?" He smiled, showing bad teeth. "I'm about out of the food she brought me and haven't seen her tonight."

Damn it. *Of course.* He'd been so intent on his goal that he'd forgotten people depended on Elizabeth for food. They were going to starve without her help.

"Uh." Niall scratched the back of his head, looking away from the man. *Great.* Not only was he now a kidnapper and mind-fucking torturer, he was responsible for invalids starving to death. "She's a little under the weather and won't be around for a while."

"Oh." The man wilted, sagging against his walking stick. "Tell her I hope she feels better soon." He turned and shuffled back down the path to his cottage.

Niall stood for a moment, watching him go. Then he tipped his head to the sky and breathed out in defeat.

Time to go harvest some food and distribute it. Just call him Mother fucking Teresa.

Although maybe he could use it to his advantage with Elizabeth.

ELIZABETH raised her head from her place on the couch at the sound of the front door unlocking. Early morning sunshine shone through the windows of the cottage, draining her of energy almost as badly as the charmed iron touching her skin. She needed to sleep. Sitting up, she squinted blearily at him. Dirt marked his jeans and navy blue sweater, covered his hands and forearms.

"What have you been doing . . . digging with your bare hands?" She straightened with a snap, cold fear jolting through her at the possibility he'd found her hiding place. She drew a careful breath and reminded herself to calm down and not give anything away. It was more likely he'd just been *searching* for them and that's why he was all dirty.

He didn't look at her as he walked into the house. His hair was mussed, dark circles marked his eyes, and dirt smudged his forehead. Served him right if he'd been up all night searching to kill her mother, because that's what the pieces represented in her mind.

Grabbing a towel from the kitchen, he wiped it over his face and then tossed it onto the table. "Yes, I've been digging. I harvested the vegetables from your gardens and gave them out to those people you keep fed." He sounded disgusted. "Good thing I tracked your movements all those nights, right? I knew where to go."

Relief flooded through her. Her people had been weighing on her mind ever since Niall had captured her. Unsure of what to say—she couldn't really say thank you, could she?—she tucked her legs up underneath her and watched him walk into the living room to stand in front of her. "But I couldn't replant. There won't be anything for them tonight, and what you gave them won't last very long."

He grunted and looked away from her. "Don't worry about it."

"All I do is worry about it."

He shot her a hostile glance and went for his bedroom. "Like I said, don't. I've got them covered, okay? They're not going to starve. I'm taking a shower."

She sat there staring at the empty space where he'd just been standing. It was hard to get a good read on this man. He apparently intended to sit around and watch her waste away, but he also meant to take care of the people who counted on her. How could one man seem so cold one minute and caring the next?

The sound of the water starting in the bathroom met her ears. She settled back against the couch and pulled the sleeves of her sweater down over her hands, taking in the steady drum of the shower and holding it close.

Being away from her element for so long was a hardship that a fae like Niall couldn't understand. She'd never spent this long away from a natural source—a lake, stream, the ocean. Time would tell how that lack would affect her. Just the steady sound of the shower right now soothed her soul and eased the weakening ache of the iron sickness that was leaching into her bones and gathering behind her teeth. The only good thing about this cottage was its steady supply of warm water. At least she had that.

A short time later Niall walked into the living room wearing only a pair of jeans. No shirt, no shoes. His damp hair stood up all over his head, and she hated how badly her fingers itched to smooth it down. She gave him a quick sweep with her gaze when he wasn't looking and hated to admit her fingers wanted to do a whole lot more than just touch his hair.

As he moved through the room, righting the chair she'd been tied to—she certainly hadn't wanted to lift a finger to do it—gathering up the rope and arranging a few other things, her gaze skated over the muscular ridges and valleys of his upper arms, chest, and stomach. Niall was definitely a man in shape.

Weighing in at around one twenty, she didn't have much hope of being able to defeat him in a fight . . . unless she fought dirty, anyway. Her father had taught her how to take down a man who was bigger than her, but that had been a long time ago and she'd never had any opportunity to practice the self-defense tactics he'd taught her.

"Thank you, I guess," she said into the sleeve of her sweater. "For making my rounds. I shouldn't be thanking you, though, since if you weren't holding me they wouldn't be starving."

"No, you shouldn't thank me," he answered without turning around. He glanced at her. "And you should have thought about taking care of those who depend on you *before* you started working with the Summer Queen."

"Stop saying that. I'm not working with the Summer Queen. I hate her. Our goals were simply in accord for this one instance."

"Pretty big instance."

She nodded, miserable.

"If the Summer Queen came to you, asked you to do something for her, and you did it, you're working with her. *Period.*"

"You make it sound as if I agree with her reasons for trying to keep the walls intact. I don't. Her reasons are frivolous and self-centered. Mine aren't."

He shrugged. "You still haven't revealed who or what you're protecting, so I can't really agree or disagree with that statement."

She dropped her hands into her lap. "Who says I'm protecting someone?"

"Someone?"

Oh, crap.

"Don't worry; I'd already guessed you were protecting a person." He turned and grinned at her. "You spend every night harvesting and distributing food to elderly and poverty-stricken nature fae. You sure as hell seem like a protector to me." His smile faded. "Maybe I don't want to know your reasons. Maybe they'd just make it harder for me to get what I need out of you."

"Maybe it would, but I'm still not telling."

"Awww, you don't trust me, baby? I can't imagine why."

She tossed him an irritated glance and bit her bottom lip.

"I know about your father and brother, by the way. About how they died."

She flinched. "How do you know about that?"

"You talk in your sleep."

A burst of ice-cold terror ripped through her. If she'd babbled about her father and brother during her sleep, who knew what else she might reveal? Her fingers gripped the inside of the sleeve of her sweater. She was fighting so hard to keep her secret safe and now there was a possibility she could give it up without even knowing it.

He bustled around the kitchen, making tea and toast. "You must hate the Unseelie Court."

She pushed her hand out the mouth of her sleeve and studied her fingernails. "Were you a part of what happened to my father and brother?" The words came out sounding casual, but she felt anything but that. The memory tightened the muscles of her stomach and made her feel sick.

She worried about Niall's answer—stupidly. Yet if Niall had played a part on that bloody day, she would be disappointed.

He turned toward her, slice of bread in his hand. "No, Elizabeth, but I'm not surprised it occurred. The Shadow King was a good ruler, but he had no mercy for those who stood against him."

"A good ruler." She made a sound of disgust. "They weren't *standing against him*. They simply didn't want to dedicate their lives to the Shadow Guard. Last time I checked, Piefferburg wasn't a dictatorship."

"Anyone who defied the wishes of Aodh Críostóir Ruadhán O'Dubhuir stood against him." He paused. "I didn't know you had a brother."

"He wasn't my brother by blood, but the link was every bit as strong." She swallowed hard. "Do we have to talk about this?"

The memory of their deaths was still fresh in her mind. Living so far out in the Boundary Lands, her family was all she had. Losing two members that same day had been devastating. Her father and brother had been Pict by genetic origin, extremely powerful warriors by birthright. They'd been commanded by the Unseelie King to join the Shadow Guard. When they'd refused, the king had sent a contingent of soldiers and his personal bodyguard, Barthe, an ogre, to beat them until they agreed.

They never agreed.

"No, we don't have to talk about it." He brought the tea and toast over to her and set it on the coffee table in front of her. "Eat. You look pale and tired. The iron sickness is setting in."

"Do you think?" she snapped at him. Stomach rumbling, she reached out and snagged the edge of the toast, bringing it to her lips to nibble. "Trying to keep me healthy as long as you can?"

"Of course I am. You die and your secret dies with you."

She raised her eyebrows. "That's the idea." Her tone was light to mock him, but she couldn't keep the note of sadness out of her voice.

He watched her polish off the tea and toast and then ordered her to sleep. That was one command she was more than willing to obey. She stood, took two steps forward, and stumbled. He caught her and she ended up pressed against his solid, warm body. Despite her fatigue, every nerve in her flared to acute awareness of his differences as a man—sculpted, hard muscle, broad shoulders, strong chest and arms.

Niall was the type of man that females responded to on a primal, cavewoman-like level. He had the kind of body that screamed power and raw masculinity—the kind of body that made a woman instinctively think he would protect her against all threats. Of course, Elizabeth knew better.

Niall *was* the threat.

Alarmed by her inappropriate reaction to him, she pushed away, but he just held her firm. "Come on, let me help you to bed. You're iron sick and awake during the day. It makes you unsteady on your feet."

She was really too tired to argue or fight. That made her distinctly worried about the immediate future, but there wasn't anything she could do about that. Not right now. Right now she needed a bed, a blanket, and hours of shut-eye.

After taking a couple shaky steps toward the bedroom, he simply lifted her into his arms like a child and carried her there. She refused to look at him, refused to touch him more than was necessary, and refused to thank him when he laid her onto the mattress. Her heart beat out a crazy rhythm, and she cursed her poor, starved libido a million times from the living room to the bedroom.

He pulled the blankets over her. "Sleep." Then he turned away, flipped off the light, and closed the door.

ELIZABETH rolled over in her bed, snuggling into the blankets. Cracking her eyes open and gazing out her bedroom window, she glimpsed the silly gnome lawn statue her brother had given her when she'd moved into her house. Evening was just reaching its elegant fingers into late afternoon, knitting purples and blues with oranges and pinks. She stretched, feeling the delicious sensation of her muscles moving after a full day's sleep.

She pushed her blankets away and admired their softness for a moment. They'd been quilted by her mother. All her blankets had been gifts from her, quilted, crocheted or knitted lovingly in her hands. Smiling, she rubbed her fingers across one, remembering the reason she'd said yes to the Summer Queen.

As she moved through her small house, she flicked lights on here and there. Outside the sprae gathered at the edges of her trim yard, lighting on the yellow picket fence that surrounded her cozy place. Her home had been built by the birch ladies and the Scottish nature fae who were their allies. She owed them a lot.

Standing in her kitchen, Elizabeth sipped a fresh cup of coffee—she set the maker to brew every day at 5 pm, right before she woke—and gazed out the window. It was going to be a nice evening, and she had lots to do.

Gazing out her kitchen window, she had a vague sense of unease, almost as if there was a presence in her house or as if someone was watching her.

Any other time she'd brush it off, chalk it up to her imagination or her nerves, but not tonight. As long as she was hiding the final two pieces of the *bosca fadbh*, she couldn't discount any sort of unease she felt. There were too many different kinds of magick within the bounds of Piefferburg, too many for her to take any niggling sensation she had for granted.

Setting her empty cup in the sink, she went back upstairs, changed out of her nightgown and into a pair of cargo pants and a sweater. Then she slipped on a sturdy pair of boots. She needed to check her gardens and she'd do it with her ATV, not wanting to roam the chilly Boundary Lands in only her birthday suit. She had clothes stashed just about everywhere, but re-forming to physical state on the freezing ground this close to winter had given her a cold more than once.

She exited the house and stood outside, the sensation of wrongness intensifying. Frowning, she headed to her ATV. She'd wanted to move the pieces tonight, but something felt off. It wasn't safe to go to them for some reason.

Standing in the middle of her yard, she stopped and lifted her face to the sky. She felt a little dumb, but she was taking no chances. Not with her mother's life. "Whoever you are or whatever you are, I know you're there. If you think—"

She gasped as the world . . . *melted*. The trees dripped green and brown and orange, the colors running like paint. The neat little yellow fence pooled onto the green grass, swirling into a stream of dissolving reality. The ground went spongy under her feet, become porous. A huge hole opened up beneath her.

She screamed as she dropped down. . . .

* * *

ELIZABETH gasped and jerked up in her bed back at Niall's cottage, panic coursing through her veins. The charmed iron of the cuff still banded her ankle. It had been another of his "scenes." More illusion. Her breath came fast and hard. She pressed a hand to her chest as though it would slow her heart rate.

Niall sat in a chair in the corner of the darkened room, elbows on the armrests, fingers steepled, face half-shadowed. "You're very good." His voice sounded low and dangerous, a little pissed off, and held a little grudging admiration.

She couldn't answer; all she could do was concentrate on breathing. Sweet Danu, she hated this.

"Everything I try, you figure it out. You can feel me through the layers." He cocked his head to the side. "You're like the princess and the pea. How do you do that?"

Swallowing hard, she pushed the blankets aside and sat up. "You're the devil incarnate," she managed to push out. "I'd be able to sense you anywhere."

"You're not the first to call me that." He stood and walked toward her. "Sleep well?"

She nodded, pushing a shaking hand through her hair. He was very close to her, a little too close for her to feel comfortable, especially with the bed right behind them. She started to stand. "I want a shower." She'd taken one not eight hours ago, but she needed to feel the water on her skin.

He pushed her gently back onto the bed.

She gazed up in slight alarm. "What?" The word snapped out in her agitation. She hated having to fight her reaction to him all the time.

He was a villain. Normal woman were not attracted to men like him.

Half his face remained caught in shadow so she couldn't read his expression. "I would never take advantage of the fact you're in my custody. You know that, don't you, Elizabeth?"

"I don't know anything about you, Niall." Her voice came out husky.

He stared at her a moment longer, his face still only partially lighted. Instead of answering her, he turned away and left the room. A moment later and she could hear him slamming pots and pans around in the kitchen.

Trying to shake off the nagging unease in her iron sick body, she took a long, hot shower, absorbing every drop of moisture into her skin that she could. She had never gone this long without becoming water self. It took a toll on more than just her body; it took a toll on her state of mind and emotional well-being.

Under the spray, she closed her eyes and tried to mimic the act of dissolving. Surrendering herself to the moisture around her, joining with it, flowing as one. *Water coursing through the earth . . . surrounding . . . flowing . . . joining with the moisture of the lakes, streams, the salty tang of the ocean . . .*

She opened her eyes. Imagining it wasn't doing it.

Once she'd finished her shower, the ache in her muscles and the fatigue she felt were worse than ever. Cranky and losing hope, she stumbled out of the bathroom with her damp hair loose around her shoulders and wearing a pair of soft jogging pants and a T-shirt. The cottage smelled of eggs and sausage.

"Hungry?" Niall asked, standing in the kitchen holding a pan of something in his hand.

She waved him off and collapsed onto the couch. "I'm a vegetarian."

"*Vegetarian*, not vegan. You eat eggs and dairy products, right?"

"Yes, but not sausage."

"This is veggie sausage. I got it for you."

"Still, I'm not—"

"You need to eat, Elizabeth. I'm not going to let you skip meals."

"It's my body and I'll skip meals if I want to." She winced at the whiny quality in her voice. "Leave me be, I'm dying over here."

"The iron sickness is exactly why you need these calories. You need strength or you'll fade too fast." Yeah, and that would limit the time he had to get the info he needed. He fixed up a plate and brought it to her on the couch. "Now eat."

She stared at him for a moment, the mingled food scents making her stomach growl. Finally she grabbed the plate and fork from him and started eating. "Is there coffee?" she asked hopefully.

He brought over cups for both of them, then sat down across from her.

Remembering what she'd be doing ordinarily tonight, she stared at the food on her plate. "What about my people?"

"Like I said, don't worry about them. I've got them covered." He sipped his coffee. "I'm not a monster, Elizabeth."

She snorted into her coffee cup. "That's in the eye of the beholder."

"Baby, most of Piefferburg thinks *you're* the monster. You're not going to be getting a medal of valor anytime soon, that's for sure. In fact, once this is all over and your name becomes known to the rest of the fae, you better start thinking about hiding."

She kept her head down and concentrated on her veggie sausage. "I do what I have to do."

"And you'll pay the price. I hope it's worth it."

She set the empty plate onto the table between them and looked up into his eyes. Holding his gaze she answered, "It is."

He shook his head, scooped up the plate and both their coffee cups, brought them into the kitchen, and started washing up. "So, what fun games should we play today?" His voice came out light and teasing.

Elizabeth wanted to punch him.

Curling her feet beneath her on the couch she said, "I'm sure there's more illusion on the way."

"You can count on that," he tossed carelessly over his shoulder.

"I should hate you for what you're doing to me."

He wiped his hand on a kitchen towel and walked into the living room. "Does that mean you don't?"

She stood with the intention of returning to the bedroom, just to get away from him. She swayed on her feet, feeling weak, and caught herself right before she collapsed. "I wish I could hate you, Niall, but we both think we're doing the right thing, don't wc? You're protecting your people and I'm . . . well, I have my reasons for doing this, too."

"Another time, another place. I think we could have really clicked, you and me."

"Do you mean we could have been friends?"

"Friends, sure." He gave her a slow smile.

She snorted. "Yeah, more than friends for a night or two, right? You don't seem like the type to stay with one woman."

He gave a loose shrug. "Depends on the woman."

She considered him for a long moment, not knowing what to think about that statement. She lacked experience, was very young for a fae, and had spent her entire life in the Boundary Lands. He was at least three hundred and seventy years old, probably older, and lived in the Unseelie court. "You were never joined?"

He shook his head.

"Serious girlfriends?"

"Several."

She laughed. "*Several*, huh? Over centuries of time? I'm impressed."

He tipped his head to the side. "Was that sarcasm?" He shook his head. "Never mind, what about you? Is there some big, strong nature fae out there missing you? Should I be watching my back for a gallant rescue attempt?"

She gave him a withering look. "You know there isn't."

He shrugged. "I did what research I could on you and your family, but there wasn't much to find. The wildlings are like that. More power to the Summer Queen. She did a great job selecting you."

"What did you find out about me?"

"That you are a rare asrai, found as a child by a riverbank in the Boundary Lands, biological parents unknown. There was no other record of any other asrai in Piefferburg at all, so you're kind of a mystery. There was even less known about your adoptive parents."

She relaxed. That was good. Maybe she could keep her mother's sprae dependency a secret and no one would ever discover her reason for hiding the pieces.

"You're an attractive woman. I'd be surprised if there wasn't some strapping Scottish tree fae or something out there ready to storm this place to rescue you."

"Well, prepare to be astonished. I do my own rescuing."

Niall gave her one of his signature grins that was half made of cocky and half of charming. When she did that she was never sure if she wanted to slap him or kiss him. "And a fine job you're doing, too."

She gritted her teeth, fisted her hands, and pushed past him. "You're a bastard, do you know that?"

"So I've been told." He grabbed her by the upper arm and drew her gently back toward him. "Bastard, the devil incarnate. Pick a descriptor."

She whirled. "You may have this cottage magicked to hell and back so I can't escape and this damned charmed iron cuff might be around my ankle, but that doesn't mean you're going to win. You're not—"

He yanked her up against his chest. "Yeah, yeah, I know. You'll die before you'll give up the location, blah, blah."

Rage rocketed through her. "*Blah, blah?* Are you serious? Did you really just say *blah, blah* to me?"

Holding her close against his chest, he smoothed a loose hank of her hair behind her ear. "I would rather pretend none of this lies between us for a while. I don't want to think about those fucking pieces or that you're my prisoner. Not right now. I really don't want to think about you dying, okay? Can we pretend, just for a few minutes?"

She relaxed against him, confused at the gentle tone of his voice. "Pretend? That would be nice, but impossible. The stakes are too high."

"Too bad." He was staring at her lips. "That's really too bad, Elizabeth."

She tried not to melt against him, but it was an effort. This man had such a powerful effect on her libido, but she didn't want him to know it. It gave him power over her, and he already had too much. She stood stiffly in his arms, as if suffering his touch, but all the while she stared at the pulse jumping in his neck, wondering at the way it sped up every time he touched her, and tried not to inhale the intoxicating scent of his skin.

The whole situation was horrifying. She was about to die a virgin, something she really didn't want to do, yet the only man around—and the only man who made her hormones leap—was the man responsible for her circumstances.

She wished they could pretend. Just long enough for her to experience what it was to be touched by a man. She didn't really have that much longer to find out what sex was like, and the only man around willing to give her the experience was this one.

With a heavy sigh of surrender, she gave into the idea, dissolving as if into water. Her body went warm and soft against his.

Absurdly, Niall's body went stiff, almost as if her subtle reaction had put him on edge. "Elizabeth, no matter how much I may want you, I will never take advantage—"

"Blah, blah." She went up on her tiptoes and pressed her mouth to his.

EIGHT

NIALL went stock-still for a moment, then slipped his hand to her nape, hungrily slanting his mouth across hers, and gave her the second kiss she'd ever had.

His lips slid over hers slowly, raising goose bumps all over her body. She relaxed, curving to fit him perfectly. Then he crushed his mouth to hers and coaxed her lips apart. His tongue slid within and it collided, stroking, with her tongue, sending shivers of need up her spine. His mouth was hot and he tasted like coffee.

She wasn't sure what to do with her hands. Sliding them up his arms, she finally curled the fingers of one hand into the hair at the nape of his neck. The other she pressed tight against the back of his shoulder.

The man kissed the way she imagined it would feel to make love. Exploring her mouth, yet stopping sometimes to carefully brush his lips across hers, as if memorizing the feel and taste of her. The masterful strokes of his tongue served to stoke the fire that was already burning hot and high within her. Any doubt that may have lingered about sleeping with him dissolved like sugar stirred into water.

He dragged her lower lip through his teeth gently once

more, and then slid his tongue back into her mouth to leisurely brush up against hers. Her nipples tightened and her body primed itself for him, making intimate areas tingle. Reaching up, he cupped her breast, rubbing his thumb back and forth over her erect nipple through the fabric of her T-shirt and bra. His cock pressed against her, showing her how much he wanted her.

If this was just a kiss, what was the rest of it like?

He rocked her back and broke the kiss, staring hard at her. "What are you doing, Elizabeth?"

"Trying to get you to take advantage of me."

He released her and stepped backward. "If you don't stop, I *will* take advantage. I want you, Elizabeth. I want to touch your sweet body. I want to watch you come. I'll love doing all that, but then I'll feel like shit afterward."

Fine, he wanted to play hardball?

She grabbed the hem of her T-shirt and pulled it over her head, leaving her in just her bra. Then she reached around and unclasped that bit of silk, letting it drop onto the floor. "I don't really care how you'll feel afterward, Niall."

Niall took exactly one heartbeat to pounce on her. He dragged her up against his chest, walked her back to the thick carpet in front of the fireplace, and lowered her onto it. His gaze roaming her bare breasts, he pulled his sweater over his head and came down over her.

Her fingers roved his skin, feeling the bunch of his muscles as he moved, enjoying the warmth of his strong arms and back. He dropped his head to her breast and covered one of her nipples with his mouth. She let out a surprised gasp of pleasure as his skillful lips closed around the hard little peak and he sucked it against his hot tongue. Her fingers tightened in his hair as he licked one nipple to a hard point and then moved to the next, pleasure shivering through her body.

So this was what sex was like. People were right to make such a big deal out of it.

Lost in a haze of sensation, she watched his head move lower as he kissed her abdomen and dropped to her belly button. His fingers caught in the waistband of her jogging pants and yanked them down. He made a hungry sound in the back of his throat when he found she wore no underwear. He skimmed her pants down her legs.

After he'd tossed her jogging pants to the side, Niall hovered over her, gaze caught with hers, as his hand glided up her inner thigh, gently urging her to part her legs.

She moved restlessly on the carpet, beginning to lose the ability for rational thought. Her body felt on fire from his touch, and she wanted more. The first stroke of his hand on her sex made her jump and moan at the same time. His fingers whispered over her delicate flesh, finding her clit and petting it until her back arched and her toes curled. Then he slipped a finger inside her, and she moaned his name.

He halted his movements, looking up at her in surprise. "Elizabeth, are you a virgin?"

She opened her eyes to find him staring down at her. "Yes. Is that a problem?"

"No. It's just a surprise." He rocked a finger in and out of her. "You're really tight, but I don't feel your hymen."

She licked her lips, trying not to moan like a sex-crazed idiot. It was hard to think with him doing that to her. "I ride horses," she managed to push out. "Kelpies. I drive an ATV. I run. I'm very active. My hymen probably broke long ago. I am in my midtwenties, after all."

He brushed her clit with his thumb. "Have you ever come?"

"Of course." She blushed, then qualified, "By myself."

He threw his head back and groaned. "*Danu*, I would love to watch you do that sometime."

She blushed even harder.

"But not right now," he continued, his voice a low, dark rasp against her skin. "Right now *I* want to make you come."

Her tongue went dry. She wanted that, too, very much.

Then he dropped his mouth between her legs and her tongue went even drier. Words left her—the ability to *think* left her—as he sucked her clit between his lips. Pleasure tingled throughout every part of her body, starting from the place where he touched her. It was so much better than any of her late night fumblings, when she'd tried to ease the natural yearnings of her body with her own hand. He added a second finger to the first and she gasped as he pressed them slowly inside her, widening her and stretching her muscles.

She imagined what it would be like to have his cock there instead, thrusting inside her, his chest pressed against hers, his mouth sealed to her mouth—and the ecstasy tripled from the fantasy of it, pleasure surging through her and bringing her right up to the edge of an orgasm. Already she could tell that when she came from his lips and fingers on her, it would be so much better than the climaxes she'd ever given herself.

His tongue eased over her swollen, sensitive clit, pushing her harder, his fingers still tunneling in and out of her. "Niall," she half breathed, half gasped, her back arching and her fingers digging into the carpet on either side of her.

Intense pleasure burst, making her cry out. Her body tensed as it washed over her, and she gasped against the waves of it rolling through her body. Niall pushed her past the threshold, extending her climax. Her orgasm stuttered, came to a close, but he pushed her straight into another. The ecstasy seemed to go on and on until finally it receded, drained away, and left her limp and breathing heavily on the floor.

She felt like she'd been wrung out like a washcloth, but in a good way that left her tingling, weak, and wanting more.

Niall crawled up her body and lay on his side, looking down into her face. She opened her eyes blearily, feeling drugged. "That was fast," he said with a cocky grin.

She gave a sleepy half-smile. "It was the first time a man's ever touched me. Don't get too arrogant."

He covered her breast with his hand and gently flicked the nipple back and forth. "Should we see if we can make you do it again?"

Reaching up, she caught his nape with her hand and pulled his head down to hers for a kiss. His tongue tangled with hers and she pulled his trick, dragging his lower lip through her teeth. He shuddered against her, and she smiled against his mouth, pleased at his reaction to her.

"Let's do it together," she murmured. Her other hand found the button and zipper of his jeans. She wanted to feel what it was like to have a man inside her.

He moved his pelvis away from her and shook his head. "All in good time."

His hand strayed to her stomach and glided between her parted thighs. Slowly, he stroked her clit until pleasure flared once more. She closed her eyes and moaned.

"I want to see how many times I can make you come in a

row. You have a lot of lost years to make up for, you poor, sexually deprived woman." He slanted a mischievous grin at her. "Let's see how we can remedy that."

He lowered his head to her breasts and explored every ridge and valley of her erect nipple while he steadily petted her clit, drawing it from its hood. It wasn't long before her sex-starved body was shuddering in climax on the rug once again.

And he wasn't through by half.

THE door opened with a metallic groan and Niall stumbled out into the cool air and dragged in a lungful of it. Sweet Danu, she was killing him. She was the one in bondage, he was the one in control, yet this woman had him wrapped around her slender finger like so much breakable tinsel at Yuletide.

Anything she wanted, he gave her.

He had not meant for this to happen. It was bad all the way around. Bad because she was in his care. Worse because it brought them closer together. Where the body went, a tiny slice of the heart followed. What he needed was distance, perspective. Hells, he was supposed to be getting information out of her, not making her come multiple times on the carpet in front of a merrily burning fire!

Gods, he was weak where this woman was concerned. At least he hadn't fucked her.

But he almost had.

Maybe he wasn't the right man for this job. Maybe the Shadow Queen needed to send someone else. This was getting out of control fast and he needed to find a way to rein it in, bring the control back to him and him alone.

Time was almost running out, anyway.

He took a couple staggering steps forward and caught himself on a tree. His cock was hard and he considered relieving himself of his erection, and then decided against it. He needed to get back in there. Leaving her alone wasn't good idea. Not even when she was unconscious.

Looking up into the star-strewn night sky, he exhaled hard, his mind working over the situation.

What to do? He needed to make this work, or he needed to let her go.

* * *

ELIZABETH woke in the guest bed, nude body swathed in softness. Her body tingled and pulsed from Niall's hands and mouth on her the night before. There was weakness there, too, sickness. Every day it grew a little more pronounced. She was still technically a virgin, but at least she had experienced what it was to have a man touch her.

He sat in the chair across the room, a brooding look on his face, eyes troubled.

"What is it?" she asked, sitting up. The blanket fell away from her breasts and he glanced at them, then away, as if he didn't want tempt himself. She pulled the blankets up to her chest, suddenly feeling chilly.

"I fucked up last night. I'm getting too close to you. I'm not the man for this job."

Hope shot a tiny blossom of light into her chest. "What do you mean?"

He stood and walked to her, flipping the blankets back. Cool air kissed the length of her bare body. He leaned over, touched her cuff, and whispered a power-laced string of words in Old Maejian. The cuff popped off. "You're free."

She kicked the cuff away like it was made of nuclear waste and stared up at him. Was this for real? Or was this just another layer of illusion? "I don't trust you."

He turned away. "Fine, then stay. But I'm out of here. I'm headed back to the Black Tower. I need to tell the queen I've failed and get someone else to come after you. Someone who can do the job."

"Bullshit." She hopped from the bed and followed him out of the room. She was still naked, but that was a secondary concern right now. It wasn't like he hadn't seen it all before . . . up close and in detail. "If you were going to send someone else, you would leave me in the charmed iron and just direct the next miscreant here to me."

He rounded on her and bared his teeth. "I touched every inch of your body last night, Elizabeth. I made you come multiple times. Is it so hard to believe that I might want to see you live? By the time the Shadow Queen sends someone back to this cottage, you'd be dead from the iron sickness. The next guy can catch you, kill you. I'm done." He stalked into the other room, grabbed a duffle bag, and paced to the front door. "Bye, Elizabeth. Good luck."

She stood in the middle of the room, staring out the front door that he'd left open. *Danu*, she wished she knew if this was real or not.

After she'd heard the sound of his SUV driving off, she hugged herself, shaking off the disgusting feeling of the iron sickness that still clung to her, and trying not to feel like she'd just had her first one-night stand.

HE never came back.

Wrapped in a blanket on the couch, she waited and waited. Also absent was the sense she was being watched. No niggling from the recesses of her mind ever came. So, finally, she stood and dissolved.

Surrender. Permeating wood, sliding through cement, finding earth. Accumulating and leaking through rock, silt, humus, minerals, decaying organic matter. A stream not far. Merge. Rushing, rushing.

Ah, it felt good. So good to be water self.

She returned to full consciousness lying on her side at the edge of a river with sprae playing in bushes and trees opposite her. Sitting up, she hugged herself against the chill and analyzed her location. Her water self had led her to a clearing near her home. Better yet, this was a place where she kept clothing, *thank Danu*.

Standing, she pulled the cached set of pants, sweater, underthings, shoes, and socks from a heavy plastic bag secreted under a bush and pulled them on.

The sensation of being watched remained absent. Yet, something didn't feel right.

More than anything she wanted to verify that the pieces were still hidden where she'd left them, but she couldn't risk it. Not yet.

Instead she went to her house.

All was as she'd left it, though her ATV was still at the garden where Niall had caught her. She'd have to go back for that, but it was almost dawn, the time when her energy ebbed and she normally slept. The iron sickness still had its claws sunk deep inside her and would take time to fade, so she would wait and rest.

Visiting her mother would have to wait until evening, too. She would have to make up a story to explain her absence, maybe something about how she'd traveled to the ocean for a little impromptu vacation. She would apologize for not telling her beforehand, would feel terrible for lying . . . and hope like hell her mother didn't give her any food that would compel the truth from her.

She made herself a dinner of stew, sipped fortifying tea, and snuggled into her bed to sleep. Dawn was just lighting the horizon when the phone on her nightstand rang.

"Hello?" she answered, already half asleep.

Silence on the other end. Finally, a man said, "Is this Elizabeth Cely Saintjohn?"

"Yes." She sat up, pressing the phone more firmly to her ear and waking up fast. The unfamiliar voice had a note of threat threaded through it. "Who wants to know?"

"I know where the pieces are. I'm going to get them right now." Pause. "Then I'm coming for you." *Click.*

Elizabeth stayed frozen for a heartbeat, then slammed the receiver down and leapt from the bed. She needed to go now, dissolve, get the pieces, and hide them again. She raced out of her house in her pajamas and ran into her front lawn, ready to become her water self and get there before the unknown man.

Maybe there was still time. Maybe . . .

Wait.

Her jaw locked and she fisted her hands. "Why would someone hunting the pieces warn me they were going to get them?" she said loudly to the air around her, turning in a circle and looking up into the sky. "They wouldn't. They would just take the pieces and then come after—"

For the second time, her front yard melted.

SHE sat up on the rug in front of the fire, still naked, body still tingling from the last orgasm Niall had given her. He stood not far away, dressed only in a pair of jeans, barefoot, and staring down at her.

"You're a class A bastard, Niall."

"You keep saying that. Can we just have a standing agreement that I am, indeed, a bastard so we don't have to talk about it anymore?"

Angrily, she stood and pulled a throw from the couch, wrapping herself in it. The last thing she wanted was to feel naked and vulnerable in front of this man. What had she been thinking, throwing herself at him that way?

Never again.

His eyes were stormy. "I'm running out of options, Elizabeth."

She collapsed onto the couch, every molecule of her body fatigued and sore. It was the iron sickness, coming on faster and faster. "Whatever," she breathed, resting her head on the cushion behind her. "No matter how you try and trick me, I'm not leading you to the pieces. You're just going to have to let me die, *bastard*."

At some point she felt him lift her and lay her in bed. "That's what I'm afraid of," he murmured and touched the charmed iron cuff around her ankle. "Tick tock, baby."

Exhaustion pulled her under.

ELIZABETH sat on the couch in the living room, staring daggers into Niall's back as he built up the fire. Over the last two days, the iron sickness had dug its claws so hard into her body that it was an effort for her to move.

She was dying.

The ache in her body and the fatigue in her muscles made it so this fact was almost a blessing—something to look forward to. Her magick was entirely eradicated. She felt certain that if Niall took off her cuff, laid her on the earth outside, and took a step back, even then she wouldn't be able to form water self. Her magick was completely gone.

Little by little, minute by minute, he was destroying her.

All she could hope for now was a swift passing to the Netherworld. At least the pieces were safe, and that meant her mother was safe. She had to stay strong in her resolve. The sickness leached her strength, but not her will.

That didn't stop Niall from trying. Illusory scene after illusory scene, he battered at her, trying over and over to trick her into leading him the pieces. No matter how sick she was or how awful she felt, she foiled his plan every time.

He brought over a glass of water from the sink and sat down next to her. Refusing to look at him, she stared into the flickering fire instead.

"Drink," he insisted, putting the glass to her dry, cracked lips.

She opened her mouth and water trickled in. Ah, water, how she missed it. It was an effort to swallow or speak. Walking was just a dream.

Not long now.

He set the glass on the table. "Nothing I do works." He sounded discouraged, and it made her crack the smallest of smiles. "The Summer Queen was right to pick you."

"Soon," she croaked. "I'll be dead and the pieces will forever be hidden, from everyone, even the Summer Queen."

"And the fae will be at the mercy of the Phaendir. Trapped in here, forever." His tone sounded as bleak as his expression looked.

She had a twinge of regret. "I wish it could be different. I wish we could all have what we want, protect everyone we love. But there are always winners . . ." She took a deep, rattling breath. "And losers." She closed her eyes, smiling. "I'm a winner." Slowly, painstakingly, she raised her hand to her forehead and made an *L* with her hand. "And you're a loser."

Niall sighed. "You'll be gone before dawn comes."

"Oh, sooner . . . I hope."

"Elizabeth, just tell me where the pieces are. I can heal you. You don't have to do this."

She sighed, resigned and surrendering. "Yes, I do."

He stayed with her throughout the night, offering her water until she couldn't swallow any longer. He pleaded with her to tell him the location of the pieces so he could take the cuff off, nurse her back to health, but he didn't plunge her into any more illusions.

Finally, she let her eyes drift closed for what she knew would be the last time.

A light feeling entered her body and she floated upward. Somewhere below her, in the dark, Niall said her name over and over, more and more urgently, trying to call her back from the edge of death. Still, she drifted upward, away, the pain, the aches, and the exhaustion falling away like a heavy winter coat.

She was free. A million times lighter . . . happy . . . everything was perfect. . . .

NINE

"ELIZABETH?"

Niall's voice pulled her up from what felt like layers of deep sleep. She woke sprawled on a hard surface of metal. A small camping lamp lit the area. Niall's face loomed in front of hers, dark stubble marking his cheeks and chin. His hair was mussed and lines of exhaustion marked his face. He was dressed in the clothes he'd been wearing the night he'd captured her and he looked like he needed a shower. She was naked, but he'd put a blanket over her.

She glanced around. They were in the big trap he'd set for her.

What was going on? Where was the cabin? *She'd died.* Why was she here?

Throwing the blanket off, she scrambled to a sitting position and crab-walked back to hit the charmed iron wall behind her. The wall was cold and very real.

Breathing in short, panicked little spurts, she took stock, trying to gain a handle on the moment. Her body felt fine. A little tired, a little achy, but no advanced iron sickness plagued her.

Looking down she saw that no iron cuff banded her ankle.

Her lip still hurt from where she'd smacked it running into the wall of the trap, but that was strange since the cut had healed days ago. Her stomach hurt from hunger, and she'd never been this thirsty in her life.

Her hair fell across her face and she stared at Niall through it. Suspicion and confusion played a symphony within her. "What's going on?"

He sat back and pushed a hand through his hair. He looked defeated. "You died." Pause. "At least, in the illusion. You went the whole way with the ruse, died, and woke up out of my control."

"Illusion?" She glanced around the box.

"The cabin. None of it was real."

"The cabin," she echoed dully, "wasn't real?"

He waved a hand as though it was nothing. "Everything from the time you hit that wall and I came in here and touched your arm. You reached out toward the open door, that's when I put you under. You've been unconscious ever since. All of it was illusion. All in your head."

"What?" She put a hand to her temple. She felt sluggish, stupid. "That's not possible."

"That fog in your head will clear. You'll see that what I'm saying is true. My magick has a certain aftertaste, especially when I create more than one layer. For you I had to create about ten layers, since you're the princess and the pea."

"I don't understand."

"It felt like you were in the cabin for more than a week, but we've only been in this charmed iron box for a little over twenty-four hours. We need to get out of here, by the way. The charmed iron is starting to affect both of us."

"Twenty-four hours," she echoed, her mind working lethargically. "No, it's been days and days."

"I *told* you. You're not listening. That was all illusion." He paused, his eyes narrowing. "You let yourself *die*, Elizabeth, rather than tell me where the pieces are."

"I told you I would." She spat the words at him, pressing the heel of her palm to her eye socket.

His full lips twisted, but there was no hint of amusement there. "Lots of people say that, but when the time really comes they go weak. They give in." He trailed off, studying her with fascination. "Not you, though."

"How do I know *this* is real? How do I know this isn't just another layer of illusion?"

"Wait for the fog to clear." He stood and walked toward the door of the trap, stumbling a little. "We need to get out of here. The Blacksmith made this place with only enough charmed iron to prevent you from dissolving, but it's still too much for us to handle for long."

Realizing suddenly that she was naked, she snatched the nearby blanket back and covered herself with it. Dumb, since he'd seen her naked already, come close to having sex with her. Of course, none of that had been real.

Supposedly.

This could just be another mind fuck for all she knew.

The door to the trap opened with a screeching whine of metal. Niall stumbled out into the twilight and didn't even look back at her.

Was he that confident she wasn't going to run?

She pushed to her feet, needing to get out of this charmed iron box just as much as he did—whether the box was in her head or not—and gingerly forced her sore muscles to work. Her bare foot touched the soil outside and she closed her eyes, savoring the sensation. The fog was clearing. Drawing deep lungfuls of air in, she took a few more steps into the woods, holding the blanket around her.

This was real. Now she could feel the difference.

Under Niall's magick everything had felt not as tactile as this, though she hadn't noticed it while she'd been under. Now, here in the woods, she felt the realness of life and knew she wasn't under Niall's spell anymore.

Unless he'd designed it to feel that way.

She rounded on him. "Is this just another layer, another trick? Did you do all that and then bring me here, upping the tactile sensations of my environment to make me think it's all over?"

He turned to study her, a grin playing along his full lips. She knew those lips very well now. . . . "I don't have that kind of power, baby. I'm done with you. You won." He motioned to the woods. "This is all real."

"I don't believe you would up give that easily."

"Easy?" He laughed, shaking his head and pushing a hand through his hair. "That was not easy. You drained my power to the dregs, and you still let yourself die." His voice lowered a degree, to a dangerous level that made the hair on her nape rise. "But don't think I'm giving up, woman. I don't do that."

She turned in a circle, making a sound of frustration. "How do I know for sure this is real? How will I know *anything* is ever real again?"

He shrugged, unapologetic. "You'll figure it out eventually."

She stared at him, a million thoughts running through her head in a jumble, mixed with emotions that ranged the spectrum. "So you're just letting me go."

"What else am I supposed to do with you? You've just proved you'd die before giving up the location of the pieces, and you're no good to me dead."

"I haven't seen the last of you yet, though, have I?"

He tipped his head to the side and grinned. "Awww, have I grown on you?"

"Like a wart." She paused. "Bye, Niall."

"Bye, Elizabeth. I'll be seeing you soon."

She needed to rest, to eat and drink. "Not if I have any say in it." She dissolved, the blanket fluttering to the ground as she sought her water self.

NIALL stared at the blanket she'd left in the leaves, then scooped it up. It was still warm and smelled like her.

"Fuck." None of that had been real, yet it was still as though they'd spent all that time together. He'd gotten to know her, grown close to her, begun to like her . . . *a lot.*

Too much.

Around him the birds and bugs whistled and chirped and a low breeze rustled the leaves of the trees. Storm brewing. He could feel it. He needed to get back to the Black Tower and tell the Shadow Queen what had happened—let her know he'd failed. Again.

It was time to bring the others in on this. He needed a new plan of action.

* * *

LIAM burrowed his hands into the soft, giving earth of the Boundary Lands and focused his magick on finding Elizabeth. He sought the pieces in this area as well, hoping to get lucky. Maybe he if could happen upon the pieces, they'd be able to leave the asrai alone.

He wasn't hopeful.

This was the fifth area he'd searched in the last twenty-four hours. He was staying close to the woman's home and the gardens she kept just because he had no other criteria to search by.

Near him stood Gideon. His band of Phaendir, robed, silent, and creepy as hell, were housed somewhere in Piefferburg City. Gideon had brought them because they were loyal to his cause and could create the hive magick he needed in here. Every night more Phaendir crept in, focused their power on Gideon, making his strength grow.

Gideon was so full of evil Phaendir juice he could just look at things and blow them up now. The fact Liam was helping them made him want to smash his fist into a tree.

Trying his best to tune out the nasty presence of the archdirector and tune into the lush beauty of the woods around him, Liam spread his mental fingers and sifted through his immediate surroundings.

The Summer Queen had provided them with the location of Elizabeth's house and where she kept her gardens. They didn't know much else. It was unlikely Niall Quinn, the Unseelie sent to capture Elizabeth, had been successful, but it was possible. If Niall hadn't succeeded in gaining the location of the pieces, they would.

They just had to find her first.

The scent of richly turned dirt and loam filled his senses, the rough feel of tree roots tripped over his thoughts. His magick traveled through the bustling, burrowing insects, to the tender roots of plants and grass, up to the air of the forest, redolent with a mixture of rot and growing things. Outward, he expanded his consciousness, searching for the woman or the two silvery chunks of preciousness all of them sought.

Elizabeth, the water fae, was protecting her mother, according to the Summer Queen. Her goal wasn't unlike his.

Elizabeth's mother would die when the walls fell because the sprae keeping her alive would disperse. His wife, Aideen, would die because long ago she'd killed a fae man. For that crime she would be reaped by the Wild Hunt and added to the sluagh when the walls fell. If they could find Elizabeth and get her to hand over the pieces, they could save both their loved ones.

But he didn't have a lot of confidence that Gideon would just let Elizabeth go after she turned them over. Gideon never missed a chance to kill a fae, if that fae wasn't of use to him.

"Find anything yet?" Gideon's whiny, impatient voice cut through the syrupy overlay of consciousness his magick always provided.

He didn't respond. Instead, he kept sifting, searching through tree limbs, the prickly arms of bushes, the soft padding of a bird's nest. Careful. Patient. Leave no stone unexamined.

There. The woman was just *there.*

Surprise rippled through him. He double- and triple-checked to make sure it was really her. Days of searching and nothing. Now, all of sudden . . .

"Got her." Liam made note of the location of the cottage where he'd located the water fae's presence and pulled his hands out of the earth. "She's gone back to her house."

"Labrai be praised. Now we can stop camping and maybe even get out of this Labrai-cursed shithole of a place."

Liam only stared stonily at him. Part of him wanted to stay in Piefferburg forever, even though he'd be trapped. If only Aideen could live here with him.

"Let's go get the woman. Once we obtain the pieces from her, we can get rid of her, too." Gideon stomped off toward the main road, where they'd parked the Jeep, pushing at tree branches and cursing nature every step of the way.

After a moment, Liam followed. He just wanted to do what needed to be done to protect Aideen.

"I'M not used to seeing you engrossed in a book, Niall." Aeric O'Malley entered the room where Niall sat slumped over a pile of dusty tomes. "It's just not like you."

Bella Quinn, Charlotte Bennett, and Bran, a nature fae who was part of the Wild Hunt, were also in the tower library sitting in various nooks and crannies, thumbing through their own volumes. All of them were looking for tidbits of knowledge about the asrai or anything about Elizabeth's family.

The queen had ordered that anyone not preparing for the coming war should help him sift through the massive amounts of information the fae had collected since Piefferburg had been created. If they could find out who Elizabeth was protecting, and why, he'd have leverage over her. At this point, Niall thought it was their only hope, but they weren't getting very far.

He slammed his book closed and glanced around the library, stretching. "A man's got to do what a man's got to do."

Aeric tossed a leather-bound book onto the table in front of him. "Emmaline found that in my forge, tucked away on a shelf. It's a book about various kinds of nature fae. She thought you'd want it."

Niall picked it up and flipped through it. "Great. Tell her I said thanks." He indicated the pile of twenty books to his right. "Tell her I could use her help, too, anytime she wants to give it."

"She's helping me in the forge. Aislinn has me making weapons twenty-four seven. It's tapping my magick every damn day." He jerked his chin toward the general direction of Bran. "I came for Bran, too. Aislinn wants him to start organizing whatever animals and birds he can for the coming conflict."

Back in the day, during the Fae Wars before Piefferburg was created, there were nature fae like Bran who could communicate with animals and use them in battle. Looked like they were nearing that time again.

"It's getting that bad, is it?"

Aeric shrugged. "No way for us to know. It's not like they send us status reports. The red caps report higher-than-usual activity at the gates. Maybe the military and the Phaendir are finally finding accord."

"That would be bad for us."

"Maybe not. The humans seem to want to show restraint. Maybe having them work with the Phaendir is better than having the Phaendir loose on our asses."

Niall grunted and picked up the book. "I need to get back to work." Not getting the pieces from Elizabeth had made him grumpy. He opened it up and leafed through it angrily.

Aeric was silent for a moment. Finally he said, "The queen's sending Ragnar and a bunch of goblins after the woman. I thought you should know."

He went still. Ragnar Joren Kvalheim had the ability to boil the water in a person's body. Not a pleasant way to go.

Niall looked up at him, rage making him clench his teeth for a moment. "What the fuck is Ragnar going to do? Evaporate her when she dissolves? How is that supposed to help us find the pieces?"

Aeric paused, hesitating before he spoke. "I think Ragnar is meant to go after the people she cares about." He paused. "You know, those people she keeps fed."

Niall slammed the book closed on the table. "What are we, the fucking Mafia, now? We're taking out people's families? Old people? Invalids?"

"We need the pieces, Niall, no matter what. The queen knows it's time to get brutal."

Like locking Elizabeth in a charmed iron box and plunging her into a waking nightmare wasn't brutal.

"She won't give the pieces up to save herself," Aeric continued, "but she might—"

"Yeah, yeah, I understand the concept." Niall pushed to his feet, rubbing his hands over his face. "I'm out of here."

Two weeks ago, the Black Tower had known nothing about Elizabeth. Not what she did at night, not about her gardens, not about the people she cared for with the food she grew. Now the Shadow Queen was in possession of all kinds of information about her . . . thanks to him.

Now all those people she fed were in danger . . . thanks to him.

He pushed past Aeric and stormed out of the library, stalking his way through the Black Tower to Aislinn's receiving room. Recognizing him, the guards let him through. Good thing, since Niall hadn't really planned on knocking.

"What the fuck is going on, Aislinn?" he burst out, coming to a stop in front of her chair. Aelfdane, a Twyleth Teg and part of the Wild Hunt, was sitting on the couch near her, along with Gabriel.

Gabriel stood. "Back off, Niall."

He glanced at him with fire enough in his gaze to burn. "I will not fucking back off. She's sending Ragnar after the asrai. Elizabeth is mine."

Aislinn's face flushed and her hands went tight on the armrests of her chair. Her eyes burned with fury, and all of it was directed at him. The heat in the room ratcheted upward with her emotions. With a swish of silk and satin, she stood. "You had your chance, Niall. Now someone else gets a turn."

"You're going after the starving, old, and sick nature fae she cares for, Aislinn? Really?"

She looked pained for a moment, then her face settled into a mask. Turning away from him, she walked to the window and looked onto Piefferburg Square, gazing past it, toward the gates. "Don't think I *liked* giving that order. Don't think I've slept a moment since I gave it." She drew a breath. "But I'm running out of options."

"This is not the way." Niall fisted his hands at his side. "We don't hurt innocent people, Aislinn."

She gave a cold, mirthless laugh. "Tell that to the military at our door. Tell it to the Phaendir. They're getting ready to slaughter hundreds of innocents." She turned toward him. "So, you tell me what I should do, Niall. Sacrifice one or two to hopefully save hundreds, maybe thousands, of us? Or should I take the high road, not pursue the pieces with every brutal tool at my disposal, and let our enemies turn our streets to blood?"

Niall let out an agonized breath of air, nostrils flaring. Sweet Danu, this was wrong. "Why pick Ragnar? He's a monster."

She smiled, but it came nowhere close to her eyes. "It takes a monster to do this job."

"Could *you* do it?" asked Aelfdane from the couch. "She had to set Ragnar loose for this task."

"Yes, I can do it." Niall looked at Aislinn. "Call him off, send me instead."

Sadness entered her gray eyes. "You're no monster, Niall, and you're too close to her. I hear it in your voice when you talk about this woman. You feel protective of her. Despite everything, you like her. Could you really go out there, threaten the people she loves? Torture them in front of her? Kill them?"

"No, I couldn't do that. Not for real. I can do it in her head, though. Let me try." He would hate it, and she would never forgive him—not for that—even if it was only a scene he created in her mind. Still, better she hate him forever than let innocent people die.

Aislinn shook her head. "She's on to your tricks now. From the moment you captured her, she'd know anything that happened wasn't real."

Sensing a crack in Aislinn's resolve because of the slight tremor in her voice, he pushed on. "I won't use myself in the scene. I'll make her forget me. I'll use Ragnar. She won't even know I'm there until it's over. It will seem totally real to her."

The queen said nothing, considering him. "We can't afford to waste any more time." She smiled. "Niall, you just don't have the kind of darkness we need for this. You didn't even think of it as an option when you captured her."

No, that was true, he hadn't. He was really fucking regretting that right now, too.

"Aislinn, I'm begging you. Call off the dogs. Send me."

Her face pale and dark circles marking the flesh under her eyes, Aislinn turned away. "I'm sorry, Niall. It's done. Let Ragnar handle it from now on."

Niall stared after her retreating form with heavy, black dread forming in his soul.

Nothing left to say, and with Gabriel and Aelfdane refusing to meet his eyes, Niall turned and smashed his way out of her chambers. Making noise made him feel better, even if he was totally fucking powerless to stop this shit storm.

"Niall!"

He turned to find Bran running down the corridor toward him. "Aeric told me what was going on with the asrai." He stopped and stared hard into his eyes. "You're not going to let that happen, right?"

"Fuck, no."

Bran nodded. This was probably the most he'd heard Bran say since he'd met him a hundred years ago. Man of many words, he was not. "I found something interesting in one of the genealogy annuals a minute ago. It's a record of a woman reported to be an asrai. There's not much info about her, but it does list an adoptive mother who is sprae dependent."

The sprae dependent were a type of nature fae that had evolved only since Piefferburg had been created. The few of them that existed lived only by the grace of the sprae, who provided them life energy.

"I think it's possible the asrai they're talking about could be Elizabeth," Bran continued. "If her mother is sprac dependent, that would be a pretty big motivation for Elizabeth to want to see the walls stay up."

Especially since she'd already watched her father and brother die and had no one else in her life.

Niall was already moving when he called over his shoulder, "Thanks, Bran."

Time to end this.

ELIZABETH tossed her damp hair over her shoulder and stuffed an armful of garments into a duffle bag.

The first thing she'd done after getting away from Niall was visit her mother to make sure she was all right. Thea had patted her cheek, asked her why she was so pale and tired looking, and then offered to make her a meal.

Elizabeth had eaten until the hungry ache in her stomach had faded, all the while spinning a story of lies to explain her absence that gave her a different kind of ache, this one right around her heart. Worse, she had a feeling Thea hadn't really bought her made-up story.

When she'd been adequately fed and rehydrated, she'd kissed her mother on the cheek and left her house to check on her gardens and deliver food to those who counted on her. Niall said he had distributed food to them, but how could she trust him? She'd never experienced black magick like his before and it scared her to the center of her bones.

Tonight, moving as quickly as she could, she'd harvested everything from her gardens and given it all away. It would be the last time she could feed people for a while, so she'd cautioned each of them to be careful with the supply. Happily, she'd found her people already with food stores. Niall hadn't lied to her about that, at least.

She needed to leave the Boundary Lands. The ocean would be the best place for her. Lots of water to hide herself in. The act of becoming and traveling as her water self always seemed easier the closer she was to the sea.

More than anything she wanted to check on the pieces, maybe move them, but it seemed too risky. At this point she was pretty sure that everything that was happening was real, but she couldn't be one hundred percent certain.

Coming home hadn't felt safe. After her time with Niall, *nothing* felt safe. She'd returned home only long enough to take a shower and pack a few necessities.

Things were going to get a whole lot more dangerous— that's the only thing she knew for sure. She wasn't safe and no one around her was safe. The only choice was to flee.

Of course, Niall, or some other Unseelie, would find her eventually.

She slung the duffle over her shoulder and made her way downstairs. Light had just begun to show on the horizon, which meant she'd be traveling by daylight. Not ideal. She could handle being in sunlight, but it sapped her energy. If she was forced to dissolve into water self, she'd find it much more difficult. It was at least a forty-minute drive to her destination. The faster she left, the faster she could find a dark place to sleep.

Taking the stairs two at a time, she entered her small foyer. At the exact moment her foot touched the floor, the front door burst open. Standing in the frame was a hulking man with long, stringy black hair and a shiny gold front tooth. He put her in mind of a pirate and—she sniffed—apparently he had the hygiene of one, too.

She dropped her duffle to the floor, ready to dissolve. Man, she hated that she'd be leaving all her clothes behind. Narrowing her eyes, she fisted her hands at her sides. Maybe she should have been scared, but she wasn't. Her experience with Niall had frightened the scare right out of her. "Can I help you?"

Out of the corner of her eye, she caught movement. Slender gray beings. *Crap.* He wasn't alone. It appeared other creatures were outside her house, probably surrounding it. Were they goblins? Quickly, eyes on the stranger, she reached out and tapped into the moisture in the air, sensing presences in the immediate area. Felt like seven to eight.

"Where are the pieces?" the pirate bellowed.

Damn. She'd thought she'd have more time.

Glancing regretfully down at her duffle, she made the decision to dissolve. The moment she hit the floor, she knew something was very, very wrong.

Warm . . . then hot. Unable to soak into the wood of the floor.

Burning.

Every molecule of her water self screamed in agony. *Evaporation. Dying . . .*

TEN

SHE re-formed, lying on her clothes and gasping, her fingers digging into the floorboards on either side of her. No charmed iron. Only wood. *What was going on?*

Scorch marks ran along her arms and legs, radiating white-hot pain. The man had some kind of magick that heated water.

"Try to escape again and I'll boil you down to nothing."

"So, do it," she rasped, swallowing hard. "Kill me and you'll never find the pieces." She sat up like nothing was wrong, wincing at the agony of her wounds, and dressed, hiding the way her hands were shaking.

Another Unseelie with magick off the charts. *Fantastic.*

"Your friend Niall told us all about your death wish. I'm here to take things a step further. We know all about the people you help." He made the words *people you help* sound like *maggot-filled apple.* His thin lips spread into a cold smile. "Brought some goblins with me."

Movement caught her eye, and a couple of the tall, skinny alien-looking creatures stepped out from behind him.

Goblins weren't necessarily as frightening as they appeared. They had their own culture, religion, customs. Leave them alone, respect them, and they minded their own business—

could even be nice. But they could be vicious, too, and they lived at the will and mercy of the Shadow Ruler, in this case, Queen Aislinn. If she had commanded these goblins to make hats from the livers of the people she loved, that's exactly what they would do.

Saying nothing, she pulled on her shoes. "Fine, asshole, you have my attention."

His creepy smile widened. "Tell me where the pieces are and this stops now. I won't touch your friends or your family."

Her eyes narrowed. He didn't know about her mother or he would have said *mother* not *family*. After all, Thea was the only family she had left. That he didn't know about Thea was good. Unfortunately, thanks to Niall, this fae likely knew the names and location of every one of the elderly and infirm nature fae she visited every night. He'd run through them like a wildfire literally.

"The goblins are already rounding them up. They'll bring them here and I'll kill them one by one until you tell me what I want to know." He smiled. "We're like kin, you and me. You can become water, travel as water, and I can boil it within another person's body. Neat trick, right? I bet you're jealous."

She stared up at him, wishing like hell looks really could kill.

He laughed. "I'll show you how it works in a few minutes." Pulling a piece of folded paper from his back pocket, he read it. "How about I start with Mr. Donnell McKee?"

Damn it. She fisted her hands so hard her fingernails dug into her palms. Niall had been taking notes, given them to the Black Tower, and now the Shadow Queen had sent this piece of work for her. Now what? She couldn't let any of her people die over the pieces, yet she wasn't ready to allow her mother to die, either.

Sweet Danu, what a choice.

She glanced into the kitchen on her right and focused on her iron skillet, hanging over her stove. The only way out of this was to defeat the pirate, right here and now. The goblins were a wild card, but she was betting that once their commander was out of commission, they'd back off.

Shooting to her feet, she bolted for it.

Searing electric pain shot through her body, dropping her

hard onto the floor. She writhed, screaming, unable to do anything but endure the fire blazing through her veins. The scorching pain was gone as soon as it had started; leaving her with a marrow-deep ache in her body that prevented her from moving.

She lay motionless, moaning, as the pirate loomed over her. He was talking and gesturing angrily, but she understood nothing. The world had gone silent except for the roaring in her ears. Her mouth opened and closed, her fingers scratching on the polished wood of her kitchen floor. The pain wiped all thought from her mind.

Something caught the pirate's attention. His head jerked up, gaze focused out the window. His eyes widened and he raced away. *Oh, crap.* Anything that could scare that guy was not good news.

Around her, chaos exploded.

From where she lay, she saw only feet—the pirate's black boots; long, bare gray goblin feet; and new feet. Polished brown leather loafers, a scuffed pair of hiking boots.

Sounds began to filter into her consciousness and started to make sense again. Yelling. Explosions. Grunts and bellows of men and creatures in pain or in attack. Battle sounds. Smoke curled along the ceiling of her kitchen and foyer.

She lay, trying to endure the aftermath of what the pirate had done to her. Becoming water self was the only way to heal, and she needed to escape while the pirate and the goblins were distracted, but she couldn't make herself dissolve. The pain was still too great, though receding, little by little, like the tide at twilight. All she could do was sprawl on the floor and hope she wasn't trampled.

Her house was on fire. The bodies of the pirate and the goblins lay scattered around.

These facts registered dimly.

Smoke filled her kitchen. It tickled her lungs, and she would have coughed if she'd been able. Instead she just choked. A big man with red hair scooped her into his arms, carried her from the burning building, and laid her outside on the grass.

The redhead turned and talked to another man who had brown hair and eyes. The second man would have appeared totally harmless, if she hadn't gotten a good look at his eyes while he examined her as she lay helpless. The second man had the eyes of a sociopath. Cold. Soulless.

Behind the two strangers, her house went up in flames.

The brown-haired man pulled a set of charmed iron cuffs from his pocket and took a step toward her. *Oh, no.* Time to go.

Dissolve . . . Nothing happened.

He took another step. Panic flared inside her.

Dissolve . . . Still nothing.

He reached down and caught her wrist.

Dissolve!

Anguish screamed as she forced water self. The moment of bursting into liquid caused bright, sharp, bone-chipping pain. The agony would have made her pass out, but the instant she became water, it disappeared. There was only cool trickling, the seeking of a wide flow and the surrendering.

No burning. No boiling. No dreaded evaporation.

She traveled away from the angry nature fae with the red hair and the small, evil brown-haired man.

Flowing. Free.

NIALL stepped over the body of Ragnar and toed his crispy shoulder. *Dead.* Definitely dead.

The smoking ruins of Elizabeth's house lay all around him. Parts of it still smoldered. The Boundary Lands, sentient thing it was, usually found a way to put out such fires before they reached the trees. It had rained recently, very heavily. Tendrils of smoke curled through the kitchen and wound their way past the bodies of several goblins.

He sniffed the air, smelling sulfur. Some magick he was unfamiliar with had done this job. He frowned. It didn't feel natural, but it didn't feel like fae magick, either. He looked down at Ragnar. Whoever had done it, he owed them a debt of gratitude.

Elizabeth was gone. Either she was now a prisoner of whoever had killed Ragnar and burned down her home, or she was on the run. He was betting on the latter. After all, he knew better than anyone how hard it was to catch an asrai. She was like fisting water—just ran right through his fingers.

He stepped into the yard, leaving the smoldering wreck of her home behind him. He'd come here to warn her, but he'd been too late. The fact that he'd raced to save her from Ragnar made him squirm. He didn't have time to examine it, though.

It was time to find her mother.

His first move was to check on her people. Niall assumed they were all right, since Ragnar was lying dead behind him, but he wanted to make sure. Plus, they all knew Niall's face, since he'd distributed food to them the night he'd caught Elizabeth, and they might be able to tell him where all the sprae-dependent fae lived around here.

There couldn't be that many, and one of them was bound to be Elizabeth's mom.

ELIZABETH flowed, her water self burbling happily down a stream. Occasionally she would meet a Lady of the Lake, a Glaistig, or a Gwragedd Annwn. Their consciousnesses would brush up alongside each other's in acknowledgment and she would continue on her way.

She couldn't quite remember what she was supposed to be doing. All she could remember was the pain she'd experienced in her corporeal self.

Avoid.

Instead she wanted to flow, surrender.

Above the streams and rivers she flowed through, the sun shone brightly. That was strange and not nice. It made her feel weak. So she just traveled, trickled, dripped, and soaked. All day she swirled in eddies and played in the currents of rivers.

It would be nice to do this forever. Forget that whisper that not all was right. Just flow.

Yet somewhere deep within her consciousness, a nagging sensation lingered. It told her to re-form. As the sun sank lower in the sky and the weakness receded, the nagging grew stronger and stronger until she finally gave in.

Re-forming at a location her water self recognized as familiar, Elizabeth found herself lying by the side of a small stream at twilight, all her memories and the full consciousness of her corporeal self restored to her. She closed her eyes, enjoying the absence of pain.

One of the perks of being an asrai was being able to heal almost any injury by dissolving into water self, almost any . . . not iron sickness. That was because charmed iron negated her ability to shift.

Traveling as water self was an enjoyable experience, especially during stressful times like now when she needed to hide or simply not think about anything. Unfortunately, she couldn't do it for too long. The longer she stayed water, the greater her chances of losing her corporeal self forever.

Sometimes she wondered if that was what happened to her biological mother. Had she lost herself somehow and merged with water forever? Was she running through this stream at her fingertips even now?

The thought made her sad.

It also made her think of Thea. The event back at her house had changed her plans. She needed to move her mother before she went to the ocean. She'd removed all evidence that could trace back to her mom from her house when she'd accepted the pieces—and now it was all burned to the ground, anyway. Yet it was still possible someone might discover her mom's location.

Elizabeth had been dreading this. Somehow she needed to relocate her mom without telling Thea why she needed to move. Her mother's cottage was only a little over a mile away. Forcing her chilled muscles into action, she pushed up and sought the heavy plastic bag she'd hidden behind a nearby rock and pulled out the clothes and shoes contained inside.

Dressed, warmer, but not feeling any more cheerful, she started for her mother's place. She needed to hurry; she'd already wasted too much time today.

Dread filled her chest with a leaden sensation. She hated lying to her mom, and her mother was not an easy person to deceive, especially when she was already suspicious about Elizabeth's recent disappearances. She'd just have to stay vigilant.

Under no circumstances could she eat any of her mother's food or drink any of her tea.

NIALL knocked on the door of the trim house and admired the profusion of flowers in the yard. It was clear that Elizabeth visited often and used her gardening skills. The sprae lighted on everything here, the trees bracketing the fenced-in yard, the brown clay shingles on the roof, and the matching wooden shutters. There were definitely more sprae here than anywhere else he'd noticed lately.

A late middle-aged woman answered the door. She had short, curling reddish brown hair, laugh wrinkles around her grass-colored eyes and full lips. She was attractive, likely had been a knockout when she'd been younger.

She gave an easy smile. "Can I help you?"

The scent of freshly baked cookies wafted from behind her. She displayed not even a hint of fear that a strange man was at her door, even though she lived way out in the middle of nowhere. *Interesting.* He'd been expecting to need to win her trust.

It could mean that Thea Jocelyn Saintjohn was not as innocent a nature fae as she appeared and had ways of defending herself. He would need to be careful.

"Hello, Mrs. Saintjohn, my name is Niall Daegan Riordan Quinn. I'm a friend of your daughter's. I was looking for her. I stopped by her house, but she wasn't there. Is she here, by chance?" She wasn't and he knew that, but it was a good opening gambit.

Luckily, she displayed no recognition of his name. Good. Less explaining to have to do. "Elizabeth? No, she's not here right now, but she'll probably be arriving soon. She usually stops by every evening."

"That's too bad. I'll have to wait, I guess. I really need to speak with her." He rubbed his hands together and shivered. "Cold evening, isn't it?" He smiled, and started to walk back toward his car.

"Niall? Is that what you said your name is? Would you like to come in to wait? I'd enjoy hearing how you know Elizabeth. She doesn't have many friends."

Bingo. He turned back to the door. "That would be great. Thanks very much."

She nodded and turned inside, holding the carved wooden door open so he could follow. Inside the house smelled of fresh baked cookies and coffee. A fire burned in the kitchen hearth. The house wasn't big, one open room with a hallway

leading to what he presumed were bedrooms and bathrooms.
The kitchen was the largest room, obviously a well used area
with shiny pots and pans hanging from the wooden rafters of
the ceiling interspersed with bunches of drying herbs.

"Would you like a cookie?" she asked. "They're oatmeal
raisin."

"That would be great." He sat down at the butcher's block
that partitioned the kitchen and living room while Thea
served him a plate with two warm cookies and a cup of coffee.

She poured herself a cup of coffee and sat down next to
him. "Now, tell me how you know my daughter. Like I said,
she doesn't have many friends, let alone attractive male
friends."

He bit into a cookie and stifled a groan of total ecstasy.
They were incredible. He pointed at the cookie. "You should
be selling these. They're delicious."

She smiled. "They're very special cookies. Old recipe. We
keep it in the family. I whipped up this batch for my daughter.
I was hoping to tempt her with them when she comes to visit
tonight." She sipped her coffee and looked at him expectantly.

She seemed like such a sweet woman. Niall had the immediate sense that she had no idea what her daughter was up to.

And for some stupid, inexplicable reason, Niall found he
didn't want to tell her.

Niall took another bite of cookie and chewed thoughtfully,
framing his answer. He was going to have to lie to protect
both Elizabeth and her mother. "I was assigned to—"

He snapped his mouth closed. *What the fuck?* He'd meant
to say he'd met Elizabeth at Donnell's house, thus dropping
another name Thea knew and cementing her trust in him, but
the truth had come out instead.

He tried again. "I was ass—" He fell into a coughing fit to
cover his gaff and stared at the cookie. Was it possible? Was it
these damned delicious oatmeal raisin cookies? He set the
cookie down on the plate and took a sip of coffee.

"You were saying?" Thea prompted. "You were assigned?"

"Ah, yes."

Okay, it appeared the mom *wasn't* as harmless as she
appeared. Now he had to tell the truth without actually telling
the truth. "I was assigned by the Shadow Queen to look for

the two lost pieces of the *bosca fadbh*. My search led me to the Boundary Lands, where I met your daughter. We struck up a . . . friendship."

Huh. They weren't really friends, were they? Yet the truth cookies had let him say that. Fascinating.

The front door opened, and Elizabeth entered. "Mom? Whose car is that . . . *Niall?*" Her eyes flicked from the plate of cookies to Niall's face and she went completely still.

Relief rocketed through him. She hadn't been captured. Niall gave her a slow smile and a wink. "Hi, Elizabeth!" he returned brightly.

She narrowed her eyes at him.

Her mother turned in her chair. "Come on in, honey, Niall was just telling me how you two met. You didn't tell me you had a new friend." Her tone said the unsaid—*who's a man*.

"I was going to tell you, Mom." She smiled. "I just hadn't gotten around to it yet." Her eyes met Niall's while her mom's head was turned, and he mouthed *liar* at her. "But I'm really glad to see that Niall is here because I need to talk to him. Right now. Outside. Would you be offended if I took a little walk with him, Mom?"

Thea immediately stood up. "Not at all! While you're gone, I'll make you both some dinner."

Niall regarded the stove warily. If the cookies made him tell the truth, what would dinner make him do? "A walk is a great idea." He stood and followed Elizabeth out the door.

Once they were traveling the moonlit path away from the small house, she whirled to face him. "What the hell are you doing here? How did you even know where to find her?"

"Don't get your panties in a bunch. I'm the only one who knows where to find your mom. A friend found an obscure reference to a sprae dependent woman who adopted a possible asrai, and I followed up on the lead. Took me all damn day." He studied her. "She's who you're protecting, right? And she doesn't know about it. She's got no idea you have the pieces."

"She knows now." Elizabeth gestured angrily at the house. "You ate her cookies."

"No, I didn't tell her you're the one hiding the pieces of the *bosca fadbh*. She has no idea you're currently the most wanted fae in all of Piefferburg."

She said nothing for a long moment, then tipped her head to the side. "Why? You could have taken her into custody, threatened her. You could have used her against me. Why didn't you?"

His jaw clenched, apparently he still couldn't lie. "I came to warn you about that very thing, but certain events have transpired since then. Walk with me."

She fell into step at his side. She wore a tight pair of leather hunting pants, popular with nature fae, a pair of scuffed boots, and a heavy black cable-knit sweater. Her red hair hung loose around her shoulders. If it hadn't been for her pale skin and her hair, she would have blended seamlessly into the night.

And she looked good.

"Have you been to your house lately?"

She shuddered. "There was a man, a big guy with long black hair and a gold tooth. He came with goblins."

"Ragnar Joren Kvalheim," Niall replied grimly. "I saw his body. Who killed him?"

Hugging herself, her boots crunching dead leaves, she led him into a small clearing and sat down on a boulder. He sank down beside her, and she moved a degree away—probably afraid of being captured by him again. "I don't know. That Unseelie did something horrible to me, felt like my veins were on fire."

"He can—could—boil blood and the water in a person's body."

"Lovely. Whatever he did, it nearly killed me. All I know is that some other people showed up, two men I didn't recognize. There was a big battle, and my house ended up on fire."

"You didn't see their faces, hear anything they said?" He rubbed his chin. Who the hell were these new players? Someone sent by the Summer Queen?

"Gee, no, sorry. I was too busy writhing in absolute agony. They tried to cuff me in charmed iron, but I managed to force myself to dissolve right before they got me."

"Why did you come back here? It's not safe."

She looked at him sideways. "Why do you care whether I'm safe or not?"

"I'm not a fucking monster, Elizabeth. I came to warn you that the Shadow Queen told me to back off, says I'm too close to do what needs to be done after all that time I spent in your head."

Apparently she'd been right, considering he was sitting here having this civil conversation with Elizabeth.

"She sent Ragnar after you instead," he continued. "He'd intended to torture and kill all the people you care about one by one until you gave up the pieces."

"*Damn it.* Ragnar is dead, but that doesn't mean she won't send others." She pushed away from the boulder and paced in front of him, hugging herself.

"Right. The Black Tower has a surplus of badass fae who have no problem hurting people if ordered. So it's time to give up the pieces before you lose the people you love."

Elizabeth stopped pacing and looked off into the distance, in the direction of her mother's house. "She'll die, Niall. If the walls fall, she'll suffocate without the sprae to give her breath."

"Then I guess you're in the same position as our queen. You have to sacrifice one to save many. It's an awful decision to have to make, but—"

She lunged at him, grabbing his jacket and coming nose to nose with him. The scent of her flowery soap wafted around him. He tried not to inhale and be seduced. "You're still under the influence of my mom's cookies, so tell me, do you have magick that could help me?"

Fuck. "Yes, I do."

"What is it?"

He clenched his jaw and narrowed his eyes, fighting the magick that was compelling him to tell the truth.

"Tell me what magick you possess that can help me save the people I care about," she asked again.

He sighed, unable to combat it any longer. "I can conceal them from anyone who looks, at least for a time."

"You can . . . hide them?"

"Yes."

She considered him for a moment. Her breath warmed his mouth and he fought a crazy impulse to lean forward and press his lips to hers. *Fuck.* He was in trouble. "You want to help me for some reason, don't you?" she asked him in a mystified tone.

"No. I don't want to help you hide the pieces. What you're doing is wrong, but I do want to keep you and yours alive."

She stared at him for a moment longer, and then turned away. When she spoke next, she sounded defeated, like she knew what his answer would be. "Do you have magick that could help my mom if the walls break?"

"I wish I did, but no. If I had magick like that, I would have already offered it to you."

Her shoulders slumped. "Do you know anyone who does?"

He went silent, considering. The Piefferburg witch was the only one he could think of. "Maybe."

She turned back toward him. "Really?"

He held up a hand. "I wouldn't get your hopes up. This fae is expensive and capricious as hell. Sometimes she'll hurt while seeming to help you. Sometimes she'll help you while seeming to hurt. She loves to sow chaos, and she doesn't give a shit about the walls coming down. Her time here in Piefferburg is like a blink of an eye to her, she's so old. Everything's a game to the Piefferburg witch."

Elizabeth's eyes glowed with hope in the small amount of moonlight. "Still, if there's even a chance."

"She could make it worse."

"How could it get worse?"

Niall rubbed a hand over his face as he stared off into the tree line. Sprae danced and cavorted in the leaves and bushes. "Look, here's the deal. I'll do the concealment spell on your mom and your people, but only for the time it takes me to go talk to the Piefferburg witch. If she's got some miracle solution for your mom, you'll hand over the pieces, right?"

She squealed and launched herself into his arms. "Happily."

He held her close, enjoying the way her body molded to his. Immediately he recalled the night on the floor in front of the fire, when he'd made her come over and over. . . . Fuck, his dick was getting hard.

He held her at arm's distance, trying to control his impulse to lay her flat on this rock and make her come for real. "If the witch doesn't have anything to help you, all bets are off. Got it?"

"I get it."

"I know who you're protecting now. I can use that against you. I would never hurt your mom physically, but there's other ways I can make you do what I want."

Her eyes narrowed. "Just when I started to think you were a good guy."

"You're making me work against my queen right now. It's making me cranky."

She raised an eyebrow and grinned. "I'm not making you do anything. You offered to do this. Why?"

"You're really fucking taking advantage of those cookies, aren't you?"

She shrugged. "All the nature fae around here know not to eat my mom's food. Sometimes it makes you tell the truth. Sometimes it makes you do a dance. Sometimes, if you've been really naughty, it will kill you."

"And your mom seemed so sweet."

"She is sweet. She's just not a sitting duck."

"Your mom is Unseelie."

"Technically. *Answer the question.*"

"I'm helping you because I want to get the pieces back with as little bloodshed as possible. Also, I like you."

"You do?"

"Against my better judgment, yes." Damn, and he'd even offered that bit of truth voluntarily.

She stepped toward him. "What about during that time you had me tricked, that night . . . in front of the fire . . ." Her voice had gone a little husky and it made his cock go hard. "Did you *want* to do that? Was it personal . . . or was it just part of the show?"

His mouth went dry, remembering the soft silk of her skin, the little sounds of pleasure she'd made. "That was intensely personal, Elizabeth, and I'm dying to make it real. Officially, you've still never come. At least, not—"

She held up a hand. "Yes, got it. *Right.*" He couldn't tell for certain in the low light, but it looked like she was blushing.

His voice came out low, husky with lust. "I still want to watch you do it yourself, as well as do it for you."

"Do you now?" She tilted her head to the side and gave him a flirty little smile.

"Oh, yeah, in the worst way. I like the sounds you make. I

love the way you look when you're experiencing that kind of pleasure, the flush of your skin . . ." Reaching out, he caught her wrist and pulled her up against his body. Cupping her cheek, he murmured, "I like you a lot, Elizabeth. I hate that we're on opposite sides of this."

"Yeah," she murmured, staring at his mouth. "I do, too. Can we take a time-out, maybe?"

That was the best idea he'd ever heard.

He moved his head at the same time she moved hers, and their lips met for the first time in real life. She tasted wild and sweet, like the cool, running water of a Boundary Lands river. He made a hungry sound in the back of his throat and plunged his hands into her thick fall of hair, angling her head to the side to better part her lips and ease his tongue within her mouth.

Her hands closed around his shoulders and slid slowly down his back. He enjoyed the feel of her warm body against his and wanted all this fabric between them to disappear. He wanted her bare breasts against his chest, wanted her pretty thighs parted, wanted to feel all that smooth skin brushing against his body.

He just wanted her, no matter the cost.

His tongue rubbed up against hers, tasting every little part of her that she would allow. His hands found the hem of her sweater and pushed up, searching out the small of her back. He rubbed his fingers over her smooth skin, back and forth, wanting to delve below the waistband of her pants for more tender parts of her anatomy.

When he was in a person's head, creating a fantasy world for them, it was pretty authentic. But this? There was *nothing* better than this—having her in his arms for real.

She broke the kiss, breathing heavily. "We shouldn't do this. This is not right."

"Feels pretty right to me. I thought we were taking a break."

"I want to, but we both know better." She stared at him for a moment in the half light, breathing heavily, lips parted and a little reddened from his kisses. "There are no breaks for us. No time-outs. We're enemies, remember?"

He shook his head, gaze on her mouth. "Nope, can't really remember that part." He pulled her close and nipped her lower lip.

She melted against him, her fingers going to the button of his jeans while she pressed her lips more firmly against his. "You taste really good," she whispered against his mouth. "Better than I remember."

"You, too." He nipped at her lip. "I want more."

He couldn't wait to get her clothes off and have her pressed up against this boulder behind them. His only regret was that she deserved better for her first time. She deserved a bed, at least, but this might be their only shot before this whole mess engulfed them in chaos once more.

His hand slid down the front of her pants, skating along the silken smooth skin of her abdomen to between her thighs. He cupped her sex, finding her clit, such a delectable little berry. He wanted it between his lips, pressed under his tongue. It would taste so sweet.

She moaned into his mouth, shuddering against him with pleasure. He pressed and rotated his finger on her clit, remembering the way she looked back at the cabin when she'd come. He wanted to make her do that again, right now.

Elizabeth shuddered again, her body suddenly going tense. Then, abruptly, she pushed away from him. "This is wrong. You keep making me forget that."

He pulled her back. "Not wrong. Nothing that feels this right can be wrong."

She shook her head. "It is."

He curled a tendril of her hair around his index finger. "Just let go, Elizabeth."

She looked up at him with clear eyes, the lust-filled haze fast disappearing, and he knew he was losing her. "Make sure you do what you promised."

"Elizabeth." His voice came out in a bark of warning because he knew what she was about to do.

Then he was standing there alone, her clothes in a pile at his feet, and one long red strand of hair still wrapped around his finger.

ELEVEN

NIALL was a man of his word, even if he had to bend the rules a bit. He'd promised to recover the lost pieces of the *bosca fadbh* for the Shadow Queen, and he intended to honor that commitment even if the Shadow Queen had told him to relent.

He'd also promised to cast a concealment spell over Elizabeth's loved ones and go to the Piefferburg witch on her behalf—essentially, he'd promised to protect her.

At first glance, Niall knew these two promises seemed to conflict, but if honoring both got him to his goal—the missing pieces of the *bosca fadbh*—he didn't see where the harm lay.

Another man probably would have felt a duty to inform the Shadow Queen that Ragnar had been killed, along with all the goblins she'd sent, but he figured that could wait awhile. It bought him time.

He parked his SUV on an empty side street in Goblin Town, which was not very far from the Black Tower. It was his goal to stay clear of the Unseelie Court, if he could. The Piefferburg witch's shop resided in an alley that curled around the base of the Black Tower, so he needed to be stealthy.

Stepping out onto the street in front of a clothing store, he

nodded at the gaping goblins that passed him by. Humanoid
fae weren't common in Goblin Town, though they were welcome. When they did come, they were almost always Unseelie.

The main street was cluttered with storefronts and bits of
refuse blowing about in the gutters. Goblins tended to procre-
ate much better than any of the other fae races. The goddess
Danu seemed to grant children to them and no one else for
some reason. As a result, the goblins were outgrowing the
area that had been allotted to them at a great rate. They had
the choice to move out of the city to the rural parts of Piefferburg, but most of them refused.

In the distance, above the tall, narrow buildings of the
commercial area, he glimpsed the shiny golden dome of
the Temple of Orna. To his right he could see the tall onyx
tower of the Unseelie Court. Taking a right, he headed toward
the massive gleaming black building.

The alley where the Piefferburg witch could be found was
flanked on one side by the smooth quartz of the Black Tower.
The other side was a brick wall, the back of the storefronts on
the next street over. Halfway down the alley he could see a
shaft of light illuminating the dark of early morning. Apparently the witch already knew he was coming. Typical.

Priss had taken the guise of maiden and stood framed in the
doorway of her shop. "Well, hello, kindred fae." She gave him
a slow head-to-toe sweep. "What brings you to my door so late
at night? Or early in the morning, I should say." She winked
and turned into her shop, crooking a finger for him to follow.

She always called him and his brother *kindred*. Of all the
fae in Piefferburg, the three of them had magick that was closest alike. No one knew much about the Piefferburg witch
other than she was very old and kind of a bitch. His magick
and that of his brother was strong and versatile and so was
Priss's. But Priss's magick came from mixing potions and
combining herbs—that's how she came by the moniker of
witch, even though she was technically fae, or so it was
assumed. His and Ronan's magick was inborn, internal, and
had nothing to do with combining ingredients outside of
themselves.

"So you knew I was coming. Do you know why I'm here?"
He stood just inside the doorway.

Each side of the room was lined with tables and shelves filled with jars, vials, and different shaped containers. It smelled of some acrid herb he couldn't place. Her shop was in a pocket of reality that also existed in the Boundary Lands and had exit and entrance points in various locations of Piefferburg City.

She turned, twirling a tendril of her reddish blond hair around her finger. It reminded him of his recent encounter with Elizabeth. "I thought you came for me," she replied, all innocence.

He gave her a slow perusal. "As lovely as you look . . . right now, no. I have other business."

It was better to flatter than offend this woman. In actuality, he would never find himself interested in the Piefferburg witch, for reasons other than the fact she spent most of her time guised as a stooped, cackling old woman. No one really knew what her natural form was—maiden, mother, or crone—and he didn't care. She was repulsive in any shape she took.

These days he was far more attracted to an impulsive, trouble-making redheaded water fae who had a penchant for protecting others and tended to land in trouble a lot.

Priss pouted. "Then why have you come?"

"I'm here on behalf of a friend. Her mother is dependent on the sprae to survive. She's worried that if the walls break, the sprae will disperse and her mother will die. Do you know any magick that could help?"

The Piefferburg witch turned, and as she did so, her form shifted to crone. Mumbling to herself, she moved around the room, checking the labels on canisters and jars. "Perhaps something to capture the sprae."

"I thought you couldn't capture them."

She shrugged. "Normally you can't." She gave him a sly look over her shoulder. "But there are ways to capture all sorts of creatures that are supposed to be uncatchable if you're clever enough, aren't there?"

So the minx did know about Elizabeth.

Niall shifted and grinned at her, narrowing his eyes. "Right, sure there are."

She moved glass containers around on a shelf, making them clink. "I'll need time." She paused, then cackled. "And money. Lots of that. But I know you're good for it, aren't you, Niall?"

He gritted his teeth for a moment before replying. "Of course."

He'd pay whatever needed to be paid in order to see Elizabeth protected. The thought came so fast, hard, and unexpected that it rocked him back a step. Was that really why he was doing this? To protect Elizabeth?

Damn, he really was in trouble.

She waved a hand in his general direction. "Then if that's all you need, you can go. I'll need time to explore whether this is possible or not. Check back later."

"Later, when?"

Dismissive hand wave again. "Later, later. Go now."

Niall had no idea if he was getting played or not. Sometimes the witch acted like she could help and really couldn't. Sometimes she tricked everyone involved, as she had with Kieran Aindréas Cairbre Aimhrea.

Kieran had had a curse laid on him that meant death to him and any woman he fell in love with. Then Kieran had gone and fallen in love with Charlotte Bennett. The witch had directed Kieran to kill himself before the curse took him in order to save Charlotte, without telling him that by sacrificing himself he was breaking the curse. Her intervention had saved both Kieran's and Charlotte's lives. That didn't automatically make Niall believe she was doing him a good turn now, though.

Tricky witch was Priss.

ELIZABETH sat on a cliff at the edge of the ocean, looking down at the waves crashing against the rocks. The place was desolate. She hadn't seen even one fae since she'd arrived.

Not far from where she sat, she'd found an abandoned cottage and was currently squatting there. She didn't have much, since she'd been forced to leave everything she'd packed back at her house, but there was a bed, now covered in freshly purchased bedding, a fireplace, and a place to cook food. The roof leaked, but, hey, it wasn't like she was going to live there forever.

She hoped.

Hugging herself, she stared out past the hazy warding that made up the far eastern part of the Piefferburg warding. Humans couldn't see it. Fae couldn't cross it. It made her sick that she was fighting to keep it up, but the thought of her mother suffocating to death made her sicker.

"Elizabeth Cely Saintjohn?"

She jumped up and whirled around, ready to dissolve into her water self. Crap, she hadn't even heard a footstep. A tall black-haired man in the rose and gold garb of the Imperial Guard stood ten feet away from her. "How the hell did you find me, and what do you want?"

"You've chosen to set up a residence less than a mile from where Her Majesty, Queen of the Seelie, the Summer Royal, Caoilainn Elspeth Muirgheal, is currently residing."

Oh, fantastic. She hugged herself. It figured she'd picked the one place that was near the queen's hideaway. Elizabeth rolled her eyes. "Does she want to borrow a cup of sugar or something?"

He didn't crack a smile. "She wishes to meet with you."

"Right now?" If she ever saw the Seelie queen again, it would be too soon. "I'm sort of busy today."

"Right now." The guard turned and started down the path that led away from the cliff.

Of course, *now.* And the Summer Queen was used to getting her way.

Relenting, Elizabeth picked her way past a clump of brambles and followed the guard. He led her down a tangled mess of pathways, looking odd as he tromped through the woods in his shiny rose and gold hauberk and with a sword sheathed at his side.

Finally they came to a clearing, the opening of a cave looming in front of them. He ushered her through the dark crack and led her through a series of caverns to a carved set of wooden doors. Clearly the Summer Queen had had this place created a long time ago. It put Elizabeth in mind of a bomb shelter—and the queen had set off freaking World War III.

The guard swung the doors open, and Elizabeth was nearly blinded by the whiteness of the room within. Of course, that was a calculated move on the Summer Queen's part. The chamber was designed to shock and awe. All that white put Elizabeth in mind of the human's notion of what heaven looked like—but Caoilainn was no angel.

She stepped onto the polished marble floor, her footsteps echoing as she walked to the center of the room, where she knew she would find the Summer Queen's throne. The first time she'd met the queen it had been in the woods, without all the fanfare, but she knew enough about Caoilainn to understand that wasn't her regular modus operandi. This place looked a lot like the throne room in the Rose Tower.

Caoilainn wanted people to worship her. She wanted to be the most powerful person around, the most feared. That's what this was about for her. If the walls fell, she'd lose all that. Swallowed up in the wonders of the wide, wide world, she'd lose her court. Her life would be meaningless.

"So," said Elizabeth, her voice echoing off the tall marble pillars and the painted fresco on the ceiling high above her head, "you've holed up in a wall just like a bug? Interesting."

The Summer Queen gave her a tight smile, and the ringlets framing her beautiful, young face quivered. "You've got the pieces hidden very well and I don't want them found. Ever. Tread carefully, girl. It might be better for me if you were dead."

Good point.

She shifted on the balls of her feet and crossed her arms over her chest. "I understand we're neighbors now."

"You're *holed up* like a wild animal in an abandoned shack not far away. My scouts reported the activity. Do you really think anything goes on in these woods that I don't know about? There were no cliffs here when Piefferburg was created. *I made them* with my magick. *I am this land.*"

"I admit you know more than other people about many things. You knew about me and my mom, and you're the only one." She paused, the thought suddenly occurring to her. "Do you know anything about my biological family?"

The queen's full, perfect ruby red lips parted in a smile. "That's information I *may* choose to give you *if* you agree to my terms."

"Terms?" She frowned, fingering the edge of her torn, dirty sweater and trying not to feel inadequate in front of the Summer Queen's silk and satin finery. "We already had our negotiations. I hide the pieces of the *bosca fadbh* for our mutual benefit. Our dealings are done."

"Things have changed." She lifted an elegant hand, arched an elegant brow, and flicked a long, elegant finger.

Elizabeth turned to find two men striding toward her. One tall, muscular and redheaded. The other average and unforgettable in most every way—aside from his cold, soulless eyes.

They were the two men who'd killed Ragnar, burned down her house, and tried to slap charmed iron cuffs on her.

She took a deep, measured breath in through her nose and out her mouth. Her first reaction was to dissolve and get the hell out of Dodge, leaving, *again*, all her belongings behind. There were other places in Piefferburg where she could hide.

But were these men friends or foes?

They'd basically saved her butt back at her house and they appeared to be allied with the Summer Queen, who was not Elizabeth's ally but did want the same thing—the walls to remain standing.

But what about those cuffs?

Taking a step back, she made sure to keep a good distance between herself and the approaching men. If they made any move in her direction, she'd be out of here before they could blink.

"Elizabeth Cely Saintjohn," said the poisonously innocuous man coming toward her with an outstretched hand, "so nice to finally meet you."

She stepped away from him and put her hands behind her back. "And you are?"

A flicker of bare violence shot through his eyes, and he lowered his hand. "My name is Gideon P. Amberdoyal, archdirector of the Phaendir."

Her mind went numb with shock. *Archdirector of the Phaendir?* "What does the P. stand for?"

He smiled, but it didn't reach his eyes. He motioned at the redhead beside him. "This is Liam Connall Deaglan Mag Aoidh, a free fae working to keep the walls erect in order to protect his wife from the Wild Hunt." Gideon paused and gave her a small, oily grin. "You two have something in common, don't you?"

"So, wait." She held out a hand as if to slow the whirling in her head. "The archdirector, a free fae, and the Summer Queen are all working together to make sure the walls don't fall?"

"Ding, ding, ding. You're a genius," replied Gideon in a voice laden with sarcasm. "And guess how much I love to be here in Piefferburg with all the fae. Talking with them, touching them, offering to shake their fucking hands."

She gave a cold and bitter laugh. "Why would I care about your discomforts, Phaendir?"

"Because you and I want the same thing." His voice came out a low hiss. He moved his hands, and she caught sight of heavy, mottled scar tissue at his wrists. *Sweet Danu.* "And the faster you turn over the pieces to me, the faster your precious mother will be safe, Liam's precious wife will be safe, the world will fill with rainbow-flavored lollipops for everyone . . . and we can *all fucking go home.* I'm most interested in that last part."

Elizabeth glanced at the Summer Queen and back at Gideon. "I'm not giving up the pieces, not to anyone. Not even to someone who purports to want the same thing I do. Especially not to the Phaen-*fucking*-dir."

She didn't swear often, but this occasion totally called for it.

"I told you," said the queen in a bored voice.

Gideon took a step toward Elizabeth, immediately making her back away. "You don't have a choice." He spat the words at her and clenched his thin, white hands at his sides. He wanted to kill her. It was right there in his eyes, clear as anything. The man gave her the creeps.

"I have the pieces; therefore I have all kinds of choices." She jerked her chin at him. "Why do you want the pieces, anyway? They're safe, hidden. You don't need to worry about them."

"I don't have to *worry* about them? Really?" He pointed to himself and raised his eyebrows. "*I'm* in charge of the safety of all the world and *I* don't need to worry about where the pieces are? That's news to me." His countenance changed, growing darker. He snarled the next words at her. "I want all the pieces of the *bosca fadbh* and the Book of Bindings. Breaking the walls of Piefferburg isn't the only thing you can do with the book, after all."

"What do you mean?" Elizabeth glanced at the queen, but got no reaction from her. "Is he saying what I think he's saying?" She turned to stare accusingly at Liam, who hadn't said one word since he'd entered the room. "How can you be working with him? He's evil!"

"He's not going to destroy the fae with it," said Liam, his face grim. "He means to destroy the fecking book, to keep anyone else from using it." He had a heavy Irish accent.

"And you believe him?" She made a scoffing sound. "How can you be sure he's not going to unleash a can of unholy Labrai whoop-ass on us? Maybe another round of Watt Syndrome, or something worse?"

Liam shrugged. "We can't be sure."

"Oh, great. *Great* plan. I'll be keeping the pieces, thanks." Her hands were shaking with a mixture of rage and fear. It made her voice sharp. She needed to get out here. After shooting an icy glance at the Summer Queen, she walked for the door.

Gideon grabbed her by the upper arm as she passed, and she dissolved in the space of a breath, leaving him holding her sweater.

Hard. Pooling. Trapped. Choking. Suffocating.

She shifted back into corporeal form and lay on her side, coughing and gasping. She slapped a palm to the marble and stared poisonously up at the Summer Queen through the fall of her hair. "There's charmed iron in this floor." There was no mistaking it. This was the second time in her life she'd experienced charmed iron, and both occurrences had been within days of each other.

The Summer Queen smiled. "Why do you think I asked you *here*?" She waved a hand airily. "I'm getting bored, you can take her now."

Liam stepped forward and scooped her into his arms, snagging her clothes along with her. She fought him, kicking and screaming, not even caring she was naked. He just clamped down on her harder . . . then even harder, so she could barely breathe.

Gideon approached her, looking very pleased with himself. Murmuring a series of words she didn't understand, he pressed his clammy hand to her forehead and she felt consciousness slowly slip away. Her eyeballs rolled back into her head as darkness closed its fist around her. She bet anything that when she woke, she'd have a charmed iron cuff on her ankle.

Only, this time, it would be real.

TWELVE

NIALL found Elizabeth the same way he'd found her before, by working a tracking spell on her. He wasn't surprised to find she'd fled toward the ocean. She'd need to be a little less predictable than that. Of course, in Piefferburg, there was a lot of ocean. His tracking spell showed she was in a hilly, uninhabited area of the Boundary Lands, about forty-five minutes from the coast.

Since he didn't have that nifty way of traveling as water, he packed up his SUV and set out to tell her what Priss had discovered.

He'd stuck around Piefferburg City for a couple days waiting for Priss to research whether or not she could entertain his request, taking a room in the *ceantar dubh*, since he didn't want to run into anyone from the Black Tower.

The city was in a state of preparation. It almost felt like they were getting ready for a hurricane to hit. Families were leaving the city, boarding up their homes and shops. The Shadow Queen had ordered the Blacksmith, Aeric O'Malley, plus a small army of fae, to make weapons and had armed everyone she could in case the Phaendir or the military came in through the gates.

And they waited. For the invasion. For the missing pieces of the *bosca fadbh*. For a miracle.

He was supposed to deliver that miracle, but it was a damn hard thing to do without becoming the monster some people thought he was.

And it was about to become harder.

Following the map he'd drawn to pinpoint her location—and hoping like hell she didn't leave it before he got there—he turned down a narrow gravel road in the northernmost part of Piefferburg. The weather had turned frigid during the last couple days and little specks of snow rained on his windshield.

Irritated, he flicked on his wipers and turned the heat up. He got that she needed to lose herself where she couldn't be found, but this was ridiculous. Navigating narrow, treacherous roads becoming more treacherous by the moment from the snow that was falling more heavily, he made his way through the forested Boundary Lands to the small cabin where she was hiding. Turning down the driveway, he spotted a dented white cargo van in front.

Stopping the SUV, he considered it, his wipers *swish, swishing* back and forth. As far as he knew, Elizabeth didn't own a vehicle other than her ATV.

So who that hell was that?

His intuition prickled. Something wasn't right here. Rolling the SUV down the road a little, he parked it behind a clump of holly bushes and eased out of the vehicle. The cold hit him like a slap to the face. Using the bushes and trees to mask his movements—and hoping like hell there weren't any magickal security systems in place, he made his way up to the log cabin. It was a large place, nice, probably some vacation getaway for a wealthy Seelie or Unseelie. The windows were half frosted over, but he found one to peek through.

Someone passed by the window right as he peered in and he ducked down, out of sight. After a minute, he tried it again. There were two men in the house, a tall, strong-looking guy with red hair who he didn't recognize and a man with brown hair and eyes who was wearing a suit—seemed kind of formal for a trek to the wilderness. Where was Elizabeth? His magick said she was here somewhere.

The brown-haired man paced in front of a couch that was turned so its back was toward the window, gesturing and talking as though agitated. The redhead sat on a chair turned backward, his expression apathetic and maybe just a tad pissed off. The suit-guy looked like he probably talked a lot. He looked like a weasel, too.

He caught sight of movement on the couch, a flash of a woman's red head. Ah, there was Elizabeth. He studied the couch, silently willing her to move or do something so he could get a sense of what was happening. Was she in there of her own free will? Was this some new twist in their ill-advised and treacherous relationship?

Or was she a prisoner?

Silver flashed near the polished wood floor and Niall concentrated on it—a charmed iron cuff around her ankle. So, prisoner, then.

A crackle of a power signature not unlike his own zinged through his awareness. In the same instant, suit guy looked up, toward the window, his eyes focusing hawklike on Niall's face in the millisecond before Niall lunged to the side, bolting for his SUV. The redheaded guy burst from the cabin behind, hollering for him to stop.

Niall climbed into his SUV and gunned the engine. He needed to get away, needed to regroup, needed to plan.

Needed to figure out who the fuck these men were and get Elizabeth away from them—and soon.

Magick exploded behind him as Niall gunned the vehicle out onto the road, spraying gravel underneath his tires. In the rearview mirror he caught a glimpse of the suit-guy standing in the road behind him, snowflakes catching on his dark lapels. The man's mouth worked as he uttered words Niall couldn't hear. It looked like he was working some kind of magick, not unlike the magick Niall wielded.

Power gathered in the air, raising the hair on the back of his neck, tasting like metal at the base of his tongue. Niall slammed his foot onto the accelerator, forcing the SUV's transmission to clunk into a higher gear and squealing the tires. An alien source of power exploded like a bomb right where his vehicle had been a moment before, uprooting a small tree and sending dirt and rocks flying.

Fuck him. Whoever that man was, he could blow things up like Kolbjorn Einar Soren Halvorson, the death dealer.

He sped down the treacherous, narrow road, knowing like a punch to the gut that the redheaded hulk would be following. Sure enough, a heartbeat later, the white cargo van careened onto the road behind him.

Taking a turn so hard he nearly rolled the SUV, Niall spotted an opening between the trees and directed himself toward it. He risked entering the woods and not being able to find a way through, but it was his only shot at getting away from this guy. The roads up here were too unpredictable to drive fast on. He'd end up going over a cliff, and who would help Elizabeth then? Plus the spits of snow were fast becoming a full-fledged storm, diminishing his visibility. Luckily, there wasn't enough on the ground yet to show his tracks.

Yanking on the steering wheel, he veered to the left, off the road and into the trees. It would be hard to navigate in here, but much harder for the cargo van. Finding the narrowest path through the trees he guided his vehicle as deep as he could into the foliage, hearing the *twang* and *thunk* of branches against the sides and undercarriage of the vehicle. He found a nice clump of bushes to hide the SUV behind and stopped, mumbling the words it took to pop a concealment spell into place. It would shield him from any locator magick either of the men might possess.

Rolling down his windows, he could hear the cargo van trying to follow, the squeal of spinning tires, silence, then the slam of a car door and lots of cursing.

"Fuck you, bastard," Niall murmured. "You'll never find me now." He allowed his head to fall back against the headrest and let out a careful breath.

The redhead was definitely fae, and from Irish descent if the accent and the quality of the cursing was any measure. The man still had a strong accent, which was . . . *odd*, considering all the Irish fae, himself included, had been trapped in Piefferburg for three hundred and sixty five years and time had bled their accent away into the lighter, more homogenous form that most Piefferburg fae possessed.

That was strange, but the suit man was even stranger. No one in Piefferburg had magick like that except himself and

Ronan, so who the fuck was he? The only other people who had a power signature like that . . .

. . . were the Phaendir.

He closed his eyes. "Oh, fuck."

ELIZABETH opened her eyes blearily to find Liam and Gideon bickering in the middle of the living room. They always bickered. They were like an old married couple that had nothing in common. But, of course, these two *did* have something in common—they wanted to break her.

Just like Niall had wanted to break her. Just like the Summer Queen.

She had a thing or two to show these people about how breakable she was.

"Why, in Labrai's name, didn't you stick your hands into the dirt and do that finding thing you do?"

"I told you," answered Liam, his accent thicker when he was angry and spit flying everywhere, "I *did* do that. The fae had some way to mask himself. He entered the fecking woods and just fecking disappeared."

Gideon grimaced and wiped some of Liam's spittle from his face. "Masking magick means mage. Mage means Ronan or Niall fucking Quinn." He said their names like he was announcing the spread of the Black Plague. "*Niall* Quinn, would be my specific guess. We should have killed those little Quinn bastards back when we had a chance." Gideon turned toward her. "You're wanted by so many men these days, cupcake."

She gave him a chilly, unamused grin. "I'm flattered. Too bad they all want to kill me."

"I don't want to kill you. *Au contraire.* I want you to tell me where the pieces are and I'll let you go."

"Right, so you can gather all the pieces and the book, and do Danu knows what with the spells inside."

"Nonsense." He gave her a wolfish smile. "It's exactly as Liam says it is. I intend to use the spells in the book to destroy the book, itself. Once the book is destroyed, Piefferburg's walls will hold forever. The Phaendir and the humans will be safe from the threat of the fae loose in the world. That's all I want."

"Sure. I believe you," she shot back, sarcasm thick in her tone. "And if Liam believes you, he's dumber than he looks."

Liam's gaze shot to her, his eyes narrowing.

She looked past Liam, dismissing him, and focused on Gideon. Despite Liam's size, Gideon was the real threat. "You'll do whatever it is you think your precious god wants you to do. I have no doubt that's genocide."

"You misunderstand me. I'm your keeper, not your killer. We want the same thing, Elizabeth. Just give in and we can all go home." He motioned at the charmed iron band around her ankle. "That's been on for three days. Things are about to get a whole lot rougher for you. That thing could even kill you." Gideon spread his hands and tried to look innocent.

Gideon was incapable of looking innocent. Evil, yes. Creepy, definitely. Every night the man took off his shirt and used a cat-o'-nine-tails on his own back and arms, ripping his flesh and letting his blood run down his buttocks and the backs of his legs. His skin was a mess of fresh and healing wounds and thick, mottled scar tissue from old ones. As he injured himself, he prayed.

It was the only time she and Liam were ever in accord. Gideon was disturbed beyond all comprehension.

She laughed, and it turned into a series of racking coughs. When it was over, she laid her head on the pillow and breathed shallowly, fighting the now familiar feeling of exhaustion from the iron sickness. It seemed to be progressing faster in real life. "I've already died once from a charmed iron cuff. You're too late."

Gideon looked confused for a moment, then sneered at her and turned away, pointing at Liam. "If death doesn't scare her, maybe pain will. She's all yours."

Elizabeth closed her eyes, thinking of Gideon's cat-o'-nine-tails.

Great.

NIALL pushed a branch aside and let it *thunk* back into place.

He really hated all of this. He hated that he was now in the position of having to save the woman responsible for hiding the pieces of the *bosca fadbh*. He hated there were fucking

Phaendir loose in Piefferburg—and there had to be more than one. No one single Phaendir was capable of wielding magick the way suit-guy had. He had to have a contingent of Phaendir secreted away close by who were sitting in meditation and powering this asshole, giving him a steady stream of juice.

That meant suit-guy was a bigwig.

The archdirector? Was this man Gideon Amberdoyal? It seemed likely.

If suit-guy was Amberdoyal, why was Elizabeth fighting them? The Phaendir wanted the same thing she did, and the Phaendir could hide the pieces much better than she ever could.

So why the resistance? Why the charmed iron? Why was she willing—yet again—to die to keep the pieces from someone else's hand?

Who was she was protecting now?

He needed to contact the Black Tower and let them know the Phaendir were somehow loose in Piefferburg. It wouldn't be the first time they'd gotten in without their knowledge. The Phaendir had kidnapped Aislinn once, in the days leading up to her succession to the Unseelie throne. No one had known how they'd entered—but they'd all left in body bags.

In *pieces* inside the body bags, since the goblins had gotten to them.

That meant the weird Irish-accented redheaded hulk might be from the outside, too. It seemed likely he could be one of the free fae who'd been giving them so much trouble.

Queen Aislinn needed to know all this, but he had no way to send word to the Black Tower right now. His first priority was getting Elizabeth out of there. Depending on when they'd captured her, she may have been wearing that iron against her skin for days. He hadn't gotten a good enough look at her through the window to judge.

Murmuring a series of words under his breath, he eased around the side of the cabin, popping a concealment spell in place. This one was different than the one used on a stationary item—like his SUV parked down the road, for example. This one cloaked him from locator magick as he moved around, but it wouldn't last long, which is why he'd put it into place at the very last minute. He had a knife sheathed at his side in case he needed it. Aside from that, his only weapon was his magick.

And a group of nature fae.

The first thing he'd done after the redhead had abandoned the cargo van to the tangled mess he'd embedded it in was seek out a few of the nature fae around these woods. He knew they would be singularly pissed off that one of their own was being held against her will, especially by the Phaendir. Of course, he'd had to slightly modify the reason for her predicament.

It hadn't taken him long to find a clutch of Scots woods fae and a few of the birch ladies. Both groups, especially the birch ladies, who were sworn to protect women, had wanted to storm the cabin right then. He'd been forced to manage them into a small army and make them vow not to attack until he said so.

The free fae and the Phaendir bastard wouldn't know what hit them.

Even better, Elizabeth would be in his arms shortly.

Sneaking up to a window, he peered inside, this time confident that suit-guy—Gideon Amberdoyal, he was certain— wouldn't see him. His eyes widened, taking in the scene. Elizabeth, shirtless, was slumped over a chair turned backward, hands tied in front and her bare back exposed. Her face looked haggard, ashen. Clearly she was deep in the throes of iron sickness, only this time it wasn't just in her head.

The massive redhead stood behind her, holding a cat-o'-nine-tails loose in one hand, his mouth snarling out words at Amberdoyal. It looked like they were arguing. Amberdoyal was gesturing toward Elizabeth. It appeared Amberdoyal was trying to get the redheaded fae to flay her open and he was resisting.

Niall took all this in for one, short moment, and then leapt into action. He shouted the command, voice hoarse with shock and panic. A man as big and strong as that one could lay soft skin like Elizabeth's open with only one lash, no matter how much he held back.

The redheaded fae never got the chance to try.

The nature fae stormed the house yelling out battle cries like Celtic warriors of old. As soon as the cabin was breached, Amberdoyal started exploding magick front, left, and center.

Niall forced his way into the cabin to find it already filled with smoke, obscuring his vision. To Niall's right, Gideon fought off a group of burly Scots fae and birch ladies with his magick while slowly inching back toward a window to escape. To Niall's left, the redhead was in a fistfight with a woods fae who was of an equal size.

Fire had erupted in at least three different places, thanks to Amberdoyal's willy-nilly, panicked explosions, he guessed. Now he knew how Elizabeth's house had caught fire. But none of that mattered to him. He had one priority and one only. He waved the smoke away, getting a bearing on where Elizabeth was located in the mess.

There!

He made his way toward her and came around her chair. She was out cold, slumped over the backrest and oblivious to the chaos around her. He worked the knots of the rope binding her wrists.

Right before he got them undone, the sting of the cat-o'-nine-tails bit into his back. His spine snapped, arching in white-hot pain. His shirt ripped from collar to hem and hot blood gushed. He stood and whirled to face the redhead.

Well, hell, apparently he didn't have a problem hitting anyone with that thing but Elizabeth.

The man held the cat in one hand and smiled maliciously. "Liam Connall Deaglan Mag Aoidh, free fae, at your service."

Ah. That explained a lot.

They circled each other warily. The rest of the nature fae were busy with Amberdoyal, leaving him alone with Liam. "So, a traitor free fae, then. I figured. Heard lots about you."

He shrugged. "A man does what he needs to do to protect those he loves."

"Including beat up on defenseless women? How noble."

Liam glanced at Elizabeth, looking almost regretful. He turned sad eyes back to Niall. "There's nothing noble in any of this. She's protecting someone, too."

The fire around them grew, snapping and crackling. The nature fae retreated, coughing. He couldn't see where Amberdoyal had gone in the smoke and that made him nervous. "We need to get out of here soon, or we'll both die."

Liam's eyes narrowed. "Nah, just you."

The cat'-o-nine-tails came toward his head with whiplash

fast speed, but Niall was ready for it. He reached up, his back screaming in skin-ripping agony, and grabbed the cat. Yanking it to the side, he pulled the man off balance and brought his fist up, giving him a solid punch to the face. It cracked Liam's head to the side and made him stagger.

Totally okay with hitting a man when he was down, Niall stepped forward and delivered a hard punch to the man's kidney. Liam's back snapped rigid as he arched with a bellow of pain. Taking advantage of his exposed chin, Niall gave him another fist to the face.

Liam stumbled back a step, dropped the cat, then fell backward with a *thump*.

Niall stood, breathing hard, adrenaline pumping. His back screamed with pain, on fire just like the house. All he wanted was to collapse, but he couldn't nurse his hurts yet. He needed to get Elizabeth out of here—*now*.

THIRTEEN

COUGHING from the smoke, he turned and quickly finished undoing the knots at her wrists. She was still out cold,
which was not helpful at all. He tossed her over his shoulder
in a fireman's carry . . . and nearly passed out from the pain of
his back ripping even further. He stopped for a moment,
breathing in smoke and forcing himself not to lose it.

Coughing and staggering, he made his way out the front door
and into the cold, fresh air. A little way from the house he gave
her over to the hands of the Scots fae and sank to the ground.
The cold, snow-dusted earth felt so good against his back.

One of the birch ladies sat down beside him. "The Phaendir
got away," she said, her dark hair shifting over her shoulders.

He nodded, watching the cabin go up in flames. "The free
fae didn't." Liam was still in there, knocked out cold.

"Is that what he was?"

Niall nodded.

"Sit up so I can see what he did to you."

Grimacing, Niall pushed up from the ground.

The woman examined his back. "You need healing."

One of the men knelt beside him. "The woman's breathing,
but still out."

Niall looked up and saw they'd covered her with a blanket. "She's iron sick." His voice was rasping from the smoke. "I need to get that cuff off her."

He pushed to his feet and staggered over to the man who cradled her in his arms. Her face was dirty from soot, her hair was tangled, and her skin looked wan and pasty. She was pretty far gone.

"Carpean mia dosic," he murmured and touched the cuff. The side of the smooth metal split and it dropped onto the ground. That was the end of his magick. It was pretty much tapped. He probably only had enough left for a low-level locator spell, and he would need to work it to find them shelter.

If Amberdoyal came calling now, they were in deep shit.

The dark-haired birch Lady came up on his side. "Come with me. We can give you shelter and heal you both."

He shook his head. "Thanks for your help, all of you." He knew they'd lost a few in there to Amberdoyal's magick. He'd seen the bodies. "But I need to take her where no one knows our location. And we need to leave now, no time for healing."

Her brow wrinkling, the woman looked from him to Elizabeth. "Are you sure? She looks—"

"Bad. Yeah, she looks real bad. But, yes, I'm sure." He couldn't run the risk of them discovering what Elizabeth had done. They'd probably want to kill her themselves.

A burly Scots wood fae placed Elizabeth into his arms. He grimaced in pain, feeling hot blood run down his back anew. No matter, they needed to get the hell out of here.

Niall looked down at the woman in his arms. Here he was helping her again. *Stupid.* This woman wielded some magick over him that he didn't understand—because what he did for her now had so much less to do with the *bosca fadbh* than he was comfortable admitting.

He turned, thanked the nature fae again, and walked to his vehicle anyway.

H E wanted to drive farther, but the weather conditions and the pain of his back made it impossible. Going as far toward civilization as he could do safely in the driving snow, he pulled off to the side and used the dregs of his magick to locate shelter somewhere nearby. Immediately he got a hit on an empty structure not far away.

Guiding the SUV to it slowly, he saw that it was another cabin, not unlike the one he'd left burning down the road. Apparently this must be a Seelie fae vacation destination. Whatever. It was shelter from the storm. He just hoped there was food to scavenge.

After kicking the front door in, he carried Elizabeth inside and set her on the couch.

Breaking into one of the upstairs bedrooms, he found a stash of clothing and selected a cashmere sweater, then returned to Elizabeth and slipped it over her head.

She roused, pushing at him, and he calmed her. "Where are we?" she murmured, looking down at the new sweater.

"Seems like every time we meet, you're naked," he grumbled under his breath. "Let me worry about where we are. Relax. You're safe."

She peered up into his face. "You look like hell."

"So do you, baby. Rest now."

A faint smile flickered over her lips. "You do know how to flatter a girl." She fell back against the cushions and closed her eyes. Dark circles marked the flesh beneath them.

He stood back and studied her. She looked close to gone. He'd figured that charmed iron against the skin of a nature fae would do its work faster and had built that into the illusion he'd woven for her, but he'd never expected the process to be *this* fast. By the looks of the weight she'd lost and the color of her skin, he'd gotten her out of there just in time.

While she slept, he cleaned and dressed the wound on his back as best he could, hid the SUV, built a fire in every available fireplace in the cabin to heat the place, and figured out what they'd do for food while she recovered. Luckily the place was stocked with canned goods.

He just hoped no one would find them before he had enough juice for a concealment spell. He wouldn't be able to put one in place for at least twelve hours.

Elizabeth slept way past that amount of time. He bundled her in blankets where she lay on the couch and checked every few hours to see if she was breathing.

Other than that the brief flicker of life she'd shown when

they first arrived, she did a really good impression of a dead person. Niall had never dealt with anyone who'd been so thoroughly dosed with charmed iron. To him it looked like a coma, or a really deep sleep that allowed her body to repair itself.

He found himself sitting near her, studying her night and day, worried not only about the hidden pieces of the *bosca fadbh*, but about the woman, herself. She was a bright light in the world. Stubborn and misguided, to be sure, but also intelligent, incredibly strong, and very protective.

She was like no one he'd ever met—and he'd lived a long time. Unique, complex, fascinating, she intrigued him on a level that went far past her physical allure. Niall had to admit he was attracted to her, but on a deeper level than he'd ever been attracted to a woman before.

For the first time in his three hundred and eighty two years, Niall felt the bite of true fear.

Finally, around forty-eight hours after he'd carried her into the cabin, she began to stir. He put down the book he'd been thumbing listlessly through and sat forward, watching her. She parted cracked, pale lips and her eyelids fluttered.

"Elizabeth . . . Elizabeth," he singsonged. "Are you in there?"

She groaned and opened her eyes a crack. Taking one look at him, she grimaced, and closed her eyes again. He'd try not to take that personally.

After fetching a glass of water, he set it to her mouth and dribbled a little between her lips. She groaned again, grabbed the glass with surprising strength, and tried to gulp it empty.

"Hey, easy," he said, wresting control from her. "A little at a time or it will all come back up." He eased the glass away from her.

She blinked and focused on his face. "What happened?"

He set the glass on the table and slumped in the chair. "You mean other than you almost dying? This time for real?"

Weakly, she pushed up and propped herself among the pillows. "I'm aware of that particular fact. I meant the rest of it. How did I get here, with you?" Her words came halting and raspy from an abused throat.

He told her the whole story, then steepled his fingers and grinned. "I saved your cute butt."

She set the water glass onto the coffee table. She was looking better by the minute, but she wouldn't be dancing around anytime soon . . . or dissolving into water self, probably. "Maybe, but you also let Gideon Amberdoyal get away."

"Way to be grateful, Elizabeth."

"I *am* grateful. Thank you for saving my butt, Niall. You're my hero."

"*Cute* butt."

She closed her eyes. "If you say so."

"Am I your hero? Are you thinking about ways you can repay me?"

She cracked one eyelid and glared at him. "You're not getting the pieces."

He grinned and waggled his eyebrows. "I wasn't thinking about the pieces."

"I'm sure you weren't." She swung her feet around to the floor and swayed a little. "I need a shower, and my stomach is trying to digest itself. I'm getting way too used to that sensation. After that, you and I have things to discuss."

His grin faded. *Priss.*

Slowly she pushed to her feet and walked unsteadily toward the back of the house.

"I laid out fresh clothes for you on the bed. I'll make you something to eat."

At the entrance to the master bedroom, she stopped and half turned toward him. "I really am thankful you got me out of there. I thought I was going to die for real that time."

"I did, too." He paused. "I'm glad you didn't."

"Me, too."

EVERY part of her body ached. It felt a little like the time she'd caught the flu. The fae didn't get sick very often, so she remembered it.

Gathering up the clothes Niall had set out for her, she moved carefully into the bathroom and ran the water in the shower. She'd never been so hungry in all her life. She was so hungry she was nauseous, so hungry she was repulsed by the idea of eating.

Clean first, then food—a small amount of food.

She washed her hair twice and scrubbed her skin until it was shiny and pink, as if trying to get the touch of Gideon Amberdoyal off her. Then she dressed in the jeans and soft sweater Niall had laid out for her. When she returned to the kitchen, she felt better, maybe even a little stronger, and saw that he'd made toast and eggs for her.

"While you were sleeping off the iron sickness, I made a visit to the nature fae around here. They provided us with some fresh food."

She sat down and studied her plate. The mix of ravenousness and illness warred in her stomach. Picking up her fork, she tested a little of the egg. She swooned. It was the best thing she'd ever put in her mouth. Her body demanded more.

Soon she was shoveling the food in and Niall had to slow her down. Finally she leaned back in the chair, the small amount of bread and eggs making her stomach ridiculously full. Ah, that was so much better.

Now it was time for business. "So, what did Priss say?" she asked.

Niall sighed and sank into an opposite chair. "There's no way to save your mother, Elizabeth."

Disappointment sank like a boulder in her chest. She'd really been hoping for some good news. That was the problem with hope. The higher the hope, the harder the disappointment. She drew a breath and looked away from him. "That's too bad."

"It is. I'm sorry. I'd wanted better news to bring to you."

"That means we're still bitter enemies."

"I'm having a hard time feeling bitter toward you."

She looked at him, trying to read his expression. Narrowing her eyes, she said, "You don't have me locked in some blasted illusion in my head right now, do you?"

He locked gazes with her. "I swear on my mother, I don't."

"You never had a mother."

"It's a figure of speech."

"*Niall.*"

He leaned forward. "You can tell I don't. Can't you feel it? You should be able to sense the difference, since you've experienced the illusion before. Reality is more real than my mind fuck can ever be."

She considered him before speaking, sensing her environment. "I can feel it, and I think you're telling the truth."

He leaned back in his chair and spread his hands. "Good, because I am."

Crossing her arms over her chest, she asked, "Where do we go from here?"

"You rest, get better. I'm assuming you can't dissolve yet."

She rubbed the center of her chest with her palm. "The iron sickness has sapped my magick." It felt like a hole had opened up inside her because of it, too. She eyed him suspiciously. "After I get better, then what?"

"I don't know. You may not feel like a bitter enemy to me, but we're still on opposite sides of this thing."

"Yes, so . . . why help me?"

"I told you already." He met her eyes. "I like you."

Trying to take his measure and sort her feelings for him, she studied his face. She was physically attracted to him, that fact was undeniable. There was more there, too. A flicker of something deeper. An appreciation for his protectiveness and desire to do the right thing, for his wit, even for that stupid cocky grin she wanted to knock off his face half the time.

"Elizabeth?"

She blinked, coming back to herself. Oh, crap. This was not a good thing.

Pushing to her feet, she swayed a little, catching herself on the edge of the chair just as Niall reached out to steady her. She pushed his hand away. "I'm going to lie down for a while. I assume there's some kind of hidey, no-one-can-find-us spell on this place."

He nodded. "Rest easy. Get well so we can go back to chasing each other around like Tom and Jerry."

She gave an uneasy laugh. "Sure."

But she had a feeling they were doing another kind of chasing at the moment.

LIAM reached out, his soot-streaked hand skimming through a pile of dead leaves. He grasped the dry, rough root of a tree and used it for leverage. He flipped to his back, and a coughing fit immediately assailed him, making him double over on the ground. A short distance away the house he'd dragged himself out of still smoldered.

Damn Gideon and his fucking hive magick. It destroyed everything it touched.

Rolling onto his back again, he stared up at the lightening sky and dragged smoke-tinged air into his burning lungs. He'd only barely escaped with his life after meeting that fucking fae, Niall Quinn. Worse, now the bastard knew what he looked like, knew his name, and he needed to go back to the Black Tower to risk himself again. Gideon had left him for dead, so it was his only move.

He closed his eyes, wheezing. Outside these walls was his small family of free fae. Good ones, bad ones. They'd all joined together, coming from far and wide, most of the fae who'd somehow managed to escape the Great Sweep and the descendants of those fae.

Danu, he missed them right now.

He'd been there the day his wife had committed the sin of murder. It had been in the early days of Piefferburg, and he and Aideen had been running from a small group of Phaendir in Ireland that had been set on capturing them and loading them onto a ship bound for the newly formed fae imprisonment area in the colonies.

They'd sought shelter at a friend's house, only to discover that the friend, Declan, had taken money from the Phaendir to turn in fae. He and Aideen had only just figured out why Declan had been acting strangely before the Phaendir had burst through the front door of the cottage. They'd fought their way free, and Aideen had stabbed Declan right before they'd fled into the woods.

She hadn't needed to do it. It hadn't been in self-defense. The killing had come from a place of utter rage and betrayal. Aideen had been livid that Declan had informed on them and had wanted him dead. Simple as that. Liam was certain Aideen's action would be considered cold-blooded murder in the eyes of the Wild Hunt.

Maybe it had been wrong, but how could he allow her to spend forever in the sluagh for what she'd done? It wasn't fair that these fae should spend a lifetime in Piefferburg, but it wasn't fair his wife should be damned for eternity for what she'd done, either.

And now, here he was, feeling as big a betrayer as Declan.

Liam pushed up and pressed a palm to the center of his chest, coughing. He needed to get his arse moving. No way was he letting Gideon have those fecking pieces. He'd acted like he didn't care in front of the woman, Elizabeth, but he did care. He had no intention of letting the Phaendir go near the book or the *bosca fadbh*; he'd just figured the best way to prevent Gideon from getting them was to stay close.

Looked like that plan was fecked all to hell. Who knew where Gideon was by now? Not mourning Liam's loss, that was for sure.

GIDEON lifted his foot out of a glop of muck that made a sucking sound and took his shoe.

After clenching his jaw for a long moment, he let loose with a string of malicious curses screamed into the fucking faery treetops.

All the sprae in the area, keeping their distance from him anyway, disappeared with little winks. The Labrai-cursed Boundary Lands were covered in snow, yet he'd managed to find the one swampy section in the whole forest.

He glanced around, beginning to think the very trees and bushes were out to get him. In a fae forest, that possibility couldn't be dismissed. He was, after all, their enemy.

Turning, he fished his shoe out of the mud with freezing fingers, all the while glancing anxiously around him. Then he straightened and strode forward, limping with only one shoe on. He was the archdirector of the Phaendir with powerful hive magick burning in his head. He could explode anything that threatened him.

He was just glad his men couldn't see him like this. They were holed up in Piefferburg City, giving him a steady stream of Phaendir hive magic, and he was out here, freezing, covered in soot and mud.

He'd actually had to flee *nature* fae. Fucking *tree* faeries. Birch ladies in their wispy white dresses.

This was the fault of the U.S. government and their frightened, weak-willed morality against allowing him to storm the gates of Piefferburg *the moment* they'd learned the fae had the book and the *bosca fadbh*. This was *their* fault.

Back when they'd first created Piefferburg, the Phaendir had assumed the New World would be the perfect place. Free of laws, wide open in terms of space. And, in the beginning, it *had* been perfect. Early America had been nicely free from conscience. In fact, if it hadn't been for their powerful magick, the fae would have been enslaved just as the Africans had been.

Yes, Gideon, thought, sighing with remembrance, for centuries things had been just lovely. Back then, no one could have predicted it would turn out this way.

He remembered those days with fondness. Hunting down the fae had been good sport. First Watt Syndrome had hit them, making them weak, pathetic, and catchable. The creation of Watt Syndrome had been one of the earliest examples of biological warfare, all thanks to the Phaendir . . . with the Summer Queen's help. The illness had hit only the fae, killing them off by the hundreds, making the rest fragile and sluggish, unable to fight off the Phaendir/human alliance.

Watt Syndrome had been key in the capture of the fae worldwide. If the fae escaped now there would be no recapture. The fae had developed an immunity to Watt Syndrome over the centuries and, even though the Phaendir had tried, it seemed impossible to engineer another bug as beautiful as that one had been.

During the Great Sweep, they'd gathered the sick fae and loaded them onto ships bound for the New World. Packed so the vessels were near to bursting, they'd died like flies on the journey. Gideon had thought it was all a big waste of time and resources. Why not just slit their throats as soon as they'd been in custody? Yet even back then there had been a misplaced sense of morality and he'd been unable to convince more than a handful of his fellow Phaendir or humans that killing them right off was the best plan—*Labrai's* plan. As if letting them die of Watt Syndrome, hunger, iron sickness, or a lack of water on the journey to their prison was any more humane.

Even though the Christian god had said it was perfectly acceptable to slaughter a million or so people during the Cru-

sades and thousands more in the Inquisitions, killing the fae
at point of capture was wrong.

In his opinion, that had been arbitrary, ridiculous, and hyp-
ocritical.

Gideon had traveled from England to the colonies in the
spring of 1647. His accommodations had been slightly more
luxurious than that of the stinky, moaning, sick mass of fae in
the ship's hold, of course. Sharks had traveled in their wake to
enjoy the regular feedings.

Those ships hadn't been unlike those of the already thriv-
ing slave trade that had carried Africans. The slaves had been
treated much worse than the fae, in Gideon's opinion. Slaves
had been shackled, forced to work, treated like property.
Their children had been taken from them, their women raped.
The fae had just been thrown into a big, secure area and left to
fend for themselves. Set adrift and left alone.

He'd been one of the Phaendir to erect the warding that
enclosed Piefferburg. He'd been there to supervise the building of the brick wall, too, the thing humans could see as a
tangible barrier.

At first the fae had had nothing. They'd lived in squalor,
built their houses from sticks and mud, fought over the game
in the forests. Many more had died, and that time Watt had had
nothing to do with it. Slowly the fae had recovered, built better
houses, formed alliances, and organized the distribution of
food.

One thing no one had counted on was the mending of the
rifts between the fae races. The war that had originally driven
them apart, outed them to the human world, and made them
vulnerable to Watt Syndrome and eventual capture was only a
distant memory. Survival had united the fae once more. Eventually the Unseelie and Seelie Courts had formed, but their
war was not a violent one. Not even now, even after the Summer Queen had betrayed them all, still, annoyingly, unity in
Piefferburg reigned.

America had matured outside of Piefferburg's walls and
feelings for—*fascination*—with the fae had begun to take
hold. The government had begun to allow shipments of sup-
plies to be delivered through the gates. Commerce had flour-
ished. And where there was money to be made, the Americans

were there to take advantage of it. "It's a slippery slope!" the Phaendir had cried to no avail. Now look where they were.

Look where *he* was.

Something moved to his right. He turned, releasing a bolt of hive energy that crackled in his head. A bush exploded, something screamed, and bits of flesh flew everywhere. Gideon stood stock-still, fists clenched, then reached up and wiped a bit of rabbit from his cheek.

Someone was going to pay for this. All of it.

FOURTEEN

———⟡———

ELIZABETH stepped out into the comforting twilight of a chilly late afternoon and heard the crunch of snow under her boots. She headed for the tree line and began to gather kindling and place it into the basket she held. It was nice to get outside and draw fresh air into her lungs. The air had an icy bite to it, and a large amount of snow had fallen. The SUV Niall had driven could still handle the roads, but barely. If it started snowing heavily again, they'd have to leave.

Over the last day she'd gained a lot of strength, though she didn't quite have enough power yet to dissolve. The iron sickness was rapidly on its way out of her body, and she hoped like hell she never experienced it again.

She and Niall had spent an uncomfortable amount of time talking during the time she'd been recovering. He'd saved her. He'd helped her. Elizabeth wasn't sure what to do with those facts or the most disturbing thing of all—she liked being with him.

Kneeling, she scooped a handful of snow into her palm and let it melt. It called to her, sparking yearning in her chest for her water self.

Footsteps crunched behind her, and she turned to see Niall. "Let me help you with that." He reached for the basket.

She snatched it away from him, frowning. "I can handle the weight of a few sticks, Niall."

He shrugged and stuck his hands into his pockets. "I can gather the wood on my own."

Not looking at him, she knelt and placed another branch into the basket. "You've been doing everything and I don't like to feel beholden to others."

"You should be resting."

"I need to get out a little, feel the snow on my cheeks and get some fresh air into my lungs."

"You still look pale."

"Who are you, my mother?"

He grinned. "No, I'm definitely not that. I don't have very motherly-type thoughts where you're concerned."

She felt her cheeks heat and turned away. Damned man was hard to resist, and with every day she spent with him, she had more trouble remembering why she should.

Reaching down, he pulled out a stick peeking from a snow-drift and set it into the basket. "Speaking of your mother—"

"No."

He raised his eyebrows. "You don't even know what I was about to say."

"I don't want to talk about her." She turned away from him.

He grasped her elbow and turned her back toward him. "We're going to have to talk about this sometime."

Her gaze met his and held. "Not today. It's a good day and I don't want to ruin it."

"Okay, why not procrastinate a little longer? It's not as if the fate of the fae world hangs in the balance or anything."

She swallowed hard. "It's not that I don't feel guilty."

"You're too young to remember." He walked a short distance away from her, looking for more branches. "You have no idea what the Great Sweep was like."

"How were you taken? Were you sick?"

He nodded. "A human man chained me in charmed iron even though I couldn't move because I was so sick from the Watt. I only remember bits and pieces of the hellish journey over here. I would have died, but my brother came with me. Ronan kept me, and many others, alive on that ship."

"He came voluntarily?"

Niall nodded. "He never contracted Watt. That's how it was for some of the fae. They came protecting those they loved."

She pulled a piece of dead wood from where it was caught on a tree branch. The basket was full, so they started back toward the cabin. "Everyone in my family was born after Piefferburg was created. I've heard stories, though, from some of the nature fae."

"Hearing stories doesn't come close to having experienced it for yourself. If you had, you wouldn't be doing what you're doing."

She stopped and turned toward him, narrowing her eyes. "Really, Niall? Imagine if it was *Ronan* dependent on the sprae to survive. Ronan, who gave up his life to protect yours? If he was sprae dependent, you wouldn't be doing what *you're* doing." She paused and jerked her chin at him. "Would you?"

He clamped his mouth closed, then took the basket from her and walked into the warm cabin. "It would be a hard call."

She stamped her boots free of snow in the entryway. "It wouldn't be a *call* at all and you know it. You and I are a lot alike. We're both protective as hell." She waved her hand to encompass the room. "That's why you're doing all this for me instead of chasing me down and torturing me like your queen wants."

"Or maybe instead of wanting to protect you, I just want to fuck you." He pointed at her and raised his eyebrows. "Or maybe I'm just protecting you *so* I can fuck you."

Her mouth snapped open. She blinked at him a few times before mustering the verbiage required to reply. "Well, *fucking* me is off the table, so you can forget about that."

He walked toward her and she forced herself not to take a step back. "It wasn't off the table . . . *before*."

"*Before* none of it was real."

"You didn't know that." He moved closer to her. "To you *all* of it was real."

"Yes, well . . ." The only sound in the room was the crackle of the fire as she trailed off, looking for something to say. "We never actually had sex, you and me. Not even in my head."

"No, it came just shy of that." He smiled as he continued to walk toward her. It was the smile of a man who knew what he wanted . . . and who was certain he was going to get it. "But you begged me, Elizabeth. Don't you remember?"

Her mouth went dry. "Yes, I remember." She remembered his hands on her, the trail of his lips over her skin, the explosive way he'd pushed her into orgasm again and again. She'd tried to put the incident out of her head, keep her mind on the task at hand. She'd kept denying the truth—she wanted him.

She wanted him for real.

He came to stand a breath's space from her, and she glued her feet in place, heart pounding. If she backed away from him, she would look afraid. In reality, she was terrified. Terrified of how badly she wanted this man and terrified about what would happen if she surrendered to her body's desires.

Reaching out as if she was some wild animal that might bolt at any moment—she probably looked that way—he cupped her cheek in his hand. The action was surprisingly gentle and seemed at odds with his thick muscled arm and shoulder. He watched her with an intentness that made her wonder if he was attempting to read her mind.

Maybe he wasn't as certain of a victory with her as she'd first presumed.

"I want to touch you, Elizabeth." The words came out like warm honey, thick and sweet. His pupils had gone dark, signaling his arousal. A muscle worked in his jaw, like he was trying to hold himself back from lunging at her.

Her body quickened at the look in his eyes, responding to what Niall clearly wanted to do to her. He wanted her bare and beneath him. He wanted her legs spread and her moans echoing through the air.

He wanted so much more than he was saying with his words alone.

Her breath caught against the rising tide of desire softening her body. She had far too little experience to deal with a man like Niall Quinn. Her lack of knowledge in this area, and the needs of her very much underserved libido, made her easy prey for a man who wanted to use her for sex.

Was Niall such a man? She studied his eyes, seeing genuine hunger for her. He'd helped her when there had been no gain in it for him, saved her life, in fact. Even though she was not used to dealing with men, she trusted her intuition where Niall was concerned.

Niall wanted her *for her* and no other reason. Incredible, but true.

Taking a step closer to him, she pressed up against his body. His hand cupped her nape as she rose on her tiptoes and pressed her mouth to his. He stilled, as if stunned. Then, groaning deep in the back of his throat, he crushed her to his body and slanted his mouth over hers.

She remembered what it was like to be kissed by this man. It wasn't anything like how she'd imagined being kissed by a man would be. Niall made love to her mouth, brushing his lips softly over hers, then nipping her lower lip and slipping his tongue deep inside to brush against hers. It made her body tighten and hum with need. It made her think of bare skin and entangled limbs, of sheets and blankets pushed carelessly aside while two bodies fused in ecstasy.

And, oh, *Danu*, how she wanted to do that with him.

He scooped her into his arms. She let out a surprised yelp and then laughed. "What about your back?"

"The nature fae fixed me up, but it still hurts like hell."

"Then put me down."

"No way. I've been imagining this for too long." Grinning down at her, he carried her across the living room and into the bedroom. A fire burned in the fireplace, and snow had begun drifting softly past the large window that looked out over the Boundary Lands. Twilight painted the world in gentle grays and light blues.

Laying her down in the middle of the mattress, he crawled over her, looking down into her face. "I didn't want to make love to you before because it wasn't real and it didn't feel right." He paused, searching her eyes. "*Now* it's real and *now* it feels right."

"How can it feel right?" Her brow knit. "I mean, it feels right for me, too . . . but it shouldn't."

"Don't know, don't care. Right now I just want you." He leaned down and kissed her thoroughly, lips and teeth meshing and nipping, tongues meeting and parting.

She pushed the hem of his sweater upward to find warm,

solid flesh and ran her palms over as much of it as she could find, enjoying the bunch and pulse of his muscular torso. A bandage covered his back from where Liam had lashed him with the cat-o'-nine-tails, but it didn't seem to slow him down any. Pulling the sweater over his head, he tossed it to the floor, and her fingers went to work on the button and zipper of his jeans while he eased her sweater over her head. Their hands knocked and competed to get each other's clothing off, his lips kissing every revealed inch of her skin that he managed to place them on. Soon they were both bare, their skin sliding like silk against each other's.

He found her throat and nipped, making gooseflesh rise along her body and causing her back to arch. He slid a hand from her stomach to between her thighs while his tongue trailed over her collarbone, headed south, where he took one erect, pink nipple into his mouth. His wickedly skillful fingers found her clit and stroked it until she moaned and moisture flooded her sex.

Seeking between their bodies, her hand found his cock and curled around it, pumping its rock-hard length. He shuddered with pleasure against her and groaned against her breast. She loved the feel of him against her palm, loved even more that her touch seemed to please him.

He speared a finger deep within her and worked it in and out, widening her. When she was ready, he added another. Pleasure radiated out, making her squirm and moan. The heat in her body seemed to be rising, and a haze of sexual abandon fell over her mind. She wanted to make him groan, to give him pleasure, and to take pleasure from him.

She pushed up, wanting to kiss him, touch him, but he spread her thighs and dropped his head between them instead. "There's no rush," he murmured. "You're a virgin, so let me take the lead."

Then his mouth was on her, and it was all she could do to keep her sanity. His tongue found her clit and nestled against it, while his fingers speared in and out of her just the way she hoped to feel his cock. Her hands fisted in the blankets on either side of her as pleasure rose, building and building, the way she remembered it had in the illusion—but far more intensely.

"You taste so good," he murmured. "You make me crazy, Elizabeth." He sucked her clit in between his lips and massaged it.

She moaned, looking down at him. The sight of his head between her thighs was almost enough to make her come, right then. He found some place deep within that felt amazing when stroked and dragged his fingers over it.

Her climax hit her hard and fast, rolling over her like a freight train. It stole her breath for a moment, her ability to think. Her body shook, shuddered, and she cried out as the pleasurable spasms rocked through her. Niall rode her through it, pushing her orgasm harder and faster, milking every last drop of ecstasy from it before it ebbed away.

"Niall," she breathed, reaching for him. "I want to feel you. Don't say no this time."

He climbed up her body. "You don't know how bad I want you, baby. I couldn't say no if my life depended on it." He guided the head of his cock to her entrance and pushed inside.

She gasped and then moaned as her muscles stretched to accommodate him. The sensation was like nothing she'd ever felt before. So foreign, yet it was so good at the same time.

He bit his lower lip and closed his eyes. "Ah, fuck, you feel good, Elizabeth. Are you okay?"

"Okay?" she moaned, her fingernails digging into his shoulders. "The only way I won't be okay is if you stop."

He pushed in another inch. "No chance of that."

"Thank the Lady."

Another inch and then another. Slowly he worked his shaft in and out of her until he'd pushed in all the way to his base. It took a while, since, although her hymen had broken long ago, her passage was very tight. She felt completely filled and possessed by him, impaled and pinned beneath him.

There was nowhere else in the world she would rather have been.

He began to move—little thrusts at first until her body had loosened enough to accommodate his sizeable girth. Then harder and faster. His mouth found hers and his tongue slipped within to mate with hers as he thrust his cock in and out of her. He possessed her mouth the way he possessed every other part of her body. Every inward stroke brushed his body against her clit. It tingled and throbbed, sending waves of pleasure through her.

He broke the kiss and murmured against her lips, "Are you okay?"

"Oh, sweet Danu! Don't ask me that again," she breathed. "I'm fine. And whatever you do, *don't stop.*"

His strokes became long and driving. Mindless with need, she drew her hands down his back, over the bandage, and cupped his gorgeous rear. It was arousing the way the muscles flexed as he thrust inside her. The head of his cock rubbed some place deep within her that felt amazing on every inward stroke. Her pleasure built, spreading through her, making her warm, ready to explode. . . .

They came together, both crying out their mingled ecstasy. His cock jumped deep inside her as he came, her name spilling from his lips.

Collapsing to the bed, he pulled her damp body to his and kissed the nape of her neck. She curled into him, enjoying the sensation of his arms around her, holding her close. She smiled. "So, I guess I'm not a virgin anymore. You've defiled me."

He nipped her ear. "I plan to defile you several more times before morning, too." His hand spanned her abdomen, then slid between her thighs to work magick. "I remember how many times you came in the illusion. I wonder how many times I can make you come for real."

"I'm up for experimentation."

"I don't want to drain you too much, though. You're tired. Are you up for a night in my bed? Maybe we shouldn't do this."

She growled and turned on her side, pushing him onto his back. "You gave me only a taste of you and I want a full meal. I'm *fine.*"

He grinned, reached up, and nipped at her lips. "You are so fucking beautiful when you growl."

Twining a hand around his limp member, she stroked him until she felt it rouse again. She raised an eyebrow. "So are you." She glanced down. "I'd like to get my lips around this."

He groaned and his cock jumped in her hand, growing harder. "I have no objections to that."

"Good. I'm making up for lost time, you know."

"Lucky me." He slid his hand between her thighs and

found her clit. Closing her eyes, she swore that if she were a cat, she'd be purring. "Does that feel good?" Niall asked in a low, sultry voice.

She nodded, her teeth sinking into her lower lip. Her body was ripening again, making itself ready for him. Her sex, while a bit sore from the brand-new activity, was also growing damp once more. Just in time, his cock was full-on rock solid now.

Lowering her head, she kissed him the way he'd kissed her before—using not just her lips, but her teeth and tongue. His breath came faster and he trapped her head, pulling her down firmly against his mouth for more. When he tried to roll her over onto her back, she slipped away from him, moving to the center of the bed on all fours. She lowered her head to the mattress, tipping her hips up to him in invitation. She knew what he saw—plump, pink, damp, and begging for him.

Behind her, Niall stared at her for a long moment, and she hid a smile, secretly loving that she had a kind of power over him. He moved to her, slipping his fingers over her folds, teasing her, then, finally, pushing them inside of her. She squirmed, moaning, and realized he had just as much power over her.

Mounting her from behind, he pushed the head of his cock inside her. Her sex having been thoroughly plundered earlier, her muscles accepted him more easily this time. His shaft slid in inch by glorious inch, his hands resting on her hips. In this position the penetration was deeper. She felt somehow even fuller than she had before. He thrust slowly in and out of her, and she closed her eyes against the delicious sensation, enjoying every single movement he made.

"Do you want to know why this is my favorite position, Elizabeth?" he asked, his voice husky with lust.

She made an inarticulate sound in reply.

He brought his hand to her abdomen and slid it south, finding her sweet spot and taking advantage of its completely vulnerable position, rubbing it back and forth with the pads of his fingers.

She shuddered, already on the cusp of a climax.

"That's why," he purred.

Steadily, his thrusts became harder and faster, until the

sound of their bodies coming together and the mesh of their breathing were the only sounds in the room.

She climaxed hard once more, her knees going weak and the muscles of her sex pulsing and rippling around his pistoning length. He came not long after, yelling her name hoarsely, his cock once again jumping deep within her body.

He pulled her down next to him and wrapped around her protectively. As insane as it was, she felt safe in his arms. It was *right* to be there. Her body felt sore in places where she'd never felt sore before—but it was a small price to pay for perfection.

The blankets tangled around their legs and the fire snapping in the fireplace, she realized that for all her talk, the weakness from the iron sickness was still with her and she fell asleep.

NIALL watched Elizabeth in her bath with a heavy-lidded gaze and lust sitting hard on his body. She let him make love to her twice the night before, pushing herself far beyond what her body could handle.

Still, he wanted more of her.

Insatiable, like a starving lion taunted with only a bite of meat, he watched the soap bubbles slide over her delectable body. Her nipples peeked between them so enticingly. He wanted those nipples in his mouth, between his fingers. The water sluiced down her perfect, pale skin when she moved. He wanted to lick every inch of her.

He fisted his hands. He wanted her, but he couldn't push her. She was so eager for the experience of sex that if he encouraged it, she would sacrifice her health to get it. This morning he'd immediately seen the toll their nocturnal activities had taken on her.

So, for the time being, he needed to put a leash on his desires.

In any case, his lacerated back ached from his exertions. The nature fae had treated him with herbs and magick, speeding his healing, but it was still sore.

She'd still been sleeping when he'd awoken and showered. While the warm water had beat down on him he'd imagined the feel of her body beneath his, the hot, silken clasp of her sex around his cock, the feel of her aroused clit against his tongue.

Gods, he was destined to have a permanent hard-on around this woman.

When she'd awoken, he'd herded her into a bath and had intended to give her some privacy. Turned out he wasn't that strong. It was all he could do not to slide his hands into the water and make her come again. She was beautiful all the time, but when she came . . . *sweet Danu*, there was no better sight—or sound—than that.

The water drained and he held out a thick, fluffy towel for her. She wrapped herself in it and gave him a glance that was almost shy. "So, after I'm well and the game's back on, what then?"

He turned away from her, rubbing a hand over his chin. "Let's not think of that right now."

"We need to think about it, Niall. You and I are at an impasse, and this little affair can't last forever."

All of a sudden he wanted to put his fingers in his ears and chant *"La, la, la. I can't hear you!"* like a child. He grunted and went for the door. "I'll make coffee."

Leaving her to get dressed, he escaped that uncomfortable conversation and banged pots and pans around, making breakfast. Sunset was just peeking on the horizon, soon to turn the world red, orange, and purple. He wasn't hungry, but she might be. Anyway, cooking made him feel better, always had. Soon the smell of eggs rose in the kitchen.

Elizabeth wandered into the room barefoot, her damp hair hanging in tidy little skeins around her shoulders. She poured herself a cup of coffee and leaned back against the counter. "Gideon intends to get all the pieces of the *bosca fadbh*, Niall, *and* the Book of Bindings. He says he intends to use the magick to destroy the book and the pieces, themselves, but I don't believe him." She sipped her coffee. "There are probably lots of things the Phaendir could do to the fae with that magick, after all. Nasty things."

He glanced at her while he scooped the food onto a plate and set it on the table for her. "I wondered why you didn't just hand over the pieces to him. You guys want the same thing, after all."

She looked up at him, her expression wounded. "You really thought I would willingly work with the Phaendir?"

He shrugged a shoulder. "You worked with the Summer Queen."

She wilted. "You're right, I did." Shaking her head, she sat down at the table. "But just because I want my mother to live doesn't mean I want the fae hurt. If there's any magick in the back of that book for that particular purpose, you know the Phaendir will use it."

"No doubt." He sat down across from her and sipped his coffee. "I wondered who it was you were protecting by defying Gideon and now I know—it's the fae."

No one knew what the pieces of the *bosca fadbh*, once united into the key it was meant to be, would unlock in the back of the Book of Bindings. All they knew for certain was there was some power contained within that would take down the walls of Piefferburg. Honestly, they didn't even know *that* for certain; it was just a legend, passed down through the generations. It was a legend all the fae had their hopes and dreams pinned to . . . well, almost all of them.

"I know where the Summer Queen is hiding," she said quietly.

He snapped to attention. All their attempts to track Caoilainn's movements or find her location had failed. "Where?"

"You should know she's working with the Phaendir."

He grimaced. "I wish I could say I was surprised."

"Do you know the sea cliffs in the northern part of Piefferburg? The ones created by magick? She's got a whole residence built into them, complete with a throne room. Apparently she thought she'd need a secure location at some point and spent centuries creating one for herself."

He studied her. "Thank you for telling me."

She shrugged. "She's working with the Phaendir and needs to be stopped. Go get her."

"You did well by not giving Amberdoyal the pieces." He looked at her. "Honestly, Elizabeth, you're one of the strongest people I've ever met."

She swallowed a bite of eggs and grinned. "You sound surprised."

"I am. I mean, you spent your life pretty much alone, way out there with only a few nature fae and your family for company. Someone raised like that, you wouldn't expect—"

"What would you expect?" Her tone had gone a little dark and stormy. *Uh-oh.*

He shrugged. "You'd expect more naivety, less maturity, maybe . . . more innocence."

She looked down at her plate. "I was pretty innocent last night, if you'll recall."

He grinned. "Maybe at first, but you displayed an incredible eagerness to learn." He recalled how she'd crawled onto her hands and knees for him and his cock went rock hard.

Clearing her throat, she glanced out the window and colored a bit. Her pale skin let every little blush be known. It was adorable. "You make it easy." Her voice had gone a little husky, aroused.

He reacted to it immediately, his hands shaking like those of a man with an addiction and no way to get a fix. Making fists, he looked away from her. "Look, I need to get back to Piefferburg City and tell the queen that Gideon Amberdoyal is loose among with us with a cadre of Phaendir."

"Ah." She raised an eyebrow. "So, we've come up against our little problem already."

"What do you mean?"

She set her coffee cup on the table and leaned toward him. "Well, I'm not going with you to Piefferburg City, that's for sure. So it's come time for our interlude to be over and for me to be on my way."

He laughed. "And go where? You're not recovered enough to dissolve and I'm taking the SUV."

She shrugged a shoulder. "I'll figure it out."

"You'll stay with me." Immediately he understood the mistake he'd made by using that tone of voice and the order that came with it. It had come from a place of concern for her safety, but no one ordered Elizabeth around. He knew that better than anyone.

Elizabeth Saintjohn had a will stronger than anyone he'd ever met. She'd told him once that she would resist him to her dying breath—and she really had.

She crossed her arms across her chest. "Not happening. I won't go willingly, and I think you're past slapping charmed iron on me, right?"

"I never slapped charmed iron on you, if you'll recall."

"Right, you just trapped me in a big box made of it."

"And I'd do it again, too."

She pushed away from the table and stood. "Listen, I better be on my way now."

He affected his best wounded expression. "So soon? After last night? I think I feel used."

She grinned at him. "Sure you do." After putting her dishes in the sink, she crossed through the living room into the bedroom, probably to pack or find suitable clothes for the journey she intended to make.

Of course, he had no intention of letting her leave. Not while Gideon was still out there. Not in the snow. Not before she had the ability to dissolve.

He stood and followed her in, leaning against the doorframe. "Don't make me use my magick on you again."

She rounded on him with an expression of rage on her face. She pointed a finger at him, a sweater balled in her opposite hand. "Never do that to me again. *Niall, promise me!*"

"You would trust a promise from me?"

She considered that for a moment. "Yes, I would."

He nodded, smiling. He liked that. He liked that a lot. She trusted him. "I promise I will never use mind fuck on you again, no matter what."

"Thank you."

"Come to Piefferburg City with me."

"No way." She turned around and continued to select clothing, clearly going for the heaviest items that would protect her skin the most. She intended to hike. "What if the Shadow Queen finds out I'm there? I'll be dead within a week, tortured, then dead."

"I won't let anyone hurt you."

"You might not have a say." She pulled an extra sweater over her head, then laced up a pair of hiking boots. "We're going to have to send these people money for squatting in their house and using their things."

"I won't let you go out there with Gideon still on the loose."

"Yeah?" She stood and pushed past him, walking for the front door. "Try and stop me." She opened the door and turned, cold air and snow rushing around her and mussing her hair. Deep red tendrils whipped around her face. "This is where our paths diverge. I wish it could be different."

"Me, too."

She gave him a sad smile. "Good luck, Niall."

"Good luck, Elizabeth."

And then she was gone.

FIFTEEN

A goblin opened the doors of the Black Tower for Niall and he walked into chaos. Seelie nobles thronged the grand foyer, mixing with the monsters of the Black.

It stopped him dead.

Staring, he took in a sight that he'd never thought to see in all his days. The Seelie mixing with the Unseelie. He guessed he shouldn't be surprised. After all, the Summer Queen was gone, labeled a betrayer of her people, and the Seelie had always been sheep. Of course they were over here at the dark end of Piefferburg Square, seeking protection and direction. It was all the more convenient that the Shadow Queen had once walked among them. Her mother was Seelie. Niall guessed that was enough for most of them in these troubled times.

Kieran came up on his left side. "Amazing, isn't it? They started arriving in groups a couple days ago."

"Fuck." It was the only utterance Niall could make at the moment.

"The military is massing at the gates. Looks like they're coming in at any moment. Probably today. The Seelie are scared and looking to the only Tuatha Dé royal left in the city."

"Fuck."

"You mentioned that, yes." He rubbed his chin.

He glanced at him. "Why are you so calm?"

"Calm? I'm not calm. I have a wife to protect, remember? A wife that went against the Phaendir and got us the last piece of the *bosca fadbh*. A wife that all the bad guys want dead. I'm headed out of the city with Charlotte today, Niall. I won't risk her pretty neck. Not for anything or anyone. In a way, you're lucky that you have no one to worry about."

Yeah, except he did.

The realization jolted him. He really did care about Elizabeth. He cared about her a lot. Damn it all to the Lady, that complicated things so much.

He shook himself out of that thought pattern. The only direction it went was *down*. "Where's the queen? I have more excellent news."

"Do I detect sarcasm?"

"Just a hint."

"The last time I saw her she was meeting in the Ivory Room with the highest ranked Seelie nobles, attempting to soothe their scared rabbit hearts."

Niall snorted in derision. "They're like humans with a breath of magick."

"Some of them not even that much. I met a man this morning whose only talent is turning yellow roses red. So useful in a fight."

"And now we get to babysit them."

"They think it's our pleasure."

Niall grunted, turned, and shook his hand. "Good luck, Kieran."

"You, too. You're going to need it with the queen."

Yes, and Kieran only knew half of it.

He found her in the Ivory Room, just finishing up with a group of well-dressed Seelie nobles who all had sour looks on their faces. Niall stepped aside to let them pass and each of them favored him with either a look of scorn or fear. As the last man filed past, Niall made as if to bite him, snapping his teeth together. The Seelie shrieked and hurried away, leaving Niall grinning.

"I'm glad someone is having fun," said the queen wearily. She stood at the large window that overlooked Piefferburg Square.

"I wouldn't say I'm having fun, exactly, but you only have so many opportunities to frighten Seelie nobles in your life and you have to seize each one." He walked into the long, ivory-colored room that was dominated by a long table with chairs.

She smiled at him and rubbed her temple. "It appears I get a surplus of them."

She'd been raised Seelie. It was probably pretty strange for her to greet them as the dreaded, dark Shadow Queen now. She was even dressed the part today, in an elaborate black and silver silk and satin gown, split up the front to reveal thigh-high goth boots. Niall thought she looked great, then instantly imagined what Elizabeth would look like dressed in those clothes . . . minus everything but the boots.

Aislinn turned from the window and flopped into a chair. "I can't wait to get my hands on the Summer Queen." She fisted her hands in her lap, her voice holding a thread of steel.

"I think I can help you with that."

"What?" She looked up at him. "Do you know where she is?"

He stepped a little closer to her . . . but not too close. "Do you want the good news or the bad news first?"

She closed her eyes and let her head fall back to hit the headrest. "The good news. I could use some of that, even if it's followed by bad."

"I know where the queen is hiding." He drew a breath. "The bad news is she's teamed up with Gideon Amberdoyal, who is loose in Piefferburg with a cadre of Phaendir giving him magickal head juice that can blow things up. Gideon was allied with a free fae, too, but I think he's dead now."

Aislinn didn't say anything for several moments. Finally, she focused on his face. "And the asrai?"

Oh, yeah, he'd forgotten that part. "Still alive, still has the pieces." He launched into the whole story, leaving out the part when he'd made a pact to help her save her mother, rescued her from Gideon, and, oh, yeah, slept with her. Twice.

"Gideon killed Ragnar and the goblins?"

"Burned them to itty-bitty cinders."

She sighed, turning to gaze out the window again. "And the asrai is gone again and no one can find her."

"I can find her."

She turned toward him and her eyes narrowed. "I told you to back off. How do you know all this?"

He grinned the most charming grin he could conjure even though he knew it wouldn't help. "Yeah, well, I never backed off."

"Why?" The question cracked out of her like a whip, and the temperature in the room dropped several degrees.

Because I love Elizabeth Cely Saintjohn. The thought slammed into his head like a freight train. Luckily he kept it from leaping to his lips. "I couldn't. I didn't back off because I care about my people, and because when I take a job, I see it through to its bitter end." His breath showed white in the suddenly chilly air.

"You disobeyed me."

"My intentions were good."

She glowered darkly at him for a moment before the temperature in the room increased a little. She had more important things to worry about than his disobedience and they both knew it. "I'm not giving up, Niall. Those bastards might be between our walls and the soldiers might be ready to beat in the gates, but I will never stop trying to break the warding." The dark circles under her eyes seemed to go a shade darker. "Lead Kolbjorn Einar Soren Halvorson to her. He'll get her to tell him who she's protecting and where she's hiding them. He'll do whatever is necessary to get the pieces."

He wasn't surprised by the name she'd given him. Kolbjorn was the likely next choice after Ragnar. Not only could Kolbjorn shoot exploding magick like Gideon, he could pulverize bones with a thought. Imagining him with Elizabeth made his blood run cold.

Niall didn't have the heart to tell the queen her plan wouldn't work. There would be no way Elizabeth would give up any information under torture . . . even if he really planned to lead Kolbjorn to her, which he didn't.

"Of course," he replied. "Right away."

He was lying and it made a black fist of sick nothing form in his gut, but he knew a way to end this situation once and for all—without causing physical harm to Elizabeth. Instead he planned to go to Thea, tell her everything. He had a feeling she wouldn't like what her daughter was doing.

He also had a feeling that Thea would do the right thing.

By doing this he knew the woman he'd fallen in love with would hate him forever, but it would also save her life. Having Elizabeth alive, healthy, and hating him was better than having her tortured and killed.

Aislinn lifted her eyebrows. "Really? No fighting me? No discussion about morals or compassion that will break my heart?"

He gave his head a sharp shake. "We don't have time to lose."

"Thank you for understanding."

His heart felt sick lying to her, for betraying his people, but he loved Elizabeth and there was no way he would be a part of her destruction. He would do anything to protect her, sacrifice anything.

And in that one moment of clarity, he finally understood Elizabeth's motivation.

Behind them, one of the Shadow Guard lurched, panicked, into the room. "It's done. They're through! U.S. soldiers are streaming into Piefferburg right now."

Sixteen

NIALL raced out of Piefferburg City at top speed just as the soldiers were streaming in. They didn't come in with their guns blazing—that was a good sign. Instead they marched and drove in, took up spots around the city like silent sentinels, weapons at the ready.

They didn't allow any Phaendir into the city. That was smart. It kept the fae from attacking . . . at least, mostly. Still, skirmishes were breaking out here and there. Likely it would only get worse. The fae weren't going to suffer an occupation.

The clock was ticking away the seconds to war. The tension in the city, already palpable like heavy fog, had ratcheted up a degree. Niall knew he had to hurry.

He sped out of the city and down the narrow roads of the Boundary Lands, as fast as he could get to Thea's house. Leaving the engine running and the door open, he raced up the walkway to the front door and didn't even bother to knock. He burst into the kitchen . . .

The cottage was empty.

No fire burned in the hearth. Everything was cold and dark. He raced through the living room to find that the bedroom showed recent signs of packing.

Elizabeth had moved her. She hadn't trusted Niall enough not to come here and reveal all. Smart woman. Too smart for her own good.

Niall sank down on the end of the bed and cradled his head in his hands.

He was out of options.

ELIZABETH walked up the path to her mother's hidden house. She moved her to a small home deep in the woods, the home of one of the elderly people she'd cared for and who had died not long ago.

Before she made it to the door, her mother burst forth, arms waving. "They're through! Elizabeth, they're through!"

"Who's through?" Although she had a sinking feeling she knew.

Her mother hugged her hard, then led her into the house. The TV was blaring in the small living room, channel set to *Faemous*. "The U.S. government has broken through the gates. They control it now, won't let any fae out and won't let any Phaendir in. The military has marched into Piefferburg to take control of the towers. There's fighting breaking out everywhere."

Elizabeth sank down onto the couch, hand to her mouth. "Sweet Lady."

"I never thought I would see this day." Her mother sat down beside her. "I never really thought it would happen." Her expression and voice grew dark. "Curse whoever has those pieces."

Elizabeth jerked as if hit, but she wasn't really surprised to hear her mother voice such an opinion. "Do you really want the fae free? Mom, if the walls fall the sprae will leave Piefferburg and you'll—"

"Die." She looked down into her lap. "I'm aware."

They fell into watching coverage of the blooming occupation of Piefferburg City, filmed from high atop a building in the *ceantar dubh*, it appeared, by a trembling Brian Bentley, one of the *Faemous* commentators. The fae were using their magick left and right, as the shaking camera showed. Shots were being fired back. Charmed iron and non-charmed iron weapons—the only physical weaponry the fae possessed—

really weren't all that effective against bullets. Even so, the humans were definitely getting the worst end of the battle.

Because, after all, bullets weren't all that effective against magick either.

Elizabeth closed her eyes and almost passed out. She'd known this would happen, but now that it actually was happening she couldn't quite catch her breath.

"Elizabeth, what's going on with you?"

She opened her eyes to find her mother staring at her. "What do you mean?" She motioned at the TV. "History is being made even as we speak. It's making me woozy."

"Bullshit. It's not that." She waved her hand dismissively at Brian Bentley, who was white-knuckling his mic. She muted the sound. "There's something else going on, and we both know it. First that strange man comes to the house. I know you don't know any men, Elizabeth, not ones you haven't told me about. He was handsome and charming, sexier than any man I've ever met, actually—except your father. You would have told me about *that* man. Then there are your disappearances. Those have been very unlike you. Then you convinced me to move—"

"Mom."

Thea continued, ignoring the interruption. "Why did you want me to move? Why farther into the Boundary Lands? You said it was because of the possibility of this." She motioned at the muted TV set. "But, please, Elizabeth, tell me the truth. Don't make me break out the cookies—"

"Mom!"

Thea's mouth snapped shut.

Elizabeth drew a shaky breath, reached over, and flipped the TV off. Then she folded her hands in her lap and lifted her gaze to her mother's face. "There is no way in the Netherworld I'm letting you die."

Her mother looked confused for a moment, then realization dawned slowly over her face. She covered her mouth with one hand, her eyes widening. "No. It can't be you. Please tell me you didn't, Elizabeth. *Please.*"

She only held her gaze, saying with silence what she'd sworn never to tell her with words.

Her mother dropped her hands into her lap, then, after a

moment of stunned quiet, reached out and grabbed her by the wrist. "Give them back!"

"No."

"You can't do this, Elizabeth. You can't!"

"I would do anything to protect you. I will not watch you suffer. I will not watch you die."

Her mother rose, grabbed the remote, and flipped on the TV. She motioned at the screen. "There are people suffering and dying out there. I don't want that on my hands. Not on my account, Elizabeth. *Not on my account!*"

Elizabeth stared impassively at the screen, doing her best to school her face and her emotions into a place of numbness. The fae were kicking some ass. At least there was that. "I knew you'd say that, but I won't lose you like I lost Papa and William."

Thea stared at her in complete dismay, then sighed and sank back down on the couch beside her. "That day is still fresh in my memory, too." She hugged herself. "You, coming back to the house. I've never seen you look that way, so completely lost. Pale." She paused. "Like something inside you had died along with them."

"It did." Her voice broke.

Her mother hadn't been there to see them murdered. Only Elizabeth's ability to travel as water had let her arrive in time. At least she'd been able to say good-bye, although the cost had been high.

She'd found out about the Shadow Guard on their way to intercept her father and brother only at the very last moment. By the time she'd arrived, it had been too late. Her father and brother had been in the forest chopping wood.

The guardsmen had used their own axes on them toward the end.

Elizabeth squeezed her eyes shut, pushing away the raw memories that her psyche hadn't been able to explore at length since the day they'd been burned into her brain. They'd done it slow. The amount of blood had been enormous. . . .

Hiding behind a tree, she'd tried to look away, tried to leave, to save herself since there was no way she could've done anything to save them. But she hadn't been able to do even so much as glance away from the carnage. It had been as if she'd owed it to her brother and her father to experience every last ounce of pain right along with them. Illogically, she'd thought maybe she could somehow lessen their hurt. As if she could take on a percentage of their suffering by sharing it. They'd known she was there. She'd reached out to them from behind the tree.

And had stayed long after it had been over and the guardsmen had left.

She'd buried their bodies in that clearing, not wanting her mother to see the condition the Shadow Guard had left them in. Then she'd dissolved, made her way back home, and grieved for a million years.

Elizabeth wiped a tear off her cheek, not willing to look at her mother.

Her mother cupped her cheek. "Thank you for loving me so much you can't let me go, my darling."

She covered her mother's hand with her own. "You're all I have left."

Her mom shook her head. "You'll go out into the world. You'll meet someone, have a family of your own."

"Stop talking about yourself as if you're dead."

"Oh, Elizabeth." She paused, her voice breaking. Then she leapt to her feet, hands fisted. "I know you don't want to let me go, but you must, my dear. *You must.*"

She sat for several long moments, looking down at the floor between her feet. Finally she stood, walked to her mother, and enfolded her in her arms. "I can't," she whispered.

Then she turned and walked out of the house.

GIDEON stalked up the steep staircase of the narrow building in the commercial district of Piefferburg City, just on the edge of the *ceantar lair*, where his men were squatting. The stench of mold and mildew assaulted his nose, making him crankier than usual. Peeling paint from the walls of the constricted space brushed the sleeves of his coat, leaving bits of yellowed white stuck to him. The place had been built for some tiny breed of fae. It annoyed him.

Everything that had happened since he breached the walls of Piefferburg annoyed him.

He flung open the door to the apartment to find the brothers kneeling in various locations around the bare room, on their knees, hands folded in their laps, brown cowls drawn over their heads hiding their faces. Gideon knew their eyes were closed; they were buried deep inside themselves, all of them funneling their meager amount of magick into the hive portion of their collective consciousness that each of the Phaendir could access.

With so few Phaendir here to feed him, it was necessary they concentrate very hard at all times, rising only to eat, drink, and defecate. The nose-wrinkling unwashed smell of them rose up, mixing with the musty scent of dilapidated building. The low hum of their murmuring voices filled the air as they repeated the mantra they used to keep themselves deeply invested in their labor.

Pride swelled in his chest as he looked at them. These were Labrai's chosen. His men, sworn to serve *him*, who was Labrai's Right Hand. His race was truly superior to all others to have such dedicated brothers.

Stepping inside, careful not to disturb them, he made his way through the room to the balcony on the other side. Sliding open the cracked door, he stepped out onto the small deck and grasped the rusty railing. It was close to midnight in the city, but the place was alive with sight and sound. The U.S. military had broken through the gates. They'd come without the use of force, here to subdue and occupy only, but some of the fae had risen up anyway and small skirmishes had broken out here and there.

The red taillights of cars could be seen in a long snakelike tangle through the city as residents fled to the countryside, fearful of violence.

As if they had anywhere to go.

They were trapped in the prison that was Piefferburg. The military let them out of the city, knowing they couldn't run far. They could flee to the ocean or the northern Boundary Lands, but they weren't getting through the warding.

He wondered what the Phaendir were doing, those outside the walls, the ones not privy to his plans. Brother Cadwyr had likely taken over and was being every bit as recalcitrant with the government as Gideon had been.

Why didn't the military just open fire? What sad, strange notions were going through their heads? Compassion? Pity? Why have any for these animals?

He would never understand the human mind, no matter how long he lived among them.

Maybe it was flat out fear. Maybe their orders were to avoid engagement at all costs, hoping the Phaendir would put an end to this uprising so they didn't have to look like the bad guys. Gideon could only conjecture.

Gazing out at the city, he could practically feel the seething fear and anticipation. The whole place seemed balanced on the edge of a knife. They all wanted to know—*what would happen now.*

It was crazy to think they were all being foiled by an asrai, one, single, slender redhead with a will of steel.

He would spend the night here, and wait for his unlikely ally to make her appearance in the city two days from now. If he couldn't get the book and the *bosca fadbh* by sneaking around, he'd do this the straightforward way. And maybe he wouldn't even need the book and pieces to defeat the fae. The presence of the military changed the landscape quite a bit.

And he hated subterfuge, anyway.

As much as he loathed the Summer Queen he was curious to see what kind of magick she packed.

He had failed. In so many ways, he had brought this situation on himself. It was time to stop blaming others for his fuck ups and take responsibility. He owed it to his brothers, to his people. Most of all, he owed it to his god. It was time to change tactics.

Oh, yes, the day after tomorrow was going to be a very, very interesting day.

Somewhere below him a window broke. Somewhere down the street a car alarm blared, people yelled, and horns honked. He closed his eyes, taking in a deep breath. Ah, the sweet sounds of chaos.

He felt certain he could make more.

Turning, he reentered the apartment and sought his cat-o'-nine-tails, hidden in the closet of one of the bedrooms. Sinking down in the center of a group of rocking, murmuring Phaendir, he pulled off his coat and yanked his shirt over his head. Then, cock hard as a rock, the way it always was when he did his devotions, he picked up his cat and swung it in an arc over his head. The first lash didn't penetrate the scar tissue, and his erection flagged. Putting all his considerable strength into it, he swung it harder.

His back snapped, bowing in, and he gave a shivering gasp of mingled pain and pleasure as the ends of his beloved cat ripped through flesh and delicious pain flared through his body. The warm rush of blood trickled down his skin. Smiling, he brought the cat down again and then again. His hard prick throbbed.

Praise be to Labrai.

SEVENTEEN

THERE were soldiers instead of goblins on either side of the doors of the Black Tower.

Liam approached them cautiously, hoping like hell they weren't going to detain him. It seemed like everywhere in the city the human soldiers just stood. Guarding. Occupying.

Waiting.

Waiting for what Liam had no idea. The good news was that they didn't appear to have orders to shoot, or imprison. Just to stand with their rifles at the ready. They talked to no one and moved for no one.

He entered the building with no trouble and made his way through the throng in the main foyer. He needed to see the Shadow Queen. He needed that book, needed the pieces. The situation was getting desperate now, and he was ready to take some chances. He had no time to lose, no time left to play with that fucking asrai.

He'd shown mercy and he'd paid the price. As much as he hated to admit it, he should have listened to Gideon. He should have whipped the bitch bloody instead of feeling all warm and kindred.

She wanted to protect her mother, yeah, well, *he had people to protect, too.*

Now his plan was to get to the Shadow Queen and reveal all he could about Gideon's plan without telling her who he really was. He'd say he'd been working on his own to find Elizabeth and had run across Gideon somehow, learned of his plan. Hopefully that would earn him some brownie points. Maybe she would let him close to her.

Maybe he could get close enough to snag something of value.

It was a long shot, but it was the only shot he had right now.

Aideen. The vision of her lovely green eyes and her long blond hair never left his mind's eye. His heart ached constantly from his separation from her.

Pushing past a gaggle of Seelie, he made his way down the corridor to Aislinn's receiving chamber. Once there, he argued with the guards to be let into the room until Gabriel stuck his head out to quiet the commotion and invited him in.

"Queen Aislinn," Liam said in a loud, clear voice.

She turned from where she stood on the opposite side of the room, talking with another woman. Frowning, she tilted her head to side. "Liam, right?"

He nodded. "You need to know that the archdirector of the Phaendir is in Piefferburg City even as we speak and plans an assault on the Black Tower two days from now for the Book of Bindings."

Saying nothing, she stepped toward him. "How do you know that?"

The dark-haired woman who had been talking with Aislinn had been staring hard at him. For the first time since he'd walked into the room, he gave her his full attention.

Oh, shit.

Charlotte Bennett, the nearly full-blooded human woman he'd fought with in Ireland the year before, the only person in the whole of Piefferburg who could identify him, narrowed her eyes and opened her mouth. . . .

He turned and ran for the door.

"Stop him!" Charlotte yelled.

The guards on either side of the door grabbed him immediately. Liam fought them, kicking and pulling, but the Shadow

Guard were about as big as he was and he couldn't fight off two of them at once. Holding him by the upper arms, they turned him to face the queen.

Ah, Aideen, I'm sorry.

The time to lie was past. It would be better for him if he told the truth.

"Everything I just said is true. I know all of that because I'm a free fae and have been working with Gideon Amberdoyal," he said before Charlotte could speak.

"Guards! Restrain his magick," commanded the queen without missing a heartbeat. Two more Shadow Guards by the entrance immediately moved to him and cuffed his hands behind his back in charmed iron. His power disappeared right away, leaving him feeling weak.

Charlotte pointed at him. "He's one of the fae that met me and David Sullivan at the Stone of Destiny. He tried to kill me to prevent me taking the pieces. He *did* kill Calum, a good man whose soul is now waiting for the Wild Hunt beyond the walls of Piefferburg."

True, all. He'd stabbed Calum in the sternum. He remembered it vividly.

The Shadow Queen peered at him like someone trying to put together a jigsaw puzzle. "Why are you here?"

"To warn you. I had every intention of telling you who I was before I saw her." *Lie.* He jerked his chin at Charlotte. He didn't bother to dampen his accent now. "I came to warn you that Gideon is working with the Summer Queen and they plan to attack the Black Tower."

Queen Aislinn's skirts rustled as she moved toward him. "And we're supposed to believe you? You and your free fae have been working to keep the walls up. You haven't done anything that hasn't benefited yourself since we first learned of you. Why tell us about Gideon's plan? What do you get out of it?"

"Gideon wants the pieces and the Book of Bindings. Once he gets them he can't be trusted not to use whatever is in the back of the book for his own purposes."

"Yet you were working with him."

"I never intended to allow him unfettered access to the book. I was only working with him to prevent the walls from falling." He leveled his stare at the queen. "But now I've been separated from him, which means I can't stop him once he gets the book."

"You mean you can't *steal* the book from him when the time comes."

He grinned. "Something like that."

"Do you really think you could have stolen the book from him in the first place? He's the archdirector of the Phaendir, powered by their hive magick."

He shrugged. "I would have done my best. I want the walls up and the fae behind them, specifically the Wild Hunt. I don't want the fae dead."

Just then Gabriel Cionaodh Marcus Mac Braire, the Queen's husband and honorary Unseelie King, entered the room. Liam narrowed his eyes. Mounted on his black stallion, Abastor, Gabriel would lead the Wild Hunt to Aideen and his friends if the walls broke.

The Shadow Queen brought her husband up to speed. Then Gabriel turned toward him, a look of fury on his face. "He's wasting our time. Throw him in the dungeon."

The guards immediately began pushing him toward the door. "Wait!" he called over his shoulder. "I can help you!"

The Shadow Queen gazed at him coolly. "Why would you want to do that?"

"Like I said, I don't want the Phaendir to have the book any more than you do. I have spent time with Gideon. I know how his mind works and what his magick is capable of. I can let you know what to expect from him when he attacks."

"How can we trust you?"

"After all I've done, you can't trust me. Not really." He grinned. "But I'm all you've got."

She stared at him, jaw tight. Finally she said, "We still don't need your help, Liam. Gideon isn't getting the book. Not in this lifetime. Guards, take him away."

Aislinn turned away from him, and the picture of Aideen he held in his mind's eye transformed to blood.

ELIZABETH scrabbled in the dirt, her fingernails breaking on the hard packed earth. When she'd knelt to check on the pieces, she'd had the eerie sense the ground had been disturbed, but she'd brushed the suspicion aside and blamed paranoia.

Apparently there was something to her paranoia.

A cold endless pit in the center of her stomach, she rocked back on her heels, staring at the hole and the dirt coating her fingers. "Not here," she whispered, her heart pounding. "How can they not be here?"

Even though she knew someone had dug them up and they were gone, she dug a hole about three feet in diameter anyway, hoping, that by some miracle, she was wrong about their exact placement at the base of the tree.

She looked around to orient herself—boulder to the left of her, oak and an elm to her right, berry bush right there. . . .

No, she had the right location.

And, now, looking around her, she saw that this wasn't the only place in the clearing where the ground had been disturbed. Someone had come here and dug at the bases of all the trees and had moved rocks, too.

Pushing up to stand on shaky legs, she stared down at the hole and panted, her breath showing white in the cold air. The pieces were gone. Someone had taken them.

Gone.

Her mother.

Of all the people in the world, Thea was the only one who could have possibly guessed the location of the pieces. That's why Elizabeth had taken such a huge chance by coming here to relocate them. She'd intended to move them to a location that not even her mother could guess.

If her mother had taken them, she'd moved fast. If it *had* been Thea, she hadn't even thought about it—not for a second. The moment Elizabeth had left her house, she'd come here to dig them up.

Elizabeth closed her eyes, feeling the onset of a headache. This was the location of her father and brother's death. Only feet away lay the double grave where she'd buried them. It wouldn't have been difficult for her mother to surmise where Elizabeth might bury something of great value, something that symbolized the preservation of the last member of her family.

After all, she'd already buried two things of very great value at this location.

She dissolved immediately, traveling as her water self with all great haste to her mother's house. Re-forming on the snow, shivering, she looked down at her hands and saw the shift had scoured them clean.

Lurching to her feet, she ran into the cottage where her mother had been staying. The fire was long cold, and there was no sign of her. She ran into the bedroom and saw that Thea's clothes were scattered over the room. She'd packed. Elizabeth's heart stuttered.

Piefferburg City. The Black Tower.

Of course that's where she'd gone.

EIGHTEEN

NIALL rounded the corner and headed for the front doors of the Black Tower. Entering the thronged foyer, he glowered at the noisy crowd. This area was Seelie Grand Central these days, a sight he'd never thought to see in all his years. Fucking *Seelie* in the Black Tower. Pretty soon they'd be hosting balls in here.

Of course, he was pretty cranky these days. Going to find Thea and discovering that Elizabeth had moved her did not make him happy. After he'd discovered that, he'd come back to the Black Tower, gathered up Kolbjorn, and had ferried the colorless freak all over the Boundary Lands "in pursuit" of Elizabeth.

Of course, somehow she always seemed to get away. Imagine that. Darn their bad luck anyway.

Now back at the Black Tower, he was busy weighing options and found them light as a feather.

Pushing past a group of well-heeled, designer-clad Rose denizens, he caught sight of an older woman, dressed in clothes that seemed out of place in the crowd, clothes that almost seemed homemade. Niall did a double take, then headed straight for the woman, who was milling around looking lost.

Perhaps his options had just gained some weight.

"Thea? What are you doing here?" His heart rate ratcheted upward. Was something wrong with Elizabeth?

Thea turned to him and grasped his forearms. "Niall! Thank the Lady, a face I know."

"Is Elizabeth all right?"

Her grip on his arms tightened. "She's fine, but, oh, Niall, she did an awful thing."

"I know what she did, Thea."

She squeezed her eyes shut for a moment. "She did it because she loves me and because she can't bear to lose any more of her family, but it was wrong." She shook her head. "I can't be the cause of this. I just can't."

Niall took her forearm in his and forced her to look at him, to focus. The babbling had to be due to nervousness; she'd been nothing but calm and confident when he'd visited her in the Boundary Lands. "Why have you come here?"

She hesitated a moment, then glanced around to make sure no one was listening. "I have them with me right now. I guessed where she hid them and I dug them up."

His blood went cold. He knew exactly what "they" were. A million questions crowded his brain, but he didn't have to time to ask any of them. Not now. Not here. "She doesn't know you have them or that you've brought them here?"

She shook her head and winced as if pained. He relaxed his grip on her arm, realizing it had tightened.

He swallowed hard, looking into the woman's eyes. Thea was younger than himself, had lived her whole life within the walls of Piefferburg. She was an aberration of fae nature, in fact—not unlike him, his brother, and the Piefferburg witch. Thea would never have been born if the walls had not been present and the sprae had not decided to pass through and congregate between them. "If you turn these over, the walls will probably come down and you will die." He paused. "You totally understand that, right?"

Her nostrils flared and she glanced away. "Yes." She drew a breath and nodded. "I know."

"You are very brave. I knew you would be, Thea. I had a feeling you'd do the right thing no matter the cost."

Thea glanced at him and he saw a sheen of tears in her eyes. "Not brave. I'm scared as hell."

"I went to your house yesterday, intending to tell you about the pieces. I figured you'd want to help me get them from Elizabeth."

"I do want to help you." Her voice sounded stronger now.

He considered her for a long moment. Elizabeth would never forgive him for this, but there was nothing else he could do. "All right, come with me. I can get you safely to the queen."

"Thank you. I had no idea what to do or where to go once I got here. I didn't know who I could trust. I just wandered around, looking for you."

He took her hand, and they threaded through the crowded foyer to the elevator. She gawped as he might expect a nature fae who didn't come into the city much. There was a lot to see in the Black Tower right now, even for those of them who'd grown up here and were used to the dark circus.

He led her up to the highest floor and to the carved black lacquer double doors of Aislinn's receiving chamber.

"The queen isn't seeing anyone right now," said one of the silver-and-black-bedecked Shadow Guard on either side of the door.

"Trust me," Niall answered. "She'll want to see us for this."

The guard hesitated, but Niall was one of the queen's closest advisors and pulled a weight that others did not. He stepped to the side.

Niall opened the door and found Aislinn inside, sitting cuddled next to her husband on the couch. She looked up, saw that it was Niall, and snuggled back down, her head on his shoulder.

"She's resting, Niall," said Gabriel, a protective hand on the silk gown covering his wife's thigh. "What do you need?"

Niall turned and motioned for Thea to enter.

Once Aislinn saw the unknown fae, she straightened, stood, and smiled. "Hello." Ever the good and gracious queen, was Aislinn.

Thea froze in the entryway, then dipped low in an old-fashioned curtsy. "My queen."

"Please, don't do that," answered Aislinn. "Not when the city is in such chaos."

Aislinn had never become used to the bowing and scraping that some of the fae did in her presence.

Niall led Thea forward, into the sitting area. "Aislinn, Gabriel, please meet Thea Jocelyn Saintjohn."

That was all he needed to say. They were perfectly aware that Thea was Elizabeth's mother. Both Aislinn and Gabriel went very still.

"It's a pleasure to meet you," said Thea, nodding at both of them.

Niall met Aislinn's eyes. "Thea has a couple things you've been looking for."

All the blood drained from Aislinn's face.

"First," said Thea, "I need your promise that my daughter will not be punished for what she did."

Aislinn's face hardened. "Thea, your daughter—"

"Was protecting her mother," Niall cut in. "Put yourself in her place, Aislinn, and pretend it was your father who was going to die. Imagine he was the only person you had left in this world because you'd had to watch the rest of your family be brutally slain, and then imagine what you'd do to protect him."

Aislinn's biological father had been the former Shadow King and there had been zero love between them—after all, the man had tried to eviscerate her soul—but Aislinn had adored the man who'd raised her, the man she'd called father from birth.

Staring hard at him over Thea's head, Aislinn pressed her lips together. "Fine. No harm will come to Elizabeth Cely Saintjohn. I'll issue her a pardon and an edict that none should harm her."

"Thank you." Thea dropped her hands into the pockets of her skirt and came out with a piece of the *bosca fadbh* in either hand.

Aislinn put her hand to her mouth. "Sweet Lady."

All of them stared at the pieces for a long moment. They appeared so unassuming. Hunks of metal, engraved with strange symbols and cut jaggedly on two sides, like puzzle pieces. They looked fit for melting down, or something one might find at a flea market and wonder what they'd once been used for.

The queen reached out and took them into her hands reverently. "We have them all."

"And the book," said Gabriel.

"I can't believe it," Aislinn breathed, looking down at them. Tears streamed down her cheeks.

"Where did you find them?" asked Gabriel.

"My daughter hid them very well. You never would have found them, but I know my girl. It wasn't hard for me to locate the hiding place she'd chosen. Once she'd admitted what she'd done, I just couldn't let her do it. I knew she'd never turn them over herself, she's far too driven and stubborn for that."

Gabriel stepped forward and drew the woman into his arms. "Thank you for bringing them to us."

"You're not aware of what she's sacrificing," said Niall.

Gabriel released Thea and she backed away, looking down at the floor.

Niall looked between Gabriel and Aislinn. "Thea is dependent on the sprae for her survival. Once the walls fall and the sprae disperse, following the other fae, she'll die."

The room went silent.

"There's nothing that can be done?" asked Gabriel.

Niall shook his head. "We've looked into ways to keep the sprae near her. I've been to the Piefferburg witch, but—"

"But the sprae are free and wild magickal beings and there's no way to do it," finished Aislinn.

"Right."

"Then we owe you a huge debt of gratitude," said Gabriel to Thea.

She raised her tired gaze to his. "It was the right thing to do. Just make sure my daughter isn't punished for what she did."

Gabriel grasped her hands. "You have our word."

ELIZABETH stood on the sidewalk outside the Black Tower, her hair loose around her shoulders and slowly drifting snowflakes catching in the strands and melting on her sweater and jeans.

She'd never put protocols in place for traveling as water to Piefferburg City, a lapse in judgment she sorely regretted now. With a lack of stashed clothes and money near the city, she'd been forced to travel here by vehicle. It had wasted time. Although, honestly, traveling as her water self would have left her with significant problems that would have cost her time, too, like locating transportation in from the rim of the city to the center, not to mention finding clothes.

It didn't matter. In her gut, she knew she was probably too late.

Steeling herself for whatever she might find inside the Black Tower, a place she'd only seen from a distance the rare occasions she'd ventured into the city, she went toward the double doors, eying the armed human soldiers that had taken the place of the goblins who traditionally guarded the Unseelie Court.

She shivered as she entered the foyer, shaking off the snow on her clothes. Her eyes widened. The place was a raucous mess of fae, both Unseelie and Seelie. The Seelie were even easier to spot than the sometimes monstrous-looking Unseelie, in their designer clothes and slightly panicked countenances.

She didn't know where to find the Shadow Queen, but she could guess. Her receiving room was probably on the highest floor, watched by the Shadow Guard. Staking out a place close to that door was her best chance of intercepting her mother. She would need to be careful. As soon as she showed her face, she'd probably be recognized and thrown in the dungeon. She didn't care. She had to find her mother before Thea handed over the pieces—if it wasn't already too late.

Heading for the bank of elevators she could see off to her left, she kept her head down, examining the polished black marble floor. Magick had raised the walls of this place, making the quartz from which it was constructed malleable enough for the enormous tower to be erected not long after Piefferburg had been created. Niall had watched this place be built and had lived here ever since.

She wondered where he was now and fought a pang of longing for him. Ever since she'd left him at the cabin, she missed the smell of him, the sound of his voice, and the feel of his body on hers. Now that she was here, ready to out herself to prevent her mother from handing over the pieces, she knew she'd probably never get to be close to him again.

It was a greater loss than she would have guessed.

Sometime between the beginning and the end of their short, doomed relationship, she'd developed feelings for him.

She guessed those feelings might even be called love.

Love really did make you crazy and sad, like all the songs sang. She wanted to be with Niall all the time, wanted to hear the sound of his voice, the press of his lips on her skin. She wanted the scent of him rubbed against her body, marking her as his. She hated leaving him because he was like a drug to her—all she wanted was another moment with him.

Even now. Even in the middle of this chaos—she missed him.

Knowing she could never have him made her chest ache, made her feel nauseous, and made her grieve. Yes, the songs were right, love was hell.

She pressed the up button on the elevator and stood back with a group of people, waiting for the doors to open. None of the fae around her paid any attention to her, too wrapped up in their personal dramas to realize they were standing next to Public Enemy Number One. They chattered about the soldiers and what was going to happen next and the war that might start and where was the Summer Queen?

The doors of the elevator car opened and her eyes widened. Within stood Niall, leaning against one of the elevator walls.

NINETEEN

HE caught sight of her, eyes narrowing, and that customary smirk spread across his handsome face.

Her stomach did a slow flip and happiness blossomed in her heart like a flower. "Niall!" she blurted.

"Fancy meeting you here."

The chattering fae moved into the car, jostling her. The elevator dinged, ready to close its doors, but she just stood there, torn between wanting to leap into his arms and wanting to dissolve to escape. Niall still stood in the car, only an arm's length away.

What would he do with her now that she was here in the Black Tower? Would he honor his queen and turn her in, or honor his conscience—*heart?*—and let her go free.

Right before the doors closed, Niall reached out, grabbed her by the hand, and pulled her into the car . . . straight into his arms.

He pressed her up against his chest and tilted her head, his mouth coming down for a kiss. His lips slid across hers, making her knees feel weak. He nipped at her lower lip and she opened her mouth, letting him slid his tongue within to stroke slowly and deliberately up against her tongue. Her hands found his arms and gripped, trying to hold on against the erotic on-slaught that were constantly his kisses.

He released her when the elevator dinged and the doors opened on another floor. She staggered back a step and looked up, feeling a little dazed. It was then she realized everyone in the car had gone silent. The other passengers all grinned at them as they filed out, leaving her and Niall alone. As soon as the doors closed, Niall hit the button that would take them to the fiftieth floor, the top of the tower.

She glanced from the button to him, panic making her stomach tight. After everything, did he intend to turn her over to the Shadow Queen? "Where are we going?"

Niall stared at her a moment, his expression going soft. "You're too late, Elizabeth."

She crumpled to the floor of the elevator, grief making every bone in her body feel soft. *Danu*, she'd *known* it.

He knelt beside her. "The Shadow Queen has all the pieces and the book."

"Where is my mother?" The words came out sounding weak and thready. She felt sick.

"Safe. Sleeping. She was up all night. We put her in one of the guest rooms here in the tower."

Sleeping. Okay, it was better that way. She wasn't ready to face her right now anyway. Elizabeth drew a shaking breath. "Why are we going up instead of down? Shouldn't you be taking me to the dungeon?"

He cupped her chin and forced her to look at him. "Your mother wouldn't give up the pieces until the queen promised that you wouldn't be punished for what you did. You're safe."

Of course she did. Protecting her little girl to the bitter end. She shook her head. "Doesn't matter. My mother is going to die."

"I'm sorry it has to be this way, Elizabeth. It was Thea's choice, in the end, to bring the pieces here. Just remember that."

Fury rose up in her, made her stomach feel hot, but grief tamped it all back down again hard and fast. Grief was stronger than rage, maybe. "Of course she turned the pieces over. She's selfless that way."

The elevator reached the fiftieth floor and dinged open. Niall helped her stand. She knew she should have been protesting this.

He was taking her to see the queen. There was no other reason they'd be on this floor. Yet the grief stole not only her rage, but her will, too. So she allowed him to lead her down the corridor to the ornate double doors of the queen's receiving chamber.

The Shadow Guard on either side of the entrance widened their eyes as they recognized her and one snarled as she passed, but they didn't leap to take her into custody, so Niall had probably been telling the truth.

They entered the room. A blond woman in a huge Victorian-style, silver and gold gown stood at a table with a handsome dark-haired man whom Elizabeth recognized as Gabriel Ciona-odh Marcus Mac Braire, the Shadow King. They looked up as she entered and their faces went stony as recognition bloomed.

"Please meet Elizabeth Cely Saintjohn, asrai, and former keeper of two pieces of the *bosca fadbh*," Niall announced.

The Shadow Queen moved toward her, her expression stormy. "Please come here, Elizabeth."

Elizabeth moved toward her, uncaring of what they thought of her or what they intended to do with her. Her mother was going to die.

"You are very good at keeping things hidden." The queen's voice had a steely quality. Had the temperature dropped in the room suddenly? It felt a little chilly.

"I had a reason," she answered, her voice breaking.

"I know you did." Aislinn's voice softened. "Sometimes when you're trying to protect those you love, others get hurt in the process. Sometimes there are hard choices to make." Aislinn's gaze met Niall's before returning to Elizabeth's. "I'm not saying I condone what you did, but I do understand why you did it."

"I know where the Summer Queen is. I can lead you right to her."

Aislinn studied her for a moment. "I thought you were allied with her."

"I only agreed to hide the pieces to save my mother. The Summer Queen is a dangerous, selfish woman who cares about no one but herself. I would really enjoy seeing you take her down."

Gabriel stepped forward. "Actually, we've known where she is hiding for some time. Our concern was the pieces. Now we have reason to believe she's moved from her caves to the city, along with Gideon Amberdoyal. They plan to attack the Black Tower." He paused. "Tomorrow."

That reached through the numb cloak that had settled itself around her shoulders. She knew how powerful the Summer Queen was, and allied with the archdirector of the Phaendir . . . She glanced at the pieces of the *bosca fadbh* lying on the table. "And you're not worried . . . ?"

Aislinn smiled, and all the warmth fled, not only from her expression and voice, but literally from the room for a moment. It made Elizabeth gasp. "The Black Tower is able to handle whatever that bitch wants to throw at us."

"You're free to stay in the Black Tower, Elizabeth," said Gabriel. "The queen has issued an edict that you're exempt from punishment. Anyone who tries to harm you will suffer the wrath of the Shadow Queen." He turned, and he and the queen went back to the table. It seemed like a dismissal to her.

Niall drew her away. "Come to my apartment. You look exhausted."

She nodded, glancing back at the king and queen. They were about to ensure the death of her mother, and there wasn't anything she could do about it.

NIALL'S apartment was decorated in a comfortable fashion, leather couches strewn with pillows and blankets, hardwood floors covered with thick area rugs. It was clear he didn't care much about decorating, but the space was definitely made to be a place for him to take his ease and relax.

He ushered her into the living room, sat her on the couch, and tucked a blanket around her. "You're freezing," he chided her when she tried to push it away.

She noticed for the first time that he was right, she was freezing.

"It's shock. You looked like I detonated a bomb on you in the elevator," he said, sitting down beside her.

"I never expected this to happen." Her voice sounded wooden. "I never expected my mom to go dig the pieces up and bring them straight to the queen." She paused, grief welling. "She just signed her own death certificate."

"I wish I could make all of this go differently."

She said nothing for a long time, curling her icy hands into the soft blanket. "Speaking of bombs, shouldn't the Black Tower be evacuated? We've seen firsthand what Amberdoyal's magick can do and now that he's teamed up with the Summer Queen . . ."

"The warning was given right after you arrived. The queen ordered that all children are to leave the tower, along with everyone who wants to leave voluntarily. It's sad because traditionally the Black Tower has been the safest place to be in the city. People have been coming here for sanctuary, even knowing that the Summer Queen and Gideon are teamed up in their bloody, unholy alliance."

"Yes, but that magick." She shuddered. "Like lightning bolts from Danu, herself."

"Not Danu, Labrai."

She nodded.

"But don't forget, Aislinn is a powerful queen. She looks all soft and friendly and, honestly, she *is* soft and friendly most of the time. But when she wants to kick ass, watch out. She can command the goblins and, between herself and Gabriel, they have the power of the sluagh. Caoilainn and Gideon had better be planning their attack very carefully."

"The Summer Queen thinks Aislinn is too young and fluffy to be a threat."

"The Summer Queen is an idiot."

Her breath shuddered out of her, and she allowed her head to drift down and rest on Niall's shoulder. *Surrender.* She closed her eyes. She'd lost. "It's over."

"No, Elizabeth, this is only the beginning."

AISLINN and Gabriel were still staring down at the pieces on the table, frowning, as Niall reentered the room.

"Where's the woman?" asked Gabriel as he approached the table.

"Sleeping in my apartment."

"You have a soft spot for her, don't you?" he asked, studying his face.

Niall shrugged. It was more than just a soft spot, but he wasn't about to admit that out loud. Not now, not to them.

Aislinn pushed the pieces closer together, lining up the grooves on each side like a puzzle. When she had the pieces in their respective spots and all she had to do was push them together to fuse them, she drew a breath and stepped back.

"It feels like there should be a ceremony or something," said Gabriel, taking his wife's hand.

She nodded. "Or at least that more of us should be here—Aeric, Emmaline, Charlotte, Kieran, Ronan, Bella . . . everyone."

Niall stared hard at the pieces. "It's better not to create a fuss. Right now we're the only ones who know that we have all the pieces. That's a good thing. We don't need any more excitement."

Aislinn nodded, saying nothing for a long time. Finally, she drew a breath. "There are three of us, so let's do it together. All of us take a piece and push them to the center."

They positioned themselves around the table and each one of them touched one of the pieces.

Gabriel looked up at both of them. "Ready?"

"No," said Aislinn.

Niall stared hard at his piece. "Let's do it anyway."

The three of them pushed the pieces together. A bright flare of light pushed them back as the pieces seared into one smooth metal object with jagged sides—the *bosca fadbh*.

"There it is." Aislinn pressed a hand to her mouth.

Niall squinted down at it. "Doesn't look like much."

She lowered her hand. "It's just a means to an end. A key."

"Speaking of the end." Gabriel walked to a nearby wall and pulled off a painting that had a safe hidden behind it. Producing a key, he unlocked the safe and took out a book wrapped in red velvet. So that was where they'd been keeping the Book of Bindings; Niall had always wondered.

He unwrapped the book, tossed the velvet to the couch, and laid it on the table. It was an unassuming tome, clearly old, with a worn, red leather cover. At the back would be the portion of the book that was locked, with a grooved indention where the *bosca fadbh* fit. The rest of the book was filled with fragile vellum pages with spells handwritten in Old Maejian.

"If we can open it up and work the spell inside right now, before the Summer Queen and Gideon attack, we can save some lives."

Aislinn nodded and opened the book, her long fingers flipping through page after weathered page of various spells. This was the book where Aislinn had first come across the magick that had pointed out her necromancy to her. She reached the end of the book, and that's where Niall saw the indention where the key was supposed to go. It made his stomach clench.

The legend was that the back of the Book of Bindings contained magick to break the warding, but no one really knew for certain. They might unlock the back of the book and find something else in there, recipes, or a spell to shear sheep, or some other useless thing.

Even though that was his worst fear, Niall didn't really believe that would happen. After the war between the Phaendir and the fae, the ancients had gone to a lot of work to hide the *bosca fadbh*. There had to be some kind of powerful magick contained in there. Whether or not it was powerful magick that would knock down the walls of Piefferburg remained to be seen. If not, many, many expectations and hopes would be dashed.

"Niall, you do it," Aislinn said.

He jerked in surprise. "Me? Why me? Are you afraid the book is booby-trapped or something?"

She rolled her eyes. "Don't be ridiculous. I was simply trying to bestow an honor on you."

He thought of all the ways he'd misled Aislinn in recent days in order to protect Elizabeth. He didn't deserve any honors. "I think the Shadow Queen should do it."

"I agree," replied Gabriel.

"All right." Aislinn stepped forward and picked up the *bosca fadbh*. Holding the object over the book, she said, "Freedom for the fae."

"Freedom for the fae," chorused Gabriel and Niall.

"May this key unlock a new era of peace and happiness." She slipped the key into the grooved section of the book, and then backed away, shielding her eyes.

Nothing happened.

Aislinn straightened, frowning. All of them took a step

toward the book. The key lay harmlessly in the grooves, but the book was still locked.

The bottom dropped out of Niall's stomach.

Oh, *Sweet Lady* . . . the *bosca fadbh* didn't work.

TWENTY

"WAIT," said Aislinn. "There's writing, but it's not in Old Maejian."

Niall took a step forward, stomach roiling, fists clenched. Writing was slowly appearing on the blank page above the *bosca fadbh*. It was written in a glowing, flowing script, but in a language he didn't recognize. It looked a little like some mutated form of Old Maejian, perhaps the language they knew as Old Maejian had originated from. Ancient Maejian?

"Can you read that, Aislinn?" Gabriel asked.

"Maybe, give me a minute."

"How could you possibly read that?" Niall asked, studying the odd symbols.

She shrugged, leaning over the book. "I don't really know. It first happened when I came across a necromancy spell in this book. It was in Old Maejian, back when I didn't speak it. I didn't understand what it was I was reading, I just read it anyway."

"That makes no sense at all."

"I think it must have something to do with my magick."

"Maybe it has more to do with your bloodline."

She looked up at him. "Maybe." Her blood was Unseelie

royalty. It made sense she'd have the power to read an ancient fae tongue.

Leaning over the book again, she squinted, her mouth working and no sound coming out. Finally, she spoke. "It says we can't open the book until the sun is at its highest point in the sky and no shadows mar the land."

"Noon." Gabriel rubbed his chin. "Great. It's just after one in the morning right now. We'll have to wait almost twelve hours to open the book. So much for doing this before the Summer Queen and Gideon launch their attack. So much for saving lives." His voice came out as bitter and as angry as Niall had ever heard him.

Niall studied the strange text, swallowing his frustration. "How do we know it means noon in this time zone? It could mean noon anywhere in the world."

Aislinn chewed her lower lip, deep in thought. "I strongly suspect it means noon wherever the book is. Of course, we can't know for certain."

"So, we hold our breath until noon tomorrow, then."

Aislinn gazed out into the black of the night through the picture window opposite them. "Yes, we wait. We hope."

"Not like we haven't been doing that for years," said Gabriel. "We can survive one more day, right?"

Niall met Aislinn's eyes and knew they were thinking the same thing, and so was Gabriel, judging from the grim tone of his voice.

Twelve more hours just might kill them all.

Aislinn gave him a slow smile. "We wait, we hope . . . we prepare for battle."

Sounded good to Niall. Kicking a little butt was just what they needed. Although, thinking of the woman back in his apartment, he knew what he needed even more.

ELIZABETH roused when Niall slid into bed beside her. His arms came around her, and she stiffened when she realized he was completely—lusciously—bare.

She turned over. "Hello."

He grinned. "Hello."

"I assume the walls haven't fallen yet?"

His expression grew serious. "I would warn you before that happened."

Grief closed her throat for a moment. Right, so she could be with her mother. "So what are you doing here? Shouldn't you be off with the queen, redirecting the future of the fae?"

"Redirection has been postponed, and there's nowhere I'd rather be than here."

She moved her hip, feeling the press of his cock. "Yes." She smirked. "So I see."

He reached up and smoothed her hair behind her ear. "Your mother is still asleep, and there's nothing to do with the book until tomorrow at noon. We have until morning, just you and me . . . this bed. I want to be with you, Elizabeth. It's all I can think about."

He ruled her thoughts as well, and when he was this close to her, his low voice murmuring in her ear, the press of his long, strong form against hers, he ruled her body, too.

She smiled and leaned forward, gently pressing her lips to his. "Sounds nice. Sounds distracting."

"Oh," he murmured against her lips. "I distract really well. Here, let me show you."

He rolled her beneath him, covering her body with his. His knee slipped between her thighs, and she was suddenly really, really sorry that she'd fallen asleep in her clothes. Yes, Niall could be exceedingly distracting.

Hooking her leg over his hip, she pressed against him, forcing his rigid cock against her. He shuddered in anticipation and pleasure and she smiled, loving the power she had over him.

"There's only one problem," he whispered against her mouth.

"What's that?"

"You have way too many clothes on."

Her smile widened. "Well, let's take care of that, then, shall we?"

Together they slipped her sweater over her head and he snaked his hands behind her back to undo her bra, leaving her breasts warm and bare against his chest. Then he unbuttoned her jeans, unzipped the zipper, and she wiggled them past her hips. Soon their bodies slid together, skin-on-skin, smooth and sweet.

Outside the wind picked up, blowing snow against the windows, but between the sheets with Niall against her, she had never felt so warm and protected. He pulled her beneath his body, his mouth coming down on hers. She kissed him back ferociously, as though she could consume him—make him a part of her body and soul forever. His tongue slipped inside her mouth and brushed against her tongue, sending delicious shivers through her body.

He worked his way downward, pulling first one rosy, erect nipple into his mouth and laving it until she moaned, then doing the same to the other.

Pressing up against him, she flipped the blankets away and pushed him over onto his back, then straddled his hips, bending over to kiss him. He tried to roll her over, gain control again—he was that kind of a lover—but she pressed the issue and he relented.

Kissing her way down his throat, she ran the tip of her tongue over the powerful hills and valleys of his muscular chest, inhaling the scent of his skin and savoring the taste of him. When her tongue made it into the lightly tangled trail of coarse hair that led down to his cock, his fingers found her hair and fisted.

Ah, yes, now he understood what she meant to do.

Her tongue touched the head of his rock-hard cock and he jerked, his grip tightening a small degree in her hair. She closed her mouth around his shaft and sucked him within. He let out a low growl of arousal that made the hair on the nape of her neck stand on end. Settling in, she took her time with him, sliding her tongue up and down his length, finding the places that seemed the most sensitive, learning his body.

She had every intention of driving him as insane as she possibly could and, judging from the groans and jerks of his body, she was doing a pretty good job. She loved that she could render this man, so powerful and strong, helplessly aroused only by the power of her mouth.

A millisecond later, without warning, he had her on her back. She let out a surprised yelp and found herself pinned beneath him. She squirmed, surprised by the sudden turn of events, and he pressed her down, parting her thighs and burying his mouth between her legs.

Her bones seemed to melt as his mouth closed over her clit, licking and sucking it until pleasure permeated her body and made her moan his name. Her fingers found the blankets on either side of her and fisted as he slid two fingers inside her and stroked them in and out, all the while toying with her clit with his tongue.

And as fast as that, Niall was back in control. She had to admit, she really didn't mind.

One of his big hands held her down as he forced her, hard and fast, toward a climax. Her mind entered that hazy place of total abandon, the needs of her body completely taking over. His tongue slid solidly against her clit over and over, her pleasure building, cresting, until she could brook no more of it. It spilled over the threshold and washed through her in wave after wave of ecstasy, stealing her breath and her ability to think. Her orgasm ruled her for several long moments and he rode her through it, lengthening it and making it more powerful.

When it was over, he flipped her to her stomach and pulled her hips up, positioning his cock at her entrance. One long, slow thrust had him root-deep inside her. Her back arched and she let out a guttural cry of pleasure.

Niall was not feeling particularly gentle and she loved every second of it. He grabbed her hips and began to stroke deeply inside her. Every inward thrust brushed the head of his cock against that spot deep within where she was extra sensitive. Her fingers sought purchase in the blankets as he took her harder and faster. He dipped his hand down to splay on her stomach, then moved between her thighs to stroke her clit.

The combination of the pressure of his fingers on her and the steady, unrelenting thrust of his cock deep within her body forced her into another climax. Her head whipped back as it hit her and she cried out, her sex pulsing and spasming in pleasure around the pistoning length of his shaft.

Her orgasm seemed to trigger his and his cock jumped deep inside her while her name fell from his lips on a deep groan.

They collapsed in a satisfied tangle on the bed. He pulled her toward him and wrapped his body tightly around hers, laying tiny kisses to her temple. "Forgive me. I was rough. I really wanted you."

She let out a short laugh. "Sorry? Please. That was incredible."

They lay together in the darkness, the sheets and blankets tangled around their legs, and watched the snow come down. His hands traveled restlessly over her body, as if he could draw needed sustenance from the surface of her skin. "I'm really happy that you're here with me tonight," he whispered.

She sighed as he slipped his wandering, magical hand between her thighs and gently stroked. "I've been thinking so much about you since the cabin."

She almost told him about how she wanted only to be with him, how much she'd missed the sound of his voice and his touch—his presence—but it was too close to admitting how deep her feelings went. She wasn't ready for that yet. What if he didn't feel the same way?

Anyway, her emotions for him were fanciful at best. It's not as if there was a happily-ever-after waiting for them.

"Have you?"

She nodded. "And now we don't have the pieces lodged between us."

He kissed her forehead and lay a hand over one of her breasts, playing with the nipple until it grew hard and aroused, making her softly moan as her sex flooded with warmth for him once again. "I've been thinking about that, too."

"Yes?" her voice came out breathless since he chose that moment to slide between her thighs. The head of his cock pressed against her entrance. She moved her hips a degree, and he slipped inside her, pushing deep. Her teeth sank into her lower lip, and she closed her eyes for a moment, savoring it.

"Yes." His voice rumbled out of him, and he stared deeply into her eyes as he rocked back and forth, driving his cock very slowly in and out of her. "I've been thinking about all I did to keep you safe and why I did it. I betrayed my queen to protect you, Elizabeth. I've never done anything like that before."

She held his gaze, pushing her hips up to meet him, slow, easy, thrust for thrust. "And why did you do it?"

"Because I love you." His voice came out warm and sweet as honey.

She stared wide-eyed into his face. "What did you just say?" Maybe she hadn't heard him right.

He pushed a loose tendril of hair away from her cheek, then searched her eyes. "I've never met anyone like you, and I've fallen totally and completely in love with you."

His words coated her in tenderness, made something respond deep in her chest, thrum like a huge bell. The sensation was like an answering note of clear brilliance, a moment of perfect harmony and happiness in the middle of a storm.

She pushed up, kissing him hard and slipping her tongue into his mouth to twine with his. The pace of his thrusts increased. He took her harder and faster. She sighed and moaned, enjoying the sensation of Niall becoming one with her.

Their gazes met and held, his hips rocking against her hips. Pleasure rose, blossoming through her body until it burst over her. She cried out from the racking ecstasy that shuddered in waves through her body. Niall came a moment after, murmuring her name. Then they fell to the bed, panting from the exertion.

She rolled over and lay her head on his chest. Rubbing her palm over his stomach, she closed her eyes, enjoying this perfect moment. Never had she expected that when she'd taken the pieces of the *bosca fadbh* for the Summer Queen that her journey would end this way. If there was one good thing about this situation, this was it.

Elizabeth raised her head and looked into his eyes. She felt brave enough to tell him now. "I love you, too, Niall. Somewhere in the middle of all this, I fell for you."

He hooked her hair behind her ear. "Stay with me."

She smiled. "I don't want to be anywhere you're not."

She snuggled against his chest and eventually they fell asleep. Not even the power of the night could keep her awake, so immense was her exhaustion from the life-changing events that had befallen her during the last twenty-four hours.

When she woke it was morning. The bed was empty, but she could hear Niall in the kitchen. Her stomach growled at the smell of the food he was cooking and she realized she hadn't eaten for over twelve hours. She stretched, then slid from the bed, grabbing a bathrobe that Niall had left hanging over a chair.

First she headed into the bathroom and took a shower,

enjoying the hard, hot spray of the water on her aching muscles. She and Niall had performed sexual gymnastics the night before—something she was really not used to yet—and it had left a sweet ache throughout her body.

Her hair combed, but still damp, she pulled the robe on and headed to the kitchen. "Yum," she said, entering the room. "I'm starving."

His kitchen was large, with a center island hung with wineglasses and pots and pans dangling from the ceiling. He was dressed only in a pair of jeans—a most luscious sight—and stood at the stove, cooking up a pan full of French toast.

She wilted in the doorway. "*Danu*, that smells amazing."

He scooped them onto a plate and set it on the table along with a bottle of syrup. "Want some coffee?"

She sat down and picked up a fork. "Are you kidding me?"

"I'll take that as a yes." He poured her a cup and then sat across from her.

After smothering the French toast with syrup, she forked some of the sugary yumminess into her mouth and almost passed out as the flavor hit her tongue. "Sweet Lady, these are good. You are an incredible cook."

"When you're as old as I am, you learn."

"Well," she said, after she'd sipped some of the delicious hot, black coffee, "maybe you can teach me."

He caught her gaze and held it steady. "I hope to have many years to do just that."

A little thrill of pleasure curled through her stomach. She'd been alone for so long, now she had someone to spend her life with. It was almost too good to be true. She finished up her meal and sighed with happy fullness, settling back in her chair with her coffee. "So, do you do this often? Seduce a woman, then make breakfast for her in the morning?"

He looked surprised. "No." Then he smirked. "Ah, that's right, you're a wildling. You don't know my reputation here in the Black Tower."

She raised an eyebrow. "And what's that?"

He leaned forward a little. "Let's just say I haven't had many long-term relationships in my life. Very few women have tasted my"—he glanced down at her nearly empty plate—"French toast."

She stifled a laugh. Niall had a streak of arrogance that never quite disappeared, even when he was being sweet and vulnerable. Of course, judging from the power he seemed to have over her body, perhaps that arrogance wasn't completely unjustified. "Gee. I guess I should feel special."

His gaze turned intense. "You *are* special, Elizabeth. I've met many women in my life, but none of them have been like you."

Her mouth went dry and her smile faded at the sound of his voice and the look in his eyes. He really meant what he was saying. He really thought she was unique and wonderful. Emotion clogged her throat. "I guess growing up sheltered out in the Boundary Lands has its advantages."

Reaching across the table, he took her hands in his. "No matter where you grew up, you would have grown up to be the exceptional woman you are. It's simply built into you. Strength. Intelligence. Protectiveness. Cunning."

"Stop it." Of course, secretly she loved it.

He pulled her out of her chair and into his lap. "Sexy as hell. Gorgeous beyond measure." He nuzzled her throat, holding her close, and she wound herself around him, closing her eyes. "Willing to risk your life for someone you love."

"Go on," she breathed.

He found her mouth and whispered against it. "Vulnerable in all the right places." He slid his hand into her robe, between her thighs. "And—"

Someone rang the doorbell.

She groaned. "I guess you have to get that."

He straightened, looking suddenly serious. "It might be your mother."

Elizabeth slid from his lap, the sense of comfort that he'd wrapped her in suddenly gone and that familiar, cold knot slowly tangling through her intestines once more. She followed him to the door and stood beside him as he opened it. Thea stood on the other side, dressed warmly in an expensive coat that had undoubtedly been offered to her by the Black Tower.

In exchange for her life.

Niall backed away from the door, and Elizabeth hugged herself, staring at her mother for a long moment, before Thea finally broke her gaze and moved inside.

Thea spread her hands, her eyes glistening with tears. "I had to do it."

Elizabeth swallowed down the sob that had lodged itself at the back of her throat, then reached forward and pulled her mother into an embrace. "I really wish you hadn't," she murmured.

Her mother backed away, wiping tears from her eyes. "Thank you for loving me so much, Elizabeth."

"Come on in," said Niall. "Sit down."

Thea gave her daughter one last long look, then went to sit on the couch. Elizabeth sat down next to her. "Did they manage to assemble the *bosca fadbh*?"

"Yes."

Thea's hands clenched in her lap, betraying her nervousness. She was a brave woman, bent on doing the right thing for the good of all, no matter what it cost her yet it was clear she was uneasy about what was to come. "So, now what? I want to be . . . prepared."

Niall nodded, rubbing a hand over his chin as he sat on the armrest of one of the easy chairs in his living room. "The Book of Bindings cannot be opened until noon today. So, we hold our breath, hope nothing catastrophic happens. Until then we prepare to battle anything that comes our way in the meantime. At noon we'll open the back of the book and—hopefully—find the magick within to break the walls."

"So," said Thea, glancing at the grandfather clock in the corner, "I have less than four hours left on earth."

Elizabeth's hands knotted together so hard she feared breaking her fingers.

"I'm sorry, Thea." Niall sounded heartbroken, but how could he be? It wasn't *his* mother who'd sacrificed her life to do the right thing. It wasn't *his* last remaining family member he was about to watch die.

Thea shook her head. "What is will be."

Elizabeth wanted to scream at her calm acceptance. She didn't possess any of the zenlike qualities of her mother. She wanted to fight for what she wanted right up to the very end. Never give up, no matter how bad it got.

Thea raised her gaze to Niall's. "Thank you for everything you did yesterday. If it wasn't for you, I don't know what I would have done. I was completely overwhelmed when I arrived here. If you hadn't met me and brought me to the queen, I'm not sure I would have ever been able to turn the pieces over."

Every molecule in Elizabeth's body went cold. Her body went rigid and her gaze snapped to Niall, who was watching her carefully. "What?" The word snapped out of her.

Thea turned on the couch to look at her. "He found me wandering the foyer yesterday, not knowing who to go to or whom I could trust. I was too afraid to tell anyone I had the pieces. I spotted Niall, and he brought me up to see the queen. He didn't tell you?"

"No, he didn't tell me."

Her gaze swung to Niall as anger clenched in her stomach. Of course Niall had bustled Thea right upstairs with hardly a thought. He wanted the walls to fall, so his actions didn't come as a surprise. Yet there was something especially awful knowing that it was *Niall, the man she loved and the man she'd grown to trust*, who had led her mother to her end. She wasn't sure she could stomach that knowledge.

"Yes," continued Thea, "he even tried to find me at the house. . . ."

Her mother continued speaking, but Elizabeth could barely hear what she was saying because of the dull buzzing in her head. *Of course* Niall had gone to her mother's house, had intended to tell her what her daughter had done. His last shot had been to try and get Thea on his side. Elizabeth should have known he'd do that.

Still, this changed everything.

Her gaze met Niall's. "You helped her kill herself, Niall?"

"Elizabeth—"

"No!" she cut him off. "You just told me you loved me, yet, just yesterday you took away my mother? How could you!"

"This is the way it has to be, Elizabeth," Niall said, rising. "I *do* love you."

Fisting her hands in her lap, she looked up at him. Her thoughts swirled just as fast as her emotions, making her feel sick.

She loved him, too. She always would. Yet this wasn't going to work. Every time she looked at Niall, she would see her mother's death. For a moment she'd actually believed they could have a relationship, but that had just been an illusion, a mirage—like an oasis in a desert.

She and Niall could never be together because too much lay between them.

Elizabeth stood, shook her head, and moved toward the bedroom. She was going to dress and get the hell out of here. Pausing, she turned toward him. "Last night was just a fantasy. Those pieces of the *bosca fadbh* will always be wedged between us, Niall. You and I can't ever be together. We couldn't before and we can't now." She paused, staring hard at him. "*Especially* not now."

Tightly leashing her emotions, Elizabeth pulled off Niall's robe and jerked on her clothes. In the other room, low voices murmured. Just as she was sitting on the bed and leaning over to pull her second boot on, something powerful hit the tower.

The force of it knocked her off the bed onto the floor. A second explosion rocked the tower, and she curled in on herself as plaster rained down from the ceiling.

TWENTY-ONE

"ELIZABETH!" Niall bellowed.

Elizabeth pushed to her feet and lunged into the living room. Another blast hit the tower. Elizabeth was thrown off balance, barely catching herself on a chair as she passed. Her mother stood near the door, hands pressed tightly to her mouth, eyes wide, while Niall stood at the window, looking down at the square.

Fear exploded through her. "Niall!" Elizabeth yelled. "Get away from the window!"

"They can rock the building, maybe do a little damage, but they'll never break through the Shadow Queen's shields." He motioned to her. "Take a look."

She had a bad feeling she knew who "they" were.

Elizabeth glanced at her mother, who had gone incredibly pale. Her curiosity getting the better of her, she stalked over to the window just in time for another volley. Niall caught her as she stumbled and she pulled away from him, giving him a cold glance before she directed her attention out the thick pane of glass.

Down in the square, Gideon stood alongside the Summer Queen. Behind them stood a small army of cloaked Phaendir, head bowed, faces shadowed, hands clasped inside the voluminous sleeves of their robes. Apparently Gideon and Caoilainn were through with shadowy collusions and secret operations.

This was a full-on frontal assault.

It made something bitter sting the back of her throat to see the Summer Queen standing in alliance with the archdirector of the Phaendir against the Black Tower.

The square had cleared of fae. Not even one human soldier could be seen. Apparently they'd retreated at the first hint of malicious magick. Smart on their part since bullets wouldn't help them much. Maybe they had orders to stay out of what occurred between the fae and the Phaendir.

Gideon and the Summer Queen had, of course, a magickal protective shield around them. There was no other way they could be standing so boldly in the middle of Piefferburg Square otherwise. Just as Elizabeth had considered the shield, a group of men rushed out from the base of the Black Tower.

Niall leaned forward. "The Fianna. Those idiots."

The Fianna were men who were descended from the original Fianna of lore, though they also possessed the blood of the Tuatha Dé. Once they'd been fierce warriors, their eversharpened swords for hire to the Irish kings of old. In Piefferburg, without the tradition of warring kings to employ them, they lived privileged, idle lives in the Rose Tower. The group of men were known womanizers and tended to get drunk a lot, fight a lot, and play sports.

From the way they were charging into the square right now, Elizabeth assumed they'd forgotten that centuries had passed since even one of them had fought anyone but each other.

"Poor deluded bastards." Niall's voice sounded grim. "I give them ten seconds."

It didn't take even that long.

Elizabeth turned her face away as magick exploded. The Fianna were left burning on the cobblestones . . . in pieces. "Sweet Danu," she breathed. "The Summer Queen just murdered members of her own court. Has she gone insane?"

"She was never all that stable." He paused. "The goblins will be next, but they're a lot harder to kill."

Indeed, as soon as he'd uttered it, goblins began streaming out of the Black Tower commanded by the Shadow Queen. In a killing frenzy, the mass of tall gray creatures swarmed toward Gideon and Caoilainn. There were too many and they moved too fast to kill, though that didn't stop Gideon from trying. Burning goblin carcasses began to fall around them.

It made a lump rise in Elizabeth's throat. The goblins, having no choice in the matter, had been used like cannon fodder over the years by the Shadow Royal.

The unharmed goblins bounced off the invisible barrier surrounding Gideon and Caoilainn like something out of a cartoon. The barrier was definitely the Summer Queen's, though her magick wasn't all that different from Gideon's.

Normally, the Summer Queen could only wield magick in defense of the Rose Tower. Elizabeth wasn't sure if this situation counted. But, after all, the Rose Tower was, indeed, at risk. The Summer Queen herself had ensured *that*.

Thwarted in their efforts to reach their intended targets, the goblins roamed Piefferburg Square, snarling and snapping. No one could envy the Summer Queen and Gideon when they were surrounded by hundreds of slavering goblins thirsting for a taste of their flesh the moment the barrier faltered. The goblins were under direct command of the Shadow Queen—part of the Shadow Guard—they wouldn't stop until they had destroyed—in this case, consumed—their targets.

Once the king and queen called the sluagh, things would go from worse to hellish for them.

Gideon and the Summer Queen lifted their hands in unison, and another wave of magick rocked the Black Tower. Both she and Niall stumbled back. Plaster rained down from above them, and a crack zigzagged through the living room wall.

She glanced at Niall. "What was that about a barrier protecting the Black Tower, Niall?"

His expression looked grim as his gaze followed the crack in the wall as it snaked up the ceiling. "Maybe it's the nature of their combined power. It's the Phaendir out there, after all. That's not all fae magick."

Elizabeth turned to her mother. "We need to get out of here."

"Great idea. Come on," said Niall, going for the door. "I'll show you a secret way out of the tower."

The corridor was a mess of fae who'd remained in the tower after the evacuation order for the children. Now the rest of them were fleeing, and she didn't blame them. Apparently everyone had received the same message at the same time— Gideon was going to bring this tower down around their ears.

Of course, Elizabeth doubted he'd really go that far. At least, not until he'd secured the Book of Bindings and the *bosca fadbh*. Even from a distance, she could see that Gideon looked crazed. He wasn't going to be denied this time.

Elizabeth just wanted to get her mother as far away from this place as fast as she could. Her goal was to get to the Boundary Lands and hope like hell the sprae didn't follow the rest of the fae if the walls came down. It was her mother's only chance.

Elizabeth hated relying on luck.

They flowed into the river of fae making their way toward the stairs and elevators, but before they reached the end of the corridor, Niall pulled her and her mother into a shadowed alcove.

"Melia, a friend of mine and a member of the Wild Hunt, was one of the designers of the Black Tower," Niall explained as he felt around the ceiling of the alcove, looking for something. "She showed me and precious few others all the secret places they built in."

He found the mechanism he was looking for and triggered it. The back of the alcove slid open and they stepped into blackness, the wall sliding back into place quickly behind them. She couldn't see anything—not even her hand in front of her face.

Another blast of magick shook the tower, throwing Elizabeth into Niall, who steadied her. "This is not making me feel safe, Niall," she muttered.

Ignoring her, he murmured, *"Illivium kar nium vatch."* A small orb of light appeared before them, illuminating the small room they stood in and a flight of narrow, shadowed stairs leading into the bowels of the tower.

Thea peered down them. "Where do they go?"

"Well," said Niall, staring down the seemingly never ending flight of stairs, "eventually they lead out of the tower." He paused. "But they haven't been used in a while, and it's a long way down."

Another blast shook the tower, knocking Thea into the wall and making the whole structure groan ominously. They stared down the pitch-black flight of stairs for a moment in silence, all of them thinking the same thing.

"Okay, let's do this. *Fast*," said Elizabeth, taking her mother's hand.

Niall insisted on going first, to clear the way for the rest of them and take on unexpected surprises, should there be any. The light of the orb floating in front of them, they headed down into the darkness as fast as they could safely move. It was a long way down. It seemed like they descended forever, every blast on the tower growing worse, making the building sigh and moan, and crumbling bits of quartz and concrete onto their heads.

Finally, just as the magick of the orb began to flicker and go out, they reached a metal door at the end. Niall opened it, and Elizabeth saw they were in the foyer. They slipped through the doorway and Niall closed it behind them. It looked just like the rest of the black quartz wall—no trace of the door remained or any visible way to open it from this side.

They watched from around the corner as fleeing fae rushed through, finding exits. Moments later the area emptied out. Elizabeth started to walk across the foyer, to the main doors that led out onto the street, but Niall raised a hand to stop her. "Something's not right."

"*Nothing's* right," she snapped over her shoulder.

"No, I mean, we got down here faster than everyone else. The foyer should be filled with fleeing people right now, but it's a fucking ghost town in here. They know something we don't."

Just then the double doors of the Black Tower burst open and magick flared in the foyer, creating a metallic flavor at the back of her mouth. Thea shrank back against the wall, hiding around the corner, as if trying to make herself small.

Elizabeth fought the urge to shut her eyes. Her feet seemed frozen to the marble floor. "They're coming in here, aren't they?"

Niall yanked her around the corner.

Gideon and the Summer Queen strode into the Black Tower side by side, the cadre of cloaked Phaendir bringing up the rear. Gideon wore a dark suit with his brown hair slicked back, and Caoilainn wore a flowing white and gold gown. It looked like a demonic wedding party.

Elizabeth knew she should move, find an exit. She'd seen what their magick could do. May the Fianna rest in pieces. They needed to escape, but she couldn't make herself budge.

Beside her, Niall seemed to be having the same problem. He muttered more Old Maejian under his breath and Elizabeth heard a little pop of some kind of magick being created around them. She hoped it was an invisibility spell.

The Summer Queen swung her head toward them and narrowed her eyes, catching sight of them. Her pale blond hair was curled and twisted on the top of her head and held in place with a thousand small golden pins. The white and gold gown that swathed her shifted with her movements, making slithering sounds. Diamonds dripped from her earlobes and twinkled from the base of her throat. Even for the Summer Queen, she was dressed to the nines today. Apparently she was certain victory was hers and wanted to look the part.

"You!" she shouted, raising her finger to point at Elizabeth. "You slimy little bitch! Traitor!" She lifted her hand and an immense blast of magick shot toward them.

Elizabeth whirled to shield her mother, but the blast hit a barrier protecting them—Niall's magick.

Gideon placed a staying hand on the Summer Queen's forearm. "Now, now, Caoilainn, that part of the story is over with. Don't waste your strength."

The Summer Queen lowered her arm, still fuming. The bank of elevators dinged, announcing someone's arrival. Elizabeth pitied those fleeing fae and the surprise they were about to have.

But instead of random frightened fae, it was the Shadow King and Queen who stepped out of the elevator. Looking regal and completely unafraid, they came to stand face-to-face with the Summer Queen and Gideon.

"Gee," whispered Niall, "I wish we had some popcorn."

Elizabeth took a deep breath, trying not to hyperventilate. "How can you be so flippant about this, Niall?"

"I'm flippant about most everything, Elizabeth." He looked into her eyes. "Except you."

Sorrow filled her chest and she eased away from him a

little, averting her gaze. How she wished it could be another
way. She glanced at her mother, who had narrowed her eyes at
her with a disapproving look on her face. It was nice to know
that even in the midst of a terrifying situation her mother had
an opinion about her love life.

"The book isn't here, Caoilainn," said the queen in a low,
steady voice.

Goblins from the square began streaming into the foyer. Not
the hundreds that had streamed out, but enough to surround
Gideon, the Summer Queen, and their creepy entourage.

The Summer Queen smiled. It was odd how angelic she
could look with her cherubic lips and clear blue eyes, like a
porcelain doll . . . of evil. "Did you hear that, Gideon? The
book isn't here. That means we can level the Black Tower."

"Goody," deadpanned Gideon, his eyes focused on Gabriel's face as though exploring all the possible ways he could
flay skin from muscle and tendon. "So, you're the head of the
Wild Hunt?"

Gabriel lifted his chin, his dark blue eyes flashing. "I am."

"You'll be working hard tonight."

"Maybe." Gabriel rolled his shoulders. "But who will reap
you when you die, Gideon? I hear no one comes for Phaendir
the way the Lady comes for the fae. How do you know your
God even cares about you?" He paused. "How do you even
know he exists, this *Labrai*?"

Gideon's entire body went tight. That was, of course, a
blow that must hurt a devout man like the archdirector of the
Phaendir. Everything Gideon did, he did for Labrai. "I know
He exists because I'm standing here, ready to take down the
Black Tower stone by stone and then destroy the fae. *Labrai*
has made that so."

Elizabeth frowned, wondering at the exchange, wondering why the Shadow King and Queen were even bothering to
talk to them. Then movement drew her eye and she spotted
Aeric O'Malley, the Blacksmith—she recognized him from
Faemous—and a dark-haired woman ushering people down a
corridor behind them and out a side door.

Ah. The Shadow Royals were buying time, getting the
tower completely evacuated.

"*Hmmm* . . . that remains to be seen, I guess." Gabriel

looked around the foyer. "After all, the Black Tower is still standing, and the fae are alive and ready to kick your ass. They are, in fact, surrounding you." He clicked his tongue. "Gotta say, I don't really see you or your brothers getting out of here alive. The moment your shields go down . . ." Gabriel grinned then took a mock bite out of the air. "You'll be lunch."

"Enough!" roared the Summer Queen. "Hand over the book and we won't level the tower."

The temperature in the foyer plummeted. Elizabeth let out a hard and fast puff of breath in surprise and it showed white in the air. "You're never getting the book, Caoilainn," said the Shadow Queen in a steady, deadly sounding voice.

The Summer Queen laughed. "You can't scare me, Aislinn. I was there the day you were born. In my lifetime, that was yesterday."

"Aislinn," Gabriel said in a strong, clear voice. "Are you ready?"

"I'm ready," she answered.

Time seemed to stop for one dark, horrible moment. The air thickened, and for an instant almost all the light was sucked out of the room, leaving long, twisting shadows and incredible cold. Thea took Elizabeth's hand and squeezed.

"What the hell is happening?" Elizabeth asked Niall in a low voice.

"They're calling the sluagh."

A low inhuman screaming began in the distance, growing louder and louder until Elizabeth and Thea were forced to sink to the floor, covering their ears. It was a sound that could shatter bone, sever tendon, make the listener go insane. The screaming faded to whispering that grew softer and softer.

All the noise stopped. It was as if the entire world froze. Universal silence. To Elizabeth, it was even worse than the screaming.

"This is getting out of hand," Elizabeth whispered shakily to Niall.

She'd barely uttered the sentence when the front doors of the tower burst open and a stream of monstrous gray creatures rushed inside. Elizabeth and her mother pressed up against the wall behind them. The scuttle of sharp curved claws on the floor nearly deafened her.

One of the creatures stopped right in front her, looking her up and down. He—or she—had long, spindly arms and legs that still managed to be sinewy with muscle, a bulbous head, and an insectlike body. Its scaly skin was a sickly gray and it had huge eyes like an alien. Tattered, ripped clothes barely covered its body, and it held a machete in one clawed hand. Its nose was like a skeleton's, really just two slits in its face. It opened its mouth, revealing long, sharp teeth, and hissed, spattering her with saliva.

TWENTY-TWO

"NIALL," Elizabeth yelled over the noise. "It's time to go, don't you think?"

"They won't hurt you unless the Shadow Queen commands them."

She wiped the spittle from her cheek. "Oh, great, that's *very* reassuring since the queen is *so* happy with me these days."

Niall paused for a moment. "Good point. Let's go."

Before they began to edge down the corridor toward the side exit they'd seen Aeric O'Malley sneaking fae out of, Elizabeth took one last look at the scene in the middle of the foyer. Between the roaming, snarling sluagh and goblins that were looking for a way into the bubble around the bad guys, she could see that Gideon and the Summer Queen looked nonplussed. They were still facing off in a battle of wills with the Shadow Royals, who stood calmly in the midst of the chaotic sea of Unseelie creatures. They were speaking, but she couldn't hear anything over the snarling, snapping, and scuttling of claws on marble.

Suddenly Gideon's face flushed red with rage and he shot his arm to the side. A huge chunk of the foyer exploded in a shower of black quartz. The tower rocked ominously and Elizabeth wondered how much more it could withstand.

"Time to hurry," muttered Niall, taking Thea's hand and beginning to pick up the pace down the corridor.

They found the side door and burst out of it just as another blast of magick rocked the tower. A chunk of quartz plummeted past them from above and crashed into the sidewalk near her. She yelped in surprise, turned her body and shielded her face. Tiny bits of shrapnel peppered her, stinging her skin.

Niall grabbed her hand and ran with both women across the street, where a crowd had gathered.

"You're lucky you got out when you did," said a dark-haired man coming up on Niall's side.

"Is the tower completely evacuated?" asked Niall, staring up at the tower with a look of mixed disbelief and dread on his face. "I'm not sure it can take this kind of pummeling."

"We think everyone got out."

"Good. Why aren't you gone? I thought you were taking Charlotte out of here."

The dark-haired man's jaw tightened. "Circumstances changed."

"Right. She wouldn't let you, huh?"

"No," the man practically growled the word.

Niall motioned at Elizabeth. "Elizabeth, this is Kieran Aindréas Cairbre Aimhrea. Kieran, Elizabeth Cely Saintjohn."

Kieran narrowed his eyes, recognizing her name. "Hello." It was one of the most unfriendly hellos she'd ever been treated to. She guessed she couldn't blame him much.

"Where's the book?" Niall asked him. "I know they got it out of the tower before Boris and Natasha showed up."

Kieran glanced at her, rubbing his chin. "Yeah, they did. It's safe."

"You can trust her, man."

Kieran snorted. "Please."

Elizabeth felt her face go red with shame. "No, I get it. No problem. I was on my way out of town, anyway. Come on, Mom." She looked at Niall. "Good luck with everything."

"Elizabeth." He caught her hand before she could turn away. "Don't go. Stay with me, at least until this is over."

She looked up and met his eyes. "This *is* over, Niall. Completely and totally." She pulled her hand away from his and walked out of the crowd, into the road to go around the crowd.

"Elizabeth!" Niall called from behind her.

She kept walking, never turned around—even though her heart was breaking.

"You're making a mistake," her mother grumbled coming up beside her. "Niall is a good man and he loves you."

"And I love him back, Mom." Her voice was choked with tears. She cleared her throat, banishing them.

"I don't understand the problem."

"Too much lies between us. Too many bad decisions. Too many regrets." She glanced at her mother, grief swamping her for a moment. "Too many bad memories." Or there would be, anyway, very soon.

"I love you, but I won't be your excuse, Elizabeth."

She only shook her head in response and kept walking. It wasn't an excuse, but she couldn't explain that to her mother. "We'll go back to the Boundary Lands, find a pocket of sprae. Maybe if you stay there, they won't leave if the walls—Mom?"

Her mother was not beside her. She stopped and turned, scanning the throng but finding no trace of Thea. "Mom?"

Nothing. She'd disappeared.

"Damn it," she muttered, heading into the crowd to look for her, panic tightening her throat. She didn't want her mother to die alone.

Just then another blast of magick, this one stronger than the others, shook the street like a mini earthquake.

"Watch out!" someone yelled, pointing at the top of the tower. The crowd took a collective breath and the noise level grew.

Elizabeth turned, looking up to see a huge chunk of the tower plummeting to the street. Directly under it wandered a young woman looking like she was lost. Elizabeth acted without thinking, realizing that she was closest to the woman since she was in the street.

Bolting to her, she pushed the woman out of the way. Elizabeth tripped, sprawled on her back, looked upward.

The huge chunk of black quartz hurtled straight toward her.

TWENTY-THREE

GIDEON'S teeth ground together, but he refused to look at the sluagh that roamed around him. The sounds of their claws on the marble were like splinters of ice through his brain. He kept his gaze focused on Gabriel's face. Beside him, the Summer and Shadow Queens were locked in a similar prison of attention.

"Look at these monsters you can call," he yelled over the sound of the goblins and sluagh around them. "How is it you think you deserve to walk among humans?"

"You don't fool anyone here, Gideon," Gabriel countered. "You don't care a whit about humanity. Don't pretend to be their guardians."

"I wouldn't be standing here, with Labrai guiding my every move, if I wasn't."

Aislinn snorted. "If Labrai is guiding you, why didn't you stop the last two pieces from getting into Piefferburg? How was it, if the almighty Labrai directs your hand, Ronan Quinn was able to create an illusion that duped you all and enabled him to carry in the first piece? The piece he stole for *you* in the first place. How is that, Gideon?"

"Oh, that's right." Gabriel barked out a laugh. "That had to be embarrassing."

Gideon's jaw locked. Those failures were bitter truths that poisoned his reality.

"In fact," continued Aislinn, "I would make a guess that the Lady Danu had a hand in allowing those pieces to come to us. Everything happened so perfectly." She paused and gave him a sweet smile. "As though it was all meant to be."

Gideon gave her his best poisonous smile. "If the goddess Danu is guiding these events, how is it you were trapped in Piefferburg in the first place?"

Aislinn locked gazes with Caoilainn. "That's an excellent question."

"If you're accusing me of something, just come out with it," answered Caoilainn.

Aislinn raised her silver blond brows. "You're helping the Phaendir to keep the walls up right now, Caoilainn. There's no reason not to suspect you didn't help erect them in the first place."

"Watt Syndrome could never have been created without specific knowledge of fae genetics," Gabriel added. "We've long suspected a traitor in our midst. Viewing your recent actions, seems likely it was you."

The room immediately plunged into a subzero temperature range. Gideon watched frost coat Gabriel's golden skin, leaching away the healthy color. Out of the corner of his eye, he glimpsed several of the sluagh slip and go sprawling on the suddenly slick floor.

"How dare you," shrieked Caoilainn. "I would *never.*"

Gideon's lips curled in a smile and he bit back the *liar* dancing on his tongue. He'd entertained the idea of throwing Caoilainn under the bus if he'd deemed it would help him. Looked like that option was off the table. Her actions spoke louder than his accusations.

"Cut the temper tantrum," Aislinn growled. Her lips were blue and frost coated her hair, starting at the crown and snaking its way down.

"I think the lady doth protest too much," Gabriel added.

"Cut the temper tantrum? You just accused me of damning my race!"

"If the shoe fits."

"You incredible bitch!" She reached her right hand out to one side and a chunk of the foyer wall exploded in a shower of black quartz. The tower rocked ominously, and a deafening crack snaked its way up the wall, past the ceiling.

"Ladies, I'm growing bored." Gideon leveled his hand at Aislinn and Gabriel. "Tell us where the Book of Bindings is or I'll kill you both right now."

Aislinn and Gabriel exchanged *a look*. Gideon couldn't interpret it, but it should have been a look of apprehension. They had little power to wield over him. Gabriel was an incubus, so unless he was planning to seduce them to death, his power was useless. Aislinn's main magick was that of necromancer, also a relatively useless skill in battle.

"Yeah," said Gabriel lazily. "We're not doing that."

Gideon didn't even blink . . . he just fired.

ELIZABETH rolled to the side a moment before the chunk of quartz hit the cobblestones. She curled in on herself, protecting her head and face from the explosion of rock. A piece of the shrapnel hit her leg. Blinding pain burst through her and blood ran hot. Elizabeth doubled over as she lay on her side, gripping her leg and crying out in agony.

Niall raced over to her with Kieran at his side. Niall knelt near her, while Kieran led the confused, dreamy-eyed fae woman away.

Niall helped her to sit up and rolled the bottom of her pant leg up to check the damage. He rocked back on his heels and pushed a hand through his hair. "We need to get this wound cleaned up *now*."

"Is it bad?" she asked, peering down. All she could see was blood. It hurt like hell. The pain throbbed in hot waves up her leg. She sank her teeth into her lower lip to keep from groaning and crying out.

"I can't tell, but I don't think it broke a bone. Seems like just a really bad, deep cut. You'll need stitches." He looked into her face. "Looks like you're not running away from me anytime soon, beautiful."

She looked away from him, really hating the little spark

inside her that thrilled at the prospect of being forced to remain with him . . . at least for a little while. "Yay," she replied, her voice flat.

"*Aw*, now no sarcasm needed." He glanced around. "Where's your mother?"

She shrugged. "Apparently trying to teach me a lesson. She disappeared."

He nodded. "Come on, let's get away from the tower." He helped her up, and she limped toward the sidewalk.

Everyone they passed thanked and congratulated her for saving the woman. The woman in question had wandered down the road, staring up into the velvety winter night sky, seemingly oblivious that someone had just risked their life for her. The lady hadn't even known she'd been in danger.

Kieran approached them, hooking his thumb after the woman. "Feeorshee."

She raised her eyebrows. "Oh." It made sense now. The feeorshee had one foot out of this world and into the next. They lived in a reality that was half a dream.

"Listen," said Kieran. "I'm sorry I reacted that way to you earlier. What you just did was incredible."

"Don't be too impressed." She grimaced. "I really didn't even think about it, Kieran. I just acted."

He grinned. "That's good. If you'd thought about it, you'd never have done it."

That was true enough.

"After you left, Niall told me about your motivation for hiding the pieces. I didn't know any of that." He paused, studying her. "Very compelling."

Elizabeth swallowed. "Look. I'm not asking for forgiv—"

"Come with us," he cut her off before she could get defensive out of guilt.

She narrowed her eyes at him. "Why?"

"Are you always this suspicious? I'm offering to trust you." He glanced down at her leg. "And we can get you cleaned up and bandaged. You won't get far with an injury like that."

She snapped her mouth shut before she said something she would regret and gave a curt nod.

Niall scooped her into his arms, and she immediately began to struggle. "Put me down. I'm not some damsel in distress.

I can walk . . . or limp, at least." She could dissolve and heal the wound, but she didn't want to do that here and end up buck naked. She'd rather endure the pain.

Another blast of magick shook the tower and the street along with it. The crowd began to scream and scrabble, running away as more pieces of black quartz began to fall like some demented, dangerous rain, crashing on the street.

Niall began to move through the throng, away from the structure. She grabbed his neck and hung on tight. "You were saying?" he asked with a sly grin.

"Be quiet," she muttered, angry that, at least for the moment, she needed him. She was acutely aware of how much that pleased him.

Niall and Kieran made their way through the fleeing people to a SUV a couple blocks away. Kieran opened the back door, and Niall slid her onto the seat. Wincing, she changed her position to one that didn't hurt so much. Kieran started the vehicle and they took off down the street.

She stared out the window, looking at the chaos erupting. The sluagh and the goblins had spilled from the tower and roamed the streets around the structure, frothing at the mouth at their inability to carry out their queen's orders. The residents of the city were now fleeing Piefferburg Square, apparently in response to some event that she was unable to see now. Something big was happening, that was for sure.

The light-headedness that she'd been keeping at bay only through a sheer force of will reared its head. Her eyes drooped and her head lolled as she fought it. Looking down, she saw she was bleeding all over Kieran's car.

So much blood.

In the distance, gunfire rang out, making her jerk erect for a moment before her vision began to fade to black. Struggling to stay conscious, she glimpsed a group of human soldiers running across the street in front of them, chasing the sluagh.

Well, *that* was exceedingly dumb.

Kieran swerved to avoid a skirmish and gunned the engine to go around another confrontation. Everything was falling apart. War was beginning. Elizabeth felt badly for the humans. They'd obviously received the order to engage, but they were going to get the worse end of this.

Niall glanced back at her, as if reading her mind. Did he know her that well? "Don't look so worried. The Shadow Queen gave orders to the goblins and sluagh that the soldiers are not to be harmed. They'll be detained, incapacitated, but not killed." He paused. "We're about to reenter the human world; we won't start out by slaughtering them."

Elizabeth nodded, unable to speak. She was only barely holding on to consciousness.

"The queen doesn't want any more bad publicity with the humans than we already have," Niall finished. When she didn't respond, he looked back at her. "Are you all—Kieran, *stop the car!*"

"I can't!" Kieran was negotiating the disordered streets like a pro. "We need to get the hell out of downtown. Everything is turning into chaos."

Niall scrambled into the backseat beside her, cupping her face between his hands. "You're pale and look ready to . . . Elizabeth? *Elizabeth?*"

Her eyes rolled shut and everything went dark.

TWENTY-FOUR

"FUCK," Niall swore under his breath. Elizabeth had passed out, either from pain or blood loss. "She needs medical attention!"

"I'm going as fast as I can go. Hold on." Kieran jerked the wheel to the left to avoid a group of fae battling soldiers.

Niall held on tight to Elizabeth's limp body, looking out the back window to see the soldiers scattering the fae with bullets. If the soldiers were packing charmed iron bullets, those fae were dead. If not, the shots might not kill them, depending on what kind of fae they were, but it would hurt like a son of a bitch.

Kieran headed into the *ceantar dubh* and parked in front of a tall residential building that Niall didn't recognize. "The book is here?" he asked as Kieran stopped the engine.

He nodded. "It's a safe house, of sorts. Only a few of us know about it."

"And you trust Elizabeth not to do something crazy?"

"Am I right to trust her, Niall?"

"Fuck yes."

Kieran turned to look at him. "You love her, don't you?"

Niall met his gaze. "Yes."

"I trust that anyone *you* trust is okay." He glanced at Elizabeth as Niall hefted her unconscious body into his arms. "Even someone who did something like what she did."

"She did it for love."

"A year ago, I wouldn't have understood that, but now I do."

They climbed out of the SUV and went into the building. It was dank-smelling, and the staircase was steep and narrow. Like most of the buildings in this part of town, it had been constructed during the early days of Piefferburg so it was very old and had been built small to be easier to heat.

Holding Elizabeth close to his chest and musing about how much she would hate the fact he had to carry her up the stairs, he followed Kieran upward, their passage lit by only a series of bare lightbulbs hanging from wires. Each of their shuffling footsteps echoed through the space.

They went all the way to the top—*of course*. Niall's lungs were burning and his arms ached from Elizabeth's weight by the time they reached the final flight of stairs. There, on the topmost landing, was a scuffed and dented metal door. Kieran knocked, and his wife, Charlotte, answered. "Thank god you're safe," she breathed, throwing herself into his arms.

After several long moments of standing there, listening to Charlotte and Kieran coo at each other, Niall cleared his voice. "I know she looks light, but . . ."

Charlotte moved, just then noticing him there. Her eyes traveled to Elizabeth, then to Kieran, recognition clear on her face. "Why have you brought her here?"

"Niall trusts her and that's good enough for me. Plus, I watched her risk her life to save someone back at the tower."

"Yes," snapped Niall, "that's how she got this injury that's making her gush blood." His tone made it clear he was losing patience.

Charlotte's gaze moved down to Elizabeth's leg and her eyes widened. "Of course, come in." She moved to the side, and Niall carried her in.

The inside of the apartment was sparsely furnished, the few pieces of furniture occupied by the usual suspects— Aislinn's advisors. Aeric O'Malley and his wife, Emmaline; Bella and Niall's brother, Ronan Quinn; plus the rest of the

Wild Hunt, Melia, Aelfdane, and Bran, who had his pet crow, Lex, perched on his shoulder. An old fireplace stood along one wall, rusty fireplace tools leaning against the brick.

Bella and Ronan were sitting on the couch and immediately moved so he could lay Elizabeth down. Bella knelt next to her, pushing Elizabeth's flame-colored hair to the side to reveal her pale face.

"She's lost a lot of blood," said Niall, ripping her pant leg up the side.

Bella didn't say a word, just moved to get all the things he needed. He didn't even have to open his mouth to ask. Lady, his brother had married an angel. A moment later and he was pressing a clean wad of material to Elizabeth's wound.

She would need stitches if she remained in human form. If she regained consciousness, she could take water form and heal the wound instantly. Anxiety clenched his stomach.

What if she didn't wake up?

GIDEON released the magick with a pop of power that tingled painfully through his body, as it did every time. The power arced toward Aislinn and Gabriel, but they dove out of the way at the last moment, and it made a crater in the floor instead. Bits of marble flew everywhere, exploding against his shield and hitting the roaming goblins and sluagh.

No matter. Aislinn and Gabriel weren't getting away. He'd never really thought they'd willingly hand the book over to save the tower, anyway. Bringing it down—and killing them—had been on his agenda from the start.

He turned, targeting Aislinn. Kill her and he'd get rid of the goblins and sluagh. In the same moment, a blast of magick not unlike a lightning bolt struck his shield.

Gideon staggered backward, his shield vibrating like a tuning fork. If it hadn't been there, he'd be a smoking heap of ash on the floor. His gaze swung to the Summer Queen, thinking she'd done it, but she was busy directing her magick toward a figure near the bank of elevators.

He was a huge man, ice-white skin blending with long, ice-white hair. Gideon recognized him and his unique power signature even after all these centuries.

So, the Shadow Queen had a champion.

Gideon swung his arms wide. "Kolbjorn! So good to see you after all these years. Still looking like a walking flake of dandruff, I see."

"Can dandruff do this?" he growled. Another lightning bolt shot toward his shield, making the whole thing shudder, shake, and whine.

The magick wavered under the force of the strike, and Gideon had a moment of unease. He wasn't sure how much trauma the shield could take, yet a glance behind him showed his loyal contingent of Phaendir behind him, heads bowed, not budging, feeding not only their shield, but his own.

He glanced at Caoilainn. It was time they stood together. His magick was twice as powerful joined with hers. Aislinn and Gabriel wanted a fight, he was willing to give them one. They wanted him to take this tower down? No problem.

Gideon and Caoilainn stepped toward each other at the same time. United, they moved toward Kolbjorn.

SOMEONE touched Niall's shoulder, and he looked up from Elizabeth's unconscious face to see Emmaline looking down at him. "That's all you can do for her right now. We'll have to hope she wakes up and can shift."

He stared down into her pale face. "I know." After a moment, he rubbed a hand over his face, pushed it through his hair, and stood. "What time is it?"

"Almost noon," answered Aeric, walking to the window and gazing out over the city to the pillar of black in the distance. "I don't know if Aislinn and Gabriel will make it in time."

Niall went to stand beside him. "By the looks of things when we left the Black Tower, I'd say that's a negative."

"Yeah." Aeric paused. "Fine, so we do it ourselves."

"Where's the book?"

"It's safe," came a belligerent voice from behind him. It was Melia.

He turned to look at the red-headed battle fae, who was standing near Bran and her husband, Aelfdane, and was glaring at Elizabeth lying unconscious on the couch. "Do you have something you need to say, Melia?"

Melia swung her gaze to his and spat out, "She shouldn't be here."

"But she is," he snapped back, "so get over it." He motioned at her. "It's not like she can do a lot of damage, anyway."

Melia narrowed her eyes and took a step toward her. Aelfdane put a hand on her shoulder to stop her. Melia's gaze snapped from Elizabeth to Niall's face. "She's already done her damage."

Bran's crow, Lex, flapped his wings from its perch on Bran's shoulder and cawed at Melia, making her turn. "Shut up, Melia," said Bran, who normally didn't say anything at all. "I know you. You would have done it to protect someone *you* love, too. Leave the woman be."

Melia glared at both of them, then turned and stalked out of the room. Aelfdane trailed behind.

Ignoring the outburst, Niall glanced around the dingy apartment. "Nice place."

"It's not the Plaza, but it's got a good view of the Black Tower from the deck," Ronan answered. He was standing near the patio doors, gazing out over the city. "Better yet, Gideon and the Summer Queen have no idea we're here or that the book is here."

A scratching sound on metal came from the other side of the door and all the hair rose on the back of Niall's neck. Everyone turned to stare at the door, silent, as the creepy scratching echoed through the room.

Niall glanced at Ronan. "Are you sure about that?"

"I was until now."

The scratching continued, but now a long, lonely howl accompanied it.

"What in the Netherworld is that?" Emmaline whispered, her hand going for a knife that was lying on the dining room table.

"Sounds like a dog," Niall said as he, Aeric, and Ronan inched toward the door.

The scratching came again.

Niall took the opposite side of the door from Ronan and Aeric, a charm ready on his tongue that could wallop the piss out of just about anyone. He nodded at Aeric, who opened the door.

In bounded two sleek black hounds, Blix and Taliesin. They were the dogs who led the Wild Hunt every night. The hounds went to the center of the room and turned in circles, whining. Niall dropped his hands to his sides, staring, unbelieving that the hounds had come to them ... and not to Gabriel, head of the Wild Hunt.

"But it's broad daylight," said Emmaline. "And why did they come here? Why didn't they go to ..." her voice trailed off, and she looked toward the Black Tower.

Aeric looked at Niall, his face grim. Clearly all of them had the same worry.

Lex cawed in agitation and lifted off from Bran's shoulder to find a perch on a nearby bookshelf, leaving his wings spread to make himself look bigger in front of the dogs. Bran went to the hounds and knelt, cooing at them and rubbing them behind their ears. "They don't know why they're here and they're confused. They sense something is amiss in the city, and they don't know where their master is." Bran looked up at them. "They shouldn't be here now. Danu has her hand in this."

The hounds both seemed to catch sight of Elizabeth at the same time and went to her, whining. They licked her face and pushed their noses under her arm, as if trying to wake her. Elizabeth roused, her eyes coming open, and Niall went to her side, kneeling.

"Elizabeth?"

Her eyes fluttered open and she winced. "Oh, sweet Lady, that hurts."

Niall kissed her forehead. "Lots going on, love. Can you shift to your water self and heal?"

She hesitated, as if taking stock of her injury, then nodded. "I think so." In a moment, she was gone. In the next moment, she was back, naked and gorgeous on the couch.

Niall glanced at the men. "Uh. Avert your eyes, please."

Elizabeth pulled the blanket that lay over the back of the couch across her body. "Sorry! I didn't know there was anyone else in the room." Niall looked at her leg, bloody and wounded only moments ago, now smooth, unmarred, and beautiful.

He held her gaze for a long moment. "I thought maybe I'd lost you."

She glanced away from him, as if unable to look him in the eye. "I'll be fine. Thanks for your help."

Bella brought Elizabeth a pair of jeans. "I packed a few things before I left the tower. I think we're about the same size."

Elizabeth stood with the blanket around her and took the jeans, thanking Bella. Then she gathered the rest of her clothes and ducked into the bathroom to change. When she emerged, she glanced at everyone in turn, clearly not quite sure of the welcome she was going to receive. She'd been knocked out cold and had woken in a room filled with people she probably thought hated her.

Blix and Taliesin trotted up to her, and she knelt, scratching them behind the ears. "I just want to tell everyone that I'm sorry I tried to keep you from gaining your freedom. It was selfish of me. Even my mother, the person I was trying to save, thinks so." She paused, rubbing Blix behind a sleek black ear and not looking at any of them. "I was scared—I *am* scared—to lose someone I love, and I did a stupid thing to prevent it."

The room plunged into silence. The muscles in Elizabeth's shoulders tightened.

"I'll leave right now," she said, rising. "I need to find my mother before—Anyway, it's better if I go." She turned toward the door, and Niall's stomach lurched. He didn't want her go. Not now, not ever.

He took a step toward her, but Bran interrupted him.

"Anyone Blix and Taliesin likes, I like," said Bran. "They're excellent judges of character."

Emmaline twined her hand with Aeric's and smiled at her. "I get why you did it, Elizabeth. I think most everyone in this room gets it, except maybe Melia."

Elizabeth spread her hands. "I won't stand in your way any longer. My mother has accepted her fate, now I need to learn to do the same."

"That sucks," said Ronan.

"Yeah." She gave a bitter laugh. "It really does."

Just then something rocked the building, making everyone stumble to the side. Immediately the hunt hounds began to howl. The explosion quieted, but continued, sounding like a low growl in the distance.

"What the hell was that?" breathed Elizabeth at Niall.

Realization slammed into him. "The tower." He raced to the patio door with everyone behind him. Back in the apartment, the hunt hounds lifted their noses to the sky and bayed.

Twenty-five

SNOW fell in big, fat flakes from a heavy gray sky, obscuring their vision. The deck was rusty and unstable, so they lingered in the doorway. In the distance, they could make out the tower with its four turrets, lights flickering on and off in the windows.

Another blast of magick shook Piefferburg City, feeling like a nuclear explosion. Wind radiated out from the blast site, buffeting their hair. The amount of magick used stung the back of Niall's throat, choking him.

The lights in the tower flickered, and then the whole tower plunged into darkness. Everything went silent and still. Not one of them on the deck of the apartment building breathed. Mixing in with the snow, corrupting it, were dark flakes of charcoal and soot from something burning.

A great crack echoed through the city . . . and the Black Tower collapsed.

Heedless of the creaky deck, Niall stepped forward and gripped the cold metal of the balcony railing, leaning forward, not believing what he was seeing and hearing. The tower that he'd watched be erected, piece by magicked black quartz piece, was now imploding into rubble in Piefferburg Square.

The rumbling stopped, and all was quiet. Smoke blossomed like some flower from hell in the place where the tower had stood. More soot and ash wafted through the air toward them, mixing with the snow.

No one said a word. There was nothing to say. All of them were stunned.

All of them were worried about Aislinn and Gabriel.

In the distance a black shape grew larger, flying toward them. Elizabeth gripped his upper arm. "What is that?"

"It's Abastor!" Bran yelled.

In a moment they saw it was true. The shape took the form of a great black horse, Abastor, the horse that led the Wild Hunt. On top of it were Queen Aislinn and King Gabriel.

Abastor drew up beside the deck, and Niall helped Aislinn off the back of the horse and over the railing, pushing her quickly into the apartment. Her dress was ripped and scorched in places; her hair had come loose from its chignon and hung tangled around her shoulders. Gabriel didn't look much better.

Niall held out a hand to Gabriel. "You two know how to make an entrance."

Gabriel climbed over, and Abastor flew away. His expression was grim. "Did you see the tower go?"

"We saw," Aeric answered. "Round one goes to the unholy alliance."

"What about the happy couple?" Niall asked. "With any luck they're buried at the base."

Aislinn shook her head. "There was a hell of a fight. They're still loose in the city, but I think they're split up."

"And Kolbjorn?" asked Kieran.

Expression grim, Aislinn gave her head a sharp shake.

"We all had to run when the tower started to collapse," said Gabriel. "The Phaendir and the National Guard have opened the gates. It's a full-on invasion."

"It's also noon." Niall glanced into the apartment, where the book was lying on a table, guarded against Elizabeth by Melia and Aelfdane. "Let's make sure we win round two."

"MOVE it," growled the Shadow Guard behind Liam, pushing him toward Piefferburg Square. Liam coughed from the dust and soot. A few moments ago they'd witnessed something thought impossible—the fall of the Black Tower. It was noon, but it looked like midnight in the square from all the smoke.

The Summer Queen and Gideon were somewhere gloating right now.

The tower had begun to collapse just as the rest of the prisoners were being brought up. They'd waited until everyone had been evacuated from the building until they cleared the scum from the dungeons.

Originally, Liam had had three Shadow Guards herding him out of the Black Tower, but two of them had been lost in the chaos.

"Move it!" the guard bellowed, pushing him forward again with his charmed iron sword, the handle biting into the small of his back. Liam stumbled forward, the iron links of the cuffs around his wrists jangling as he caught himself on the base of the statue of Jules Piefferburg, founder and architect of the place.

All around him, fae keened.

The tower behind them was just a smoking ruin. The building had collapsed in on itself, making a tidy, tall pile of rubble where it had formerly stood, but debris and dust scattered a wide perimeter.

The guard grunted and swore, pissed that Liam had halted for a moment to catch his balance. The handle of the sword connected with Liam's back again, making pain blossom. Anger rose in the pit of his stomach, fast consuming him. He lowered his head and gritted his teeth. It was past time he got rid of this gobshite.

Feigning a coughing fit, he doubled over. The guard shifted impatiently. Liam pivoted on the balls of his feet, bringing his hands in a swooping arc straight into the guard's jaw.

Blood flew from the guard's mouth as the cuffs made solid contact. He staggered to the side and fell under the weight of his armor.

Liam jumped on the guard, swinging his hands again and hitting the man in the cheekbone. He felt the split of meaty flesh and the crack of bone. The man went limp beneath him.

Breathing hard, his hair in his eyes, Liam searched for the keys to the cuffs quickly. The fae around him were watching the spectacle—his was just one more act of violence in a city run rampant with it—but he didn't trust someone not to be a hero. Once he'd found the keys, he grabbed the guard's sword and lurched off into the shadows before someone could try.

Once his cuffs were off, he rubbed the back of his hand across his soot-smeared forehead. Every inch of him was covered in the ash of the tower. If he was a poetic man, which he wasn't normally, he might think of death and the cremation of a body.

Kneeling in the debris and coughing on the dust, he worked his hands through the scattered rubble and pressed his palms to the cold cobblestones of the square. Magick radiated through him as he searched for Gideon. Where had the fecker gone?

Immediately he had a lock on his location, since he wasn't far. Dragging the sword behind him, Liam pushed up and stumbled through the smoky, snowy air toward him, dodging onlookers who were covering their mouths with their sleeves and walking around looking stunned.

In the distance he could hear skirmishes—fighting and the sounds of gunfire. He'd heard someone say that the gates had been opened to the Phaendir. From the sounds of it, that was definitely possible.

He made his way around to the far end of the square, dodging a slavering sluagh, who snapped at him as he passed. He didn't even need magick to find Gideon. All he needed to do was follow the trail of frustrated, bloodthirsty goblins and sluagh. They roamed this area like lions denied their prey, confused and befuddled by the protection magick that surrounded the Phaendir and the Summer Queen.

Liam would love to see their protective shields fail—how fast they'd become goblin food.

Finally he made out the group of cloaked Phaendir. They were standing in a little clump, murmuring under their breath and swaying back and forth. His steps faltered. Liam had lived almost a century and it was one of the creepiest things he'd ever had the misfortune to see.

Gideon stood not far away, talking to more Phaendir, Liam guessed. So, it was true, the Phaendir had entered the city full force. The Summer Queen was nowhere to be seen. If the bitch was under the rubble, Liam wouldn't cry for her.

"So you're not dead," said Gideon, catching sight of him.

"Yeah, neither are you." *More's the pity.* "Where's the book?"

"Not in my possession." Gideon ground the words out.

"Where's the queen?"

"Off to find the book, I suppose. I don't know. I'm not her fucking keeper."

"Huh." Liam considered him. His suit was ripped and dirty. Soot covered his face and all exposed skin. His thinning brown hair was sticking up all over the place. He looked like he'd been through hell and back. "Aren't you a little worried about what comes next?"

"What do you mean?" he snarled and motioned at the tower. "We took down the damned Black Tower!"

"Yeah." He paused. "But I doubt the book was in there when it fell." Even now the Unseelie queen could be somewhere in the city, working the spell. "Where's the book, Gideon?"

"I don't know where the fucking book is," Gideon snarled into his face.

Liam snarled back, "Then what fecking good are you?" then whirled and stalked away.

Behind him came the sound of snapping jaws, growling and screaming. Liam turned, hoping to see the sluagh tearing into the archdirector, but it was the goblins and sluagh tearing into a group of arriving Phaendir instead. Guess they didn't have any of those nifty shields.

Liam glanced back to see Gideon watching placidly as the creatures ripped his men apart. Maybe he didn't want to waste the power it would take to protect them. Maybe Gideon just wanted to see them die. Liam didn't know and didn't care. It appeared it was up to him to find the book and stop this mess.

Kneeling, the sound of death behind him fading to the sounds of eating, Liam plunged his hands into the carnage of the Black Tower and concentrated on the Unseelie Queen. Wherever he found Aislinn, he would find the book.

TWENTY-SIX

THE Book of Bindings lay on the table in the small apartment in *ceantar dubh* and the clock said high noon, though the dark skies outside made it look closer to midnight.

Aislinn opened the book, and all the air seemed to leave the room for a moment. The Shadow Royals and their advisors stood around the table, while Elizabeth hung back, clearly not feeling as though she had a role to play here.

Niall kept glancing at her. Her face appeared stony, expressionless—resigned. She kept glancing past the patio doors, wondering, perhaps, where her mother had gone, wondering if Thea was all right.

She'd tried to leave to find her mother, but Niall had pointed out the obvious—Elizabeth had no idea where she was and it was a big city, full of fighting and chaos. It was too late. What a load of sorrow was that?

Thea was going to die alone.

Elizabeth went to stand by the patio doors, hugging herself and looking out at the dirty, soot-smoked city. The beauty was gone, and all that was left was ashes.

"It's time." Aislinn flipped past all the mysterious spells to the back of the book, where the grooves for the *bosca fadbh* guarded the locked portion. Taking the key from Gabriel's fingers, she slid it into the grooves. No fanfare or grand pronouncements this time. All grim business.

They held their breath.

Nothing happened.

Aislinn frowned and glanced out the window. "It said it would work when the sun was at its highest point in the sky and no shadows marred the land. Shadows definitely mar the land. Maybe . . ."

"Aw, holy fucking—" Niall began.

Light exploded from the book in a flash so bright, they all turned away to shield their eyes. The flash was so brilliant it probably spilled from all the windows and doors of the apartment, lighting the building like a Roman candle.

Not exactly discreet.

The light faded, and they all looked down at the book. The *bosca fadbh* was gone. What remained was a single sheet of velum with swooping golden writing in the same strange, ancient language that the instructions had been written in. Maybe it was the language of the ancients. Whatever it was, it was old. When a fae couldn't remember what something was or where it came from, that meant *really* old—older than humanity, older than the dinosaurs.

Niall leaned over, trying to understand what it said. After a moment, the words flowed into his head even though he still couldn't read the text. "These words are meant to free the bound, should this spell, once lost, be found."

Aislinn took a step back from the book, her face pale.

"What's wrong?" asked Gabriel.

She motioned at the book. "We have no idea what this spell will actually do. This book was created before time was recorded. Why should it work for our specific circumstances? What if we speak this magick and it makes things even worse than they already are?"

"We've been working toward this moment for years, Aislinn," said Gabriel. "We can't ignore this power."

Niall stared at the book, then glanced at his brother, Ronan. "Ronan and I are familiar with this type of spell. I think the book is meant to fashion itself based on the immediate needs of the owner of the *bosca fadbh*. *These words are meant to free the bound* . . . our most pressing problem is being bound and this magick will free us. Would you agree with that, Ronan?"

Ronan took a step closer to the book. "We can't know for certain, but I think Niall is right. If the Phaendir had been in possession of the *bosca fadbh* and opened the back of the book, the spell revealed may well have destroyed the fae."

Aislinn hugged herself. "So let's be happy the Phaendir didn't get the book and take our chances with it, right?"

"Right," said Gabriel.

Aislinn stepped toward the book. "Let's do it, then." She picked up the sheer, iridescent sheet of paper and steadied herself. All of them moved in closer to her. Niall wasn't sure why he felt the urge to be closer to Aislinn and the book, he just did. He suspected everyone felt the pull. Even Elizabeth rose from her perch on the armrest of the couch and took a step or two closer to the group, her face now animated with curiosity, her bright green-gold eyes shining and wide.

Aislinn scanned the text. After a moment, she began to read in a foreign language that none of them recognized. Tendrils of magick reached out and caught each of them, drew them closer and held them in thrall, like a tractor beam. Somewhere deep within Niall, a compulsion to join in with Aislinn tickled at him, growing more and more intense.

One by one, each of the fae circling the table joined in with Aislinn, chanting words that were strange to their minds and their tongues without even reading the text. Niall felt suddenly cemented in place, the tendrils curling around him, through him. He tried to move and found he couldn't.

Just as all of them, except Elizabeth, were locked in and chanting, the door burst open, practically ripped from its hinges. The free fae, Liam, stood in the doorway in all his enormous glory, chest heaving, body, face, and hair black with soot, and looking pissed as hell.

Oh, good, and just when none of them could move to defend themselves or the book.

TWENTY-SEVEN

OUT of the corner of Niall's eye, he watched Liam take a half second to orient himself and spot the book. Immediately the man seemed to realize the magick held all of them in thrall—and made them defenseless.

Now he understood why it was called the Book of Bindings.

In a heartbeat Liam was headed toward them, clearly intending to snatch the paper from Aislinn's hands. Aislinn tensed, but she was locked in by the magick from the book and helpless to stop him.

Out of nowhere, Elizabeth grabbed the poker from the fireplace tools and swung with a battle cry, catching Liam in the head.

Liam bellowed in surprise and pain, staggering backward, blood gushing from a huge cut in his forehead. He stood for a moment, looking dazed, and pressed his hand to the wound that had bloomed like a red flower. Niall thought maybe he'd pass out, but his confusion cleared and his gaze focused on Elizabeth.

Brutal intention transforming his face, he lunged at her. "You bitch! I spared you back at the cabin!"

All of the muscles in Niall's stomach tightened and he strained to free himself from the magick that held him, but it was like being caught in cement. Liam was ten times Elizabeth's size. And even though Niall knew—better than anyone—how fast and how hard she was to catch, he feared for her with every fiber of his being.

Elizabeth darted away, coming around behind the bigger man quicker than he could track and whopped him in the back with the poker. Liam bellowed again, this time in rage more than pain and grabbed for her. She ducked out of the way just in time, looking like a rabbit avoiding the swipe of a bear's paw.

As she squatted to avoid the sweep of his hand, she brought the poker around, right into the back of his knees. Liam went down with a grunt.

They were nearing the end of the spell; Niall could feel it in his bones. The tendrils of magick tightened harder, and soon he couldn't even move his eyes. All he could hear was the sound of the fight between Elizabeth and Liam under the drone of the indecipherable words pouring from their mouths.

Out of the corner of his eye, Niall saw Liam grab Elizabeth from behind and try to pin her arms down, but she thrust her elbows back, catching him in the solar plexus, twisted free of him as he *ooofed*, and brought the poker around to smack him in the side of the head.

Liam collapsed to his knees, blood coating his face.

Lady, he was getting spanked. Niall guessed he shouldn't be worrying for Elizabeth—he should be worried for Liam.

The building shook under a blast of power. The floor moved beneath their feet. Dust and drywall fell from the ceiling and walls.

Oh, goody, looked like Gideon had arrived.

THE floor lurched sickeningly under Elizabeth's feet. She tried not to fall off balance, her gaze cemented on Liam, who'd collapsed to his knees, stunned from his latest bash to the head. *Stay down, stay down,* she chanted in her head.

The metal of the poker felt hot in her hand as she gripped it tightly. Her muscles ached from moving so fast to avoid Liam, and her breath came in pants from the exertion.

Slowly Liam pushed to his feet, looking pissed as hell and creepy as anything with the blood running down his face, mixing with the soot. "Why are you doing this, Elizabeth? Help me." He motioned toward the book. "This is our chance! We can save the people we love."

Elizabeth hesitated, glancing toward the book. Suddenly the poker felt heavy in her hands. For one dark, dangerous moment, she almost put it down.

She shook her head, forcibly moving her gaze away from temptation. "No. What's done is done. This is meant to be, for the good of all fae." *Minus one.*

Liam brought his meaty fist toward her head, but she darted away, bringing her poker around like a fighting staff and smacking him in the back. It made him grunt, but not much more. The man was a locomotive.

He advanced on her, and she backed toward the open patio doors. Liam wanted the book, the others were in no shape to prevent him from getting it, and her luck wasn't going to hold out forever. She needed to get Liam gone *right now*. She was pretty sure Gideon was below them on the street, so luring Liam out onto the creaky, ancient deck was either stupid or brilliant, but one thing was for sure—it was her only shot.

"You and I want the same thing, Liam," she said, holding the poker in her hand and backing up slowly. "I feel for you. I really, *really* do, but we can't always get what we want."

"Stop fighting me, Elizabeth. Help me get the book. There's still time to stop this. We can save your mother."

"And then what? Gideon gets the book? What happens then? Would my mother want that, your wife? Would they even survive if that happened? Maybe we'd all be dead."

He shook his head. The blood from the gash in his head had slowed, but coated his face and his hair red. "I would never give that snake anything."

Another blast of magick shook the building, making it sway. A crack sounded and two of the walls in the living room began to fracture. The place was going to go down just like the Black Tower . . . and soon.

Her heart lurched into her throat . . . *Niall.* She drew a steadying breath. *One thing at a time, Elizabeth.*

She stumbled to the side, catching herself on the doorway

of the deck, then darted through, luring Liam out. The deck groaned under his additional weight, and Elizabeth noticed it had a slant it hadn't had before.

Liam had heart, but he wasn't all that smart. After righting himself from the most recent blast of power, he followed her.

Of course, seeing the scene in the street below, Elizabeth doubted her own powers of deduction. Gideon stood below with the Phaendir fanned out around him. Ranging the area were the sluagh and goblins, snapping their jaws and growling.

Dear Lady, she was taking a huge chance.

Her stomach did a slow flip as Gideon's brown eyes focused on her and Liam on the deck. "All the exits are guarded. You're trapped. Throw the book out to me or I'll level the building with everyone in it. You have exactly one minute."

"Never, Gideon," Elizabeth called. "We'll die before we hand the book over to you!"

Gideon shrugged. "Fine. I'll pick the book out of the rubble." Then he raised his hand and sent a blast of magick at the already shaky deck.

Elizabeth had one moment to lock gazes with Liam. A part of her felt kindred to him, joined in mutual desire. A part of her regretted this deeply.

Liam's eyes widened, the drying blood on his face cracking grotesquely. *"My wife."*

Then the deck gave way and they fell through space.

Right before she hit the ground, Elizabeth gave over to her water self. She collided with the cobblestones with a splash instead of a squish.

It took every ounce of her ability to draw in, gathering her water self from such a hard hit, and sink into the stone, finding a way to travel through the ground, away from Gideon and his bloodthirsty Phaendir.

Above her she sensed Liam—cold and broken on the street, *gone*.

This time for sure.

Deep within her normally detached water self, sorrow niggled. The tiny part of her that remained emotional wished it could have gone another way.

The rest of her focused on a man named Niall. Worry blossomed, growing more and more intense.

* * *

GIDEON'S body hummed as he released a shot of power toward the deck where Elizabeth and Liam stood with a lazy flick of his wrist. Neither of them was any good to him anymore.

The deck collapsed, and the sickening sound of Liam's body thumping to the street could be heard along with the groan, creaks, and crashing of the metal and wood. The asrai transformed midair, leaving only her clothing to flutter to the street.

Oh, well, at least he'd gotten one of them.

Liam lay mangled in the wreckage, twisted in ways no human or fae body ever should be. He hadn't escaped death this time.

Gideon turned his attention to the structure. He'd wanted the book, but it looked like the only way he was going to get it was by pulling it from the destroyed structure. So be it. He knew they were in there opening it. He'd seen the flash of light. He had no time to waste.

Channeling all his available power, sucking the cadre of brothers dry of their power—he drew a deep breath and savored it for just a moment. Then, smiling, he released it.

The building imploded.

TWENTY-EIGHT

THE screech and crash of the building exploding blew Niall's eardrums. At the same time the deathly blast of magick hit the structure, the Book of Bindings flashed in another blinding display of power.

Deaf and blind, Niall hurtled backward.

He expected to hit things. Painfully. Bloodily. Bone-breakingly. But nothing stopped his dark, quiet fall into nothingness. Were the rest of them experiencing this strange plummeting sensation?

Was this what death was like?

Would he meet Elizabeth in the Netherworld, or had she escaped her fall from the apartment's deck? Maybe in the Netherworld they could finally be together—there would be no *bosca fadbh* between them, no hard decisions, no putting anything before each other and their love.

Niall got no answers. He only continued to plummet.

LIGHT flashed just as the building exploded. Gideon's heart-beat stuttered for a moment as he considered he may have been too late.

Too late.

He'd been too late eliminating Brother Maddoc. Too late discovering Emmaline's treachery. Too late with his phone call to stop Charlotte.

Too fucking late.

Then the building collapsed in on itself with a horrible, deafening sound. Dust rose. All became quiet. In the wreckage, not a creature stirred. Nothing lived. No magickal book threatened.

Gideon let out a pent-up breath of relief.

He immediately checked within the recesses of his mind for the space he shared with his brothers. There he found strong magick, pulsing and bright. He also found the power that built the walls of Piefferburg; it remained impenetrable and unyielding. Gideon smiled, sweet satisfaction filling him.

Not too late. *He'd won.*

Labrai had been with him. He turned, joy pouring through his body, pumping his fist in the air at the hooded Phaendir behind him. "All praise Him!"

Their circumspect demeanor broke, and they cheered. "All praise Him!"

The book was under the rubble among the bodies, theirs for the taking. The Shadow Queen was dead. The . . .

Gideon's smile faded. If the Shadow Queen was dead, the sluagh should be gone and the goblins should be leaving him and his brothers alone. Yet the sluagh was still a slavering presence around him and the goblins roamed, snapping hungrily at all the Phaendir they couldn't reach.

He turned and considered the rubble, cocking his head to one side. The Shadow Queen, somehow, some way, was still alive in all that mess.

Perhaps Labrai wasn't with him at all.

Gideon blinked.

It was just a seed of an idea, like a tiny sliver under his skin, but it was poisonous seed, a *deadly* sliver. It spread infection. Gideon's nostrils flared. He tried to put the tiny doubt from his mind, but it wouldn't go. It was like trying to will a drop of poison from his bloodstream, but all it did was travel straight to his heart.

He'd done all this. He'd broken into Piefferburg, allied with the Summer Queen, channeled more Phaendir hive magick than any of them could ever remember an archdirector channeling, and he'd blown this building up when he'd known—*known*—the Shadow Queen, her flunkies, and the book were all inside.

He'd thought he'd won.

Yet she lived on.

He remembered thinking before he'd entered Piefferburg that no one but Labrai, Himself, would stop him from achieving his goal. Labrai had stopped him. The defeat of the fae was not His will.

Labrai was not with him. This time he was sure.

Gideon stumbled back, hand to his head. What was going on? Why was he having these doubts? He never had doubt, not where his god was concerned.

Labrai was not with him. Labrai did not want this. Perhaps Gideon had been working against his god's will this entire time.

Or perhaps Labrai didn't exist at all.

Gideon turned to regard his brothers, who stood in a clump not looking as celebratory as they had a moment ago. They shared a hive mind, and it was possible that one little seed of unease in his brain had grown roots and spread like an ivy of doom.

"No," Gideon whispered. That couldn't be allowed. It was their faith in Labrai—*their faith*—that kept the walls up around Piefferburg.

If their faith faltered, they would lose their ability to imprison the fae.

Gideon turned to the destroyed building with a start of realization. This was the doing of the Book of Bindings. This was magick affecting him now. He *had* been too late.

His god had deserted him wholly and utterly.

Gideon closed his eyes and raised his hands to the sky. "Oh, Labrai, Father of us all, give us strength in our time of need. Deliver us from this threat in our midst. Everything I do, I have done it in Your name, oh, great Father . . ."

Nothing. Silence.

Labrai doesn't exist. You're praying to no one.

It was a whisper in his mind, a sickening breeze blowing through his consciousness.

"Labrai!" Gideon fell to his knees, the rubble from the collapsed building digging in, slicing his skin open and making blood run. "Hear me! Shine Your light upon us. Hear our cries!"

Silence. The Phaendir behind him moaned, and Gideon scrabbled in his mind, searching for the place where their consciousnesses met. Coldness touched his skin.

The walls were wavering.

Gideon leapt to his feet and whirled. "No, my brothers, we cannot allow this. Hold fast, hold strong!" He glanced around at the sluagh and goblins. The monsters seemed to sense that the Phaendir were troubled and that maybe, just maybe, the magick that protected them was faltering.

One of the hooded Phaendir stepped toward him, arms outstretched. "Labrai has forsaken us."

"No! It's an illusion! It's only faery magick! We can fight through this! Labrai is with us!"

But even he didn't feel the truth in those words.

Gideon lowered his arms as his Phaendir brethren turned, wandering away from him, looking abandoned. In that moment, he knew it was lost. Everything was lost. The small niggle that Gideon could feel of their shared hive mind blipped out of existence, just like one might turn off a television.

The barriers collapsed.

The sluagh and the goblins descended on the Phaendir in a pack. Snarling. Ripping. Screaming. It happened all over the city. Blood flowed and gobbets of flesh and slivers of bone flew.

Gideon watched, uncomprehending, then fell to his knees once more. This time not in supplication to his god, but in despair.

He screamed as the sluagh and goblins descended on him. Claws shredded his suit, left bloody furrows in his skin that reminded him of the marks left by his cat-o'-nine-tails. Teeth ripped into his arms and legs, tearing away chunks.

The last things Gideon saw were the alien mouths of the sluagh chewing his flesh, snarling around mouthfuls at each other for their share of the feeding.

TWENTY-NINE

"NIALL!" Elizabeth re-formed, gasping his name.

She pushed up from the cobblestones and glanced around, seeing she wasn't far from Piefferburg Square. All the stores had been looted, their doors thrown open and their front windows smashed.

Her heart stuttering with panic for those she cared about, she darted into a vandalized clothing boutique and helped herself, carefully noting the name of the place and vowing to send money to the owner for the things she took.

She quickly dressed in a pair of jeans, a heavy black cable-knit sweater, and a pair of boots, then hurried through the side streets to the square. The fastest way back to Niall was cutting through the heart of the city to reach the *ceantar dubh.*

All around her people were screaming that the walls were broken, the fae were free! But others were yelling that the Phaendir were loose in the city, the Shadow Queen was dead, and all was lost. Everything had devolved into total chaos, and she didn't know what was true.

The only thing she knew was that she needed to find Niall and her mother.

Concern for both of them tightened her stomach and made

her chest ache. Never in her life had she been so worried. She really hoped that Niall and the others had managed to escape before Gideon had taken the place down.

But she doubted they'd had time.

The thought of Niall being crushed in a pile of rubble broke something deep inside her.

"You bastard," she muttered as she pushed past a group of fae who were fleeing in the other direction. How dare he make her love him? How dare he make her care so much?

A tall water fae with blue-tinged skin stopped, grabbed her by the shoulders, and shook her. "The walls are coming down!" The woman's eyes were shiny with excitement. "I can't believe it! We're finally free!"

In her head it sounded like, *Your mother is somewhere choking to death all alone.*

Elizabeth glowered at the water fae for a moment, then pushed past her. The next person who grabbed her and yelled in her face was going to get smacked. Forcing her way through the half-celebrating, half-fleeing throng, she continued on.

Near the statue of Jules Piefferburg, someone grabbed her by the shoulder. She rounded on the person, a diatribe ready on her tongue. As soon as she saw Niall's face, her scowl turned to joy.

She threw herself into his arms. "Sweet Lady, Niall, I'm so happy to see you! I worried that building . . . *Gideon.*" Her words trailed off and she fell silent, gripping him as hard as she could, tears pricking her eyes and emotions clogging the back of her throat. "I thought you were dead."

He cupped the back of her head and held her close, murmuring into her hair, "And I thought you hated me."

She pushed away from him. He didn't have a mark on him, not even a spot of soot or rubble. "I wish I did. It would make things easier. What happened? Have the walls fallen like everyone is saying? What's going on?"

Niall shrugged. "My guess is as good as yours. All I know is one minute we're chanting the spell from the Book of Bindings and Gideon is outside slamming the building with Phaendir juice. Next thing I know the building explodes, I'm falling into nothingness, then, *pop*, we all show up here in the middle of the square. Me, Bella, Bran, Aeric . . . everyone. Even Blix, Taliesin, and Bran's stupid crow."

He motioned to his right, and Elizabeth saw the Shadow Queen, Gabriel, and everyone else. The Shadow Queen had begun collecting a crowd of fae from every social stratum, all looking for leadership.

She frowned at him. "What happened to the book? To Gideon?"

He shrugged again. "The book is gone. The Phaendir also appear to be gone, or at least scattered. Literally." He paused, wincing. "We keep finding pieces of them everywhere."

"No one knows what happened?"

"Not for sure. The fae who were near the building in the *ceantar dubh* say that after the building collapsed, the Phaendir began wailing about how Labrai had deserted them, then Gideon's barriers gave way and the sluagh and goblins broke through."

Elizabeth swallowed hard and hugged herself. "That means it's true. The walls have fallen."

"We haven't seen any Phaendir around that are, well, whole. If there are no Phaendir—"

"There are no walls." Cold fear fisted in her stomach. Where was her mother?

"I didn't understand the words of the spell we chanted, but Aislinn says she did. She says the spell in the back of the Book of Bindings created a mental illusion for the Phaendir. Essentially, it took away the Phaendir's faith in Labrai long enough for them lose their hold on the wall. She thinks when they lost the power of their hive mind and their protective magick, that's when the sluagh and goblins moved in."

She looked around, still seeing the sluagh wandering. "But the sluagh is still here." A seed of hope for her mother bloomed. "If—"

Niall shook his head. "The Summer Queen is still alive. They're waiting for her protective shields to falter."

"Oh."

"I'm sorry."

"I wish you would stop saying that."

"I wish I had other words to use. Better ones." He pulled her against him and wrapped his warm, strong arms around her. She closed her eyes. "I don't."

"Elizabeth! Niall!" It was the Shadow Queen's voice.

They turned to find the crowd in front of the Unseelie Queen part, everyone looking at them. The only person Elizabeth saw was Thea, who stood at the base of the statue. The moment Elizabeth recognized her, she broke away from Niall and ran toward her. "Mom!"

She came to a skidding halt, flying into her mother's arms. Thea embraced her, holding her close. It took everything for Elizabeth not to sob. Her mother didn't need that extra emotional weight on her right now. She had more than enough to bear as it was.

"Elizabeth," her mother whispered. "The walls have fallen. I can feel it." There was happiness in her voice instead of the grief and fear she would have expected.

Elizabeth raised her head and took a step backward. Her mouth worked, but she couldn't think of a thing to say.

Her mother's gaze met hers and there was sadness there. "It's time. The sprae are starting to leave."

A moment later Elizabeth's eye was caught by a twinkling. Elizabeth looked around her, staring into the sky. Lights flickered and twinkled all over the city as the sprae rose. She backed away, turning in a circle. "No," Elizabeth breathed. "Don't go." Fisting her hands at her sides until her fingers ached, she watched helplessly as they went no matter her wishes on the subject.

Oh, sweet Lady, this is not fair.

Her mother came to stand beside her, watching them leave.

A strong hand squeezed her shoulder. She looked up to see that Niall was there, with a hand not only on her shoulder, but one on Thea's as well.

Shoving off his touch, she whirled. "You don't get to be here, Niall. This is your fault."

The accusation wasn't fair and she knew it, but she needed her anger right now. Rage rose up within her and she embraced it, wrapped herself in it like armor. It was better than feeling grief and fear, better than the dread of the certainty she was about to watch her mother die right in front of her.

Thea bristled. "Stop it, Elizabeth! You're making things worse than they need to be."

She turned toward her mother, fighting tears. "I'm not the type to just accept the inevitable."

"You are a fighter, but you have to know when to bend during winds of change. If you can't bend, you're going to snap in two. Everything changes, my girl. You have to learn to let go." Thea looked at Niall. "You'll be there to catch her, won't you, Niall? You love her. I can see that. No matter what she says, what accusations she hurls, *you love her.*"

Niall's gaze had fastened on Elizabeth's face. "More than anything."

"She loves you, too," Thea answered. "Don't let her run away from you."

Niall smiled, his face softening and his eyes filling with love. Elizabeth's resolve wavered. "I don't scare that easy," he said. "Don't worry, Thea."

Elizabeth looked between them. They were ganging up on her, not allowing her the rage that comforted her in the face of what was to come. Thea stood in the middle of the square, the Black Tower smoking behind her, face upturned to the afternoon sky and a small smile playing around her mouth. Snowflakes fell gently onto her cheeks. All around them the sprae rose, like embers of a fire, swirling into the air and taking her life force with her. Still, Thea seemed calm—at peace.

If her mother couldn't be mad at Niall over this . . . how could she?

Elizabeth let out a long, slow breath and closed her eyes. The rage leaked out of her body, little by little. It was like transforming into her water self—giving in, surrendering. Letting go. Flowing.

"Elizabeth."

Her eyes opened to see Thea swaying on her feet. Niall was there, catching her before she fell. He lowered her to the cobblestones.

THIRTY

SHE raced to her mother's side. Thea's breathing was shallow and growing shallower by the minute. Her face had gone pale and her lips were turning blue. Elizabeth took her mother's hand and stared down into her face, teardrops squeezing from her eyes and hitting Thea's cheek.

Thea struggled to take in breaths, suffocating from a lack of life force. She reached up with a pale, shaking hand and cupped Elizabeth's face, then she smiled. "It's all right, Elizabeth. I'll see you again, no time soon . . . but eventually."

Elizabeth smiled down at her, thankful her mother seemed to be at peace with this. "I love you," she whispered. "I'm going to miss you so"—she drew a shaky breath—"*so* much."

Thea took Elizabeth's hand and put it into Niall's. "Not . . . alone," she managed to force out.

Her head fell back onto the cobblestones and her eyes went wide for a moment. She gasped and clutched at her throat, unable to draw any air at all. Then a curious calm overcame her features. Her eyes focused on something neither she nor Niall could see, and her body relaxed. She smiled. Slowly, the light died in her eyes until they were glassy and vacant.

Then she was gone.

Elizabeth rocked back on her heels, pressing her free hand to her mouth. Tears filled her eyes, obscuring her vision. She squeezed them shut and the drops rolled down her cheeks. When Niall extricated his hand from hers, she realized she'd had a circulation-cutting grip on it.

He leaned forward, kissing Thea on her forehead, and then he gently closed her eyelids.

Elizabeth stared up into the sky. The glowing embers of the sprae were nearly gone, just one flitted here or there. Now only snowflakes fell against the gray velvet of the afternoon sky.

Sounds that had seemed to disappear while her mother had died grew louder in her ears. Laughter. Yelling. Gunshots in the distance. The crackle of the fire In the remains of the Black Tower behind them and the magickal efforts of the fae to quench the flames.

"Elizabeth."

She blinked, the numbness slowly turning to pain. "Niall." She didn't know what else to say.

"The Wild Hunt will come for her soon."

"I know." She looked down at her mother's body. A faint smile marked her pale, breathless lips. "She'll be off to the Netherworld to see my father and my brother." She glanced at Niall. "Do you think it was them she was smiling at as she died?"

Niall shrugged. "There are more mysteries in this world than I can explain. Maybe so."

"I want to think that."

He stood and held out his hand to her. "Elizabeth, the walls have fallen. We're free. Will you come with me?"

There was so much more to that question than the obvious.

She stared at his hand. If she took it, she was committing herself to him. She would be forgetting the past and forging a new future . . . in a new world. She would be leaving the *bosca fadbh* behind, his decisions behind, her decisions behind. She would be forgiving him for leading her mother to the queen . . . and, as an extension, to her death.

Forgiveness of the past. Forging a new future together.

Could she do it? Did she love him enough? She looked up into his face and saw the note of fear and uncertainty in his expression. He was worried that she would walk away from him right now. Her heart swelled as she looked into his eyes.

She was done walking away from this man.

Reaching up, she took his hand and let him help her to her feet. She cupped his face in her hands and held his gaze. "I love you, Niall."

Niall's face crumbled in a rush of emotion, and he dragged her up against his chest, burying his nose in her hair. "I love you, too, Elizabeth. More than I've ever loved anyone." He cupped her face between his hands and kissed her hard. She tasted teardrops on her tongue and wasn't sure if they were hers or his. "I want you to be with me always."

She kissed him, her tongue skating into his mouth to meet his. Breaking the deep kiss, she feathered her lips across his and breathed against his mouth, "I want that, too. Let's leave this place behind."

Leave all of it behind.

"Elizabeth?"

She turned in Niall's arms at the sound of the queen's voice. Aislinn's face held a gentle expression. "I'm so very sorry you've lost your mother. She wants you to know that she's fine and she loves you."

Elizabeth stiffened, then remembered that Aislinn was a necromancer, able to communicate with the dead once they'd passed.

"She's here with us right now," the queen continued, "waiting for the Wild Hunt." Aislinn smiled. "Honestly, she seems excited about what happens next. None of us know, you know. Not a necromancer like me or even the leader of the Wild Hunt."

Elizabeth gazed out over the square, feeling the warm presence of her mother's soul at her side, and watched the fae. They were no longer fleeing or screaming. Now they all celebrated, jumping around, laughing, and dancing. Even the human soldiers who had been there to keep the peace had thrown down their weapons and seemed to be having a blast, fear forgotten. The *Faemous* crew roamed the area, interviewing excited fae who yelled and laughed into the camera.

For the first time since the Summer Queen had come to her with the pieces, Elizabeth could see beauty in Piefferburg.

She twined her hand with Niall's. Yes, what the queen said

was true on more than one level. None of them knew what came next.

A sparkling caught her attention and she looked down at her feet to see her mother's body shimmering with an internal light. "What's happening?" she asked, stepping away.

Aislinn was quiet for a moment, speaking, Elizabeth presumed, with her mother's disembodied soul. "The sprae are no longer here to maintain her physical structure, so it's disintegrating."

Elizabeth knew that the body at her feet was not her mother; her mother's soul was standing right next to her, after all. Still, even though the disintegration was a beautiful shimmering, sparkling event, Elizabeth choked on a bubble of grief as her mother's body turned to ash,

Niall pulled her toward him and shielded her face as a brilliant flash of light enveloped them. When Elizabeth looked back, even the ashes had blown away. Niall gently kissed the top of her head.

"Gabriel, Aeric, Melia, Bran, and Aelfdane have been called by the Wild Hunt even though it's daytime," said Aislinn. "Gabriel told me he'd never seen the Hunt arrive with so many horses."

Of course. That was because today the Hunt would ride all over the world. All the free fae who'd died since the Wild Hunt had been imprisoned would finally be reaped, along with those, like Liam's wife, who had committed murder.

"Your mother will be in the Netherworld very soon."

"Where is the Summer Queen?" asked Niall.

Elizabeth jerked; she'd totally forgotten about her.

Aislinn's face grew grim. "Gideon is dead, and the walls have fallen. She's defeated." She turned and looked pointedly at the Rose Tower. "I have a good idea where to find her. Shall we? She still needs to be dealt with, after all."

"With reinforcements," Niall answered. "Sure." He motioned at his brother, Ronan, who stood with his wife, Bella, not far away. Ronan and Bella joined them, as did Charlotte and Emmaline.

The group made their way to the opposite end of the square, where the shiny rose quartz tower still gleamed in the falling snow. The double doors were thrown open. Elizabeth entered with Niall by her side and tried not to gawp. The only times she'd ever seen the interior of the Rose had been on *Faemous*, and that coverage had never done the place justice.

Walking into the Black Tower had been like having the enormous wings of a raven enfold her. Walking into the Rose Tower was a little like entering the human idea of heaven.

The foyer was made of polished rose quartz and marble shot through with warm veins of gold. A sweeping staircase stood directly in front of them, and two long corridors stretched off on either side. Except for the roaming, frustrated sluagh the place was completely empty.

"I called off the goblins," said the Shadow Queen, her voice echoing through the place creepily. "As living creatures with lives and children, I don't like putting them in harm's way unless it's absolutely necessary. The sluagh can do what needs to be done next."

She meant the destruction of the Summer Queen. Elizabeth hated Caoilainn, but she couldn't suppress a shiver of dread for the woman's ultimate fate.

Their footsteps echoed as the Shadow Queen led them to the right, down a long corridor to a set of elaborately carved doors.

Elizabeth frowned. "Where is the loyal Imperial Guard? I saw at least twenty of them back at the cliffs."

"They've either deserted her, or she's sent them away," answered Aislinn. "I wouldn't doubt the latter. Caoilainn is a sore loser and can be unpredictable when her will is thwarted." She stopped in front of the throne room doors and drew a breath, as if marshaling her strength. "Remember that unpredictability and be ready for anything."

She pushed the doors open.

WHITE light poured from the Summer Queen's receiving chamber, making Niall blink. He pulled Elizabeth against his side as if he could protect her, all the while with a defensive charm ready on his tongue. All around him, claws scuttled on the marble floor as the sluagh scrambled around them to enter the chamber.

When his eyes had adjusted to the brightness of the room,

he saw Ronan and Bella beside him. Charlotte and Emmaline were a little bit behind, walking side by side, Kieran not far behind. Aislinn was in front, leading them all to the Summer Throne, because, of course, that was where Caoilainn would be spending her last bit of time in Piefferburg, reliving the glory days.

This place was nothing like the small, friendly room where Aislinn received people. This was a cavernous chamber with broad, tall pillars scattered throughout, a cold marble floor, and gorgeous, elaborate frescoes painted over the arched ceiling. This was a room meant to awe the visitor, make them feel small and put them on edge.

All it did was piss Niall off.

"Why should I let you live?" asked Aislinn in a steely voice. It echoed through the chamber.

As Niall rounded a pillar, he finally caught a glimpse of the Summer Queen sitting on her cushioned rose quartz throne. Like Aislinn, she looked like the loser of a prize fight. Her gold and white gown was smudged with grime and torn in numerous places. Soot marked her cheeks, lips, and forehead, and her hair had half come down from its formerly tight coif at her nape, the gold pins once securing it hanging free on tendrils of loose blond hair. One of her diamond earrings was missing.

"You won. Leave me alone," she snarled.

They all stopped at the foot of her throne. "Sorry," answered Aislinn. "We can't do that. We don't know what else you might have planned, and, after all, you already brought down the Black Tower."

"Gideon, that spawn of the underworld, *he* did that, not me."

"I was there," Aislinn snarled with sudden and surprising vehemence. "You did it together—the Summer Royal standing side by side, *allied*, with the *archdirector of the Phaendir.* I saw it, and so did many of the other fae." Aislinn shook her head. "You'll never survive this, Caoilainn, no matter how much magick you wield. It doesn't even matter that you probably helped the Phaendir create Watt, this action alone wins you a death sentence."

Power swelled in the room, bigger and stronger. The room went so cold that frost gelled on the marble floors, made their breath turn white in the air. Niall pulled Elizabeth toward him, suddenly worried something was coming—something big. Something he couldn't protect her from.

"Your subjects have deserted you, Caoilainn," Aislinn continued. "They've come to *me* for guidance and direction, the *Shadow* Queen." She motioned at one of the roaming sluagh. "And your shield won't hold forever. Eventually it will break, and the sluagh will devour you. It's over and you know it. That's why you're sitting here all alone. This is the end."

"It ends when I say it ends!" the Summer Queen roared, her tense white hands gripping her throne and her face going red with rage.

The building began to shake. Harder and harder. The pillars started to break free of their moorings. One of them began to crumble. A moment later, it fell, crashing onto the floor. A crack appeared through the fresco above their heads.

All of them retreated toward the door. The Summer Queen had gone completely insane. It appeared she was going to take down the Rose Tower, too.

"Don't do this!" cried Bella, her breath showing white in the chilled air. She and Aislinn had grown up in this court. Ronan was pulling her back toward the exit, but she was fighting him. "You may be tormented, but leave the Rose alone!"

Caoilainn stood, managing to look regal despite the wreckage of her dress and hair. *"I am the Rose,"* she bellowed. "If I go down, so does this tower!"

Another pillar crashed to the floor, splitting open. Razor-sharp shards of rose-colored marble slid across the glossy floor. Charlotte turned to run—what they were all doing now—and slipped on the floor that had become icy from the Summer Queen's fit of emotion. Niall grabbed her before she fell and righted her, helping her and Elizabeth out of the room.

THIRTY-ONE

THE corridor beyond the throne room shook as if experiencing an earthquake. Huge fissures cracked the walls, snaking over the ceiling and floor. Behind them, nipping at their heels, came the incredible cold radiating from the Summer Queen, freezing the walls, paintings, statues, and furniture, and turning the marble floor to a sheet of ice. The evidence of the Summer Queen's despair froze the skin of their heels, the backs of their legs, and tipped their hair with frost.

They ran flat out down the corridor with the fingers of winter grasping at them and the fist of destruction closing all around them.

Niall had Elizabeth's hand, Emmaline beside him. In front of them ran Charlotte, Kieran, and Aislinn with Bella and Ronan. The tower was literally coming apart. Bits and pieces of the ceiling fell, crashing around them. When a chunk seemed aimed straight for Bella's head, Niall yelled, *"Amanthrall!"* and knocked it off course. But it was hard to catch all the debris, and by the time they reached the front doors of the tower, they all had minor, bloody injuries.

They ran out of the tower and as far into the square as they could. They didn't look back as the now-familiar screeching, crumbling, whining sound of a building collapsing echoed behind them.

Beside him, Elizabeth tripped, and he went down with her. They rolled onto their backs and watched, stunned, as the Rose Tower collapsed to a rubble heap. Now the Rose was part of a matched pair with the Black. Niall's heart missed a beat.

And there was a true end to Piefferburg.

"It's over," whispered the Shadow Queen above him. He could barely hear her over the tumult in the square.

He looked at Elizabeth. Dust and soot marked her face and hair. Her eyes were wide as she stared at the wreckage of the building they'd been standing in only moments before. She turned and looked at him, forehead creased, breath coming fast. A tendril of hair had fallen over her mouth, rising and falling with her inhalations.

He reached out and smoothed it behind her ear. "All right?"

"No," she breathed.

He leaned in, pressing his mouth firmly against hers and tasting dust, teardrops, and a little blood. "It will be," he murmured against her lips.

She stood and held out a hand, helping him to stand. They remained for a long time, surveying the settling rubble as the wind and the snowflakes cleared the dust away.

Elizabeth turned to Aislinn. "Do you think she stayed in there? Do you think the Summer Queen is really dead?"

Aislinn narrowed her eyes at the structure. "I don't see the sluagh, but that doesn't mean she's dead. With Caoilainn you never can tell what's illusion and what's truth. It's possible she really did let the building come down on her head." She paused, then shrugged. "It's also possible she just very stealthily staged her own death, escaped out the back door, and the sluagh followed her. Personally, I'm betting on the latter. And if anyone can find a way to give the sluagh the slip, it's Caoilainn."

"One day I have a feeling we'll find out."

"If she is still alive," answered Aislinn, "we'll know soon enough. She won't be able to hide her light under a bushel for long."

Elizabeth let out a short, surprised laugh. "That's for sure."

"Well," said Niall, pulling Elizabeth back against him, "I love to see you two bonding, but, in case you weren't aware, the walls of Piefferburg just fell. Maybe we should, oh, I don't know, *reenter the world*?"

All of them went very still and silent.

"Gabriel is already out there," Niall added quietly.

Aislinn cleared her throat. "I know. So are the rest of the Wild Hunt, the sprae, and probably half the inhabitants of Piefferburg by now." Pausing, she swallowed hard and then offered her arm to Bella, her best friend, who had come to stand on her opposite side. "Shall we?"

"I think it's way past time, don't you?" answered Bella, smiling up at Ronan, who'd come to stand beside her.

Kieran and Charlotte stood watching them, their arms slung around each other's waists. "I can't wait to show you all everything about the human world that you've missed," said Charlotte, beaming. She nodded at Emmaline. "She can help me with that."

"I miss going to the movies, especially for the popcorn," answered Emmaline. "I can't wait to take Aeric."

"I can't wait to take Kieran anywhere," replied Charlotte. "Even if it's just to the grocery store."

"We'll have to teach them how to use cell phones."

Charlotte nodded. "And computers, oh, and—"

Niall cleared his throat. "Okay, already, can we go now?"

"Wait," said Elizabeth. "I can't leave. There are people in the Boundary Lands I need to help, take care—"

"It's done," said the queen. "I already sent a contingent of Shadow Guard to go to their aid, Elizabeth. They'll be fine. I promise."

Elizabeth studied the queen suspiciously for a moment before asking, "Why?"

"Guilt," Aislinn answered right away. She offered a trembling smile. "Those people I threatened will be taken care of *for life*. Trust me."

"Thank you."

"It's my way of making amends."

"Okay, now that that's settled. Charlotte and I will take my cycle," said Kieran, grinning. "See you guys on the other side." They turned and walked into the smoke.

The rest of them found Niall's SUV where he'd left it on the far side of the Black Tower. It was covered in dust and rubble, and had a dent in the passenger side door, but was otherwise uncrushed. He climbed in the driver's side and Elizabeth gave up the passenger seat to Aislinn, out of deference to her rank. Elizabeth, Ronan, Bella, and Charlotte piled in the back—Bella on Ronan's lap.

"Say good-bye to Piefferburg," said Niall as he started the engine.

The vehicle was quiet as it rolled slowly through the streets of the city. The fighting had given way to celebrating. Those fae who didn't have cars were traveling by foot in laughing groups.

Niall wasn't sure what they'd find when they reached the gates. The Phaendir weren't an issue any longer.

But what about the military?

The U.S. soldiers had held their ground, fought the fae when all the hell had broken loose. He'd seen the military shoot fae in the middle of the street firsthand, yet they'd seemed to stand down toward the end, some of them had even joined in the festivities.

As they approached the gates, he'd half expected to find a war zone. If that happened, of course, the military wouldn't be much of a match for the fae—not without the Phaendir to back them up. Niall thought the humans were intelligent enough to realize that.

When they reached the end of the road they found the gates thrown open and the fae streaming out. The soldiers stood to the sides of the road, armed, looking a bit nervous in some cases, but noncombative.

Niall stopped the vehicle in the middle of the road, hands tight on the steering wheel, taking it all in. The entire car had gone silent. For all of them save Charlotte, it was a surreal sight, previously only viewed in their imaginations.

He remembered his arrival in Piefferburg. He'd been sick as hell with Watt Syndrome. Couldn't even move. They'd just thrown him past the warding and left him for dead. He'd woken in the forest, rolled over, and looked up through the tree limbs at the blue sky beyond. The sunlight had dappled through the green leaves. All around him the breeze had rustled the tree limbs like a lullaby and birds had been calling to each other. Breathing shallowly, his lungs on fire, he remembered he'd thought the place was pretty.

Pretty.

That had been the fever talking, or maybe he'd just been happy to have survived the journey. Those first years had been hell. After the fae had stopped trying to break the warding and had accepted their situation, little by little they'd cleared some of the trees, built a shantytown, then, eventually, built a city. He'd been there to see every brick and stick of that city go up.

Now he was leaving it.

The car behind him honked, and Niall realized he'd been sitting there, remembering, and not moving. The fae wanted out, and he wasn't going to be the one to stop them.

Elizabeth put her hand on his forearm. "Are you all right?"

He looked over at her. The rosy first fingers of sunlight breaking through the cloud cover were reaching through the windshield and caressing her cheek. She looked concerned for him, tired, and grieving—but she was the most beautiful woman in the world to him.

And she was his.

He smiled. "Baby, I've never been better. I love you."

She smiled. "I love you, too."

The car behind them laid on the horn, and he waved a hand back at them. "Okay, okay, I'm going." He paused, then looked over at the Shadow Queen. "We're going."

"Yes," she whispered, gaze focused straight ahead. "We're going."

He smiled. "Okay."

He drove past the gates of Piefferburg and into a burst of sunlight.

EPILOGUE

ELIZABETH sat on the balcony of their Parisian hotel just around the corner from the Champs-Elysées, one bare foot dangling off the side, staring at the Eiffel Tower not far away. The spring sky stretched above, a brilliant shade of blue, a fresh baked bit of French bread, already nibbled, lay on a plate at her elbow next to a small, yet potent, cup of coffee.

Even better? She wasn't alone.

Niall stepped out onto the balcony wearing only his robe. Placing his hands on her shoulders, he leaned down and kissed her cheek, then sank into the opposite chair to enjoy the view. Sunset swirled the horizon in a tumult of oranges, reds, purples, and pinks. The sun caught the tower and it glinted, just for a millisecond, like a star.

It was one of those perfect moments, the kind that are remembered and cherished forever. She and Niall had been having lots of those since they'd decided to travel the world. They were busy seeing all the places the Phaendir never hoped they'd set foot. Every time they landed in a new country, Niall saluted Gideon Amberdoyal in hell with his middle finger.

They'd been to Australia, China, and Russia and were now making their way through Europe. They were saving Ireland for last, thinking they just might settle there. Lots of the fae had already. Ireland wanted their fae back. So did Wales, Great Britain, Germany, Scandinavia, and the Brittany region of France.

"Had an e-mail from Ronan," Niall commented once the sun had sunk low in the sky, dragging most of the light with it. He said *e-mail* a bit uncomfortably. Neither she nor Niall were fully comfortable with computers yet.

"Mmm?" she answered around her last bite of breakfast.

"They've nearly got the fae court arranged in Dublin." Since the Summer Queen had offed herself—well, maybe— and taken the Summer Ring with her, Aislinn held court for both the Seelie and Unseelie. Of course, not everyone was happy with that. Some of the Seelie had already formed a splinter group, and everyone was certain there would be a new Summer Queen soon, Summer Ring or no.

She brushed the buttery crumbs from her fingers and sighed contentedly. "The troop are there, too?"

"Being welcomed with open arms in Ireland, at least."

The goblins and some of the other more nightmarish fae had disappeared into the uninhabited places, in just the same way as they'd lived before Piefferburg. They wanted little to do with humans, and the feeling was reciprocal.

The HCIF, Humans for the Continued Incarceration of the Fae, had gained membership since the fall of the walls, and were trying to raise a human army against the fae.

Luckily, their flip side organization, the HFF, Humans for the Freedom of the Fae, were all over that and were helping the fae wage a successful public relations campaign that seemed to be winning over the hearts and minds of humans all across the world. It helped that many of the fae had grown incredibly wealthy over the centuries, Niall included, and were helping to foot the bill.

"What else did Ronan say?" she asked.

Niall looked over at her. "He wants us to come to Dublin soon." He paused, then broke out into a huge smile. "Especially since Bella is pregnant."

"What? That's incredible!" Beaming, she clapped her hands together. "You're going to be an uncle!"

"I know." His lips quirked. "How strange." The goddess Danu

had suddenly decided to grace many fae wombs with children. It was a literal baby boom in the fae community, whereas before and during Piefferburg, fae pregnancies had been very rare.

"Of course," she said, tipping her head to the side and smiling a little, "*uncle* isn't all you'll be."

She laid a hand on her stomach.

Dear readers,
Curious where Piefferburg is located?

Visit my website for an interactive map:

www.anyabast.com

GLOSSARY

Abastor The mystic black stallion that leads the Wild Hunt.

Alahambri The language the goblins speak.

Black Tower A large building on one end of Piefferburg Square that is constructed of black quartz. This is the home of the Unseelie Court.

Book of Bindings Book created when the Phaendir and the fae were allied. The most complete book of spells known. Contains the spell that can break the warding around Piefferburg.

bosca fadbh Puzzle box consisting of three interlocking pieces. Was an object once owned by both the Phaendir and the fae, back when they weren't enemies. When all three pieces are united, they form a key to unlock part of the Book of Bindings.

Boundary Lands The area where the wilding fae live.

ceantar dubh Dark district. This is the neighborhood directly buttressing the Black Tower.

ceantar láir Middle district. Fae "suburbia," it also borders a mostly commercial area of downtown Piefferburg where the troop live and work.

charmed iron Iron spelled to take away a fae's magick when it touches the skin. Used in prisons as handcuffs and by the Imperial and Shadow Guards, it's illegal for the general fae population to possess it. Charmed iron weapons were a major reason the fae lost in the war against the Milesians and Phaendir in ancient Ireland.

Danu The primary goddess of the Tuatha Dé Danann, both Seelie and Unseelie. Also followed by some other fae races. Danu is accompanied by a small pantheon of lesser gods.

Furious Host Those who follow the Lord of the Wild Hunt every night to collect the souls of the fae who have died and help to ferry them to the Netherworld.

Goblin Town The area of Piefferburg City where the goblins, a fae race with customs that differ greatly from the other types of fae, live.

Great Sweep When the Phaendir, allied with the human race, hunted down, trapped, and imprisoned all known fae and contained them in Piefferburg.

Humans for the Continued Incarceration of the Fae (HCIF) An organization of humans working with the Phaendir to ensure the fae are never given freedom.

Humans for the Freedom of the Fae (HFF) An organization of humans working for equal fae rights and the destruction of Piefferburg.

iron sickness The illness that occurs when charmed iron is pressed against the flesh of a fae for an extended period of time, eventually fatal.

Joining Vows Ancient, magick-laced vows that twine two souls together. Not often used in modern fae society because of the commitment involved.

Labrai The god the Phaendir follow.

Netherworld Where the fae go after they die.

Old Maejian The original tongue of the fae. It's a dead language to all except those who are serious about practicing magick.

Orna The primary goddess of the goblins. Accompanied by many lesser gods.

Phaendir ("Fane-dear") A race of druids whose origins remain murky. The common belief of the fae is that their own genetic line sprang from the Phaendir. The Phaendir believe they've always been a separate—superior—race. Once allied with the fae, the Phaendir are now their mortal enemies.

Piefferburg ("Fife-er-berg") Square Large cobblestone square with a statue of Jules Piefferburg in the center and the Rose and Black Towers on either end.

Piefferburg, Jules Original human architect of Piefferburg. The statue honoring him in Piefferburg Square is made of charmed iron and can't be taken down, so the fae constantly dishonor it in other ways, like dressing it up disrespectfully or throwing food at it.

Rose Tower Made of rose quartz, this building sits at one end of Piefferburg Square and houses the Seelie Court.

Seelie ("Seal-ee") A highly selective fae ruling class, the Seelie allow only the Tuatha Dé Danann sídhe into their ranks. Members must have a direct bloodline to the original ruling Seelie of ancient Ireland and their magick must be light and pretty.

Shadow Amulet The one who wears the amulet holds the Shadow Throne, though the amulet might reject someone without the proper bloodline. It sinks into the wearer's body, imbuing him or her with power and immortality, leaving only a tattoo on the skin to mark its physical presence.

Shadow Royal Holder of the Unseelie Throne.

Sídhe ("Shee") Another name for the Tuatha Dé Danann (Irish) fae, both Seelie and Unseelie.

Summer Ring Like the Shadow Amulet of the Unseelie Royal, this piece of jewelry imbues the wearer with great power and immortality. It also sinks into the skin, leaving only a tattoo, and may reject the wearer at will. This ring determines who holds the Seelie Throne.

Summer Royal Holder of the Seelie Throne.

trooping fae Also called the troop, those fae who are not a part of either court and are not wilding or water fae.

Tuatha Dé Danann ("Thoo-a-haw Day Dah-nawn") The most ancient of all races on earth, the fae. They were evolved and sophisticated when humans still lived in caves. Came to Ireland in the ancient times and overthrew the native people. The Seelie Tuatha Dé ruled the other fae races. When the Milesians (a tribe of humans in ancient Ireland) allied with the Phaendir and defeated the fae, the fae had to agree to go underground. They disappeared from all human knowledge, becoming myth.

Twyleth Teg ("Till-eg Tay") Welsh faeries. They're rare and live across the social spectrum.

Unseelie ("UN-seal-ee") A fae ruling class, the Unseelie will take anyone who comes to them with dark magick, but the true definition of an Unseelie fae is one whose magick can draw blood or kill.

water fae Those fae who live in the large water areas of Piefferburg. They stay out of the city of Piefferburg and out of court politics and life.

Watt Syndrome Illness that befell all the fae races during the height of the race wars. The sickness decimated the fae population, outed them to the humans, and ultimately caused their downfall, weakening them to the point that the Phaendir could gather and trap them in Piefferburg. Some think the syndrome was biological warfare perpetrated by the Phaendir.

Wild Hunt Comprising mystic horses and hounds and a small group of fae known as the Furious Host, led by the Lord of the Wild Hunt, the hunt gathers the souls of all the fae who have died every night and ferries them to the Netherworld. The identities of the Unseelie fae who make up the Wild Hunt are kept secret.

wilding fae Nature fae. Like the water fae, they stay away from Piefferburg proper, choosing to live in the Boundary Lands.

Worshipful Observers Steadfast human supporters of the work the Phaendir does to keep the fae races separate from the rest of the world.

Turn the page for a sneak peek at
the first book in the new
Brotherhood of the Damned series
from Anya Bast

EMBRACE OF THE DAMNED

Coming May 2012 from Berkley Sensation!

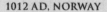

1012 AD, NORWAY

OTHER people's blood seeped into Broder's wounds, making every slash and scratch on his body burn.

He was alive. He'd survived.

His muscles were weak from disuse, but the drive to live—the drive for revenge—had made him deadly for the time he'd needed to wreak this carnage. Now that it was over, the will to kill leaked slowly from him, not unlike the last decade of his life.

It didn't matter. Nothing mattered anymore. The moment he'd stepped foot in this enclave, his life had been worth nothing. Before then, even . . .

Ignoring the fiery pain of his injuries, his chest heaving and his eyes wild, Broder turned in a circle, a sharp sword clenched in one sticky hand, an ax in the other, and surveyed the bodies around him. The sight gave him no pleasure, no peace, but he didn't regret any of it. He'd do it again if given the chance, even though the act itself was more blur than memory.

He'd delivered retribution.

He barely remembered it. He'd heard tales of men caught up in battle carnage, wild with bloodlust, unknowing of the deeds they committed. Man, woman, child, it mattered not to them, all fell beneath the crazed warrior's blade. That's how he'd spent the last five minutes . . . had it been ten? Or had it been an hour? He wasn't sure. Images flashed through his head—blood, bone, flesh—the sharp, silver edge of his blade rendering it all into so much meat.

Movement caught his eye. He turned, ready to launch into another attack, and caught the sight of a decapitated body sliding slowly from an ornate gold and green chair to the floor, making a lifeless heap. He relaxed.

It was over. Soon, he, too, would be over.

Blinking barely focused eyes, he lowered his sword and lifted his head, stretching muscles of his body that had long gone unused. He limped to a nearby chair and sat. He needed to leave this place because he didn't want to die here and he didn't have much time, but now that the insane rage which had animated his half-dead body had ebbed, he could barely move. His nose twitched, stinging from the stench of unwashed body and death.

Slumping against a heap of silken pillows, his blood staining them dark brown, he closed his eyes. Just for a moment. His hands still gripped his weapons, as though secured there for eternity. One wound burned brighter and hotter than the rest. He looked down at his side and examined the crescent-shaped slash.

He wouldn't survive it.

Every movement made the congealing blood covering him—his own and other men's—crack like dried mud. The images of what he'd done crowded his mind. It made him sick, but he didn't want to take it back. He looked around, his lip curling with hatred. If anything, he wanted more.

"Broder Calderson!" His name echoed through the quiet chamber.

In spite of his wounds, Broder leapt to his feet, turned toward the voice, and reflexively threw the ax in his right hand. The man who stood at the entrance of the chamber didn't move, didn't even blink as the weapon circled through the air, swooping end over end lazily, as if time had slowed it, the blade headed straight for his forehead.

The ax passed through the man as though he were made of mist.

The man—tall, slender, black hair slicked back from his angular, handsome face—smiled. He swished his forefinger back and forth, grinning. "No, no, Broder. Bad boy."

Broder frowned at the unfamiliar language and accent, and backed up, the sword dropping from his hand and clattering to the marble floor. The man wore outlandish clothing, he now noticed.

He looked him up and down. He wore no tunic and his trousers were more than passing strange. There was an odd, sharp cut to his clothing and his shoes were too shiny. Some sort of extra long bit of material that served no purpose hung from his neck. He'd never seen the like of such clothing—or fabric—in all his life. A black swath of some hard material Broder couldn't identify balanced on the man's nose and wrapped around the upper part of his face, concealing his eyes.

"What are you?" Broder asked in a voice that hadn't been used in a very long time. It came out broken and rough.

"Not what, *who*. You don't recognize me? I am Loki." The man walked toward him, unusual shoes crunching broken pottery, treading through pools of blood. His strange, shiny shoes never seemed to be affected. His voice held a strong note of derision. "Surely you must know who I am. I am known for the tricks that I play, and I have played many of them." His voice went serious. "But I am not playing now."

Of course he knew Loki. Broder felt the blood drain from his face. He'd just tried to kill a god. "Am I dead, then?"

Loki laughed. "Not hardly. Not yet, anyway." He removed the odd black thing covering the upper part of his face and his cold blue eyes skirted Broder's body, taking in the parts of him covered with Broder's own blood. "You won't be dead for a very, very long time. If ever."

Broder struggled to make sense out of those words. It was clear to Loki and to himself that he'd be dead in a few hours. It had only been a need for revenge that had kept his body full of life up until now. He'd had his revenge; now it was time to join his loved ones. He welcomed it.

Loki took a step forward, his polished shoe crunching on the remains of an invaluable piece of pottery. "You've had a more than a little fun here, I think. Are you thirsty?" He gestured to a half-broken pitcher on a nearby table, sitting in a pool of the blood he'd shed. "Need libation, perhaps?"

"It wasn't . . . fun." Broder frowned, trying to translate the odd manner of his speech. "I had reason for this violence."

"You offend the gods, you ungrateful barbarian!" Loki's voice boomed from him, echoed into the reaches of Broder's head, made the blood leak from his ears. Broder swiped at it and stared at the coating on his fingers. *"You'll not avoid reprimand!"*

Broder staggered backward, his head and side pounding out an intense rhythm of pain.

"You must be punished for this. You know that, don't you, Broder?"

Punished? He'd just spent the last ten years of his life in torment. And before that . . . hadn't he had enough torment?

"Wah, wah, wah," Loki sneered. "Don't think I can't read your thoughts. If you offend the gods, you suffer for it." He pointed at him. "And, you sir, have offended most heartily."

Broder winced, pain flaring through the wound in his side. He just wanted to die. He wanted to collapse to the floor, close his eyes and never wake up. However he had a very bad suspicion his wish would not be granted. There were punishments worse than death. Anyone who believed in the gods knew that much and this was Loki, the most deceitful of all the gods.

Loki held up a hand. In his palm a small blue light sputtered to life and formed the shape of a sword, then narrowed to a sharp, pointed sliver than looked like a narrow spear.

Broder tensed. Surely that supernatural weapon was meant for him.

"I'm impressed you don't run," said Loki. "Most of them do."

He threw the blue sliver at Broder. Even though he moved to avoid it, the sliver found his chest, burying deep like the thinnest dagger made of pure ice. It pierced his heart, spreading agony to every part of him. Freezing and burning in equal turns, it dropped Broder to his knees, snapping his head back, arching his spine. A bellow of torment ripped from his throat.

The sliver formed a cold hollow of nothing in the center of his chest, shearing away all the flickers of humanity he'd managed to hold on to during the last decade. Soon nothing remained.

And nothing truly meant *nothing*—no warmth, no love . . . but no fear or anger, either. He breathed into it, relaxing completely for the first time in years. Yet at nearly the same moment the pain ebbed, something else rushed in to fill up the peaceful emptiness. Something foreign. Something that didn't belong there.

Something from Loki.

In the center of his soul a mark of despair burned. He knew without being told that he was Loki's—his possession—and that could not be a good thing. He'd traded one Hel for another.

Broder pried his gummy, blood-crusted eyes open and saw that he'd fallen on his hands and knees to the floor, shards of pottery cutting into his shins and palms. Grunting with effort, holding one arm to his chest as though he could compel the icy sliver and Loki's mark out of him, he forced himself to look up into the grinning, gloating face of the god.

"You are hereby punished for your crimes, Broder Calderson. Eternally."

Broder had no doubt of this, but he could barely rouse himself to care.

"Don't be disheartened," Loki continued. "I am not an evil god with no sense of the human heart. Exactly one thousand years from now, if you have been a worthy warrior you will have a woman. Not just any woman, the woman of your every desire."

And then Broder truly knew he was damned.

ONE THOUSAND YEARS LATER . . . TO THE DAY

JESSAMINE'S boots clicked on the pavement of the parking ramp, echoing through the empty structure. It was late and she was alone. If she'd had any other choice, she would have been home and in bed right now with a good book, rather than walking through this creepy parking garage with every bad movie cliché about such places riffing through her already freaked out mind.

Her totebag, stuffed with all her paperwork, rested over one shoulder. Her hand was secured in her pocket, pepper spray unlocked and at the ready. She didn't take any chances. Not these days. Life had suddenly grown too unpredictable for that.

Her hands still trembled from what she'd just done. She wasn't certain she could ever do it again. How she'd managed to do it all still eluded her. She hadn't received any concrete answers from the risk she'd taken tonight, but sometimes lack of information was meaningful, too.

And, wow, she'd taken a huge risk.

Now all she wanted was to get home, sort through the confusing results of the evening and figure out what to do next.

As she rounded one of the thick concrete walls, a man stepped out from near the elevators. Jessa hesitated, watching him carefully, her hand ready on the pepper spray. He was a good looking guy dressed in a black linen shirt, a pair of jeans and black boots. His face had a GQ-handsome quality to it, light blue eyes and well trimmed facial hair around his sensual mouth. His hair, black and slick, was styled to perfection. Her best friend, Lillie, would have swallowed her tongue. Just her type.

Normally she'd think *yum*. Tonight he set off every warning in her body. He was the type of polished man that usually put a woman at ease, but her mind never strayed from *Ted Bundy*. He'd been a handsome, polished guy, too.

He watched her with attention beyond that of some guy waiting for an elevator. His fascination with her every move did little to flatter her. She walked past him doing her best to hide her impulse to break into a run.

"Be careful, tonight," said the man in a rich voice that reminded of her warm chocolate.

She missed a step, tried to smile but was too on edge. "Excuse me?"

He turned toward her. "They know what you are." He paused. "They've been watching you."

What I am? She pulled up short, stunned by his words. The comment sent a shiver through her, a jolt of fear followed by a sharp jab of anger. "Are you trying to scare me or are you just crazy?"

The edges of the man's mouth quirked up and he slid his hands into his pockets. "My name is Dmitri. I'm a friend."

"A friend, sure. The kind of friend who wants to rape and murder me, maybe." Her hand clenched hard on the pepper spray. If he took one step in her direction, he'd get it full in the face.

For a moment it appeared as though his eyes went completely black. It rocked her back a step. *Impossible.* "I'm not the one who means you harm. I'm just trying to warn you, Jessa."

Now she was really scared. How the hell did he know her name?

Jessa said a whole bunch of words she would never normally say and broke into a run, checking over her shoulder constantly to make sure he wasn't following her.

Normally she would be highly disturbed by an encounter like that, but she would brush off the man's comments as inconsequential to her life. Just some crazy guy. These days what the man had said made a kind of sense she didn't want to examine very hard. She had no idea who Dmitri was, but it was possible he was telling the truth.

Maybe they *were* watching her. Maybe they did know what she was. Maybe they did mean her harm. It wasn't paranoia if they were really after you, right? She wished she knew who *they* were.

She wished even more she knew what she was. Her whole life she'd felt out of step with everyone else. Only recently had her differences really taken a turn for the bizarre.

How much strangeness could a woman handle before she went insane? She was afraid she might be about to find out the answer.

When she determined Dmitri wasn't following, she slowed her pace, rounding the corner that brought her to the lot where she'd parked her car.

She approached her black sedan with a sigh of relief. No echo of a man's measured footsteps had resounded behind her, no gloved hand had come from behind to cover her mouth and draw her back into the shadows. There was her car, she was safe. Yay. She tried to muster some enthusiasm for that happy news and failed. She was exhausted.

Pulling her keys from her other pocket, she unlocked her doors remotely. Just as she touched the door handle, someone cursed loudly. Her head whipped up and she spotted a man with medium-brown hair holding a briefcase on the opposite side of the row of parked cars. He looked harmless, like some accountant or businessman who'd been working late.

In one hand he held a briefcase and he was using the other hand to shade his eyes as he peered into the driver's side window. He swore again, his voice sounding squeaky and distressed.

She almost ignored the worried man, got into her car and drove away, but she hadn't been raised that way. "Are you all right, sir?" she called loudly from her safe place beside her car's driver side door.

The man glanced at her, seeming surprised to find her there. He adjusted his glasses on the bridge of his nose. "I locked my keys and my cell phone in the car. Stupid," he muttered. He turned back to the automobile, staring into the window as though he could reach through the glass and grab his stuff. "It's late, the building is closed and—"

"No problem," Jessa called to him with a reassuring smile. "I've locked my keys in my car before, too. I'll call a locksmith for you. I'll tell them it's a green Impala on level three of the Handburg parking garage. They should be here soon, okay?"

She opened her car door, intending to sit down and fish out her phone to make the call, but the man walked over to her instead.

No. He didn't walk, he ran . . . or something. Damn, the guy could move *fast*. One minute he was way over there, now he was right beside her.

She backed away from him, alarmed.

"Wait. That will be expensive. Do you mind if I just call my wife? She's got an extra key."

He flashed a bland smile at her, a bland smile on a bland face. She looked down and saw the gold wedding band on his left hand wink in the dim light.

"Sure." She dug into her bag and pulled her cell phone out. "Here you—" The cell phone clattered to the cement as bland suddenly turned brutal. The veneer of nice, harmless man peeled away like an aging patina.

Oh, no.

Jessa stepped backward as the man's thin lips peeled into a gruesome smile, revealing sharp white teeth and . . . were those . . . *fangs*? How could that be?

"Jessamine Amber Hamilton?" Even the man's voice had changed. He ripped off the glasses and threw them to the pavement.

She shook her head, unwilling to answer, and took another step back. Her fingers closed around her pepper spray. He was between her and her car. That needed to change. Getting to her car meant she made it out of here alive.

Rage blossomed inside her. *She just wanted to go home!* Jessa stopped retreating. "Get the hell away from me right now." Her voice came out a whole lot stronger and more assertive than she felt, but she needed to treat this man like the dog he was—and show him who was alpha. If she didn't act afraid, maybe he'd back off.

The man tipped his head to the side, looking oddly alien. Then he smiled a waaaay creepy smile and said, "No."

"Fine. You asked for it, asshole." She pulled the pepper spray from her pocket, aimed it at the man's face, and pulled the trigger. The pepper spray hit him straight in the eyes, but he didn't flinch. All he did was swipe a hand across his face and leer at her. It was like she'd shot him with a water pistol. Then, if the fangs weren't weird enough, his eyes bled black . . . *completely black*. Hellspawn obsidian *black*.

Okay, that was not normal.

The smell of the pepper spray stung her nose, made her eyes water. It was potent. Any normal human should be writhing in agony on the floor of the parking garage by now. Why wasn't he?

The man narrowed his creepy black eyes and smiled, revealing—unmistakably this time—two shiny sharp fangs.

It appeared she had her answer; this thing wasn't human.

A growl issued from the back of his throat that raised the hair along her nape. She dropped her bag, turned, and ran. He tackled her immediately, rolling her over and looming above her. She fought him—punching, biting, scratching, but his strength was as unnatural as his teeth. And his grip was cold, *freezing*. Where his skin touched her, she went numb.

His mouth, with those shiny fangs, descended toward her face, icy cold saliva dripping from their knife-like points.

She screamed.

HE could feel her.

Her presence burned through every fiber of his body, screaming at him to find her. It had rushed though him the moment that Loki had untwisted the cosmic laws that bound him—unlocked Broder's ability to be with a woman. His chastity belt. That's what the Brotherhood of the Damned called it, a darkly comedic term for the magick that kept them from intimate contact with any other person.

You could call Loki many things, but not a liar. At least not this time. It was exactly a thousand years since the day Broder had been taken for the Brotherhood. Just as Loki had promised, he was free—at least for a time—to taste the fruits of which he'd been forbidden.

He could feel her.

From the moment he'd been freed, she pulled him toward her. This was the one woman allowed him in all the world and nothing was going to keep him from her.

He raced his cycle down the rain-slicked streets of Washington, D.C., the reflection of the lights from the intersections he rode through gleaming on the wet pavement and the ends of his long, spelled leather coat flapping behind him.

His blood sang hot with the supernatural scent of her. She wasn't far, just a few blocks away. His body tightened with need, his heart rushing with adrenaline caused by her nearness. She would be human, that's always how Loki did it. Not valkyrie, not witch. *Human.* It complicated things for the Brotherhood and amused Loki, the bastard. He never made things easy.

Of course, a witch, for Broder at least, would have been far more complicated.

One thousand years he'd been in the Brotherhood of the Damned. One thousand years of offing Blight, one by one, hoping to find that single agent from whom the sliver had been taken that pierced his soul. If he could find that one agent, he would be free to die.

Most humans dreamed about immortality, but most in the Brotherhood dreamed of death—of peace, of rest, of change of any kind. Love was just a dream . . . death, something to strive for.

Immortality for the Brotherhood was hell.

Kill the agent of Blight from whom Loki had extracted the sliver lodged in Broder's soul and the sliver would die, too. The countdown clock of his physical life would resume.

But this. This was a new goal. This was different from the last thousand years of his life. This woman promised warmth, companionship . . . pleasure. A respite from the endless cycle of killing and death.

He was close now. He gunned the engine of his cycle, ran a red light. The city was empty, winding down into night. To his left was a parking garage. In it was his woman.

Broder gunned the motorcycle inside, his blood a torpedo headed straight for her.

FROM *NEW YORK TIMES* BESTSELLING AUTHOR

ANYA BAST

DARK ENCHANTMENT

THE DARK MAGICK SERIES

Accounting consultant Charlotte Bennett normally doesn't lose control. Yet when she's seduced in a dream by a handsome, rugged man, she decides to let pleasure and desire lead the way. But she quickly discovers her "safe" night of passion has dangerous repercussions . . .

M963T0911